Editor's

I am pleased to introduce readers to this second instalment in our *New Australian Stories* series. Once again, I strove to select a wide range of stories in order to provide a snapshot of what's happening in short fiction. Moreover, given the limited opportunities to publish short stories in book form these days — whether p-book or e-book — one of the central aims of the anthology is to offer new and emerging writers the chance to appear alongside more established names.

Those dwindling opportunities for single-author collections concern me, both as an editor and as a reader. Many of the foremost novelists in Australia today — Gail Jones, Kate Grenville, Peter Carey, Joan London, Peter Goldsworthy — began their publishing careers with story collections, but that trajectory no longer seems available. Yet short stories are vital training grounds for our writers: they allow a flexibility and scope to experiment with an idea or a character or a voice — to perfect something in miniature.

Scribe Publications would like to thank all the writers who submitted their work either directly to us or to our partners. For *New Australian Stories 2* we collaborated with Varuna, the Writers' House, for general submissions. Varuna received 825 stories from a total of 330 writers. Ultimately, I chose stories by Claire Aman, Sonja Dechian, Anne Jenner, Jane McGown and Jennifer Mills.

We also teamed up with the Ned Kelly Awards, which in 2009 introduced the S.D. Harvey Short Story Award in memory of the fearless investigative journalist Sandra Harvey, who worked first for *The Sydney Morning Herald* and later for the ABC's *Four Corners*. Scribe has committed to publishing the winning stories: Scott McDermott's 'Fidget's Farewell' in 2009, and Zane Lovitt's 'Leaving the Fountainhead' in 2010.

On a personal note, I want to thank Ian See for his meticulous copy-editing, his invaluable advice and his constant good humour.

Short stories are often much more open-ended than novels: they kickstart your imagination, whereas a novel gives you the whole flight path. I hope these stories will send you off on many satisfying and unexpected journeys. Happy reading!

Aviva Tuffield

New Australian Stories 2

EDITED BY AVIVA TUFFIELD

SCRIBE
Melbourne

Scribe Publications Pty Ltd
PO Box 523
Carlton North, Victoria, Australia 3054
Email: info@scribepub.com.au

First published by Scribe 2010

Copyright © this collection Scribe 2010
Individual stories copyright © retained by individual copyright holders

All rights reserved. Without limiting the rights under copyright reserved above, no part of this publication may be reproduced, stored in or introduced into a retrieval system, or transmitted, in any form or by any means (electronic, mechanical, photocopying, recording or otherwise) without the prior written permission of the publisher of this book.

Typeset in 11.5/13.5 pt Adobe Caslon Pro
Printed and bound in Australia by Griffin Press.
Only wood grown from sustainable regrowth forests is used in the manufacture of paper found in this book.

National Library of Australia
Cataloguing-in-Publication data

New Australian Stories 2.

Edited by Aviva Tuffield.

9781921640865 (pbk.)

Short stories, Australian–21st century.

A823.0108

This project has been assisted by the Australian government through the Australia Council for the Arts, its arts funding and advisory body.

www.scribepublications.com.au

Contents

PADDY O'REILLY	HOW TO WRITE A SHORT STORY	1
GEORGIA BLAIN	FLYOVER	3
SONJA DECHIAN	THE CATS OF UNSPEAKABLE KINDNESS	18
TONY BIRCH	AFTER RACHEL	26
PETA MURRAY	INDIGESTION	35
FIONA McFARLANE	EXOTIC ANIMAL MEDICINE	38
JON BAUER	REWARD OFFERED	56
PEGGY FREW	NO ONE SPECIAL	66
ANNE JENNER	THE WAY WE WED	75
MARION HALLIGAN	IT'S THE CHEROOT	81
SUSAN MIDALIA	PARTING GLANCES	94
JENNIFER MILLS	MOTH	104
KATE RYAN	THE GOOD MOTHER	111
SCOTT McDERMOTT	FIDGET'S FAREWELL	119
JANE SULLIVAN	FALLEN WOMAN	124
RYAN O'NEILL	FOUR-LETTER WORDS	133
JACINTA HALLORAN	THE SIXTH CYCLE	151
MELISSA BEIT	INSEPARABLE	161
DEBRA ADELAIDE	WRITING [IN] THE NEW MILLENNIUM	167
A.G. McNEIL	RECKLESS, SUSCEPTIBLE	184
MYFANWY JONES	BIRDSONG	193

PATRICK CULLEN	HOW MY FATHER DIES IN THE END	197
RUBY J. MURRAY	OUTBACK	202
TEGAN BENNETT DAYLIGHT	LIKE A VIRGIN	210
MARK O'FLYNN	TALES OF ACTION AND ADVENTURE	224
BROOKE DUNNELL	BLUE WATCHES	233
JULIE GITTUS	THE PLACE BETWEEN	241
CATE KENNEDY	STATIC	248
JANE McGOWN	PAPAS' LAST COMMAND	262
MEG MUNDELL	THE CHAMBER	269
ZANE LOVITT	LEAVING THE FOUNTAINHEAD	279
CLAIRE AMAN	LOUIS	293
KAREN HITCHCOCK	BLACKBIRDS SINGING	301
EMMA SCHWARCZ	HARRY	309
CHRIS WOMERSLEY	THEORIES OF RELATIVITY	324
LESLEY JØRGENSEN	THE TREES	336
ABOUT THE AUTHORS		342

How to Write a Short Story

PADDY O'REILLY

Ingredients
A person
Another person or more people
A place

Method
Take the first person, gender her, name her, crack her, separate the body from the soul and set body aside. Place Meg's soul in a bowl and whisk to a soft peak.

Put the remaining people into the place. Name the people and the place. Leave Tanya, Laird and Pauli to marinate in the Fitzroy share house for at least a week.

Preheat the situation to at least 250 degrees, or 230 if fan-forced.

Fold Meg's soul back into her body, making sure not to overbeat or the air will go out of her and she will be flat.

Transfer Tanya, Laird and Pauli into a large bowl. Beat well. Add Meg slowly, stirring after each addition.

Grease the share house. Pour everyone into the house and place in the superheated situation. Cook for 2500 words.

Test whether the story is done by inserting a reader. If the reader comes out clean, the story is done. If the reader comes out sticky, place the story back into the situation for another 500 words.

When cooked, remove the story from the situation, turn onto a piece of paper and allow to cool.

Serve with a title and bio. For a special occasion, sift a few asterisks in Copperplate Bold over the transitions.

Flyover

GEORGIA BLAIN

Sometimes, as I wait in a line of traffic near the turn-off to Glebe, I glance up to the three apartment blocks pressed tight against the tangle of roads. I wonder which of the windows in which of these buildings looks out from the room where I once spent the night with a man I didn't know. I have no idea, although I think perhaps he was living in the first block, the one closest to the flyover.

I had just turned nineteen when I stayed with him. Sydney was new to me, and I had no work, little money and only two friends, both of whom had come from Adelaide as well. Each Friday night we went to a bar that had once been a funeral parlour. Upstairs the music was loud, a deep thud in the smoky darkness, while downstairs it was quieter, and you could sit in armchairs and drink.

He was the barman.

He was certain he knew me, or so he said the first time he took my order. He leaned across the counter, his long black fringe falling over his eyes, his skin pale in the blue light from the mirrors behind him. He had given us double shots, he told me, and I could taste the bitterness of the gin before I even had a sip, the inside of my mouth dry with the memory of what was to come.

The next time he asked me what I did, and I said I was looking for a job.

'Modelling? Acting?' He slid the money I was offering back towards me, one hand still on top of it.

I said that I wanted to be a journalist, ignoring the notes he had pushed across the counter.

Cate was bemused by my refusal. 'It's not like we don't need it.' She examined him, eyes narrowed. 'Not bad-looking,' she decided. 'But not my type.'

She was the only one of us who had a job. As a production assistant on a television show, her wage wasn't high, but she was earning, and had hopes of a rapid ascent to something better. Loene and I were staying on the floor of the house she was minding until the end of the month, nibbling away at the edges of our savings, anxious about each dollar we spent.

And so I ordered for us again.

'Where do you live?' His fingers rested on the damp cardboard coaster, as he tilted his head to flick his hair out of his eyes. He shrugged away my offer of payment, and this time I accepted.

We were looking for a place, I said. I reached for the drinks, unable to avoid touching his hand, his skin soft.

He told me I reminded him of someone.

'An actor,' and he leaned towards me.

'That's so corny,' and I shook my head in embarrassment.

'Want to do something when I finish my shift?' His hand was on my arm. 'It's only an hour away.'

I said I was busy, despite knowing it would soon be obvious I had no plans other than staying here and getting drunk.

'I won't give up,' he told me.

And he didn't: the next Friday he asked me out again.

'I have Tuesday nights off.' He held his hands in prayer position.

It had been a bad week. I had been called in by a magazine, only to be told by the editor that she had asked to see me not because she had work for me, but simply to give me some advice.

'You're wasting your time sending a CV like this around.' She tapped my neatly typed pages with the tip of a long crimson fingernail. 'You have no experience. None at all. Your whole approach is wrong. The way to get into this industry is either contacts, or you start at the bottom of a down-market publication.'

She was right. It had been a waste of time. Worse, she had succeeded in making me feel small, but I thanked her for trying to help me.

'I could take you out for a meal,' the barman pleaded. 'At least give me your number.'

I could see the back of his head reflected in the mirror, obscuring my own face. In the dim lighting, my arms appeared to come from his body, and I smiled.

'That's yes?'

What would it hurt? It wasn't like my life was particularly good as it was. I took the pen he gave me and wrote my name and number on the back of the coaster, the ink barely legible as it bled into the damp.

A few weeks ago, when I was waiting in the airport lounge for the plane back to Sydney, I thought I saw him again. I don't remember much about him — the exact location of his flat, his name, and the finer details of how he looked are all gone. There is only a vague sense of his dark hair and the white of his skin. But as I sat there with my work files unopened on the table in front of me, a plate of wilted salad on my lap, I found myself staring at a man two seats to my left. He looked up and I glanced away. Moments later, he caught me staring at him again.

Embarrassed, I tried to smile. He turned back to his magazine. He was pale and slightly overweight, his shirt stretched a little too tight around his waist, his hair still falling foppishly across his forehead.

The announcement for the flight echoed through the lounge, and I stood, forgetting the salad on my lap. The plate thudded onto the soft carpet, the contents leaving an oily stain as I tried to pick up the mess.

I was one of the last on board, and in the cramped aisle I waited for another passenger to force her bag into the overhead locker. When I finally took my seat, I saw that he was sitting by the window.

I apologised while trying to extract my seatbelt from the gap between us. As he shifted his weight, I noticed the softness of his hands, a single gold band around his wedding-ring finger.

I was forced to tug the belt out from underneath him, and he looked across at me momentarily. I wanted to say then that I was sorry for having stared at him in the lounge, and that I wasn't sure if I knew him. The thought, however, of opening up what could be an awkward conversation, with no escape for the next hour, kept me silent; instead, I took the magazine out from the seat pocket and flicked through articles I had read on the way down a week earlier.

I had been covering a conference on global warming, filing stories on a regular basis and working on a feature for the weekend edition. As an industrial reporter, this was not a job I would normally have taken, but in the last month Jason had decided to return to his wife and children. It was a decision we had discussed for some time, moving from a bleak awareness that his wife's illness meant this could be necessary, to realising that this was, in fact, the inevitable place to which we had come. At first we had talked constantly, picking over and over the decision until, weighed down by the inadequacy of words, we had pared back all discussion to the cold practicalities. This was the week in which he was going to pack and organise a truck to clear out all he owned from our house. It would be easier if I wasn't there and he could just get the job done.

Now, at the end of what had been a busy five days, I was bracing myself for the return to Sydney. Ultimately I would be all right. But there was first the space between now and a time somewhere in the future when we would have either let each other go, or negotiated some form of friendship. That was what made me anxious.

Once again, I glanced briefly at the man next to me, wanting to distract myself from the thought of my homecoming. I was careful to keep my head lowered and my eye contact barely noticeable. He was gazing out the window at the tufts of cloud that wrapped us, grey and insubstantial, drifting like floss around the plane. I wished I could remember his name but I couldn't, and I knew I had no hope of even touching on the edge of what it might be. Nothing out of the ordinary, that was all I could recall. Robert, perhaps? His hands were resting in his lap, fingers curled tight into the palm with a tension that seemed at odds with the softness of his flesh. As he turned, I glanced away, careful not to be caught out again.

Robert, and I will call him that because it is a name as good as any other, phoned me the morning after I gave him my number. I had woken, my sheets pulled back to reveal the bare mattress on the floor. The lounge room where I slept still smelled of cigarette smoke and the sour wine we had drunk before heading out the night before. Through the gap in the curtains I could glimpse a sliver of sharp light that hurt my eyes.

When I first decided to move to Sydney, I thought I would find work almost immediately. I saw myself in my own house. I envisaged friends. Lately I wanted to go home, back to South Australia, but I could go no further than a general desire to return because there was, in reality, no family house to go back to, no work there, just a few friends who would welcome me but would probably not shift or adjust their lives to fit me once again within the fold. I had my sister, who lived with her husband and children in the foothills. They went to our church each week, and talked a language I had never understood, one of Christ and heaven and hell, and absolute rights and wrongs. My mother was in the granny flat at the rear of their house, although she would soon have to go to a home. Sometimes she knew who we were, sometimes she didn't. She sat in the lounge room and called the grandchildren over to sit on her lap, making up different names each time and wondering why they never answered. She was only sixty, but she seemed so much older.

Next to me, Loene stirred, snorting slightly as she rolled to one side, her hand flung out onto the floor; while upstairs Cate slept in the one bedroom, a narrow white chamber with a small window that looked over the back lane.

Outside, in the brightness of the courtyard, I sat on the step and drank a cup of tea, staring at the gate, loose on its hinges from drunks and junkies trying to break in.

We were meant to be inspecting a house for rent in less than an hour, and I knew I should wake the others, but I wanted to shower first, ensuring that I got some of the hot water from the small tank out against the back wall. I tiptoed into the darkness of the lounge, careful not to trip over the edge of the mattress, lurching for the phone as it rang.

Robert — he is becoming that name as I use it more frequently — wanted to meet me at a café in Glebe. I wrote the address down on a scrap of paper, although I knew the place he suggested.

'What are you up to today?' he asked.

I told him we were house-hunting. 'It's what we always do,' I said.

'Whereabouts?'

'Darlinghurst, Newtown, Glebe.'

He wished me luck. He said he was looking forward to seeing me. 'Tuesday,' he reminded me. 'Seven o'clock.'

I hung up and crumpled the paper in my hand.

'Who was that?' Loene wanted to know, and I blushed as I admitted it was the barman. But she didn't wait long enough to hear my reply. She had pushed past me, closing and locking the bathroom door behind her before I had time to protest, leaving me waiting in the corridor.

When I arrived the following Tuesday, he was already at a table. I could see him through the window, and I felt only a desire to walk away and go home, but I stood there watching him turn the menu over and over, the plastic coating slipping between his fingers. He saw me and stood, beckoning me inside.

The café was crowded, and I had to squeeze past other tables to get to where he waited for me in the corner. As he tried to kiss me on the cheek I pulled back, but he held my hand firmly, drawing me close.

'How is it all going? The house-hunting? The looking for work?' There was a wetness to his lips that I noticed as he slurped the soup from his spoon, leaving a fine coating of liquid over the metal.

I shouldn't have come. This, too, was not going to be what I had tried to fool myself into thinking was possible. I had never liked him in the bar and being alone with him in a café hadn't changed that. But still I continued to try, hoping that, at some stage in our conversation, a magical transformation would occur, lifting the veil to reveal a man whom I could find attractive.

When I told him I had had no luck with either, he sat back in his chair and wiped at his mouth with a paper serviette.

'Perhaps I could help with one,' he said.

I didn't see how.

'I was the personal assistant for the editor-in-chief of *The Australian*. I could introduce you or, at the very least, give him your CV.'

Why, I thought, had he gone from a job like that to working in a bar? Even if he was telling me the truth, an introduction or a CV into the right person's hands still wouldn't be enough. I had no experience. Not even volunteer or student work to suggest that I could possibly be a journalist. It was hopeless, I told him.

'You can't think like that. Let me help,' he said.

'Sure,' I replied, wanting only to end the foolishness of the conversation.

He ordered dessert. A cake to share, he suggested, and despite my saying I wasn't hungry, he asked the waiter for two forks.

'When I first came to Sydney, I knew no one,' he said. 'It can be a lonely place. I'd like to take you out. I know all the clubs. I can show you some fun.'

He named a few places I had heard of, and I told him I wasn't really into clubs.

'I'm not a good dancer,' I confessed.

'What about the theatre?'

I didn't like plays.

I was making it hard, he said, and I knew I was. Each time he tried to prise the door open a little I would pull it shut, unable to bear the thought of letting him in. Now, I wonder at my cruelty, but at the time I thought my behaviour was justified. He was too cocky, too smooth, and therefore not worthy of more gentle consideration.

At the end of our meal he offered to pay, and I let him.

'Shall we go somewhere else?' he asked.

We stood outside the café, people walking past us on the pavement, cars slowing down in search of a park, the faint sound of music coming from the record shop two doors down. Across the road from us, a couple argued, her in the car, him still on the road. She slammed the door on him and he kicked at the bumper bar. Moments later, Robert asked me if I wanted to come home with him, the directness of his request throwing me off balance.

So, it has come to this, I thought, both surprised that he could think it was possible I would agree and yet also aware that this was, of course, the inevitable conclusion of our evening out. He wanted to have sex with me.

I'm not so sure, I tried to say, but my protest was feeble. If this was the place to which we had been headed, I might as well just give in and go there. Perhaps sex would finally bring the transformation I seemed to want to continue believing was possible, despite all evidence to the contrary.

He had parked his car, a dented old Toyota, in a side street. He cleared papers and cigarette packs and a jumper off the front seat before opening the passenger door for me, his body still stretched across the driver's seat as I sat down, his hand touching my leg. And then he opened his window to the night air as we drove, in silence, towards the apartment blocks that line what has now become a tangle of roads.

A few weeks ago, as I sat on the plane next to the man who I thought was Robert, I wondered at the loneliness of the person I had once been. I found it hard to recall the feeling. Even in the last few months, as it became clear to me that Jason needed to go back to his wife and that I was going to have to let him go with grace, I never felt the complete cold emptiness I had experienced in those early days of living in Sydney.

Robert was still staring out of the curved window, arms crossed, and I shook my head as though trying to dispel the shame of remembering the girl I used to be. It was then that the plane shuddered, suddenly losing altitude. In the aisle, the flight attendant tried to steady the drinks trolley. Her face was turned away from me, but there seemed to be no visible change in her posture, no reason to feel panic, and I leaned back in my seat. Moments later, the plane dropped again and the captain asked all passengers and crew to return to their seats as further turbulence was expected.

Robert was staring directly at me.

In the dim light of the cabin it was, at first, difficult to tell if there was panic in his eyes. But when the captain announced that the plane would need to return to Canberra, his anxiety was unmistakable.

'I'm terrified of flying.' He grimaced in an attempt to smile.

'Ladies and gentlemen' — the flight attendant's voice was calm — 'the captain informs me that there is a minor technical fault, which unfortunately means we need to land at the closest airport. As we will be flying into some weather we ask that you all remain seated until the plane has safely landed. We do apologise for any inconvenience.'

'It will be all right,' I told him.

But he wasn't listening. His pupils were glassy and his voice tight. He said he'd had a bad feeling from the moment he got on the plane. 'Did you hear that?'

I hadn't.

'The strain in the engine.'

I tried to ignore the panic that surged as we dropped altitude once more. Was this the end? It was impossible. In the back a woman's scream was followed by a man's nervous laughter.

The captain spoke now. 'Ladies and gentlemen, I do want to assure you that there's no reason for anxiety. As Damien mentioned to you earlier, we are simply experiencing some bad weather. Unfortunately, we're having to fly directly into it in order to return to Canberra to rectify what is really a very minor fault with the backup navigation system. It has no impact on our safety but it is something we are obliged to fix under aircraft laws and regulations. If I could just urge you all to stay seated and calm, we should have you landed within the next twenty minutes.'

'It's worth trying to believe him.' I kept my voice level in an attempt to convince both myself and Robert. 'Doubting won't help any of us.' My hand gripped the armrest, and I could taste the acid fear at the back of my mouth.

Robert was white, and his pupils had flooded, black, into the darkness of his eyes.

I asked him if he lived in Canberra or Sydney, and he told me neither.

'Melbourne,' he eventually said, voice soft.

Behind us, in the dim glow of the cabin, I could hear other passengers talking. We were all trying to convince each other there was no need for alarm.

'Were you working in Canberra?'

Robert nodded. He was a lobbyist, for the music industry. He was there often.

'I usually drive,' he confessed, trying to smile at his own panic.

'And Sydney?' I asked.

It was where most of his clients were based. 'And my son. He lives there with my first wife.'

The plane lurched again and whatever calm had begun to still him dissipated. 'Are we going to be okay?' he asked, clutching the armrest between us.

'Of course we are.' I spoke quickly, not wanting to let my own fear in, but it was there, searing and raw as I laid my hand on top of his and held it tight.

Robert's apartment was like a cheap hotel room. He opened the front door and stepped back to let me in.

'Drink?'

I shook my head.

The plastic vertical blinds were drawn across the only window, but I could just make out a small two-seater couch, a glass coffee table, and in the corner a large television. To our left was a galley kitchen and on our right, a closed door that led, I presumed, to Robert's bedroom.

'I can't do this,' I suddenly said.

In the distance I could hear the faint rumble of traffic and, from somewhere along the corridor outside, the thud of a door as it closed.

'Of course you can.' Robert stepped close, the smell of his aftershave sweet as he kissed me, his lips soft on mine.

Of course I could, I told myself.

As he began to undress me, the thickness of his fingers fumbling with my bra strap, I said I needed to go to the bathroom first.

Under the brightness of the fluorescent light, I undressed myself, avoiding my reflection in the mirror. I gathered my clothes in a small pile and then walked to where he waited in the bedroom. He pulled back the cover, and I got into the bed with him, the sheets cold beneath me.

'Wait,' I told him as he moved towards me.

Unbuckling my watchstrap I took that off as well, leaving it not on top of my pile of clothes, but on the small bedside table next to me.

Later, when I realised I had left it behind, I wondered why I had taken it off in the first place. I had no intention of spending the night there, and could have just kept it on my wrist. Habit, I suppose.

'You're not leaving?' Robert reached for me as I sat up only moments after we had sex. My legs were cold, and I almost relented.

'Tell me more about yourself,' he asked.

'There's not much to tell,' I replied.

'Your family?'

'They are very religious.'

'And you are the black sheep?'

It wasn't that simple. I didn't follow their faith, but I was not an outcast.

I pulled my top on and tied my hair back as I told him I was going to head home.

'At least let me drive you,' he offered, but I declined.

'You know' — and he touched my arm — 'if you relaxed with me you might get to like me.'

In the darkness, it was hard to read his expression, but there was a momentary plea in his eyes.

'Can I call you?'

I explained I'd rather he didn't.

'I don't understand.'

I was surprised, thinking he must have been aware I had no desire or attraction for him. I was with him because I needed to take myself right to the hard centre of the loneliness, and I had used him for that purpose only. Surely he could see that? And having seen it, why would he want to know me?

Outside in the cold, he waited with me for a taxi. As I shivered, he tried to rub my arms. Stop, I wanted to tell him.

This is not how it is between us. There is no affection. But I let him try to keep me warm; I even let him kiss me goodbye as I got into the taxi, sinking back into the seat, the sickly smell of sweat, vinyl and alcohol a welcome relief from the sweetness of his skin.

The next evening, when he rang to tell me he had my watch, I had already decided to let it go.

'You can pick it up at the bar,' he suggested. 'Or I could meet you somewhere.'

I was standing in the hallway, aware that Loene and Cate were both in the lounge room, drinking cheap champagne, and able to hear every word.

'Can you post it to me?' I asked him.

'You really don't want to see me that much?'

Looking down at the carpet, I said I was sorry. 'It's just the way it is.'

He was silent for the first time.

I gave him my address.

Loene was laughing. She was drunk already. Cate was trying to decide which skirt suited her better. They turned the music up another notch and I heard the pop of the cork as they opened the second bottle.

'I'll post it,' he told me.

I thanked him.

'Well. I hope you have a nice life.'

Wincing slightly at the anger in his tone, I said I hoped he did, too, and hung up, relieved to have come to an end in our dealings with each other.

Two days later, the watch turned up in the mail, wrapped in tissue, with no note or return address on the envelope.

When the captain told us we were ready to land, I finally let go of Robert's hand. I hadn't really been aware I was still holding it, until I felt the tension in his fingers ease a little, my own hand relaxing on his.

For the last fifteen minutes we had talked. Rather, I had

asked him questions, and he had answered. He had told me his son was ten years old. His marriage had come to an end because of differences that could not be repaired, and then, when he explained to me that he lived with someone now, in a marriage of sorts, 'although we can't get married', I began to wonder whether he was gay.

When I told him my name, he showed no recognition. I kept talking. I said I was a journalist and I mentioned where I worked. I gave him no details of my personal life. I didn't think he really took in anything I said: his whole being was attuned to the immediate danger of our predicament. My own anxiety was only just under control.

In fact, I had suppressed my panic to such an extent that it wasn't until much later, as I lay on top of the quilted bedspread in the room in the hotel near the airport, that I began to really breathe again, slowly, deeply. I closed the brocade curtains on the cold darkness of the Canberra night, and I switched off the main light, leaving only the small bedside lamp on.

The room was old-fashioned, ordinary, decorated in a deep plum and cream, with a soft carpet beneath my feet. It was a twin share, and I had taken the bed closer to the door.

I had a bath and poured myself a straight scotch, wanting that burning warmth, before I picked up the telephone.

Jason was still at our house. I had guessed he might be, waiting for my return so that he could say goodbye.

I was all right, I assured him, because he had seen the news. From first reports, it appeared we had been in greater danger than the pilot or flight attendants had admitted, although it was still unclear as to what the problem had been.

I told him I had sat next to a man I thought I knew from years ago. 'He was terrified, and so I just talked to him, the whole way back. I kept wanting to ask whether it was him, but I never did.'

On the other end of the phone, Jason was silent.

'You know,' I said, 'there was a moment when I prayed.

Just quietly, to myself. It was the prayer they used to say in our church when I was young. It was running through my head as I kept asking him inane questions about his life. I could still remember it, word for word.'

And then, in the quiet of the hotel room, I began to cry.

'I'm okay,' I assured him. 'It's just a delayed reaction. I distracted myself, the whole time, talking to that man, but I guess I was scared as well.'

He tried to comfort me, cutting in over the rapid flow of my words as I kept insisting I was fine, never giving him the space to say what I knew he wanted to say. He would miss me. I would miss him also, but this would lessen. The facts were such that we had no choice.

His wife's degeneration had been rapid. Soon she would be incapable of caring for herself, let alone the children. He was going back to her because he was a good man, and I was relinquishing, trying to cut loose all the small threads that had linked and tied us for the past two years, because I, too, wanted to be decent. Older now, we had realised the importance of trying to behave like adults, even when we wanted nothing more than to cry out like a child.

The Cats of Unspeakable Kindness

SONJA DECHIAN

Most likely the number of cats on my street is not above average. It feels like it though. They do the normal things cats do: emerge from behind a gate, slip gently between fence posts with their tails curled or pointed — affectionate or vigilant. I don't mind so much that they talk to me. It's just that they have so many expectations. That's a tough thing to deal with each day.

They're lively in the early morning and I keep my eyes straight ahead and march to the train station without acknowledging any of them. It makes no difference; they shout back and forth. Insults and questions.

'Matty's had a hairy!'

That's what they said this morning. There's a shabby black cat about three houses along, and she started up the chant in her husky smoker's voice.

'Well, look at this then? Matty's had a hairy!'

The Persian in the next yard joined in. Her collar bell tinkled as she trotted out onto the street behind me.

'Hairy! Hairy! Hairy! Hairy!'

I slipped in late last night. I've learned to do it around dinnertime when the cats are being fed or lapping up owners' attentions. No one noticed my haircut then. I had suspicions it was too short and I stood in front of my bathroom mirror, weighing up the overall look. The front was a little high above my eyebrows. Maybe my ears stuck out a bit. My hairdresser thought it suited me. Emphasised my jaw, giving me a more rugged look. Her smile was generous so I had no reason not to believe her and every reason to hope that she really did find me rugged.

'Your girlfriend will hardly recognise you!' she'd exclaimed. Which was pretty much how I'd been feeling for weeks. Unrecognisable, or just unrecognised.

The last cat to confront me this morning was the scabby-faced tabby. His nose is pink and laden with skin cancers. Over the past six months I've watched the cancer eat away at his nostrils so he breathes with some difficulty and a snotty wheeze. You'd feel sorry for him if it wasn't exactly what he deserved.

'You look stupid,' he said to me this morning.

I kept walking.

'What the hell were you thinking?' he went on. 'Did someone tell you that looks good? Because that does not look good. Goddamn it, Matty, that haircut makes you look retarded.'

In my head I barked retorts, but we were getting close to the train station so I kept my mouth shut.

One time about three months ago I got caught by an elderly lady who was validating her train ticket. She must have heard us arguing. Or she just heard me, I guess.

'Shut up, Cancerface!' I'd yelled. 'Terminal fucking Cancerface!'

The woman was not going to work or anything, but dressed for grocery shopping or maybe volunteering in a thrift store. She was wearing a pretty straw hat and when she looked around the corner from the station all she would've seen was me shouting at a cat.

'Terminal!' I'd screamed.

So I said nothing to Cancerface this morning. I said nothing to any of them. I just boarded my train and tried to catch glimpses of myself in the shadowy window reflections. They were right about my hair. They were usually right, at least partly.

When I got to work I started an email to Marla. *Hey*, it began. *I have a new haircut. The cats hate it, but I think they might be exaggerating and it will probably be okay if I give it time to grow out a little.*

There was nothing I could say to Marla that did not sound stupid and desperate, including this. The subtext of my messages to her was always so obvious. *The cats hate the way I look too, but maybe they're wrong about us.*

I went and made a cup of tea while I reconsidered the message. By the time I returned I'd resolved not to email Marla anymore, but then I pressed send anyway. What the hell.

Marla used to be my girlfriend. I could hardly believe that my life of mundane deskwork and silent public-transport travelling had been touched by something as uncanny as the presence of Marla. She was funny and kind and interesting. Marla knew stories about explorers who died in horrible and tragic ways on very long treks. Usually they were just half a day from their destination when they were eaten by a dingo in their sleep, or their camel fell down dead and they died of thirst rather than slice open the flesh of their only companion. Marla loved explorers because they dedicated themselves to one thing above all else. I loved Marla just because.

When I told her about the cats she was very understanding. I knew she would be. That's why after about six weeks of knowing Marla I decided the time was right. We sat on my bed one night, and I started talking. It was probably the best night we spent together. Marla's hair is dark brown, which matches her eyes, and I remember how much they were shining, her hair and eyes, as the sun went down outside, and we climbed under my blankets with our clothes on.

The next morning Marla woke early.

'Let's walk together,' she said. I didn't want to walk to the train with her because the presence of the cats put me in a difficult position. It took a lot of focus to ignore them, and

I wasn't sure I could maintain a normal conversation with Marla at the same time. But I said okay. Now that I'd told her the truth it didn't seem right not to.

'Just ignore them,' she whispered, gripping my hand. 'Focus on me now.'

The sight of the two of us together had whipped the cats into a frenzy. They'd seen Marla before. It hadn't taken long for them to put things together.

'Got yourself a girlfriend, I see,' the black cat had announced. 'Quite a girlfriend! Enough for two girlfriends!'

Cancerface had loved it. 'I bet you had a good time with her last night. I heard you … Yeah, outside your window. Oh, oh, Matty, Matty, Matty! Yeah, I'd like to show that bitch! I could really show that bitch!'

I'd never acknowledged them — but the morning I stepped out with Marla it went off the scale.

'Matty and Fatty!' the white Persian chanted. 'Look! Matty and Fatty!'

A variety of cats followed us; some I'd never even met before, regaling me with long stories about what they'd like to do to my girlfriend. I gritted my teeth and picked up our pace.

'It's okay,' Marla said quietly. 'I'm here and none of it matters.'

She was trying really hard, but I just wanted it to be over. I walked even faster.

Cancerface spotted us about fifty metres from the station.

'Well, well!' he shouted. 'If it isn't the screamer. In the flesh! And look at that flesh. She's got a big arse, Matty. Have you got her on a diet? I'd get her on a diet.'

Marla and I kept on. Cancerface trotted by Marla's feet.

'I can see up her skirt, Matty. Whoa. That's quite a bikini line. Christ!'

I could see he was making Marla nervous. She quickened her pace and almost tripped, but caught herself as we reached the station's steps.

'Lucky!' Cancerface called out. 'If she'd fallen on me I'd be a goner! Big one like that! Whoa, lucky escape, nearly got fell on by a whale! Boom! A big hairy whale!'

I was seething with anger, both at Marla and the cats. She shouldn't have insisted. Things were just fine before that, just perfect.

On the station platform I stayed quiet. I tried to calm myself down. *Just let me stay quiet.*

Marla interrupted. 'Matthew?'

I ignored her. *Just let me stay quiet.* I needed a few minutes. It would pass.

'What is it?' she insisted. 'What were they saying?'

'Nothing,' I said, through gritted teeth.

'It's okay, you can tell me. I think we should be open about it. Let's not let these silly cats come between us.'

That's when I snapped. The idea that Marla could ever understand!

'Just stop it! They're not saying it to you; it's not about you. This is my thing, okay? They're my cats.'

'If they're saying things about me I have a right to know.'

'Do you? Do you really?'

'Yes. Yes, of course! I mean it, if you don't tell me …'

'Then what? You'll leave me?'

She paused and lowered her voice. 'I'll have no choice. I just want us to get through this together.'

'The cats said you're fat,' I blurted. 'They said you're fat and hairy and they made a whole lot of sexual jokes about what it must be like for us to have sex. That ugly cat, the tabby with cancer that nearly tripped you up? He looked up your skirt too.'

The train arrived then, so I wasn't sure if she'd heard all of what I'd said. The roar of the train tumbled over my words and her response. I couldn't hear what she was saying, but I saw her face contort, horrified and ashamed.

The train stopped at the platform, but we didn't get on.

'Is that what you think about me?'

'No. No, it's not. It's just what the cats think.'
She didn't believe me.

That was the last time we spoke in person. The email I sent today was just one of many I've sent Marla over the last few weeks. I've explained everything. I told her the truth about the cats, how I don't really know what they are and I can't guarantee I'm not crazy or that the things they say aren't my thoughts after all. Of course I reassured her that I find her unbearably attractive and that I have never thought that she was at all overweight. She really isn't, or if she is then I haven't noticed because Marla is truly ideal in every way — with the exception of her sensitivity to the attitudes of the cats. I explained how, given my uncertainty about the cats, I'd tried medication, counselling and owning a dog, but ultimately my only choice was to get used to the cats and to hope that, one day, someone else would get used to them too. I tried to make it sound like a singular adventure. The type explorers committed themselves to and risked their lives for.

Marla has never replied.

I caught the train home today. I braved the walk from the station with typical resolve. I kept my eyes down as if nothing was different.

'Looking good with that new hair!'

'Still hasn't grown back then?'

'Did you think that fat chick of yours would come back for your new hair? Ha! Not likely! She's never coming back.'

'Never coming back, Matty!'

I waited until I was a third of the way down the street, then I broke into a run. They followed me.

'Never coming back!'

A black cat darted in front of me. My neighbour's Persian trotted out to meet us. I bolted into a stranger's yard and did the first thing I could think of. I grabbed the garden hose and I twisted it on as far as I could. The cats were still coming towards me so I turned the hose on them. I sprayed them all then I focused on Cancerface. Got him right in the nose and I saw his eyes roll back in pain as the jet of water crashed through his broken skin straight into his cancer. He coughed water, his head tipped back, choking. Then he fled. All the others ran too. In a rage, I turned on the only cat still nearby. The fluffy white Persian yelped as I whipped the hose in her direction. She twisted and rolled, unable to make sense of the threat. I backed her into a bush, saturating her fur as her body spasmed and her stupid eyes widened in fear. She didn't even run. Just rolled over and over and over.

I threw down the hose. It convulsed in the grass and the Persian fell still and cowered. As I hurried home the front window of my house reflected my clumsy frame — uneven shoulders and sticking-out ears. Stumbling up to the front door I went for my keys. They weren't there. I figured I must have dropped them in all the commotion. I had a coating of wet grass almost up to my knees and I just wanted to get inside and into the shower.

I doubled back and headed across to the neighbour's yard. No sign of the white Persian, but my keys were there so I ran over, relieved. I bent to collect them. When I straightened up I saw him. Cancerface. He was at the edge of the lawn, his paws unhappily wet, his mouth drawn in a dour expression. I stood my ground.

Cancerface was quiet. Completely silent.

I opened my mouth to say something, but Cancerface just turned and walked away. I went after him.

'Hey,' I called. 'Hey!'

He went on walking.

The cats weren't talking to me. I guessed they were so angry they didn't want to know me anymore. I could have been happy about it, but I wasn't. I ran and caught up to Cancerface and, although he kept on ignoring me, I saw something in his expression.

'I'm sorry,' I said. 'Cancerface! I'm really sorry.'

He paused. When he spoke his voice was small. 'We just wanted to protect you, Matty.'

Cancerface must have sensed my doubt. He sighed and walked on. I called out again, but he had nothing to say. None of them did. The silence around me felt so huge then, so foreign, and in the space left by their voices I suddenly understood: they never thought Marla was fat. They thought she was as beautiful as I did and that's why they drove her away. The cats knew someone like Marla wouldn't love someone like me for long.

The wet grass squelched under my feet as I went home. I imagined the voices of the cats:

You get what you deserve, Matty!
We're never coming back, Matty!

I unlocked my door, took off my wet shoes and went in. I stuck my head outside and looked around one last time.

'See you in the morning, Cancerface!' I shouted into my darkening front yard. There was no reply, but I knew it was true. He'd be back. They were my cats. I knew they'd be back.

After Rachel

TONY BIRCH

I wasn't surprised when Rachel left me. I'd seen it coming in her mood swings and long unexplained absences from the house. But when she finally broke the news to me, in a note she stuck on the fridge door before leaving for work one morning, I felt betrayed. I thought the least she could have done was to let me know in person. I don't recall much of what was in the note, as I tore it into pieces and flushed it down the toilet after reading it. But I do remember she commented several times about needing her 'space'.

I thought I'd be okay on my own, but my life quickly fell apart. I stopped eating and found it hard to sleep. One of the other attendants at the city car park where I was working at the time, Alan, noticed I'd lost weight and was chain-smoking. He invited me for a beer after work. I wasn't keen, but he insisted. We went into a crowded bar across the street. We shared some small talk before he put a hand earnestly on my shoulder and asked if there was something wrong.

Without a couple of beers to loosen my lips I would never have confided in Alan. I hardly knew him. I skolled half a pot of beer, wiped my mouth and told him about Rachel's decision to leave the note on the fridge door.

He knowingly nodded his head, as if something similar had happened in his own past.

'Space? You know that's a code word?'

'For what?'

'Rooting. I'd bet my last pipe of weed she's fucking another bloke.'

The thought of Rachel sleeping with another man shocked me.

'No. It's not like that. She just needs some time to herself.'

'Whatever,' he said with a smirk. 'A few months down the track, you'll run into her on the street, a café or somewhere, and she'll be with some fella, probably a bloke you already know, one of her mates from work, most likely. She'll blush and pretend that this thing between them has only just started.'

He looked into the bottom of his glass with one eye as he kept the other on a tall blonde woman who had just walked into the bar.

'Don't you fall for that bullshit. I bet it's already on. Like I said, with someone you know.'

We had a few more beers before I left alone. I walked to the train station in the rain. When I got off at my stop it was still pouring. I was wet to the bone and felt miserable with the thought that all I had to look forward to was an empty house.

The day Rachel left, she insisted I stay away from the house while the removalists came. When I returned home that night I heard her absence as soon as I put the key in the door. And as I walked down the hallway my footsteps echoed throughout the house, reinforcing my sense of abandonment.

There was little furniture or ornament remaining in the house, which was not unexpected. I'd arrived two years earlier with a backpack stuffed with clothes and a cardboard box full of paperback novels. Previous to moving in with Rachel I'd lived in a share house in Richmond. None of the furniture there was mine, either. I was a literature student at university but dropped out during third year. The other tenants had dropped out also, from one venture or another. We did not have a serious dollar between us, the house was falling down, and we drank from jam jars and sat on stolen milk crates.

Rachel rescued me from this mess. We met at a seminar organised by a job centre. While I didn't get anything of value out of the seminar itself, Rachel and I hit it off straightaway. We talked all afternoon. She said I had 'potential', and I believed her.

Even though the double bed belonged to her, she'd left it in the house for me, along with a clean fitted sheet, two blankets and a pillow. That first night, I sat on the bed and hugged the pillow to my chest as I considered how generous she had been. But now, following the conversation with Alan, I woke in the middle of the night, troubled by the thought that since she'd left her bed with me then logically she'd moved to someplace where a bed was waiting for her.

A bed she was probably sharing with another man and, as Alan warned me, 'rooting' in.

She had also left her kitchen table, two wooden chairs, the fridge she'd stuck the note to, and enough cooking implements to get by on. Not that I'd done any cooking once she'd gone: I was living on black coffee, cigarettes and toast.

There were some pre-made meals in the freezer, casseroles and soups that had been lovingly prepared by Rachel before being labelled and stacked away. She once told me they'd come in handy on wintry evenings, after we got in late from a romantic walk through the park or along the river. We would warm a meal on the stove and sit on the couch in front of the TV.

Well, winter had arrived, and the couch and the telly and my girlfriend were gone.

I did pull a frozen block of pea-and-ham soup out of the freezer one night, but couldn't bring myself to thaw it, let alone eat it. I forgot to put it away and found the container on the bench the next morning sitting in a pool of water. I threw the meal in the bin, made myself a cup of coffee and smoked a cigarette.

I'd been off the smokes since meeting Rachel. Deceiving myself that I hadn't taken up the habit again, I bought my cigarettes loose, in twos and threes, from Ali at the local milk bar. I'd smoke the first of three as we chatted out the front of the shop and the second on the walk home. I shared the precious third cigarette with a cup of coffee on the back porch as I looked over the garden.

After Rachel

It had become unkempt since Rachel's exit. With the exception of an olive tree that continued to thrive, most of the plants looked sadly neglected. I couldn't summon the energy to care for it. The best I could manage was to look at the garden as I took a drag on what I truly believed was my final cigarette. I'd then sit at the kitchen table for an hour or so before giving in and making another trip to the milk bar.

I was on my way to Ali's one Sunday morning when I noticed a rickety wooden ladder leaning against the trunk of an olive tree that grew outside a block of flats at the end of the street. A yellow plastic bucket was sitting on the nature strip, next to the ladder. Closer to the tree I noticed a pair of legs wearing thick woollen socks and a scuffed pair of slippers on the top rung of the ladder. I looked up and saw an old woman picking olives from the tree and throwing them into the bucket. She looked down at me and nodded. I nodded back and walked on.

At the milk bar Ali suggested I increase my supply to four or even five cigarettes.

'I'm no pusher, man. But you buy more and you will come back not so quick. It is better for you.'

As I paced the footpath outside the shop he stood in the doorway complaining about his son's recent trip back to Egypt.

'The bastard, he rings me reverse. Reverse charges. I say "no", but his mother, she is too soft. Always, she takes the call.'

A teenage boy brushed by him and went into the shop. Although it was a cold morning he was wearing only a singlet, a pair of track pants and no shoes or socks. As we chatted Ali looked over his shoulder, keeping a watchful eye on the boy. He came out a couple of minutes later, empty-handed. He was about to walk away when Ali grabbed him by the neck.

'The pockets, little thief. Empty your pockets.'

The boy tried to free himself. They scuffled. A bottle of

tomato sauce fell from his side pocket onto the footpath. Ali let go of him, reached down and picked up the bottle. The boy ran off and stopped at a laneway. He turned and called Ali a 'wog prick' before disappearing down the lane.

Ali laughed as he studied the bottle of sauce.

'No offence, my friend, but this country has no culture.'

I lit another cigarette, said goodbye and began walking home. When I got to the olive tree the old woman was down from the ladder. She was picking up the few loose olives that had missed the bucket. It was almost full. I reached my front gate before I stopped and walked back up the street.

'I have a tree. In my yard.'

She stared at me, blankly. I wondered if she understood English.

'I have a tree,' I repeated. 'In my backyard there is an olive tree, just like this one. I live at number thirteen. You can come and have a look if you like?'

'Thirteen?'

'Yep.'

She shrugged her shoulders, picked up the bucket and walked off.

I hadn't been home long when there was a knock at the door. It was the old woman. She had an empty bucket in each hand. A man in a checked flannel shirt, work pants and muddy boots was standing behind her, leaning on the wooden ladder. She introduced him as her husband.

They had come to see my olive tree.

When I opened the side gate and took them into the yard, they smiled with joy as they walked around the tree, admiring the abundance of fruit. I watched from the kitchen window as they worked together. They spoke in Italian, English and, occasionally, something in between. I went out into the yard and lit a smoke. One of the buckets was full. They were busily working away, shaking at the tree like a frenzy of birds. I didn't want them thinking I was spying, so I pretended to tidy up around the yard. I picked up a broken terracotta pot but didn't know what to do with it and put it down.

I wandered over to the corner of the yard and stopped outside the garage. In the two years I'd been with Rachel I'd never been inside. I forced the wooden door open. The room was empty except for a piece of furniture sitting in the corner. It was an ancient record player — a 'three-in-one'.

The old woman called out to me from the yard.

They'd finished picking the fruit from the tree. Her husband, who didn't say a word, had the ladder slung over his shoulder. He was carrying the fuller bucket of olives in his other hand. She tried explaining the process of washing and preparing the olives to me, only some of which I understood.

She smiled at me as they were leaving.

'I will come back, a week, maybe two. I have olives for you.'

I stood outside the garage and watched as they walked from the yard. He was a little taller than his wife. Carrying her bucket in one hand she reached up and rested a hand on his shoulder. They rhythmically waddled from side to side as they left.

That night I dragged the record player into the kitchen with the idea of listening to the radio. It would keep me company. The three-in-one was covered in dirt and cobwebs. I cleaned it with a damp cloth. As I wiped its smoked-plastic lid I noticed an album sitting on the turntable. I plugged the player into the wall socket and flicked the switch, half expecting an explosion or an electrical short at the fuse box. Nothing happened. For the next hour or so I tried everything I could to get the radio working, pulling wires out of sockets and checking loose connections, with no success.

While mucking around with the wires I accidentally knocked the arm of the record player. The turntable began turning. It was not until I moved the needle across to the vinyl and heard the crackling notes of the first track that I remembered that my parents had once owned the same album.

I picked up one of the wooden chairs, placed it in front of the record player, sat down and listened as the album spun around. The music saddened me a little. Not particularly because of the words or the melody, but the memory of my parents arm in arm together in my childhood lounge room, a place full of people and the sounds of life.

True to her word, the old woman knocked at the front door a fortnight later. It was a Saturday morning. The jar of olives she nursed in her arms was enormous. I stepped onto the porch.

'Your husband? Where is he?'

'Oh, he fell down from ladder. Sore back.'

'I'm sorry.'

She waved my concern away. 'Better soon.'

I invited her into the house. She hesitated before following me down the hallway. She looked around the near-empty kitchen, and her eyes settled on the record player and chair in the middle of the room. She was not impressed.

'The house is empty. You live alone?'

'Yes. Alone.'

She shook her head. She looked as sad as I felt.

'You' — she pointed — 'enjoy the olives. They bring peace. They bring luck. They bring happiness. Eat.'

Before I was able to comprehend what she had said she turned around and marched out of the house.

I had no idea what to do with the jar. As I didn't want to offend her I hadn't told the woman that I didn't eat olives. I'd always thought they were a little too *exotic*. I rested my back against the kitchen sink and looked across to the jar. I walked over, bent forward and peered through the glass. There were hundreds of olives in the jar, along with pieces of chilli, peppercorns and delicate flakes of sea salt.

I unscrewed the top of the jar, reached in, took out an olive and rested it on my tongue. It tasted both warm and fresh. I bit into it. The olive held many flavours, but most of all it tasted — not like the sea — *of* the sea. I ate a second olive, followed by a third.

I quit smoking the next day, and not because I'd taken a pledge to give up. Each time I took a puff on a cigarette I could taste burned rubber in my mouth. I also decided to weed the garden; I stocked the fridge with food. I even picked up a comfortable two-seater couch from the Salvation Army store.

Within a week, just as I was fishing around the bottom of the jar for the last of the olives, the old woman returned with a fresh supply. She told me I looked a lot healthier. 'More fat,' she said, laughing, as she grabbed her well-proportioned stomach and jiggled it up and down. 'Yes, more fat,' I replied, as I showed her out of the house.

Not long after she left there was another knock at the door. I was surprised to see Rachel standing on the doorstep. She looked different. Her hair had blonde highlights through it, and she had lost weight, a little too much, if you ask me. She was dressed differently too. She wore tight jeans, black leather boots and a T-shirt with bold letters across the front — *LIVE FOR THE MOMENT.*

Before she could say anything I pointed to the T-shirt. 'What's that mean?'

She tugged at the letters. 'It's sort of like a Buddhist thing.'

I was surprised. Rachel had been more secular than Richard Dawkins.

'Have you become a Buddhist?'

'No. I said *like* a Buddhist. You know, the idea that what's happening now is what matters most.'

There was a car parked in front of the house, a late-model sedan. A man was sitting behind the wheel.

'He with you?' I nodded in his direction.

There was a nervous twitch in her eye. 'Yes. That's Robert from the front office at work. You know him. He's been fabulous, helping me get resettled. That's why we're here. I don't know if you remember, but I had an old record player in the garage. We saw one just like it at a garage sale last weekend, and Robert thinks it might be worth something. I'm going to auction it on eBay.'

Robert got out of the car. He rested his hands on the roof as he watched me closely. He appeared concerned, like maybe I was going to abuse Rachel. In an attempt to reassure him I smiled and waved. He appeared relieved and waved back.

'I'm real sorry, Rachel, but I did a clean-up after you went and gave stuff to the Salvos. I gave them the record player. I thought you'd taken everything you wanted. I've still got your bed here. Maybe you need that?'

'No. Just the record player.'

'Well, if it's any help I think the van was from the Salvos store down on the highway. Maybe they haven't sold it?'

'That's okay. It was just an idea.'

She looked me up and down. 'You well? You look like you've put on weight.'

'Yeah, a little. I'm good. Keeping myself busy at work.'

'At the car park?'

'Yep. At the car park. It's always busy. Cars coming and going.'

I waited until they'd driven out of the street before closing the front door. I unscrewed the lid on the fresh jar of olives and scooped a few into a teacup with a large spoon. I sat down in front of the record player and moved the needle to my favourite track. I tapped my foot to the beat and waited for the chorus. When it came I joined in, singing as loudly as I could.

Indigestion

PETA MURRAY

She was the childless aunt, and at the children's parties she was never quite sure where to stand, so, over the years, she had settled for a place in the kitchen. It was so much quieter there, away from the inevitable tears and collisions, and more tears, and the shock of the balloons bursting like random gunfire. They made her jump. In the kitchen she could hide from the small talk and the inane games, from the terrible moment when her own inappropriate gift was opened in front of the entire family. As a reward for her initiative, she became known as *the catering aunt*. She would arrive just a little bit early, pop her apron on and power up the urn — her sister had one, naturally, for large gatherings — then get the oven warming, and find a large enough pot to heat the pink saveloys through, starting them off in cold water, and easing the flame up under them, so they didn't burst their skins. There was nothing more unappetising than an exploded saveloy. But when heated correctly, and with toothpicks offered beside them in a small pottery dish, and the brilliant red sauce, they could be quite appealing. There was an art to it.

There were perks, of course, to her title. A hot cup of tea with her sister before the trays were passed round, and if her brother-in-law remembered her, a glass of champagne. And even if they all forgot about her, as they had, it seemed, today, there were other compensations. The hundreds-and-thousands that stuck to her buttery fingers as she plated up biliously cheerful little triangles of bread. The honey joys that she stuffed into each cheek, as she doled out the licorice allsorts. If she kept her head down, she could eat one after another till they melted away. Still more could be slipped into apron pockets, or into her handbag while no one was looking. They would do for later, and they always kept well.

But best of all, as the catering aunt, she was in charge of sausage rolls.

They had always been a weakness. It had started in childhood, with tuckshop lunches on Mondays. *A sausage roll and a cream bum.* How they'd trembled with laughter, she and her sister, as they scribbled their orders on their brown paper bags in 2B pencil. They never wrote the rude word, but they always had to say it out loud. The cream bum was over-rated, really, just a vehicle for a groove full of whipped cream and jam to probe out and lick from a finger. But a sausage roll? Warm, plump and greasy, the pastry flaked in your mouth, and the meat left a peppery smear on your lips and a coating of fat on your tongue to comfort for hours after.

She could smell them now, which meant they were almost ready. She took up her tongs and her oven mitt, lowered herself gingerly, opened the oven and slid out the rack. There they sat, party-sized, row after row of proud little pillows, irresistible. She popped one into her mouth, for a test, and then another, and then, because there was still room, three more.

Party's started, has it?

She looked up. Her sister was standing at the door, champagne flute in one hand, pinwheel sandwich in the other, watching. She stood, as elegantly as she could, picked up a single pastry, extended her tongs.

Sausage roll?

Small flakes of spit and dough bounced from her mouth.

Cream bum?

Her mouth was too full of sausage mince to let any sound through, but she laughed, a silent, quivering laugh. *Cream bum. Cream bum?* Tears brimmed, and her whole body shook with helpless laughter. She waited for her sister to join in.

Oh, for Christ's sake, Glenda, look at you. You're the size of a house. Do you think you could leave some party food for the children this year? Or is that just too much to ask?

Her sister swivelled on a heel and left the kitchen.

Honest to god...

The catering aunt popped another sausage roll in her mouth. These days they gave her terrible indigestion. But so did life, for the most part. She found it utterly indigestible. Yet she kept on living, didn't she? So, she reasoned, there was little point trying to avoid the sausage rolls. They were required to be eaten, as life was required to be lived, and one must simply go on, knowing there would be consequences.

She replaced the rack and turned the heat up to high on the oven, then did the same at the stove. The gas jet flared under the glistening saveloys. They bobbed and bumped against each other in their pale pink soup.

She popped a honey joy in each cheek, picked up her handbag, and sashayed to her car.

Exotic Animal Medicine

FIONA McFARLANE

The wife was driving on the night they hit Mr Ronald.

'My first drive since getting married,' she said.

'First this, first that,' said her husband. He looked at her, sitting high in the seat: her hair was flimsy and blonde in the late sun. It was ten-thirty and still light. These were the days for marrying — the long days, and the summer. It hadn't rained.

'You've got to be thankful for the weather,' the registrar had said to the husband. The husband was thankful for the weather and for everything else. He carried his shoulders inside a narrow suit and his wife wore a blue dress. They came out of the registry office into the pale summer, and St Mary's rang the hour.

'Listen!' said the wife. 'Just like we've been married in a church.'

It was midday, and because they were in Cambridge, the college bells rang.

Their witnesses — two friends — took photographs. The four of them went to a pub on the river to celebrate among the tourists and the students who'd just finished exams. The tourists pressed around them, clumsy at the bar; the students slipped in and were served first. The bride and groom were rocked from side to side in the crush of people. They cooperated with the crowd, and liquid spilled over their glasses.

They began to drink.

Their friend Peter swayed above their table. He motioned over their heads with his benevolent arms.

'I suppose I'm best man,' he said. 'By default. So, a toast: to David and Sarah. To Sarah and David. I'll make a statement about love. I'll say a few words.'

'You've already said more than enough,' said the other witness, Clare.

'Not nearly enough,' said Peter, and sat down. By now it was four in the afternoon, and the June town was keeping quiet. The scent of the roses in the college gardens increased, and the black East Anglian bees responded, hanging lazily above the scent. The lawns maintained their perfect green. The river was laid out straight like a track for trains. David and Sarah and Clare and Peter walked along it to find another pub.

The swans idled on the brown river, the ducks chased punts for food, the geese slid against the wet banks. Tinfoil barbecues were lit on Jesus Green, one by one, and the smoke hung in morose columns above each group, never thick enough to form a cloud. The husband and wife and their friends picked their way among the barbecues. They encountered dogs, friendly and wayward.

'Stay well today, canines,' said David. 'Stay happy and healthy.'

Sarah was on call that night.

'I'm not worried about them,' said Sarah. 'It's the Queen of Sheba I'm worried about. But he'll be good.'

(At the surgery, the Queen of Sheba lifted his haunches and lowered his head to stretch his grey back. He walked figure eights in his cage the way a tiger would.)

'He'd better be good,' said David.

'That bloody cat,' said Sarah, happily.

(The Queen of Sheba sat in his cage and looked out at the ferrets and iguanas. He looked out at the tanks of scorpions and turtles. He settled, sphinx-like, and crossed his paws. The nurse poked her fingers through the grille as she passed Sheba's cage and Sheba, blinking, ignored them.)

The crowd at the pub seemed to part before the bridal party, and they found an outdoor table, newly abandoned. Their happiness was good luck. Sarah said, 'Just one more drink. I might have to work.'

'You might,' said Peter. 'And you might not.'

'Remember, this is your wedding reception,' said Clare, and she placed her arm around Sarah, coaxing.

Sarah looked up at David. 'Just one more then,' she said.

'We'll make it vodkas,' said Peter.

'My first vodka as a married woman,' said Sarah. She sat against David and felt the day carry them towards each other. The hours passed at the pub, and they didn't think of going home, although this was what they looked forward to: the privacy of their bed against smudged windows, its view of small gardens and the beat of trapped bees against glass that shook as the buses moved by. Their bed was a long way from the colleges and the river, but the bells would still come over the roads and houses, and they would be alone, and married. The day moved them both towards the moment in which they would face each other in bed, utterly familiar, and see that despite their marriage there was no change, and that this was just what they wanted.

Sarah's phone rang. She knew it would be work, and so did David. He creased his face at her, disbelieving, but found that he wasn't disappointed. This way he would have her to himself. They would drive in the car, and she would tell him her impressions of the day: the mannerism she had disliked in the registrar — a tendency to blink too often and too hard. He would rest his hand on her warm leg and lean his head back on the seat and watch the way her driving forced her to keep her usually animated hands still. This animation would pass instead into her face, where her eyebrows would knit and rise across her forehead. She would crane forward to look left and right at intersections, as if she needed to see vast distances. Sarah drove as if she were landing an enormous plane full of porcelain children on a mountaintop.

'What a surprise,' said Sarah. She placed her phone on the table. 'The Queen of Sheba needs a catheter.'

Clare said, 'There must be someone else.'

'No one else,' said Sarah, standing now, slightly unsteady on her feet, but graceful. 'Sheba's all mine. He's a friend's cat.'

'And does this friend know you got married today?' asked Clare.

Sarah laughed. No one knew they had been married today.

'Your wedding night and you have to go stick something up a cat's dick,' said Peter.

(Sheba rolled in his cage, snapping at the nurse's fingers. The pain felt familiar to him, but newly terrible, a hot pressure. He flicked his paws to shake it off, shake it off. He couldn't.)

Sarah led David from the pub. He leaned against her the way he did when he was on the way to being very drunk. In fact, he was just perfectly, amiably, generously drunk, inclined to pause in order to kiss his new wife. He looked at her and felt grateful. He felt an expansion in his brain that he enjoyed — a feeling that finally he had found his life, or was finding it, was on the verge of finding it, although he was still a graduate student and suspected he always would be. He said to himself, 'This is my youth, at this moment, right now,' and because he was drunk, he also said it to Sarah.

The walk home wasn't far, but they took their time doing it. Sarah felt a sense of urgency about Sheba but couldn't translate that urgency into hurry. She felt the way she did in those anxious dreams when she was due somewhere important but was unable to find the items she needed to bring with her. They spent whole minutes standing on the side of the road in order to watch a woman move around her lit basement kitchen, ironing.

As they approached their apartment, David said, 'You know I'm coming with you,' and she didn't argue. They changed their clothes, and it felt to Sarah, briefly, as if it had been David's suit and her dress that had married each other earlier in the day. David followed her to the car. Before lowering herself into the driver's seat she shook her head, just a little, as if she might clear it. She didn't feel drunk.

It was an old car, friendly but unreliable, that flew with dog hair when the windows were down. It required patience, particularly in the winter; even now, in June, it demonstrated a good-natured reluctance to start. Sarah turned the key; the engine kicked in and then out. David played with the radio to find a good song and when there were no good songs, he turned it low. As if encouraged by this decrescendo, the car cooperated. Cambridge was lit with orange lights. They passed through the city with exaggerated care and were in the country very suddenly, with the lights of airplanes far overhead. England became a long dark road, then, with bright windows visible across wet fields and trees against the sky.

'What's wrong with this cat?' said David.

'Urinary tract.'

'I know that. But what's *wrong* with it.'

Sarah grew defensive on behalf of Sheba. 'He can't help it.'

'Why call a tomcat Sheba?'

'They let their kid name it,' said Sarah. 'It's the name of a brand of cat food. It uses real cuts of meat rather than by-products.'

'Crazy.'

'Don't.'

'It's crazy. It's like your mum naming your brother Leslie and your dad doing nothing to stop it.'

'It's a family name. It's a boy's name! And I don't want to think about my mother. Right now I'm pretending she doesn't exist. I left my phone at home,' said Sarah. 'If she calls, I don't want to tell her we're married, and I don't want not to have told her.'

'So just don't answer.'

'I'd have to answer. I couldn't not answer. And then — you know.' She spread her hands in order to indicate her predicament and then quickly placed them back on the steering wheel.

David lifted in his seat to feel at his back pocket and said, 'Shit. My phone's still in my suit.'

'What do you need a phone for, darling? Call all your girlfriends?'

'I've given them the night off.'

She hit at him with her left hand.

'Watch the road!' he said, laughing.

She watched the road. 'My first drive since getting married,' she said.

'First this, first that,' he said.

At this moment, Mr Ronald pulled out of a dark side road and turned directly in front of them. Sarah's veer to the left met the back corner of his car; trees moved in front of the windscreen, tyres made a long noise against the road; the car jolted over the grass and stones of the verge; they hit a low wooden fence and felt the engine splutter and stall. And as this took place they were aware of something more urgent occurring behind them: the spin of Mr Ronald's car, its dive into a roadside tree. Sarah and David remained still for a moment and then noticed the way they were both hunched over, preparing for an impact that hadn't come.

'Fuck,' said Sarah, looking back down the dim road. The muted lights of tiny Cambridge hung orange at the bottom of the sky behind them. The car radio continued to play.

'You're all right?' asked David, but that was obvious. He opened his door and stepped out onto the road. Mr Ronald's car reminded him of a cartoon dog, excessively punched, whose nose had folded into its face for a brief and hilarious moment before relaxing out again, essentially unhurt. He watched Sarah run towards it and then ran after her. The driver's door had opened in the crash, and Mr Ronald sat, his legs pinioned, but his right arm rested against the doorframe as if he were about to casually lean out and make a comment on the weather. He wasn't moving.

'He's alive,' said Sarah.

She kneeled beside the car and held Mr Ronald's wrist,

and when she released it she wiped her fingers against her skirt. David stood by the tree and passed his hand across his face. He felt the air press in around him and he wanted somehow to press it back. Sarah had found Mr Ronald's wallet on the front passenger seat.

'His whole name is just three first names,' she said, inspecting his licence. 'Ralph Walter Ronald. He's seventy-six.'

Sarah looked at Mr Ronald reverently, acknowledging his age and misfortune. She felt that his awkward name had lifted him out of a past time in which she played no part and deposited him here, in his crushed car.

'Which way to the nearest house?' asked David.

'I don't know.'

'Forward or back?'

'I don't know.'

'This is your drive to work. You drive this way almost every day.'

'It's dark. I haven't been paying attention.'

'All right, all right. Should I try the car? Otherwise I'll have to walk for help. It seems like ages since we saw a house.'

'Nothing in England is ever very far apart.'

'Maybe I should cross the fields. Do you see lights to the left?'

'I don't see anything.'

It began to rain, very lightly. The rain seemed to rise out of the ground and lift up into their faces, a cheerful mist.

'All right, try the car, quickly,' said Sarah. 'I'll sit with him. His car won't blow up, will it? Or is that just in movies?'

'It would have blown up by now. Right?'

They stood helpless in their combined ignorance, considering Mr Ronald's car and Mr Ronald trapped within it. The passenger's seat was whole and healthy, although the accordion-fold of the front of the car left almost no leg room. Sarah brushed glass from the seat and slid in beside Mr Ronald, tucking her legs beneath her.

David pulled himself away from the tree with great effort and crossed to the car with mid-city caution. It wouldn't start; it would never start when he was late for a seminar or a critical train; it required tender solicitations after particularly steep hills. Of course it wouldn't start now, when his need was desperate. Perhaps it was finally beyond repair — and then there would be the panic of finding money for a new car. David tried again. It wouldn't start and wouldn't start. He ran back to Sarah.

'No good,' he said. 'Fuck it. I'll run. I'm sure I'll find someone. Another car.'

'Go forward, not back,' said Sarah. 'Keep following the road forward. I think there's a service station. God, I have no idea of distances on foot.'

'Baby,' David said, leaning farther into the car. 'It wasn't your fault.'

'I know,' she said. 'It was his fucking fault. But, darling, I'm a little drunk.'

She watched him comprehend this. He was drunker than she was. His eyes filled briefly. There was a scar above his right eye, half hidden in the eyebrow, left over from childhood chickenpox. He often walked through their apartment on his toes, adding to his height, bending down over her as she lay on the couch. He would put his head on her stomach and look up at her face, and when he did this he reminded her of an ostrich. This is how he looked at her now.

'I'll be back soon,' he said. 'It's going to be all right. I love you. Don't be scared.'

He bent down to kiss her, bent his long, beautiful bird neck, and then began to run. Sarah was amazed at how quickly he vanished into the vanishing light. She looked at Mr Ronald. He wore corduroy trousers and a neat shirt, a woollen vest, and bulky glasses over thick eyebrows. He lay with his head thrown back and to the side, facing Sarah, and his facial expression was bemused and acquiescing. She felt again at his wrist. His legs were caught up with the buckled car, and it was impossible to tell what damage had been done. She sat on her side, looking into his face, and felt the faint breath that hung around his mouth. It smelled like a doctor's waiting room: just-extinguished cigarettes and a human smell rising up through disinfectant. She heard David try the car again, and she heard the car fail. Then his footsteps on the road, and then nothing. Sarah felt loneliness fall over her quickly; and fear.

'The Queen of Sheba,' she said.

(Sheba paused in his tiger-walk, his head lifted towards the surgery door, waiting. No one came through the door, and he dropped his head again, letting out a low small sound that startled the macaws opposite into frantic cries.)

Sarah was married and no one knew but herself and David, Peter and Clare. Her mother didn't know. She wondered now about the secrecy — how childish it seemed. They only wanted privacy. They wanted a visa for Sarah, to match David's student visa, and they didn't want to bother about the fuss that went with weddings. The last of the vodka wound itself up against the side of Sarah's head that tilted against the seat; it hung there in a vapour. Mr Ronald's burned breath came in little gusts up against her face. Was he breathing more, or less?

Sarah pulled the door as far as it would go behind her in order to feel safe, and to guard against the slight chill in the wind. This was summer, she thought. You waited for it all year, shoulders pushed up against the cold and the dark, and this was your gift: the sun and the bells, the smoke over Jesus Green, geese on the river. A midday wedding. A cat's catheter, and Mr Ronald by the side of the road.

Mr Ronald's eyes opened, and Sarah pulled back from his face. They studied each other. His eyes were yellow at the edges. They were clever and lucid. They looked at Sarah with calm acceptance; they looked at the windscreen, shattered but half in place, and at the proximity of the tree.

'I've had an accident,' he said.

'Yes, you have. How do you feel? Stay still,' said Sarah. She felt composed. Everything she did felt smooth and immediate.

'I'm all here,' said Mr Ronald. 'Everything's attached, at least.' He gave a small laugh. 'It happened so fast, as they say. I see I've hit the tree.' He said *the tree* as if there were only one tree in the whole country; as if he had always known he would hit it.

'Good of you to stop,' he said.

'Of course!' cried Sarah.

'Plenty wouldn't. Decent of you. I don't suppose he even thought for a minute about stopping.'

'Who?' asked Sarah. She looked into the back of the car in panic, as if there might be someone else crushed inside.

'The lout who swiped me.'

Sarah remained quiet. Then she said, 'My husband's gone to find help.'

She had been waiting to use this phrase: *my husband*. Her first time.

'Ah,' said Mr Ronald. 'I don't suppose you happen to be a doctor. That would be convenient.'

'Not a human doctor,' said Sarah. 'An animal doctor, though.'

'My leg, you see. I think it should hurt, but at this moment it doesn't.'

'You're probably in shock.'

'You're not British, are you. Antipodean.'

'Australian.'

'I thought so, but didn't venture it. For the first few sentences you might just as well be a New Zealander.'

He pronounced it *New Zellander*. Sarah found this charming.

'No, no!' she protested. 'We sound completely different.' She demonstrated the difference: 'Fish and chips,' she said. 'That's us.' And then, 'This is a Kiwi: fush and chups.'

'Nonsense,' said Mr Ronald. 'No one speaks that way at all.'

Sarah felt chastised. She didn't resent it — there was something so pleasantly authoritarian about Mr Ronald, who seemed to her like a school principal driving home from church, or the father of a boyfriend, to whom she must be polite at all costs.

'A veterinarian,' said Mr Ronald. 'Dogs and cats.'

'Actually I specialise,' said Sarah. 'Exotic animal medicine. But dogs and cats too, sometimes. Mostly for friends.'

'What counts as exotic these days?' asked Mr Ronald. She could see that he was keeping himself occupied as he moved his right hand slowly over his chest and towards his legs, testing for pain and damage.

'Chinchillas,' said Sarah. 'Ferrets. Hermit crabs. Monkeys.'

'Monkeys?' said Mr Ronald. 'Good god. Does anyone in England actually own a monkey?'

'You'd be surprised.'

'And is it legal?'

'I'm afraid it is.'

'And people will bother to spend thousands of pounds curing a hermit crab?'

'People become very attached to their pets,' said Sarah. She had defended her clients on this subject before, at parties and college dinners, and whenever she did she saw them all in the surgery waiting room, bundled against cold and worry, holding cages and carriers and shoeboxes with holes punched in them.

'Yes, you're right,' said Mr Ronald, and he mused on this for a moment. 'Dogs I understand, and cats too, in their own way. I grew up with a bull-mastiff. He could knock me down until I was eleven, and then I could knock him back. Once ate the leg off a rabbit.'

The bull-mastiff walked through Sarah's mind, eyeing her with care. Hip dysplasia, thought Sarah. Hypothyroidism. A heavy dog. Need help lifting it.

'And you've treated a monkey yourself? You seem very young.'

'A capuchin once, yes, with a broken leg.'

This mention of a broken leg seemed to remind Mr Ronald of his situation. His face altered, suddenly, in pain.

'Do you feel it now?' asked Sarah. The skin whitened around his mouth and he let out a sound that reminded her of a tiger she had seen on television once, whose roar sounded like a long and drawn-out *ow*.

'It won't be long,' she said. 'My husband will be back soon.'

She looked out of the window. The road was dark in both directions and overshadowed with trees. There were dark shapes in the trees that looked like small monkeys, escaped from backyard sheds all over England, swarming with their rotten teeth and cataracts.

Mr Ronald seemed to have recovered from the attack of pain and now lay back against the seat and breathed quietly. His head appeared larger than most people's. This gave it a resilient look, although it reminded Sarah of a puppet. There was a band of sweat across his forehead. Without thinking, she placed her fingers on his wrist in order to measure out his heartbeat. It was steady now, and slow. She kept her hand where it was despite feeling revolted by the dampness of his old skin. They sat together listening for cars. Someone will come in this minute, thought Sarah; but the minute passed.

'A capuchin, you say,' said Mr Ronald. 'A kind of monk, isn't it?'

'Well, a monk, yes, I think. But also a kind of monkey.'

'I once saw an orangutan in the Berlin Zoo painting on the wall with a dish brush. Looked just like my wife cleaning the shower. But here Douglas is against primate testing. I can't go in for that. Douglas calls me species-ist.' Sarah decided not to ask who Douglas was. 'If they cure Parkinson's then it's worth those gorillas, I think. Not a popular stance, I'm told. I myself can't stand vegetarians.'

'I'm a vegetarian,' said Sarah.

'Well, in the abstract. It makes sense for someone like you. A veterinarian. Why heal them and then eat them? But

I always say vegetarians ought to eat meat when it's served to them. Imagine being a guest in someone's home and turning down food that's offered.'

This reminded Sarah of her own grandfather: perplexed and indignant in the midst of his self-imposed wartime privations, carried on unendingly and with pride. Food might run out — eat what you're given. Life might be lost — don't mind the monkeys.

Sarah liked to argue on this topic, calmly maintaining her position, but in this case she would not.

'Oh, but I'm sure you're a charming guest,' said Mr Ronald. 'And here you are, helping an old man in distress.' He chuckled and the pain came again, stronger this time. It lifted him from the seat a little, and this lifting caused more pain. He shut his eyes against it.

Sarah waited for this to pass, as it had the last time, and when he was quiet she asked, 'What can I do? Anything? Is it your legs?'

He laughed again, sucking in his cigarette breath, and moved his wrist away from her hand. The rain grew heavier and the trees on the road began to move their monkey arms, high above the fields. The fields grew damp and gave up their deeper smells of night mice and manure. No cars passed by. Sarah worried about David in the rain. He couldn't have been gone for longer than ten minutes, she reasoned; perhaps fifteen. She wondered briefly if the woman was still ironing in her house.

She asked again, 'How are your legs?'

'Funny,' said Mr Ronald, and his breath was shorter now. It left his throat unwillingly. 'Funny, but one of them's not even a leg. Left leg, below the knee. Plastic.'

Sarah imagined him at other times, rapping his fingers against the plastic of his leg, knocking it through his neat trousers while chatting on a bus. The war, she thought, he must have lost it in the war; she saw him and other men running over a French field. Poppies blew in the grass, and he was a young man, strong of limb, and the sea was behind them all as they ran.

'Diabetes,' said Mr Ronald. 'Didn't know, did you, that it could take your leg off?'

Sarah shook her head, but she did know. She'd seen diabetic dogs; cats too. She'd cut off their legs. The French field fell into the sea, and the rain still fell against the roof of the car.

'Started as a blister, then an ulcer,' said Mr Ronald. 'Just a mishap. A blister from new shoes. No one tells the young: be careful of your feet. Feet should last a lifetime. What can be prevented? Everything, they say. No they don't. They say not everything.'

He laughed harder now, in a thin straight line, and his cheeks drew in over the laugh so that Sarah could see the shape of his skull and the crowded teeth, nicotine-stained, that swarmed in his mouth. Perhaps this wasn't laughing, but breathing. The steady rain and wind moved the car slightly, back and forth, and it felt as if they were floating together gently at sea. The branches of the tree against which the car was pressed were black shapes at the corner of Sarah's eye, like Sheba at night, stalking rats with his stomach full of jellymeat.

(Sheba himself lay panting in the corner of his cage, overwhelmed by a calm fury and a pain on which he concentrated with a careful doling out of attention. He kept himself steady, but his small side rose and fell, rose and fell, higher and then deeper than it should. His eyes moved toward the door, and his mouth sat open, showing pink.)

The laugh was a clatter behind Mr Ronald's teeth, a rough edge over which his breath moved hectically. Sarah huddled close to him as he moved against the back of his seat, placed her arm around his shoulders, and touched his damp forehead. She felt her hair lift away from her skin, all along her arms and the back of her neck. The summer passed through the car, windy and wet.

'Hold on,' said Sarah. 'Just hold on.' Her mouth was against his ear. David would come soon. You could swear at a cat that rocked this way, crowded close in pain and confusion; you could talk softly, not to the cat but to the idea of the cat, to the faces of the family you must explain to about the cat. You could sing to the cat and if you had forgotten its name you could call it kitty — you could say 'hold on, kitty' while your hands moved and your neck craned forward and the parts of you that understood the machinery of a cat, its secret and moving parts, worked beneath the cat's terror. You could set the leg of a monkey and watch it, later, as it limped across the surgery floor, scowling and shaking its funny fist at you.

Noises came from Mr Ronald's throat now, and these sounds seemed accidental, the by-product of something else. They continued past the point Sarah felt certain he had died; they rattled on in the can of his throat. Sometime after they had subsided she became aware of the sound of a radio playing. In her own car, or this one? Who could Douglas be? A son? A grandson?

Sarah was now unsure of how long she had been sitting beside Mr Ronald, and how long it had been since he had stopped making any sound at all. Gently she laid his head back against the seat. His wife cleaned the walls of their shower, and he had been to see orangutans in Berlin. He was too young to have been in that war.

Without warning, David filled up the space in the passenger door of Mr Ronald's car. She had been so certain she would hear his footsteps on the road, but he was here in the doorway, as if she'd summoned him out of the field.

'I'm sorry, I'm sorry, I didn't find anyone.' He was breathless and wet. 'I ran and finally found a house, but there was no one home. I thought about breaking in. Kept going for a bit but no sign of life. No cars on the road, even. So I headed back to try the car again.'

He looked at the stillness of the man in the driver's seat. He saw the blood on Mr Ronald's trousers and the way that it crept towards his belt and shirt, and searched for blood on Sarah.

Sarah concentrated carefully on David's face, which swam in the sound of the rain and the radio and the end of the vodka. My husband. She smiled because she was happy to see him. Then she placed the wallet in Mr Ronald's lap.

Sarah moved to step out of the car, and David made space for her.

'How is he? Has he woken up? How does he seem?'

When a cat died during an operation, when a newt was too sick to be helped, when it was necessary for a macaw to die, then Sarah must tell its owners. It was difficult to tell them this true thing, and so along with it she added other, less true things: that the tumour caused no pain, that the animal hadn't been frightened to go under anaesthetic. Still, it was difficult. It made no difference to Sarah that words were inadequate to her enormous task. Of course they were. There might be a time when she would have to tell her friends, Sheba's owners, that he wouldn't survive his infection. Their grief, she knew, would be altered by a slight embarrassment that they felt it about a cat. Each loss of which she had been the herald seemed now to lead to this new immensity, her own: Mr Ronald, dead in a car. But they didn't know Mr Ronald. David had never even spoken to him. They had been married that midday, with no rain. There were no witnesses.

'He's dead,' said Sarah. She stood and shut the door behind her.

David fought the desire to lower his head and look through the window. It seemed necessary to make sure, but more necessary to trust Sarah. He held his hands out to her and she took them.

'My god,' he said. She shook her head. He knew that when she shook her head in this way, it meant: I'm not angry with you, but I won't talk.

'What now?' he asked. 'Should we take him somewhere?'

It seemed to David that Sarah owned the wreck, owned the tree and piece of road on which Mr Ronald had died, and that he need only wait for her instructions, having failed to find help. He thought of her sitting alone with the unconscious body of an old man, and he thought of the moment at which she must have realised that he was no longer unconscious: that he was dead. David saw with certainty that Sarah was another person, completely separate from him, although he had married her today. His wife.

'We'll try the car again,' said Sarah. 'We just have to get to the surgery.'

'And use the phone there,' said David.

Sarah crossed the road, and he followed her. She didn't look back at the wreck. Waiting on its grassy rise slightly above the road, their car had a look of faithful service, of eagerness to assist. It started on the third try with a compliant hum. Sarah had always been better at coaxing it; even before trying the ignition she'd been sure it would work. She was uncertain if this resurrection was good or bad luck or if, beyond luck now, it was simply inevitable. Now that she could see the rain in the headlights, she realised how soft it was, how English. She missed home, suddenly: the hard, bright days and the storms at the end of them, with rain that filled your shoes.

It grew dark in Mr Ronald's car as Sarah's headlights passed over and then left him, and it remained dark as she left that piece of road and that tree. David watched Sarah drive. They didn't speak. As the distance between their car and Mr Ronald's grew it seemed that the roads were all empty — that all of England was empty. It lay in its empty fields while the mice moved and the airplanes flew overhead to other places, nearby and faraway.

They reached lit buildings and then the surgery so quickly it seemed impossible to David that he couldn't have found help within minutes. Sarah walked calmly into the building, and she spoke calmly with the nurse. She didn't look at the telephone. There was no blood on her clothes. David watched his wife as she made her way towards the Queen of Sheba, who rubbed his head against the bars of his cage. He was waiting for the pain to stop. And then he would be let out, healed, to hunt mice in the wet grass.

Reward Offered

JON BAUER

The old man smiles. This is his favourite bit.

He opens their garden gate, brings the dog in, turns and closes the gate, a curtain twitching inside the house. The old man's stomach a helium balloon in the sky.

The sudden squealing of children, the kelpie straining on the string now, not wanting to sniff anything.

The front door flings open and a woman beams, faces appear round her legs, little hands gripping on and lifting her dress inadvertently higher, the dog lurching forward, its tail batting the old man's legs.

He extends the lost-dog sign in his hand, corrects himself and lets go the string, the family falling on the animal then squinting up at the man as if at the sun.

'Thank you *so* much. Where did you find her!'

Back outside the house now, biscuit crumbs on his clothes, his hair sticking up from rough and tumbling with children. He waves enthusiastically at their steaming-over of the lounge window, turns and opens the gate, steps through, whistling, shuts the gate — glances up, but the children are already gone.

He makes his way as far as the next corner, out of sight, rolls himself a smoke, his face concentrated, the pleasure of the good deed already fading from his chest. He attempts to hold on to it, tries to stop it seeping out between his ribs.

As he licks the paper his gaze is on the hills in the distance. Forty or fifty kilometres away, but there he is looking at them in the blink of an eye. What was distance when you had eyes? When you could see what you were missing.

At the corner the old man joins the main street and its usual morning hubbub of food-delivery trucks and the

Reward Offered

unsteady old. Lapdogs are tied up outside the miniaturised supermarket, cafés are full of laptops and blue collars mixing with white — foccacias, lattes and *Great, thanks, how are you?*

He travels among the throng, as ignored as if this was an old sepia photo and he's that smudge of a person moving through the background.

Outside the pub, he sits with a beer and a *Winning Post*, people wafting like bees in and out of the supermarket over the road — a woman coming along towing a chocolate labrador, the dog's underbelly littered with distended teats.

The old man puts his beer down and watches dog and owner pause outside the supermarket, then go on.

He relaxes again, picking the paper up and shaking it straight, returning to the column he was reading for the third time. Staring at the picture of the writer.

An old lady ties a dachshund up outside the supermarket, the dog issuing its outraged yapping at the automatic doors — making them indecisive. The dog jumping back, confused too. Both dog and doors making each other stutter. Both of them seeming panicked.

The yapping stops and the old man looks up, noticing the chocolate labrador tied up there now.

He leaves his paper and beer, waits at the crossing, hammering the button.

The lights change and he's marching before the beeping's started.

On the other side he steps over the dachshund, becomes entangled with it — hops on one leg, the door juddering against him, the labrador at the full extent of its lead, wolfing down some Friday-night vomit near the ATM.

The old man peers into the supermarket for the owner, then quickly unties the lab and crosses the road with it, darting between moving traffic and away.

Once home he inspects the labrador's collar: *Chocolate*, it reads. A phone number. He removes the collar and heads outside with it, crossing the expansive parking lot at the end of his street — checking for any obvious observers before wiping off the evidence with his hanky and chucking both in the bin.

Back indoors he turns on the radio, horseracing commentary coming at him. He likes it on in the background. The snaffled excitement of the voice. He only hears that on the radio now — that familiar voice.

He stands at his front window for ages, peeking through the drawn curtains. The dog watching him. The racing commentary turned right down now to just a bubbling stew on the stove or a waiting taxi.

Eventually he gives up his window vigil and surrenders to the TV in the corner, the labrador by his slippered feet, unsettled but playing the part at least.

Spring carnival is around the corner and that familiar voice is a face on the news, talking about the influx of overseas contenders and *Can Australian racing stand the competition?* The chocolate lab plonks her head on his lap, and even though he could never think the same way about dogs again after what happened in the hills those months ago, he leans over the animal and buries himself in the solace.

Next morning he shuffles out of his bedroom in slippers, lifts the kettle from its throne, gives it a wiggle, shuffles over to the sink, his hair squiffy. His head fogged over with last night's scotch. He turns on the tap, letting it run into the kettle, gazing out at the back garden and groaning at the piles and piles of unearthed soil and chewed bamboos that once supported the first creeping of beans. The dog out there too, looking at him, jowls on paws. The man's own jowls to-ing and fro-ing as he shakes his head, standing with his hands on the stainless steel of the sink, the kettle grumbling.

He's outside later, traipsing about the garden in his dressing-gown, using a small shovel to fill in holes and pick up dog-dirt. The lab sulking, or twisting round occasionally to fuss over her breasts that are almost neon with rawness. Small cries filling her throat.

Reward Offered

The old man can't recall seeing a dog like that, mammaries hanging down. More naked somehow than when male dogs get their erections in the park — cantilevering behind some bitch with her bum on the ground.

It's been three days now and still no posters up. He looks for the collar in the parking lot bin but it's been emptied of everything but stench.

In the newsagent's he picks up the special-edition *Winning Post* and the daily papers, both of which have a picture of a glistening racehorse on them.

FREE Cup Day Form Guide!

He scans the sports sections of the nationals and there it is, a column in *each* paper. He's aflame with pride. His smile sustaining all the way through the usually curt transaction with the shopkeeper.

He sits at the pub with a celebratory beer and smoke. Reads the articles both. Then reads them again. Raises his beer to the hills. *Cheers*, the old man's mouth says, and a little girl in the back of a car looks like she'll remember it forever. A lonely old man with nobody to cheers.

People come in and out of the supermarket with armfuls of alcohol. Men and women go by in the garb of pageantry. Every other car is a taxi.

The man sees the woman sticky-taping a sheet of A4 to a power pole then moving on, a stack more of them under her arm.

Back home he hurriedly unburdens himself of keys and newspapers, the sticky tape from the poster catching on his sleeve, the old man arrested for a moment by the dog's agonised yelps.

He opens the laundry door and she remains distressed, the smell of ammonia, a puddle on the floor. She comes out, stopping to lick at her underbelly, walking away, a perfunctory wag of her tail, then pausing again to fuss and fuss at her swollen teats.

Please help, the poster says (a picture of Chocolate with an array of snuggling, suckling puppies, their eyes closed). *Her puppies and family miss her! Reward offered.*

He takes the piece of paper to the phone, shutting both the back door and the one in the hallway against the yelping.

Ordinarily he'd wait, give it a few days. But it's Cup Day, his first without an invite to the hills. Last year it was little Jerome and Daniel cheering the telly, the dog barking, the old man laughing — their dad working his busiest day of the year.

He shaves again, drinking from a bottle as he does. Runs a towel under a hot, hot tap and puts it to his face, dancing a little in the bathroom. He brushes his hair. Dresses in his suit, chooses a tie. Takes the suit jacket off. Looks at himself. Puts the jacket back on. Takes off the tie. Goes out and pats the dog panting on the lawn, listless, whimpering.

He opens the cupboard and tries to remember which of the dangling leads is Chocolate's. He chooses string instead, for authenticity.

They leave the house, Chocolate putting on a smile despite her discomfort. That same dachshund yapping at the automatic doors outside the supermarket, working them open and closed like its bark is a clicker.

As he turns the last corner he can see the woman at her gate, her hand up to her forehead to keep out the sun. Then she's coming along the footpath, halfway between walking and jogging, Chocolate straining on the string until the old man lets her go and her claws click-clack away, teats swishing.

There's a tangle of hair and fur and wagging tails, the woman looking up from the embrace to smile at the man's approach, then turning back to Chocolate, checking her over.

As he gets close she stands, holding the string, Chocolate attending to her teats again. The woman keeping her hair behind her ear. A kind smile.

'I can't tell you what a relief this is!'

'As I said, right out in the middle of the road.'

'It's crazy, I was only in the shop two minutes.'

Reward Offered

'Maybe she slipped her collar?'

She shakes her head. 'It would have been left behind. No, someone must have taken her then thought better of it and let her go. I've given up trying to understand what motivates some people.'

'Well all's well that ends well, I suppose.'

'I suppose,' she says. 'We've got a house full for Cup Day but, come in and meet the puppies?'

'I've just finished work, and —'

'Sarah, by the way.' An outstretched hand. 'Don't you want your reward?'

'Ted. No need for a reward, Sarah. Any decent person would have done the same. I love dogs.'

He wipes his feet before entering the house. Does his hair again. Struck by the sheer homeliness of everything. All the different-sized shoes by the door. The faces posing together on the walls. The distant sound of voices, as well as yelping. The aroma of damp newspaper, and that sickly-sweet puppy smell.

He catches up in time to see Chocolate let loose and racing to the wooden board barricading the puppies in the laundry, all of them jumping up towards her face. Little tails thrashing. A garden of people through the windows, the barbecue going.

'Hopefully they'll get a moment together before the kids notice,' she says and removes the partition, the pups standing on each other's saggy faces to get to their mum. Chocolate licking and licking at them then giving in to the nudging and rummaging for nipples, her body moving on the lino with the seven heads pushing into her side — Sarah turning to Ted and beaming at the moment, bottles and little rubber teats drying on the draining board.

'I can't tell you what the kids've been like. And the pups. Lucky it's pretty much time for weaning. D'you have a dog?'

'Haven't been able to face having one since … He was a chocolate lab too, actually.'

'Oh you poor thing.'

'It was my son's.'

'Did it go missing too?'

He shakes his head and says to the lino, 'An accident. My grandchildren were in the car at the time. It was always a bloody stupid mutt, chasing car tyres. They *encouraged* it.' And their faces come back to him, the way they looked just after. His car still running.

Sarah's hands are up covering her open mouth, Chocolate giving a warning snarl at one of her pups.

'I haven't driven since. Haven't seen my grandchildren, either.' He gazes at the row of wagging tails. 'I suppose he's just busy, my son. Sports journalist.' Ted's face urging hers to understand — her hand down now but her mouth still a little open. 'Posh house in the hills.'

There're squeals then as the kids come in and happy-hell breaks loose, Sarah looking at him looking at the children.

He loiters in the garden, an outsider among the inclusive throng. He doesn't know how to feel. On the one hand here he is, their new best friend and hero, people getting him sausages and does he want mustard or red sauce? *Beer, Ted? This is Ted, everyone. Ted's the one that brought Chocolate home.* Inebriated cheers.

But behind the smile and the polite platitudes of his replies there are those hills staring at him.

… *She came home with nipples like brake lights!*

He goes into the relative quiet of the house, watching those swigging aliens through the window. The light in their eyes. He sets his beer down on the kitchen surface, feeling drunk suddenly. His innards sagging.

He wanders through and has a look in the laundry, the barricade there, the puppies back inside now having been paraded and cooed at — chased round the garden. Or left to put tiny puncture marks in things, like four-legged ticket inspectors.

They're curled up now. Seven yins. Or yangs. Sprawled

all over one another like they're one organism, pink skin on their bellies. Breathing quickly as if excited to be alive even when they're asleep. Giant paws. Everything dawning and new and beginning for them. Sagging skin, but sagging with capaciousness.

A little TV is on in the kitchen, showing footage of children at the racetrack, releasing hundreds of helium balloons into the air. The children's excitement backed by manipulative music and shots of the multicoloured balloons shrinking into the sky.

There's bedlam in the kitchen, people moving in a tacit congo through to the big TV in the lounge, turned up loud for race time. Like it's New Year and close to midnight. Betting slips and drinks jutting from hands, children shooshed sternly but weaving themselves in among the tense, excited bodies of adults. The TV blaring and Ted walking out to the garden but Sarah fetching him in again — telling him he can't miss the race.

So he stands at the back, ready for that voice. The excitement in it like his son is a child again. Like his voice in the days he wasn't yet old enough to chide Ted.

You left them, Dad. I don't care if it was to get him to the vet … You can't be trusted with them if you panic like that. You can't even be relied on to drive.

But it was just a son getting his own back for his childhood, Ted thinks, watching the families around the TV. He takes an urgent slug of drink. That was parenthood for you, eighteen years of giving everything but still feeling it isn't enough. Then the rest of your life waiting for them to realise. The rest of your life waiting for them to take their love away.

SLAM. The gates open, hooves on the ground, divots flying, gaping nostrils, the whites of the eyes. That voice galloping along too and everyone in the lounge happy and bouncing and delighted. The children wrapped up in adults. Fingers in half-open mouths. Laughter. Screaming. Ted in the corner, the crystal glasses tinkling in the cabinet beside him from the vibrations.

He leaves his beer on a coaster, slips out of the lounge, then the front door. Walks down the path, not wanting to leave but unable to stay. The street quiet. *The race that stops a nation.* Ted moving through the open gate.

'Ted?'

He stops, still focusing on the footpath. Sarah's tentative hand appearing on his shoulder. He turns a little, eyes downcast and wet.

'What is it?'

'I don't deserve your hospitality.'

'After what you did for us! Wait here, just for a moment. Then you can go. Promise me you'll wait.'

He fidgets in the sunlight while she's gone. His son's voice calling from indoors. Ted feeling unsteady now, his hand on the gate post. All those households listening to his son.

Sarah reappears with three sleepy brown bundles in her arms.

'Sarah, I can't.'

'Now, Ted,' she says, a gentle forcefulness in her voice, the sweetness of alcohol on her. 'Choose one.'

'But I —'

'No matter what you might think, Ted, all I see standing here is a dear sweet man who misses his grandchildren. Now, choose one. Or two, if you like. Maybe they're ready for another by now? Anyway, what are *we* going to do with seven little terrorists.'

Wednesday — *The day that jades a nation.* Ted wakes earlier than usual, showers, shaves. Gathers up all the empty bottles and rollie stubs in his lounge.

He's hungover and dry-retching as he clears up the small messes in the laundry, a clumsy chocolate-drop chasing his shoelaces round the house. Ted shooing her off then picking her up and letting himself be licked in the ear — wiping it off again, tiny puncture marks on his formidable earlobes. The radio sitting silent in the corner.

He carries the pup and her sweet smell out to the garden, his mind occupied with a soup of feelings in his stomach, the dog's tiny pulse fluttering insistently against his hand, and a heart-shaped balloon floating high above him in the blue, heading for the hills.

No One Special

PEGGY FREW

'Have fun.' Dixon kisses me and goes back to the recipe book.

'Thanks.' I stop at the door and watch him, the way he bends urgently over the table, glasses slipping down his nose. 'Dix.'

'Yeah?' He doesn't look up.

'Don't worry too much about dinner. Bec might not even come. You know what she's like.'

He straightens, pushes his glasses back up. Looks at me. 'Kath. It'll be fine. If she doesn't come we'll just eat it.' He smiles, flaps his hand. 'Go on — off you go. Don't forget the wine.'

I go, but all the way to the tram stop I still see him, his finger on the page, marking the line. His sweet preoccupied face and the crease between his eyebrows that had softened for a moment, at the thought of her not coming.

Bec's waiting on the corner of Bourke and Swanston, under the shelter of the tram stop, hands in the pockets of a grey-green coat I haven't seen before. Her smile leaps out at me from the swarm of faces, and we fall into step together, heading up into Little Bourke, the narrow hectic red-and-gold of Chinatown.

'How was the conference?' I say.

'All right.'

'How's Sydney?'

'All right.' This she says with a lifting and dropping of her hand, a dismissive gesture that's wholly hers. For a while, in my early teens, I tried to copy it, until my mother one day grabbed my wrist and stopped me. 'It's not glamorous, that waving-off thing your sister does,' she said. 'It's actually very rude.'

So she's cut me off, and because of this we go along for a while in uncomfortable silence. I watch my feet and press my lips together over the feeling of shame that's spurted so readily at her rejection. In my head I try out and dismiss some things to say.

Then we reach an Asian grocery, and she tugs me by the arm inside. 'Should we get a present for Dixon?' she says, and taps at a jar of wizened, greyish, pickle-shaped things. *Sea cucombor* it says on the label, underneath some Chinese characters. 'What do you reckon?' She turns to face me and lifts an eyebrow, and I smile, ready and willing, because I know this is the closest she'll come to apologising.

Back out on the street, some winter sunlight comes down between the looming buildings, and we both tilt our faces to the narrow strip of sky. A sliver of eggshell blue shows through the clouds, and a platinum blaze of sun. I lower my gaze, and there we are, reflected in the shop window: our hips, our shoulders set at the same angle, each with the right arm raised, hers holding her hair down in the wind, mine shading my eyes as I stare into the glass.

'So.' She sighs, blowing on a little round cup of tea from the self-serve urn. 'Melbourne. Freezing old Melbourne.' Though I notice, if anything, her pale skin is paler than ever, despite all the Sydney sunshine she's supposed to be basking in.

My mother's voice comes into my head. 'Yes, Rebecca's in Sydney now. Doing very well. She's in finance.' Sydney. Finance. The far-off world of Bec and her success.

I clear my throat. 'Will you ... Are you still going to come for dinner?'

She narrows her eyes in the steam from her cup. 'Of course,' she says, as if she always does what she says she'll do. She taps her bitten-down nails on the table and picks up the plastic menu. 'So,' she says again. 'How's Dixon?'

And there it is, the tiny flick of a look, the split-second of acknowledgement. I look back, and we share it. An adjustment, a blip, and then it's over and we resume.

'He's good.'

'Good.' She drinks more tea.

They always happen, these moments, every time we see each other. Every time we talk about Dixon. And then, later, when he's there too there'll be another one. Recognition. Awkwardness. Throbbing there in the spaces between us.

The waitress comes for our order, and when that's done I take a risk. 'Mum says you've got a new boyfriend,' I say, looking down at my cup.

Bec shrugs. 'No one special.' She picks up her paper napkin and spreads it on her lap.

I tip the cup, watch the tea leaves twirl.

'So,' says Bec. 'What movie should we see?'

In the cinema, in the dark, I sneak a sideways glance at her, and it opens up again, that yawning space, the blankness that is the time they had together. We don't talk about it, me and Dixon. And Bec certainly doesn't talk about it — with me or with anyone, as far as I know. And I hardly ever think about it, really. Only times like this, when I see her again after a while.

It didn't last long. Like all of her relationships. And I wouldn't have even got to meet him — because of course she never brought boyfriends home — except I bumped into them on the street one night, and she was forced to introduce us. Which she did in her typical breezy don't-you-dare-start-talking way — 'Dixon, Kathy; Kathy, Dixon' — and then rounded him up and moved him along as soon as she could. And then I guess they broke up. And then I started hanging around with this girl, Sarah, I met in my first year at uni; we'd go to these parties, and he'd be there, Dixon. At first we kept our distance. But it kept happening, we kept running into each other, and Bec had moved away — not to Sydney yet, but across town, so we hardly saw her — and Dixon was so real and close, and it just felt right, and, well, it just happened.

And now our time together — mine and Dixon's — has gone on so long, and looms so big all around us and trails such a strong and bright and full history of its own that that other time — his and Bec's — is just a speck way off in the past, really.

That night though, when I first met him, when they were together. As they walked off I looked over my shoulder and I saw him put his arm around her. I can still see that, clear as if it was yesterday, if I ever think about it.

At our house, Dixon opens the front door before I even get my key in the lock.

'Oh, hello,' he says. 'Thought I heard the gate.' He runs his fingers through his hair, jabs at his glasses, rubs his nose.

'Hi, Dixon.' Bec reaches up to peck his cheek, and he receives it shyly, one hand lifting towards her shoulder but not quite making it, so it hovers for a moment like some sort of uncertain benediction.

'Hi. Hi, Bec. Haven't seen you for ages. Nice to see you.'

We all stand for a second. Rain starts to fall, rattling on the tin verandah roof above.

'Oh — come in.' Dixon steps back. 'Quick, you must be freezing. I've got the fire going.' Bec moves past him and up the hall, and Dixon flashes me a quick smile. 'Come in, come in,' he says, as if I'm another visitor.

In the living room Bec slings her coat and bag onto the floor and sits right at one end of the couch. 'Something smells amazing,' she says.

'Roast lamb,' says Dixon. 'Shouldn't be too long.' He opens the wine and pours, spilling some on the coffee table. 'Whoops.' He hands glasses around and raises his own. 'Cheers.'

We drink and stare into the fire.

'How was the movie?' says Dixon.

'It was okay,' I say, at the same time as Bec says, 'Great.'

We all laugh.

'I think Kathy let me choose because I'm the visitor,' Bec says. 'I think she'd've preferred to see something, you know, *serious*.'

I roll my eyes at her. 'You were always into crap films.'

She shrugs, lifts her glass. 'I like to be entertained. Not traumatised.'

'Fair enough.' Dixon gets up and goes to the kitchen and comes back with a dish of olives. Then he starts poking at the fire.

Bec looks at him. 'Sit down, will you, Dix!'

'Sorry.' He grins and sits down on the couch, at the other end from Bec. He sinks into the cushions with a loud, obvious sigh of relaxation, but almost straightaway gets back up. 'I'll just go and put the greens on.'

We watch him go.

'So.' Bec moves down off the couch and onto the floor, closer to the fire. 'How's your Masters going?'

'Okay. I guess. Driving me crazy.'

In the firelight the lines I'd noticed on her face for the first time today are gone again. Sitting with her legs drawn up and her arms around her knees, neck straight, eyes on the flames, she looks as she always has: contained, untouchable. 'Good old Bec,' our parents would say. Striking out on her own. Always so independent. They told stories of her as a child, of her sense of justice, how she'd take on the bullies in the playground, how her little face would puff up with rage at the sight of unfairness or persecution. 'Even as a baby she knew her own mind,' my mother would say. 'Kathy would go to anyone, but Bec — if Bec didn't want to do something there was no making her.'

There's a muted flutter of notes. Bec reaches for her bag, pulls out her phone, glances at the screen, tosses it back again. She takes an olive and puts it in her mouth. The muffled ringtone sounds out a couple more times and then stops.

I get up. 'Just going to the toilet.'

Out in the kitchen Dixon is rummaging in the saucepan

cupboard. The rain drums on the low roof.

'How's it going?' I say, but he doesn't hear me. I slip past.

In the bathroom mirror my face is flushed, my lips purple from the wine. I press my wet hands to my cheeks. A vision comes to me — Bec's eyes, up close, reflecting green from the grass we are lying on. Freckles on her skin. Her face still round, babyish. Lying so close we can feel each other's breath.

I move closer to the mirror, angle my face into it, my eye. Under the glistening outer layer I can see the sclera with its veins and yellowed patches; the coloured fibres of the iris, their gradations and flecks; the black hole of the pupil. The things you only see right up close, that as an adult you no longer examine in anyone, except maybe a lover.

'Five minutes,' says Dixon as I go through again.

'Okay. Want some help?'

'No thanks.' He fiddles at the stove, adjusting the gas.

I stop at the doorway and look in at Bec, at the straight back of her neck, her level shoulders. I think about Dixon giving her the glass of wine, the way he lowered his head to her, supplicating.

She's always been in charge, socially. I still find it amazing that someone can control others so effectively by doing so little. That way she has of closing up her face. It tightens — the eyebrows drawn into smooth curves, the eyes slightly widened — and seals itself over with a kind of cool impassivity. And whoever it was saying whatever it was she didn't want them to say just stumbles to a halt.

I think perhaps this defensiveness, this expression, is what our parents are referring to when they describe her as tough. She freezes them out too, as much as anyone, if not more. I've seen their gently frowning, wounded faces, their eyes sliding helplessly off that intractable stoniness, the questions half-asked and trembling on their lips. And then they just give up. 'Bec's always been a bit of a closed book,' I've heard them say. And my mother might laugh a sketchy little laugh, as if it's a funny thing that your own daughter could be so unknowable.

I lean against the wall. Bec's hand reaches out, lifts the glass, and she dips her head to drink. The back of her neck shows, frail as a child's.

She must've been about sixteen — and me fourteen — when I first saw the cuts on her legs. We were forced to share my room for a while because hers was being painted. And so I saw them as she swung up onto the top of the old bunk bed, as her nightshirt flared out: short ugly red scratches, deep ones, in the soft white flesh at the tops of her thighs, just near the elastic of her underpants.

And then, smoking on the garage roof, she showed me how to press the heated metal top of a cigarette lighter down on the skin near the inner elbow, leaving a burn mark like a grinning face, a curved U-shape and two small circles above it. Smileys, they were called. Kids did them at school, or at the train station, but not Bec. She did them only at home, ignoring my presence and my murmured protests. Screwing her eyes up, a cigarette hanging loose between her lips, she would hold the lighter there until I'd try to grab her arm, and even then she registered this disruption only faintly, with a flicker of her eyebrows. My smileys were barely a pale pink, and gone within a day. Eyes stinging, already sick from the smoke, I could only hold the lighter down for a split-second. But her arms inside her sleeves bore dark scabs that took ages to heal.

At the dinner table our mother commented on Bec's hands, on the way she chewed at the skin around the nails so the tips of her fingers were red and swollen. 'Darling, your nails look terrible,' she said — or something like that. And Bec gave one of her usual brick-wall replies and did her piss-off flick of the hand, and the conversation was shut down. I sat across from her and wondered what other marks were there, under her clothes.

A quiet has fallen. The rain's stopped. Outside the windows everything sighs and drips.

Dixon rattles some cutlery. 'Dinner!' he calls.

Bec puts her knife and fork together and checks the clock. She draws a hissing breath in between her teeth. 'I should call a cab.'

'You could always stay here tonight,' I say.

'No.' She pushes her chair back. 'I'm getting this nice hotel room for free. And anyway it's closer to Mum and Dad's. I said I'd have breakfast with them before my flight.'

We all go out the front to wait for the taxi. Everything — the raggedy wet bushes, the sky blown clear, the cold air — is clean and sobering, and we stand in silence until the yellow car swishes up.

'Bye,' Bec says. She kisses us both quickly. 'Thanks for dinner, Dix.' Her steps are light and quick down the path. She gets in and puts down the window. 'So nice to see you both,' she calls. 'Kathy — you should come to Sydney for a visit sometime.'

'Yeah. That would be great.' I wave as the car drives off.

'Bye!' Dixon and I both call again, even though she won't be able to hear us. And then we just stand there for a while, not talking.

I did try to visit her once, booked flights and everything. But she pulled out at the last minute, claiming something had come up at work.

Sometimes when I call or send a text message, and she doesn't answer or reply — which happens often — I picture the phone in her hand. Her watching my name light up on the screen. And then her putting the phone down again, still ringing or with the SMS unopened.

In the doorway of my study I stand and look at the piles of papers, the blank screen of the computer, the wobbly old swivel chair. There's a quiet in the house that feels solid, heavy. Immovable. I take my hand back off the light switch and close the door again.

Back in the living room I sit down beside Dixon. He pours me the last of the second bottle of wine.

I drain my glass as fast as I can. I feel too clear still, too sharp-edged and open.

We sit there, side by side. We don't look at each other.

'Dix.'

He doesn't answer.

I wish I could cry because it feels like that would make this easier, whatever it is I'm trying to do. I turn to face him. 'Dix.'

Dixon puts his hands to his face and rubs it. His glasses get pushed up to sitting on the top of his head. Then he takes his hands away but still he doesn't turn to me. 'I'm tired,' he says. 'I might go to bed.'

I wait, but he just looks into the fire.

'Okay.' I blink. My eyes are still so dry they hurt.

'Goodnight.' And now he does lean towards me, his face naked and weary. Without meeting my gaze he kisses me. A neat, chaste, goodnight kiss, but for a moment I feel his lips and taste him, and I smell him, his skin, his hair, his breath, and it's so familiar it's like kissing my own self, or a brother, or a sister.

The Way We Wed

ANNE JENNER

Back in the 1960s shotgun weddings happened a lot. You couldn't go so far as to say it was the fashion, but enough of my friends were doing it to make me see it as a reasonable lifestyle option. Anything would be better than my job as a mail clerk in a dim corner of the Department of Lands, where I'd ended up after flunking out of art school. And I had the means at my disposal: a young and healthy body, a willing boyfriend and a total lack of common sense or reliable contraception.

'You silly, silly girl,' my mother said, between outbursts of weeping. Weeping tended to be my mother's instinctive response to life's dramas, one that gained her a lot of attention if nothing else. 'You've ruined your life, I hope you realise.'

'What do you think you're going to live on?' my father asked, not unreasonably since Doug was still at uni, and my earning capacity was clearly going to be curtailed. In those days they tended not to like pregnant women hanging around the workplace. Or hanging around anywhere much at all. You were supposed to cover your expectant state in a voluminous smock, so as not to inflict your fecundity on the world. Not like these days, where the baby bump has become a celebrity status symbol.

'We don't need much,' I said. 'Anyway Doug's getting a job.' I tried to ignore Dad's snort of laughter.

'Doing what?' he said. 'Donating sperm?'

'That's not funny, George,' Mum said, dabbing at her swollen eyes. Someone should have told her the unfortunate effects of crying on the over-forties complexion.

These family councils took place around the dinner table after the plates had been cleared away. My younger sister and brother were excluded from the proceedings by virtue of their innocence, which they resented at first, especially as they got lumbered with the washing-up. Then they realised being in the kitchen gave them a chance to eavesdrop, which they did shamelessly.

'Why did Mum say you can't be a bride?' my sister Jennifer asked one night. We were sitting in my bedroom out the back of the house, which, although neither Jennifer nor my parents knew, had been the scene of the crime. My bedroom was what would now be called an extension to the Housing Trust brick-veneer box that was our house. It was really a tack-on to the back porch, a sort of dog's-leg protrusion into the backyard. This meant that it was cut off from the rest of the house by the back door, the laundry and the no-man's-land in between, which served as a repository for brooms, shoe-cleaning utensils and chooks' food. Although my window directly overlooked the Hills hoist, I liked this arrangement because of its privacy. Once the rest of the family had retired for the night, an orgy could be going on in my room and no one would know. What did go on was Doug. When we got home from a date, he'd drop me off out the front and accelerate away, ostentatiously revving his muffler-challenged bomb, only to park around the block and creep down the side to be let in the back gate by me. From there it was but a short step into my bedchamber and regular episodes of teenage sex.

'Mum has this idea that brides should be virgins,' I said.

'Oh yes, we learned about those in school, in ancient history,' Jennifer said. 'Aren't they sort of like angels?'

'In a way, yes. Anyway I'm not one so I can't wear a long white gown according to Mum.'

'Can't you even have a veil?'

'No, I don't think so.'

'So what will you wear then?'

This was a good question and was in fact becoming a real bone of contention between my mother and me. Mum was very sensitive about the whole issue of sex. In fact, if it hadn't been for the threefold evidence to the contrary, I could well have believed she was still a virgin herself. She was insistent that, as I was damaged goods, it would be the height of hypocrisy for me to appear in the holy portals of the church in anything remotely bridal. Perhaps she'd have been happy if I'd rocked up in scarlet satin. As it was, after a lot of unpleasant public wrangling in various dress shops around town, she got her way. The chosen creation was a cream-coloured lace affair quaintly called an *ensemble*. Contrary to what consumers of today may think, this was not a bed-base-and-mattress combination, although it may just as well have been. It comprised a shapeless dress covered by an even more shapeless coat sort of thing: perfectly acceptable for a matron of advanced years but absurdly and appallingly hideous on me. To top this off, in place of the forbidden veil, on my head was to sit a confection resembling a small inverted cabbage.

Once the contentious issue of what the un-bride would wear was resolved, my mother turned her attention to more important things.

'I'm too young to be a grandmother,' she said one night, seated again at the empty dinner table. 'Why is this happening to me?' A couple of sniffs portended another descent into lachrymose lament, so I refrained from saying it wasn't happening to her, but to me. If she insisted on taking credit, who was I to argue. Not getting any satisfactory response to her question, she turned to me with a worried look. 'You know what really bothers me about all this, Jane?'

'No,' I said. 'Apart from the fact that I'm ruining my life, and bringing shame, ruin and destitution on myself and my nearest and dearest.'

'Don't be smart, my girl. I don't think you even love Doug. Do you?' She looked at me, her eyes a watery rebuke.

'I'm not sure I even know what love is,' I said, telling the truth for once. 'Besides, I haven't seen a lot of examples of it around here recently.' At this there was another outburst of weeping, which diverted my father's attention from the newspaper he'd been reading under the table.

'Come on now, Jane my girl,' he said. 'That's not fair. Doug's not such a bad bloke.'

Did he know something I didn't?

So the family drama raged on while I buried myself somewhere inside my hormones and gestated. I was eating for two now and thinking for no one. According to Doug, similar histrionics were playing out at his house, except that his mother was beating her breast about him having to drop out of uni. As though he was some sort of academic ivory-tower material, when in all the time I'd known him I'd never seen him pick up a book. That's when she wasn't railing against him for marrying someone she considered sluttish. This was not, as may be supposed, because I was clearly a non-virgin, but because I'd turned up at the breakfast table once, when I was spending the weekend at their house, wearing eye make-up. She could have done with a bit of cosmetic assistance herself but apparently regarded all such debaucheries as instruments of the devil.

Of course one of the worst aspects of this gauntlet I'd so inconsiderately thrown down before my parents was how the hell were they going to pay for a wedding? Mum was brilliant at budgets and each payday religiously put aside, into small labelled plastic containers, allocated amounts for all the foreseeable household expenses. A wedding for her eighteen-year-old daughter was not one of these. Therefore, the whole thing had to be done on the cheap.

'Well, we can get the church hall for nothing,' Mum said. 'Seeing as I'm on the church ladies' guild. And we can get the CWA to do the catering; that won't cost much.'

'But the church hall's a dump,' I said, remembering the last time I'd been in there. It resembled nothing so much as a large public toilet: freezing in winter, sweltering in summer, and smelling of mouse droppings.

'It'll be nice once we put a few floral arrangements around,' Mum said. 'Beggars can't be choosers, my girl.'

The Way We Wed

'But flowers cost money, don't they? Unless you're planning to strip the neighbours' gardens.'

'We can probably run to a bouquet for you and a couple of corsages,' Dad said with breathtaking extravagance.

'Yes,' Mum said. 'And we can use the flowers left in the church from the Sunday services. In this cold weather, they should last a week.'

I could see it was pointless to argue. What did it matter anyway? I should have, though, over the photographer, who turned out to be an old army mate of Dad's who took photos for a hobby. He hadn't yet progressed to colour film so he ended up hand-tinting the photos — badly. I am well nigh unrecognisable in the resultant creations, having somehow been rendered with jet black hair and eyebrows when I am in fact a honey blonde. Still, who was I to complain?

Finally the wedding day dawned. From childhood I'd had a fantasy of getting married in Westminster Cathedral, possibly to Prince Charles. What I got was Doug in a prison haircut, and a nondescript suburban church. The musical accompaniment was a wheezy electric organ and a wobbly rendition of 'O Perfect Love' by my great-aunt Mabel.

It was one of those grey days in midwinter when the sky droops over the landscape like a public servant's cardigan. Sad is the bride the rain falls on, they say, but sadder still the bride who hangs about under a threatening sky that does nothing more than emit a constipated drizzle. Just enough to turn her fine hair into rat's tails. Coiffure, however, was the least of my worries. In the grip of morning sickness, which consumed each morning in a single gulp and spat it out all afternoon, evening and night, I looked like death.

Despite having managed to empty my stomach of any potentially troublesome contents before we got to the church, as I tottered down the aisle on Dad's arm I was assailed by an ominous buzzy feeling. Breaking out in a cold sweat, I clutched at Dad's elbow. 'Dad, I feel funny,' I hissed. 'I think I'm going to faint.'

With impressive presence of mind, Dad stepped on my toe. The shock of this was enough to get the blood rushing back to my head and keep me upright long enough for him to donate me to Doug.

I would like to say it all worked out well after that, even with the rocky start. And really it wasn't so bad. If you don't count the reception where my little brother ate so many of the CWA ladies' lamingtons that he vomited over his new shoes. Or the fact that the bride's and groom's mothers refused to appear in any photos together, because somehow they'd ended up wearing the same hat. Or that Doug and his best man, Bruce, having made total messes of themselves at the previous night's bucks party, decided to see who could down the most hairs of the dog, and ended up passed out in the gents. Doug revived enough to consummate the marriage that night, although it was pretty much a moot point by then.

It's the Cheroot

MARION HALLIGAN

It's the cheroot, he said, tapping it with the scarlet painted nail of his middle finger, it's the cheroot that will solve the mystery. We looked at this smoked-down stump, soggy in its plastic bag. Not this, he said, this is a cigar, true Havana; I am talking about a cheroot. He stood up and walked away. His short swingy red jacket showed off his small waist, his slender hips rolled very neatly as he walked in his brief skirt and stiletto heels. He turned as he reached the end of the wharf and flashed a smile, the whiteness of his teeth dazzling in his plum-dark face.

Not your problem, he said, and walked up the steps to the boat, his heels clicking on their wooden planks, the muscles of his calves made round and taut by the highness of the heels, and stood in the prow while it cast off and headed down the river.

We watched the old steam launch lumbering through the oily swell. No, it was not our problem. We went on with the card game. There wasn't a lot of money at stake, none of us had any to speak of, but that made the prospect of even a small amount more enticing. I picked up my newly dealt hand; the boat was nearly at the bend of the river. It blew its horn, a melancholy sound, old and patient and elemental as the river itself. My cards looked promising. I stared out at the greenish water, the greenish mangroves along the bank, the absent boat. Not our problem. She was young, and pretty enough; she should have had a life. I concertina-ed the cards in my hand. The death of one diminishes us all. The beautiful young man with his clue — or perhaps it was a warning — of the cheroot might not have said that, but he would act accordingly.

The Lizard lost as usual. He mooched off down the wharf. Spangle as usual won. He picked up the small pile of coins and slid them into his pocket. Every week we played cards, and it seemed as though Spangle always won. Was he a better player? I didn't think so. But luck was with him, and that was all that counted. He had a pretty wife, too. He took his winnings home and gave them to her. Maybe that was what protected his luck. I went and stood beside the Lizard, where he leaned on a post, gloomily staring at the greenish water heaving itself around the piles of the wharf. Even the water is tired, in this place. I imagined I could see a shimmer at the bend of the river where the launch had disappeared. It wouldn't be back for another week. No one much wants to come here. And nobody seems any good at leaving.

Sometimes I imagined the Lizard bending over and just sliding into the water, like some scaly amphibian. Except of course he wasn't, did not even look like one, not like his namesake even. The water was deep here, and as with most of the people who lived along the river he couldn't swim. The water did not make you want to get into it for any reasons of pleasure.

Suddenly he said, with surprising vehemence, How can she work, like that? It's not natural, I don't see how she can do it.

After a minute I guessed him to be talking about Andrea. Like the rest of the people here he thinks she is a woman. You mean the heels, I said. It's a skill they have, women.

Still seems funny, for a police, said the Lizard.

Plain clothes, I said, and he laughed.

Spangle's wife came up the track. She was wearing high-heeled sandals, with skimpy shorts and a shirt tied at the waist. Her skin was very brown, we're all burned by the sun here, but hers was somehow natural-looking, as though she'd have been born like that, and her eyes were enormous and dark with bluish whites. She took little steps, sort of mincing, that's what the high heels did. See, I said, they just can.

It's the Cheroot

She paused by the store, which in this place is pub, and café, post office, grocery, you name it; if it is to be bought it has to be bought here. There's a sign across the front, painted by Slide, the fat man who owns it. *Emporium of Broken Dreams*, it says, in dripping red letters on an old piece of timber. I heard Spangle's wife say once how she thought it sounded like a poem.

Slide's boy was carrying in the boxes the launch had unloaded on to the end of the wharf. A lot of grog. Tins of food. It's grim if the stores run out, and I'll say this for Slide, things might run down but they don't usually run out. You might end up eating hearts of palm out of a can when what you wanted was baked beans, but at least it's food.

I once asked Slide, How come hearts of palm? He replied, Why not? There are a lot of things in the world, Ken.

The opium doesn't run out. So far it hasn't, and everybody has faith that it never will. Nobody ever questions its just always being there. Maybe they're superstitious; better just to go on having faith. Maybe things would be better if it did, I said to Slide once. He laughed at me. After everyone had killed each other, you mean?

Andrea never notices the opium. Well, I suppose he notices, just pretends he doesn't. The fact is the place runs smoothly. Well, until the girl was murdered. It'd be good to think that it was some passer-by, but we never have those. No tourists come here. The boat is the only way in. Occasionally there's somebody who may be official, but they don't stay, they leave on the same boat. It comes in, unloads the stores, takes the venom and goes again.

The Lizard has a tent, quite a fancy affair with its own verandah. Spangle and his wife live in one of the shacks; Slide has the best of them. The fisherman's is okay. There's a guy called Tarantin who lives round the bend of the track with his old mother. The Chinese have a kind of compound of huts and lean-tos and canvas shelters; I am never sure how many of them there are. Sometimes I squint at it, when the sun is glinting off the flattened paraffin tins that form their roofs, and see a fabulous palace of many pavilions, but that's hard work even for my imagination.

That's about it, except for a couple of old-timers further down the river. And the hippies that live by the creek, further inland. Creek; more of a swamp. There are kids with bites all over, but they don't seem to notice. And of course me; I was lucky there was a shack, more tumbledown even than most, but it was vacant. It belongs to Slide; I expect everything does. He put a tarp over the roof so it's fairly watertight.

Slide's store is closed by a wooden shutter that folds down to the counter. The shutter has a huge padlock that he never clicks home; even when it's down it doesn't necessarily mean that the shop is shut. On the evening of Andrea's visit he beckoned me over to what he calls the terrace, and put a bottle of his whisky on one of the rickety tables. I know if I sit with Slide often and long enough I'll learn all there is to know about this place. Slide's okay to talk to, the others are hopeless, you have to play cards. When you drink with Slide you know he's totting it up, it'll end on the slate with all your other purchases. Only yours, he doesn't expect you to pay for his.

Sometimes the whisky is some terrible moonshine that comes from a still somewhere off in the mangroves. Tonight it's halfway decent, not Scotch of course but some okay colonial imitation. The stomachs are strong here. I sometimes think that Slide likes me, and that's probably why the others accept me. We all look the same: me, Slide, the Lizard, the fisherman, Slide calls him the Fisher King but I've never thought he was that good at his job. If we depended on his fish to feed us we'd get pretty hungry. We're all burned mahogany by the sun, our eyes a bit watery, dressed in singlets and shorts and thongs, our bodies worn and sinewy. Even Spangle, who's probably the youngest, looks a scrawny old bird.

The dead girl is the daughter of the fisherman. If he's the

It's the Cheroot

Fisher King does that make her the Fisher Princess? She used to flit, down to the shop, along the edge of the river, a thin and child-shaped little woman with a great red frizz of bushy hair on her head and a poignant little face. She wore dresses like nightgowns and it's as well she didn't go out after dark or you'd have taken her for a ghost. I thought of her in the whisky as I took a pull of it, a kind of memorial toast. Wondered if maybe now her figure would flit through the dark nights of the river, really a ghost. I wished her spirit rest. I suppose you can't expect that until her murderer is caught.

Know what a cheroot is? said Slide. He pumped the paraffin lamp and lit it, casting a yellow gloom over the tables, the beaten earth of the terrace, the single tree that leaned over his yard. The whisky looked very brown in the glasses. I read somewhere that whisky in its natural form is colourless, that the brown is caramel. I suppose it's to make you think of peat and amber-coloured mountain becks. I often think of words like *beck*, and *brook*, when I look at this oily river and its sluggish creeks. But we can't choose the words we live with.

You smoke it, I said, it's like a cigar.

It comes from India, he said. It's open at both ends. Originally from India. Could be anywhere now.

Andrea said it would solve the mystery.

Andrea will solve the mystery. He's a clever girl.

I nodded. So Slide knew about Andrea.

Not least because he isn't a girl, said Slide, and no one twigs. You know, he said, his mother called him that. Apparently there's some Italian painter of that name. She looked at books of beautiful pictures before he was born; supposed to give her beautiful thoughts and so she'd have a beautiful baby. It's a bloke's name, there, apparently.

Slide looks sceptical at the best of times, and at that moment even more so. You have to wonder, he said. Maybe in Italy, but not here. It could have an effect.

Why doesn't anyone else know?

They don't know much, Ken. Better like that.

I suppose he is quite beautiful.

True.

Slide took out a packet, a yellow box with some pattern in red and gold. He opened the lid and slid back cellophane. Cheroot? he said.

Where did you get these?

I've got a lot of things in there.

He lit it for me. It was quite coarse, but it didn't taste stale, as it might have done, I thought, being something Slide had had forever. Do you sell a lot of these?

Not a lot, no.

I said if I sat drinking with Slide I'd eventually find out what there is to know about this place. But I should also have said that it could take a very long time.

Cheroot's a French word, he said. They got the word from India.

Slide's got three books in the store, has had for a long time, I reckon. The same three. But you often see him sitting on his terrace, reading. Not one of the three. I suppose that's where he gets to know about cheroots and such.

Why do you stay here, Slide?

Got to live somewhere. He blew fragrant smoke into the air. Why do you, Ken?

I shrugged. I was writing my book, but I didn't want to tell people that.

One day you'll finish it, he said. Then you'll see. Whether you leave or not. Can, or want to.

So he knew that, too. I laughed. But I could feel my cheeks getting hot. Shame-faced. I turned it towards the river, secretly flowing past the wharf. This immense burden of water, always flowing, always and never the same.

People are funny, he said. They get fond of the places they live in. Even so god-forsaken as this.

I looked along the track. The shacks were dark. Nothing to do at night, nobody reads, there's no television, they just go to bed when the light goes and get up when it comes back.

The opium is not a night-time activity. Only the Chinese palace showed wavering slits of lamplight, or candle flame.

Why do we say god-forsaken, I wonder? I think God is more here than in most places I've been. What do you say, Ken? Will we find God here?

Maybe, if we look for him.

Good point.

We'd got to the stage where the conversation had become lazy; our voices were, and my brain, but the subject matter was too energetic for me. The level of the whisky had dropped considerably. I wasn't sure I could afford much more. I stood up, and stretched.

To our cots, said Slide, our virtuous cots. He drained his glass and stood up, too. He raised his hand and padded with the slow gait of the fat man round to the back of his emporium, the bottle under his arm.

When I first came here I used to get up at dawn to watch the harvest, but there's not a lot to see. The snakes begin to stir in the grey morning twilight, and the men suddenly sinuous as ghosts disappear into the scrub and come out with hessian sacks with the creatures inside. They keep them in boxes under the wharf, for coolness, and then just before the launch is due they milk the venom. It's a skill these people have. The money's okay, not a lot but not bad for the amount of effort involved. They'd say it was dangerous work, but they make it look easy. Not that you'd catch me trying.

Slide told me that at one time, when there were a lot more snake catchers on the river, they'd make dry ice with carbon-dioxide cylinders so they could milk them straightaway and freeze the venom. But they decided they didn't need that much effort; the launch just brings a sackful of the stuff, and they put the newly harvested venom in that. I said to Slide that some entrepreneurial person could probably get them a much better price, organise a market that would make them a lot richer.

Entrepreneurial, said Slide, pronouncing the word in a set

of small bites as though he'd never heard it before, let alone pronounced it, and wasn't sure he could manage it now. He squinted. What would be the point of that? he asked.

More money, I said.

What would be the point of that? What would they spend it on, here?

They could use it to get away.

Then they wouldn't be venom hunters. Logic, he said, logic, Ken.

I've given up getting out of bed at dawn to see the snake catchers melt away into the scrub, I've kept my old habits of late to bed and late to rise even though it means buying a lot of paraffin, but I do sometimes still watch the milking. Spangle is the best at it, the forked stick, the grasp of the head, the opening of the mouth. Tarantin's mother is the next best. She smiles so widely her teeth nearly fall out and she makes a strange violent action with her arms, but she gets the job done slickly, in the end.

There seem to be certain days for the opium-smoking: they happen in their own time, people know though it never seems to be discussed. I wonder where it comes from. I guess the Chinese grow it, in the hinterland somewhere; they'd be the ones you'd expect to have the skills. I don't know, and I don't ask. I don't smoke it either. I thought of what Slide said, about me not leaving. He's wrong there. I'll go, when the time's right. It isn't yet.

Once he said to me, Ever think you'd like to find Xanadu. Staring into a glass.

Xanadu, I said, my voice a bit husky from the drink; it was moonshine that night, I remember thinking they should colour it pale blue, as a warning.

Not just a fragment, the whole thing, Slide went on. No interruptions here.

It was then I realised he was talking about the Coleridge poem. I had thought about opium, what it might do for me,

It's the Cheroot

but there were too many bad warnings. No happy endings. As Slide said, the poem was only a fragment. And anyway I'm not a poet. Doesn't it take more than it gives, I said.

Maybe, replied Slide.

I'd learned that conversations with Slide didn't have ends. All my time in this place, I realised, would be just the one dialogue. It was like a piece of music, with themes uttered, dropped, reiterated, not always articulated but never lost. There was never any hurry to move it along. Another day Xanadu, or opium, would come up. Afterwards I wondered if he'd had thoughts along those lines, himself. I thought I should have said, What about you? It might have been polite.

I supposed the venom hunters spent their profits on opium. The food wouldn't cost much. Sometimes the hippies brought in fresh vegetables that they'd grown, and fine green stalks of marijuana, but people didn't have the habit of fresh much, around here. The grass was good, healthy, out of the ground; I sometimes took on a bit of that. Opium. If I took up opium I'd have to become a venom hunter.

The day after the launch left it came back again. We were sitting by the wharf, on Slide's terrace, playing cards. Spangle was winning. The launch turned the corner of the river and its melancholy horn sounded. I nearly said, How sad is the sound of the horn in the mangroves, but I thought, I'm not that silly. I might have, to Slide.

We all looked at the launch, it never comes except once a week, and for a moment I wondered if it was yesterday, if somehow the intervening events had been a moment of hallucination, and here was the launch arriving, and Andrea would step off in his high-heeled shoes and his flirty red jacket and tell us, The cheroot is the clue. But if it hadn't happened yet, how did I know it.

Andrea did step off, but today he was wearing jeans like a second skin and a silk shirt the colour of cream, with little red shoes like ballet slippers on his feet. He skipped down the steps and sat with us. Lizard said, Back already. Andrea said, Alas, and Slide came out of the emporium, pulled a chair from the other table and sat on it, back to front. We finished the game. Slide said, Deal you in? Andrea shook his head. Nobody said, Why are you back here so soon? I suppose they knew. Slide got up, in his ponderous yet efficient manner and got a bottle of whisky. The good stuff.

Slide brought a bunch of shot glasses, spread them out, and filled them, pushing them in front of us. Andrea smiled. On duty? Picking it up and taking a mouthful. Spangle shuffled the cards, neatened them, and put them on the table. The launch gave a cough of steam.

Spangle's wife came along the road from their shack, in her short shorts and tied-up shirt, her high-heeled sandals quiet on the dusty track, her long brown legs forced into small steps. She came up to the table and looked at Spangle. He didn't catch her eye. No woman has ever looked at me like that, and I don't think I would want one to. It was a naked look, raw, full of longing, love, desire, all moiling together, and with utterly no hope. She dropped her heavy dark lids over the splendid brown and bluish white of her eyes, but she couldn't hide the tremble of pain in her mouth. She bent her head so her swags of dark hair fell forward beside her face. Andrea stood up swiftly and brought a chair, placing it with a kind of gallantry at the table, filling one of the little glasses with the good whisky for her.

Slide filled the glasses again. Everybody drank, not tipping it down as you do with a shot glass but slowly, even contemplatively. Andrea's face was sorrowful. No venom today, he said. That can follow the usual timetable. We all sat and drank. It was like a very dull party, where there is nothing to say, except it wasn't, because there was so much tension in the air; I imagined everybody felt as strung up as I did.

Andrea leaned back in his chair, his body a fluid curve across its round metal back. Still got those cheroots, Slide, he asked. Slide nodded. And you're still smoking them, Andrea said to Spangle. He nodded. But not you, Mrs Spangle. She shook her head. People didn't smoke much tobacco here. Their rations of opium, that seemed to do them.

Mrs Spangle. I supposed she had a name, but I didn't know it. She looked at Andrea. I'd like to put a dress on, she said. He nodded, and she walked off; we watched the taut movement of her calf muscles as she picked her small steps down the track.

She came back after a while, wearing a dress of some stiff shiny material that creaked as she walked, in a bright purplish pink colour, the colour of hibiscus, if there had been any about. It was strapless, in a boned heart shape that fitted against her chest. She wore the same sandals, and it occurred to me that her walk was as though her body was shackled, that chains prevented the free long steps that her legs were made for. She carried a white plastic handbag, very shiny and cheap-looking, and when she sat down she put it carefully in her lap and held it tightly between her two hands. It had an orange plastic buckle that clashed with the dress. I don't think I've ever seen a sadder object than that clumsy white plastic handbag, so big, so shiny, so ugly. Andrea put more whisky in her glass and she took a long sip.

Everybody seemed to know what was happening. Well, up to that point. I wondered that nobody needed to speak of it, but there was evidently an understanding. She held the handbag tightly in one hand and undid the buckle, sliding the other inside the bag. She felt for a moment, and brought out a tarnished brass compact. I'd never seen her wear make-up; powder in that climate would set like mud after rain with creeks of sweat running through it. Andrea's fine dark skin was never touched by it.

She put the compact on the table, and her hand back in the bag, felt around, and pulled out a snake, a small and, I knew, particularly poisonous one. People took breaths and drew back. Her other hand pushed the bag away, and with a quick movement pulled the boned top of her dress down, so her round brown breast popped up over the top of it, and in the same moment she applied the snake to it. All the men stood up, chairs fell over, and then they remained where they were as she dropped the snake and fell back in her chair. She looked up at Spangle, that look of love, and longing, and no hope at all, then slid down into the dust. He kneeled and held her, and after a while she was dead. Not an easy death, or a pretty one, but at least Spangle held her tight through all the indignities of it.

Andrea and Slide and the rest of us walked down to the end of the wharf and looked at the boat. Nobody seemed to think of trying to save her.

Of course not, said Slide. Not a hope.

Don't you have antivenene in the fridge, I asked. After all, this was a community of poison hunters. They must be prepared for accidents.

His gaze shifted to the bend in the river where the launch had disappeared, taking Andrea and the stretcher that had appeared out of its depths and carried off the shrouded body of Spangle's wife. We'd laid her on it and wrapped a worn white sheet around her, the creaking hibiscus-coloured dress springing out as we tried to enfold it. Slide shrugged.

It bit her fingers, he said, in the bag. That would have been it, she wouldn't have needed to apply it to her breast.

Did she have a name, of her own?

Aurora.

Aurora. I wondered if anybody had ever called her that. Had Spangle? I'd never heard it, all the time I'd been here.

I wanted things spelled out. So you all knew, I said.

What?

That she'd done it.

Again Slide shrugged.

I spoke again, mainly to myself. That she, that Aurora, murdered the girl. I thought Slide's look meant yes. I went on, Why?

Slide still gazed at the bend in the river.

Because, I said, Spangle had been on with the fisherman's daughter, and that was the clue of the cheroot. And everybody knew Andrea had come to take her away. But he didn't know she was going to kill herself.

Well, said Slide. And I suddenly thought, he is disagreeing with me. Andrea did know. That was his kindness. And why nobody had run and got antivenene.

So, I said, justice is done. Slide raised his eyebrows. I went on, softly, to myself, Aurora has paid, and Spangle is okay, except that he has lost his wife and his lover. And maybe his luck.

Ah, said Slide, you think that possibly he will lose at cards now.

Parting Glances

SUSAN MIDALIA

She knew it would be the middle of summer, but Moscow was meant to be swirling snow, luxurious furs, huddling by a fire with smoky tea from a gleaming samovar. Even the forecast she'd read at home, thirty degrees and humid, had failed to convince her: so she'd packed three jumpers, five pairs of fleecy socks and a hot water bottle. When she stepped off the plane, the heat rushed maliciously towards her. And then the stifling terminal, packed tight with prowling men straight out of gangster movies, and busty young women with peroxide hair and 1980s platform shoes. There was concrete everywhere and not a word of English on the multitude of signs. Twenty sleepless hours in the air to get here, and a four-hour wait in Dubai, where fat westerners had swarmed along rows of duty-free whisky, diamonds and Chanel. Petra had sat in a café and watched them, these waddling lords of the earth, coming at her like prehistoric beasts in logo-ed shirts. Now they waited with her in the terminal, their faces unsure, uneasy, in the relentless crowd.

 The immigration official was a stout young blonde with gold braid on her shoulder pads, a red star on her cap and a brittle expression. Petra tried one of the few Russian words she'd been able to learn, *zdrahstvooytee, hello*, in what she hoped was a friendly tone. She made a point of looking blank, remembering the advice of her translator friend, Marie. *Don't smile,* she'd said. *Muscovites think you're simple, you know, a little retarded, if you smile at them.* Petra handed over her passport, her official letter of introduction, her confirmation of hotel bookings for every night of her ten-day visit, her holiday with a difference. The official glared at her and then looked down at her papers, up again at her face, down again, up again, wordless and stiff, as if I'm a criminal, thought Petra. She's taking her time, making me wait, shuffling my papers grimly. The woman glared at her again, held up a rubber stamp for ten, fifteen seconds, and then thumped it down on the passport. Petra felt her legs untighten. Ah, welcome to Moscow, she thought: mindless bureaucracy, state-sanctioned surliness. Two cultural stereotypes before she'd even left the airport; four if you counted the gangster men and the vaguely whorish girls. It was a relief to be dismissed with a toss of a head and a parting glance of official contempt.

Finding the commuter train wasn't any easier. There were forests of arrows on every wall, indecipherable signs. Petra remembered the word for *train*, *poheest*, two simple syllables, but people barged past her or shrugged their shoulders when she asked the way. Marie had warned her about this as well: *notoriously unhelpful*, even, at times, *deliberately obstructionist. They don't care about our tourist dollars. They've got plenty of tourists from the provinces, and a hell of a lot of oil*. Petra's suitcase felt suddenly heavy, despite its sturdy wheels, and she gave herself up to the surge of the crowd, let herself be pushed through a turnstile and hoped for the best. And there it was, a platform, open space, blue sky, a gaggle of English speakers, looking startled by their good luck. An overdressed middle-aged couple began consulting a map and quarrelling; two red-faced, swaggering young men were loudly thirsty for a beer. Petra cringed, her eyes fixed on the ground. I won't say a word, she thought. I'll be silent, unfriendly, un-Australian. She waited until they'd hauled their luggage up the steps of the train and chose a compartment further down the line.

The journey felt heavy with the whoosh of the engine, the guttural words of passengers, the images on an overhead TV displaying Gucci, Armani, Dolce&Gabbana. Through the window Petra glimpsed brutal, decaying high-rise apartments and then, unexpectedly, flashes of leafy, graceful trees streaked by the afternoon sun. Were they elms or poplars, silver birch? She'd never been good with nature. It could easily have been

England, where she'd lived for a year half a lifetime ago. She let herself blur with the passing of the trees, remembering the green and pleasant land where she'd backpacked and worked and fallen in love, where she'd cried at the airport when it was time to go home, cried in the plane for hours. She'd been clinging and desperate, a chain-smoking wreck; he'd looked relieved to see her go. *I know we'll meet again,* he'd said, like an old war movie, trying to be kind, with the bluest eyes she'd ever seen. They hadn't been in touch for ten or fifteen years, and, of course, they'd never met again.

The train braked and sent her lurching into the seat in front. She was aware of a man staring at her, his eyes slitted, and she clutched her handbag more tightly to her chest. She reached her hotel in a daze of traffic and taxi-driver shouts, registered at reception with surprising ease, hardly saw her threadbare room or felt the baking, stuffy heat as she levered off her shoes and slumped down on the single bed. She was asleep in less than a minute.

What would she write to those back home? Three days in Moscow and an email was due, one of those generic travellers' tales she'd become quite skilled at devising. The sights, of course, in some detail; the food, the weather; a witticism or two, perhaps a bad translation to amuse her literary friends. Like the sign in the hotel bathroom, exhorting guests not to steal the towels: *EARNEST REQUEST* written in bold capital letters. People seemed to like her emails: *interesting, amusing,* they said, although she preferred writing postcards, enjoyed selecting images for particular friends. *Postcards are for old ladies,* her niece had declared, and then blushed with what might have been contrition. So Petra would be electronic, would comment on the food (rather too salty and potatoes with everything) and mention her health for the sake of her elderly mother, say she was fine, walked everywhere briskly. Anything to avoid the underground, despite what her nephew had told her. *They've got marble floors and whopping great statues of the workers! Stained glass and massive chandeliers, you have to see it, Aunty Pet!* But she would not see it, none of it at all. In London, in her youth, she'd been groped in the underground, a hand sliding up and down her groin. She'd felt sick with the press of humanity and fled from the station in shame. And those were the days of the IRA, bomb scares and actual bombs, urgently wailing sirens. She'd tried again to take the Tube but had stood on the platform, unable to board a crowded train, crying like a fool. A woman had stopped to ask if she could help and Petra had said, stupidly, *I'm Australian.* Now, here in Moscow, she felt the trains shuddering beneath her, imagined the long, steep escalators crawling slowly down into the earth.

But she would try to describe the city for her nephew. Matthew was her favourite, a history boy, fifteen, her sister's youngest. Smart, restless, *dying to see the world*, he said. No one in his family had ever travelled further than Bali (twice), and when Petra told him of her trip to Russia, he'd taken books from the library and shown her what he'd found. Moscow razed to the ground by Napoleon's army and then rebuilt, *a stricken giant resurrected*. St Petersburg, a miracle built on water and, according to legend, constructed in the sky by Peter the Great and then lowered like a giant model onto the ground.

In the airport café Mattie had sat slumped and dejected, kicking one sneakered foot against a chair until his mother snapped at him to stop. He'd finally voiced his longing, how *all his life* he'd wanted to see Lenin's tomb. *He's decomposing, Aunty Pet*, he'd explained, leaning forward on the table. *In a few years' time he won't be there at all.* He'd ignored his sister's shrieks and his mother's look of alarm. *He changed the course of history and you can see him, in the flesh. How amazing is that?* Before she knew what she was saying, Petra had made an arrangement: *I'll go and see Mr Lenin, and if he's still there in two years' time, I'll take you to see him for yourself.* Her sister had looked even more alarmed, and Petra had smiled, the extravagant spinster sibling, the self-indulgent maiden aunt, who'd taken early retirement as a teacher and decided to see the world. She'd gone at two-year intervals to the predictable destinations — Paris, Florence, Rome, each time with a different friend — and had found each journey instructive (she had photographs to prove this). But no one wanted to travel to Russia: it was, apparently, too dangerous, and none of her friends could see the attraction. Petra had found it difficult to explain. Russian novels and *Dr Zhivago* (all that swirling snow); a long-ago lover who had told her stories of imperial treasures; some unformed, melancholy sense of a suffering history. At the airport, she'd clasped Mattie's hand. *I promise*, she'd said, knowing her sister thought she was mad, knowing that was part of the pleasure.

The hotel's internet café was full of high-spirited backpackers who glanced briefly at her lined face as she entered, at her too-youthful summer dress (yesterday's desperate purchase in the searing heat). And then she was invisible, free to compose her news. The days had been very hot, she wrote: diminutive Japanese tourists huddling under bright umbrellas, pretty young women sweltering in stockings and lace. Her hotel room was adequate, and served up ancient episodes of *Skippy*, ludicrously dubbed, on Russian TV. The ubiquitous babushka dolls were, well, ubiquitous. And, no, there were no cunning pickpockets or Russian mafia on the streets. The only sign of organised crime was the McDonald's near Red Square, which charged exorbitant prices for indigestible food. She'd queued for hours to see the Armoury: the coronation robes and thrones, studded with turquoise, rubies, pearls, lapis lazuli, were marvels of excess, but the Fabergé eggs she'd found rather crass. The jewel-encrusted wheels of the imperial carriages could have fed a million serfs. The Pushkin Museum of Fine Arts was, unfortunately, closed. Churches everywhere were being restored as part of a religious revival, and she'd never seen so many crucifixes — gold, silver, diamond — in so many conspicuous cleavages.

She'd lingered in a bookshop to watch a man talking to a group of eager listeners. He was tall, with endearing pixie ears, and had his audience eating out of his smoothly gesticulating hands. They laughed, applauded, laughed some more; one man even toppled sideways in his chair. Petra thought the pixie man must have been a comic writer, or at least an amusing speaker, but either way, of course, she had understood nothing, not a word. As she recalled it now, she remembered how this had pained her, how she'd felt like an impostor, a fraud.

And she had to confess that in the brightness of daylight, Red Square had felt curiously blank. She'd tried to picture it — the tsar and his milling, worshipping subjects; the famous military parades; the jubilant workers' rallies; even, as her niece had enthused, the thousands who'd cheered Paul McCartney and the Red Hot Chili Peppers. But she saw only endless, dull paving bricks, tourists being posed for photos — the provocative minx, the scowling son, the squirming toddler — and, flanking one side, the world's largest shopping centre, smoothly marbled, blandly bourgeois, GUM, pronounced *Goom*, as in *book*. St Basil's Cathedral was an architect's bad joke, its psychedelic onion domes like something out of Disneyland. And, no, she hadn't yet visited Lenin's tomb, guarded by impossibly handsome young men, all high cheekbones and military bearing, in sleek dark uniforms. But she had promised Mattie; she would go tomorrow, on her last day in Moscow. As she sent off her email, she had an image of her nephew, long-haired, curious, excited, sitting opposite her at breakfast. They would puzzle over the menu and plan the day's itinerary; he would ask strangers to take their photo in front of famous buildings. It pleased her to imagine such things.

After another hotel dinner of borscht and dumplings (she'd always been unadventurous with food, indeed took little interest), Petra retired to her room. She'd planned another evening walk in Red Square, where it stayed light until eleven, packed with desultory strollers, entwined young lovers, parents with pushers and skipping children. She'd enjoyed her walk the night before, its aimlessness, the pearly sheen of the sky, even the garish lights of GUM, a neon galleon sailing in a sea of happy crowds. Such endless light, such a radiant sky: here, for once, something, some marvellous trick of nature, had briefly met her vague desires. For as she brushed out her hair (looking rather lank, she saw in the mirror, in need of shampoo), Petra had to admit that Moscow had somehow failed her, had not lived up to her expectations, such as they were. She lay down on the bed, the hairbrush hanging loosely in her hand, too tired to meet the evening, wondering why she had come here, where history was mocked by American cafés and icons of Elvis Presley, where waiters ignored her, where she couldn't speak the language. Her feet ached from so much walking and her head was throbbing from too much sun. Petra felt weighed down, tiny as she was, a short, thin, insubstantial woman looking up at the ceiling, knowing she must get up in the morning, have breakfast and queue to see Lenin's tomb. The forecast said thirty-four degrees, and she would have to take the day more slowly, measure it out before catching the overnight train to St Petersburg, already booked, a first-class compartment. She thought of all this and wished she could stop thinking, could fall asleep, fully clothed, her face unwashed, unsoothed by her night cream, fast running out. She had to remember to use it sparingly; they didn't seem to sell her brand in Moscow.

The queue for Lenin's tomb was already long by ten a.m., the day already hot. Petra was prepared: she'd had a nourishing, familiar cereal and orange juice for breakfast, put sunscreen on her face, neck, arms. But even though the summer crowds were down (the global financial crisis), there were still plenty of tourists to annoy her, for that's what she was feeling now, annoyed, irrationally so, she knew, for was she not one of them, impatient in the blistering sun amid the pushing and shoving and gabbling about their stock-market losses, the mile-long queues and their latest camera with an automatic zoom, the one they were forced to leave at some check-in that no one had told them about, how they'd wasted an hour while foreigners barged in front of them until they got angry and barged right back. At least she didn't carry on like this, at least she wasn't an overstuffed pig drinking Coca-Cola and complaining, at least not out loud. She felt herself sighing, a sigh that seemed to keep her up long enough to move forward as people elbowed her along, past the security screen, unencumbered by a camera, released at last from the crowds.

She wandered through the grounds of the mausoleum, looking at the granite busts of Soviet heroes. There were scores of them, and most she'd never heard of. Generals, her guidebook said, political leaders, astronauts, writers, their names carved in the Cyrillic she wouldn't even try to translate. Somewhere, she knew, she would find the bust of Stalin, but what would it matter if she saw him or not, came face-to-face with his hawk-like eyes and imposing moustache, with his dates of birth and death carved mightily in stone. To tell her friends, tell Mattie, she had seen the image of the brutal tyrant, to be able to say, I was there, I saw it, all these unknown luminaries, the red carnations on the tombstones, the squealing teenage girls tottering on high heels, their disrespectful chewing of gum. She'd wanted to feel the weight of history, wasn't that why she came here, to this place that everyone warned her would be difficult and dangerous, a silly old woman flaunting her rebellion, her scorn of package tours and cruises, her fling with the mysteries of East-meets-West. For it was a fling, she saw it now. What did she think she was doing, standing in a mausoleum, surrounded by the busts of the glorious and infamous, feeling nothing more than irritation. She was no better than the silly girls, the fatly moaning tourists, Miss Prissy High-and-Mighty, she'd been this way all her life, unable to feel what she wanted to feel, whatever you were meant to feel, that even now, especially now, eluded her. Oh, she had friends, she loved reading, of course, she'd had a decent career of sorts, and now her travels, belated, some kind of treat or reward for something, for endurance, perhaps, when all was said and done. Her sister had admonished her: *You should be more careful with your money.* Petra had laughed, as she often did in her sister's company. *Don't worry*, she'd said, *you won't have to pay for my funeral.*

She reached the black marble steps leading down to Lenin. She was here now; she should make the effort to see, even if it struck her, as it surely had her niece, as rather ghoulish, voyeuristic. V.I. Lenin, the man of letters he had called himself, a man of the people, who had asked to be buried next to his mother. Even in death he had been cheated, thought Petra; revered, embalmed, preserved for posterity, opposite the modish merchandise of GUM. Stepping down, grateful for the cool, the dark, the unusual silence, she drew in her breath. Around a corner it came into view — deep red drapes, a marble coffin, the body laid out, a ghostly, creamy face in profile. You were not allowed to stop, you had to keep walking in a mute semi-circle, tourists in front of you, tourists behind, you had just enough time to catch a glimpse of the past. As she came face to face with Vladimir Ilyich Lenin, Petra saw that one of his hands was clenched, the other loose, and that his face was small, almost dainty and oddly alive, his brow slightly furrowed. It made him look perplexed, as if his dying thought had been a quizzical question, some faint, persistent stirring of desire. Petra felt the hush of her surroundings, the cool of the room on her drying skin, and for just a moment, just the smallest rush of time, the circle of people dissolved around her, everything solid melted into air. She was utterly transfixed, touched by the curled-up hand; the smooth, almost boyish complexion; the expression, above all the expression, of Lenin lost to some dream of history, even, perhaps, to himself.

Then it was over, and she was returned to the heat and light of the world, hearing the shudders of people sweeping past her, a teenage girl flapping and shrieking: *gross me out, I'm never gunna look at a dead guy again.* Petra had to smile at this youthful conviction and the flailing girlish arms, at her own sombre, unexpected reflection, her moment of touristic grace. It had all happened in the blink of an eye, the flash of a camera if one had been permitted. Lenin was a dead guy, and she needed to get out of the sun, and tonight she would board the train for St Petersburg, home of the world's largest museum. The Hermitage, she'd read, housed so many objects that it would take ten years to merely glance at each one.

As she set off for the hotel, in need of water and rest, she thought once more of waxy Lenin, and wondered what her nephew would make of that strangely moving face. She could picture Mattie's own face, his blue-eyed brightness, as she asked him again to accompany her to Russia, to help her see the sights and to help her with the language, to walk down together to Lenin's crowded tomb. *It's an earnest request, Mattie*, she would say, and they would laugh, already beginning to make their plans.

Moth

JENNIFER MILLS

I slept in the dark although I was afraid of it. The lamp would attract moths. If I leaned to one side of my bed I could watch the moths flash around the streetlight. I tried to count them, white bellies, fearless feather wings. I got quite good at this, and listening. Counting helps me hear better, hones my focus.

After they thought I was asleep my mother would talk about wanting a baby. Something in her had broken when I was born, and she couldn't have any more kids. I'm not saying I broke it, just that I was the end of the line for us. Not a good end, either. These talks would finish with my mother whimpering. She would cry and my father would say, we'll work something out, or we'll figure it out, as if it was a maths problem. I am the best at maths in this family, but no one asked me for my opinion. They didn't know that I was listening. They didn't know that the moths were listening too.

Another thing I liked about sleeping with the lights out is that it made the shadows walk around the room. I was an only child and I liked to count them while they danced. Sometimes I would take a torch and read under the covers from the *Child's Book of Poems*. When I looked out from under the covers I would see them, the little people. I had outgrown the book and I didn't believe in them but it was familiar and I liked reading the rhymes out loud under my breath like a chant:

Come away, O human child!
To the waters and the wild
With a faery, hand in hand,
For the world's more full of weeping than you can understand.

If anyone had invited me, I would have gone, even though I was past believing. But no one asked.

I was an only child until I was almost ten, until the discussions between my mother and father got louder, and then quieter, and one day at dinner they gave me a Talk about wouldn't it be *exciting* to have a little baby brother or sister, and I said no, I didn't think it would, and they said there are poor children starving to death all around the world, and we have plenty of room to spare in our family, and I thought to myself let them starve, but I didn't say it aloud. I said no, we don't, but even that I whispered. I scraped the gravy with my fork and my dad didn't even ask me to stop, so I knew they were serious.

It turned out it *was* a maths problem. There were more talks and a visit from a man with glasses who didn't want tea, and the problem was worked out on pieces of paper. A few weeks later, Mothling arrived. He didn't arrive in the normal way, like you or me, tugged from our mother's bellies. He came out of an office, and Mum and Dad had to pick him up. Before that, he was from a poor country with a lot of extra children. Mary has nine apples, and Johnny only has one.

When they brought him inside I peeked into the baby carrier and saw that Mothling was a silky, grey-brown colour. His eyes were closed and his forehead was as wrinkled as a witchetty grub. I prodded him, but he didn't stir. He didn't look right to me, all still and folded, but what would I know? It was late, and I was soon sent to bed to listen to them coo over him. Before I turned the lamp out I counted the small dead moths in the bottom of the light fitting. There were twenty-six. When I switched it off the streetlight came shining into the room like a cold electric moon, and I could see the moths dance spells around it.

The moths are called bogongs. I looked them up on the internet. They are migrants, fat and hungry. They come in huge numbers every spring, on their way to aestivate in cool dark caves in the mountains. Aestivate means summer like hibernate means winter. They aestivate in a prolonged torpor. They are pressed up against each other in a pattern like roof tiles, still and close and folded.

Mothling was a very quiet baby. He hardly ever cried. When he opened his eyes they were solemn, like the boy in the poem. At first my uncle Keith thought he was soft in the head. He told me so with beer-breath at the showing-off barbecue. I asked my father if the baby was soft in the head. They are all soft-headed when they first arrive, my father told me. You're not to squash or hug too hard or press down on his head, he said. Mothling's eyes always looked where the light was. I practised turning the lights on and off in the hallway and watching him turn his slow fat head towards them like a bug.

In some of those caves there are 15,000 moths per square metre. That is a lot of moths. If you spread out your hand and pushed it into the cave wall you would squash an average of 150 moths. When you lifted your hand again it would be covered in brown dust, and the moths would fall in a soft heap. They leave their dead on the ground. In some of these caves the bodies of moths are over a metre deep.

The head of Mothling hardened but his body stayed larval, so soft you could poke through to the guts with a matchstick. I sometimes did this if I caught a moth in my room; pressed into the long, furred abdomen, and a wet white goo would come out, and the moth would crawl along with its guts leaking, stuck onto the ground. Then I would have to crush it altogether.

Are there mountains where he is from? I asked my father. Yes, he said. And caves in the mountains? Yes, he said, and then he looked doubtful. I think so. It's very dry there. It's mostly desert.

Mothling hated water. The first time we tried to give him a bath he was very still, very quiet, until Mum got him near the warm water, Johnson's at the ready, and he began to scream. The scream came from his body like a shadow, like a flapping blanket, like wings. Mum couldn't bear it.

I thought I would get more tolerant of a baby crying, not less, she said. But I can't stand it. Not just this baby. Any baby. It's true, she'd hover over prams in the street, gurgle at strangers, give other mothers looks of dismay which were only a bit sympathetic. It was embarrassing and it meant that when I was a baby, she didn't use to mind that much.

When Mothling cried he meant it, and everyone heard. The neighbourhood shook. It was 5.6 on the Richter scale. Mothling, stop crying, I said from the doorway. Shut up. My father stood beside me and placed one heavy hand on my head. Call him Matthew, he said. That's his name.

Mothhew, I said.

Properly, he said, but he went in to lift the crying baby and left me in the hall.

That year there was a plague of them. They liked the school hall. The teachers said they got in the old air vents and headed for the light. On Diversity Day we had to watch international dancing in the hall, which meant it was assembly until the start of recess. There were moths crawling on the ground and packed into the corners. Other girls squealed in the aisles. I sat in the back of assembly next to the Year 6 boys. They didn't talk to me but they let me sit there because I had punched Leah Nolan in the mouth the previous term and made her lip bleed.

We crushed moths with our shoes until we got bored. Then we gathered them up into piles. The boys put them on the backs of people's necks in the row in front. I pocketed mine and felt the shimmering dust creep over my hand as they burrowed for pocket safety. Someone in front was talking about refugees. Why are refugees like sperm, whispered Jaydn West beside me. Heaps of 'em get in, but only one of 'em works. The other boys laughed. I wriggled into my chair and wiped the moth dust on my uniform.

Then Jaydn West leaned over and spoke to me. Hey, isn't

your baby brother a reffo? he said. No, I said. He's not my brother. Why don't you throw him off a boat, Jaydn asked. He laughed. He's not even my brother, I said. He's not even — but I couldn't say it out loud.

At the end of the day I ran to the road before the bell went so that I could see my mother arrive. I got in the car before anyone saw Mothling curled in his chrysalis in the back. It's not like he was my brother. He wasn't even human. Was I the only one who could see it?

As the days grew hotter, and the bogongs began to thin out, I wondered when he would disappear, go with the mass migration to the mountains. Instead he just slept a lot. Summer was tiptoes, lots of Milo sitting on the top of cold milk, and the morning sun like a light switched on in the kitchen. Dad and I had breakfast together, and I ran out into the heat when the bus came. It stopped right at the top of our cul-de-sac. I looked down the new-laid street at our house of mottled brick and red tiles, thinking of the moths that were gathering in the mountain caves. Maybe now he would go with them. The bus heaved me off to school, brought me home again. Soon it would be holidays.

The heat got to all of us. We were all tired; when I slept in on Saturdays, Dad said I was growing. But Mothling slept the most of all. Slowly he got fatter and paler and mothier. His eyes were too wide apart for a baby. His hair grew dark brown, silken, and tufting out like feelers. His skin had a brown shine on it like glittery powder that would come off on my hand. I tried not to damage him, but it was impossible not to get the dust off him. I always had to wash my hands afterwards.

Mum called it *down*. His down would grow back the next day. The dust shine was like a fine fur. Up close in certain lights the brown was rainbow colours like the glaze on my grandmother's teacups which I wasn't allowed to touch. It was pretty and gross at the same time.

The longer the days got, the more Mothling slept. He

only woke at night to feed. Mum dragged a camp bed into Mothling's room. She got pale and fat and she became nocturnal. My father and I hung around the house all day with these soft fat lumps breathing at the end of the hall. He was frightened of that baby, I knew it. I sat at the pine table and did my homework. I heard the fluttering of mothy breaths.

At night my mother prowled around the house. She carried Mothling wrapped in a blanket on her chest. He was usually asleep but sometimes in the night he liked to look out over her shoulders with his big sorrow-dark eyes. Sometimes I got up and followed them. They never noticed me; they were under some kind of spell. Mum had her whole body curled around the baby, and Mothling had his eyes fixed on the windows. He peered towards the streetlights outside, waiting for something. Waiting for his real family to come.

Sometimes I walked home from school past the shop. Once I ran into the Year 6 boys. It was almost holidays, they were almost at high school. I almost ignored them, but then Jaydn waved and I paused, took half a step towards him. Hey, he said. Tell your little brother something for me? Yeah, I said. Tell him fuck off we're full.

I ran home without going into the shop. I ran into Mothling's room and stared at him for a while. Then I opened his window. I swear that is all I did. Opened a window. I stood in the room with Mothling and I willed him to leave. I counted the posts on his crib and the rings on the curtain rail and then I started on the lines in the carpet. Finally I wiped the dust from my hands and went to bed.

I turned off the light and waited. The streetlight outside flickered on, and I could see the last of the moths lingering around it, reluctant to leave the bright circle. But it was the end of the season for them. It was time for them to leave.

In the morning I woke up early to the sound of crying. It was a peaceful sound. There were no moths left anywhere in the world.

It's almost a year since Mothboy disappeared, and now I am almost eleven. An only child. Mothboy took half of my mother with him and half of my father too. I didn't know he would do that. Now another winter is over and the moths will soon return. I wonder if there will be a plague this year. I wait for them at my window. I wait for them alone.

There is only one at first. One enormous moth on the glass. I peer at it. The round belly, sticky feet, the perfect featherstripes underneath. She is a queen. I put one finger to the glass where the moth is sitting, wonder if she can feel my warmth. Bring him back, I say. The wings flicker, but the creature stays closed and folded. She stays on my window all night. All night she doesn't move. Now I sleep with the lights on.

The Good Mother

KATE RYAN

It was around six or so, the twins had been fighting, I was going mad and Andy wasn't back till late. He was off to a film with a friend, probably a drink afterwards. It was a new thing, him going out straight from work. It came out of our counselling, his need to do something for *him*. My moods and desires, my desperation for him to get home did not, we had eventually established, mean that he had to.

Anyway, so the twins were half fighting, half playing a game where they were simultaneously chasing each other, laughing and crying, the pitch of both of them getting higher and higher so it was impossible to tell who was hurt or if anyone was. Twice I screamed at them, '*Will you stop it!*' A vicious voice, shrill and scary as if the words were going to break out of my head, but which for a second offered a kind of relief.

They kept playing, if anything maybe more frenzied than before. They jumped onto our bed and pulled all the sheets and the doona off so that the torn underblanket was showing and a couple of snotty hankies that Andy always seems to leave lying around — he's had so much hay fever lately. I looked at them and thought I really hate those hankies, and then I turned around and decided to leave the twins to it. I said to them as I was leaving the room, quietly so they couldn't even hear — they were standing up and hitting each other with pillows — 'You can bloody well kill yourselves for all I care.'

I had already given them dinner. 'Yuk! I hate couscous!' Gemma had said and she'd actually started sobbing in horror as I grimly poured myself another glass of wine and through gritted teeth said, 'Oh well. Why don't you make yourself a piece of toast then.'

'I love it, Mum,' Paddy said, basking in the glory of being the good twin. Then just at that moment Eve dropped her glass of milk — stupid of me to give her a proper glass not plastic — and it fell, *smash*, milk flowing everywhere and bits of broken glass all over the table and on the floor, the children with their bare feet and all the meals virtually untouched. It's a small table and you couldn't tell exactly where the glass went so I had to throw the lot out.

It took ages with the clearing and the wiping and the sweeping and the too-loud calls for everyone to keep still and not pick up any glass or stand on it. I made them all toast then and sliced up cucumber, cheese and tomato and opened a can of tuna. God knows why I didn't just do Vegemite. Somehow it happens like that when I'm exhausted and overwhelmed: instead of cutting corners I actually do more. Thank god at least they all liked it, but maybe because they did there was a lot of tuna and cheese dropped everywhere, smeared glasses and tomato seeds all around.

It all seemed to take ages, what with Gemma eating so slowly and Paddy eating so quickly and Eve watching it all. I tried to sit there when they were all chewing away and laughing and spreading food around and I tried to just breathe, let things go. But the tight feeling in my chest was still there and when I thought of getting them all to bed, books and baths and pyjamas, I just wanted to put my head down on the table and cry.

Paddy was telling me the plot of the latest *Star Wars* film and Gemma was colouring with one hand and eating with the other and Eve was standing up, half leaning over the table to get things and to see Gemma's picture. Every minute I had to tell someone not to do something or get a glass of water or answer a question, and every minute I thought someone would knock another glass over and it would all start again.

And then because Paddy finished first, he asked for ice-cream, and I said no for a while and in the end said all right and it seemed so pointless I wondered why I'd even bothered saying no in the first place. Then Gemma didn't want a cone and Paddy did and they all wanted different flavours — it was Neapolitan — and on it went. So then finally I was herding them upstairs feeling dread in my stomach about how much was involved before I could actually slump down in front of the TV by myself, let alone cleaning up the kitchen, which looked like an utter bombsite.

Those were the things that happened before the twins were in our room having their pillow fight, and the reason I decided to leave them to it. I got Eve into the bath. It was more peaceful in the bathroom despite the overflowing dirty clothes in the basket and the half-finished tiles and the vague smell from the bin that I knew I should have emptied because it probably had Eve's last night's nappy in it and god knows what else — probably a decomposing pear; Paddy never takes his food scraps downstairs to the bin in the kitchen.

I tried to ignore it all. I even had a nice-ish time with Eve and I sang *'Row row row your boat'* in a tight sort of way and she splashed away talking in different voices to a cow and a plastic horse that had ended up in there, though I doubt they're meant to get wet. I leaned my back against the toilet and watched her and I even closed my eyes for a minute and tried again to breathe.

After about ten minutes, I persuaded her to get out and I wrapped a towel around her soft wet body and she let me brush her teeth. She often makes this quite hard because she doesn't like the toothpaste we have and I had forgotten to buy another, but tonight she didn't. I smelled her foggy hair and looked at her little pink feet with her perfect toenails, see-through like the blood flowed evenly at the same pace to every part of her body. She was stamping a bit because she wants to learn to skip like Gemma, and I thought she was just perfect, if I could just gaze at her it would be okay, I might even be happy, even though I haven't got a job or a prospect of one and all I do is look after everybody day in day out, clean up and start all over again. So I dried her, even doing the spin dry three times the way Andy does, little sprays coming out from her hair and her joyous laugh making me want to cry.

I still had the dull feeling in my chest but I thought I could do it. Even with Andy gone for the whole evening and the twins out of control and the prospect of Eve waking up at about two or three a.m. because lately she'd been scared. I thought: I can do this. But I did feel tired all of a sudden, maybe it was because I'd relaxed a bit — I knew the two glasses of wine had been a mistake.

I followed Eve into her room to get her pyjamas on. She was pink from her bath and her bum was all mottled and her legs round and I felt I would die of my love for her, it seemed to course down inside me like a liquid. She was holding a teddy, concentrating, trying to get it into a cardigan that was too small. I said brightly, 'Come on, Eve, let's get your nappy on.' She ignored me, they all ignore me at least three or four times when I ask them to do something. I go through all these stages from a hopeful *maybe it'll be easier this time*, to this tightness and then sometimes to a full-on rage which I suppress as best I can. 'Come on, Evie,' I said. 'Just lie down and I can put your nappy on and then I'll read you a story.'

I could hear the twins downstairs opening cupboards in the kitchen and Gemma shouted out, 'Mum, can we have a biscuit?'

I didn't reply the first couple of times and then she called out again and I shouted back, 'No! It's bedtime.' Then I said, 'Evie,' soft again, the good mother, 'come on, let's get your nappy on.' She sat down and I somehow levered the nappy under her and then she wiggled back and said in the firm flat little voice she has started using lately, 'No,' and she kicked the nappy away. She was still fiddling with the buttons of the cardigan, trying to get it done up over the teddy's chest, despite the fact that she can hardly do buttons. I was sort of admiring her persistence when I heard Gemma from the kitchen again shouting, 'Mum, can we have a biscuit, *please?*' even louder this time and the sound of the fridge being opened. I felt the tightness right up into my throat. 'Eve … please,' I said.

'No,' she said.

I'd been holding her by the waist and then suddenly I just let go. I shouted, 'Fine. Don't put your nappy on then.' And I stood up and put my hands over my face.

I hadn't thought I was supporting her. She is three, so she can sit perfectly well but somehow she lost balance and fell back onto the carpet and she started to cry. At least her mouth opened as if to cry, but it was silent at first, building up in her throat like someone before they are about to sing. But it wasn't like that. I waited, feeling a wash of horror; I had so rarely got angry with her and now I felt I had tipped over into the realm that I had come to exist in with the twins, the one that was terrible and from which I could never get back. There was a *neee neen ee* sound coming out of her.

'I'm so sorry, darling,' I said, gathering her up in my arms. 'I'm sorry to shout.'

But when I picked her up she was really crying, hard and high and inconsolable as if she had gone to some other place too. She was holding one of her arms at a weird angle and the cry was one of pain and she didn't want me to hold her and it wasn't just because I'd given her a shock. And I felt it going into my brain with a sort of looseness like fog or alcohol. I'd hurt her. 'I'm so sorry, darling, I shouldn't have let you go like that.'

'Oww oww oww,' she said. And there was the sharp cry like a cat's. She kept crying and I didn't even try to get her dressed now, just sat with her on my knee without moving and pulled a blanket off the bed to put around her. I sat there and Eve cried and I thought I don't know what to do. I could see her arm hanging there awkwardly as if it was without nerves. So I sang nursery rhymes and wished I could cry myself and then eventually I laid her naked under her doona on the good side, and even though she said every now and again, 'My arm hurt, Mummy,' mournfully more like an adult than a child, with the nursery-rhymes tape on, she did fall asleep.

When I came downstairs, I was so relieved Eve had gone to sleep that when I found the twins on the couch eating Teddy Bear biscuits by the handful I just said in a dead sort of voice, 'Come on, you two, it's time for bed.' We went upstairs and I even read them a chapter of *Pippi Longstocking* and though Gemma asked for another and I said no, they accepted it. I tucked them in and then looked in on Eve. I stood for a minute, looking at her, and I wanted so much to crawl in next to her and hold her small warm hand — but instead I went downstairs.

By that stage I felt as if I had been in a war or a car accident and my head wasn't healing. I sat on the couch and turned on the TV. I flicked around and found a telemovie. Some young girl's father had kicked her out and there she was wandering the streets at night. It was all sinister yellowish lights and swishing rain and the girl with her big eyes pulling her inadequate jacket around her, being passed by creepy-looking people. She went into a café and was too embarrassed to ask for a coffee because she didn't have quite enough money. There was a close-up of the board with the prices and the girl's palm with its coins and her lips being licked and the rows of cakes and salads and wraps in the glass case. And the shop guy saying, 'Can I help you, love?' and the girl shaking her head, turning around and walking out.

After half an hour or so it looked like she was going to be raped for sure, down in some warehouse near the docks trying to find somewhere to sleep and the sky all dark, and my heart started beating too much so I had to turn it off.

I sat for a minute and then walked upstairs, so tired I could hardly do it. I checked everyone and they were all asleep. I put my head right close to Eve in the dark and listened to her breathing. She seemed okay.

I woke when Andy came home, him too hot and big and beery in bed, and just after that Eve woke. It was the cat's cry again and it cut straight to my gut and I pushed off the covers as if I had never been asleep. I gathered her up, she was crying and I brought her back to our bed, saying 'It's all right, sweetie,' over and over as if just by saying that it would become so, but inside I felt like the world had changed: it was dark and frightening and terrible now and I was the cause of it. I turned on the light and Andy sat up.

'What's wrong?' he said, a bit blurry and half drunk, and I felt so alone, maybe more than I ever had.

I said, 'She fell back when I was trying to get her nappy on and she landed weirdly on her arm.'

'Let me see,' Andy said.

'No Daddee, no,' Eve said, her voice all quavery and high.

'She won't let me touch her arm, but she fell asleep okay. I thought she'd just jarred it,' I said.

'You'll have to take her in. I've had too much to drink,' Andy said.

I didn't say anything, just left Eve with him, threw my clothes on and went and grabbed clothes for Eve, came back and got her dressed. I draped her favourite coat around her shoulders, but she wouldn't let me put it on.

'Oh god, oh god,' I wanted to say. But instead I said, 'It's all right, sweetie, I'm going to take you to see a doctor at the hospital to look at your sore arm.' I didn't look at Andy then, I couldn't. I knew if I did I would hate him for having said we should have a third child, that it was nice, the chaos of a big family, how he had always wanted that. I carried Eve downstairs with her whimpering and crying a little and Andy following in his undies and I got the keys and handed Eve back to him and opened the front door. I crossed the road, got in the car and started the engine. I drove around and double-parked the car outside our house. I went in, Andy passed Eve to me and I got her in the car. She was still whimpering and I put the blanket over her and only then did

I realise that I hadn't put socks on her. There I was, bundling my wounded child into the car at ten-thirty at night, the hazard lights blinking and as horrible as it all was, it was almost a relief to be outside.

Fidget's Farewell

SCOTT McDERMOTT

The pub is hot with bodies and brings the stink out of him anew. Smudges of grime cover the glass that all but disappears inside his big, oily palm.

The talk around Bartlett is loud and insistent, but his mind is captive to a Zen riddle, and none of it registers. He doesn't know shit about Zen or Buddha or any of those slanty-eyed religions but he knows what a Zen riddle is. One hand clapping and all that shit.

Across the room the Fidget shouts a round. The pay packet from which he draws a twenty bears a name that isn't his. Its rightful owner doesn't exist except as a name on a roster. The Fidget is one of the ghosts, men you won't see between paydays. It's an open secret. Better for the company to part with the extra wages and have the work done than not have it done at all. So the ghosts get paid like those that work. They take their cut and kick the rest along to the union office on Lorimer Street. If the Fidget has a real name, nobody seems to know it. He is just the Fidget; a small, twitchy boy that grew into a small, twitchy man.

The pub is a payday obligation. Sweating jugs are pushed at you to refresh your glass quicker than you can empty it. The dockers have the run of the pub. Any other bloke that wanders in by mistake doesn't stay long.

Whelan's kid is selling the skirt behind the bar on the idea that if you look close at the sleeve of *Exile on Main Street* you can see him in one of the photos. She asks whether he's the one with golf balls in his mouth. He says he thinks they might be eggs, but anyway that's not him. The kid is all lank hair and attitude and doesn't know when to shut up. Anywhere else he'd get his head punched in. He's

Whelan's kid though so that's not going to happen. Whelan is the union welfare officer and takes up the collections for the old blokes and the sick. Union or not, touch his kid and he'll send you to the emergency room. If you're union, the difference is it'll be Whelan that organises flowers for your wife.

Bartlett's father was also a docker, crawling over and into the great steel hulls berthed at Webb Dock as Bartlett does now. He attaches an importance to this that his wife, understanding though she is, cannot appreciate. She is distrustful and more than a little scared of the men that work the docks. She knows better than to call them crims and couches her reservations in softer terms. They're a rough bunch, she says.

The docks attract men with histories. His father spent time inside, and on his release only the docks would have him. The chance to work, however, comes loaded with the sorts of opportunities that men who've done prison time tend to attract. Sticking to the straight and narrow is no easy thing.

The Fidget is trying to empty his beer to leave. When a bloke fills your glass you don't leave it half drunk. This is understood. His eyes dart around the room, and his weedy frame spills nervous energy.

Bartlett catches a whiff of himself. Even in a room abundant with the pong of men at the end of their shift, he stinks bad. Cleaning a fuel-oil tank leaves you covered in muck from arsehole to breakfast-time, and though he has scrubbed his skin to redness the grime is deep in his pores. He knows from experience he'll sweat it into his bedsheets and catch hell from his wife. He doesn't mind working though. There is satisfaction in the stiffness he stretches from his back and arms in the early mornings when he rises. Better to work and be clear of any obligation to the men that control the rosters, the union men that can tap you on the shoulder and offer you a place around the pay truck while

Fidget's Farewell

working days become your own. He knows better than to look upon ghosting as a free ride. It is a due paid on your loyalty and on any occasional service this might require.

The Fidget has put himself in the service of the current union administration and has proved himself as a triggerman more than once. Maybe the lack of threat in his size and skittish demeanour means they don't see it coming. Maybe he's just been lucky. Whatever the case, he has form: a fortnight ago, when a page-three story ran under the headline *Shotgun Pair Found in Scrub*, the chatter around the docks pegged the Fidget as the shooter.

What would Hawkey make of the docks? His halftone likeness stares out from a newspaper left on the bar. Robert James Lee Hawke is approaching three years into his term as president of the Australian Council of Trade Unions. Defender of workers' rights, Rhodes scholar and yard-glass champion, he is a superhero by any Australian standard. There are places, however, that even superheroes know are best avoided. Kryptonite places.

Outside, the after-work traffic has thinned, the last of the day's tide of family men and women drawing back to the suburbs. Drink has taken hold of Whelan's kid, and he leans across the bar, attempting a grope at the barmaid. She pours him another at no charge and tells him to enjoy it because he'll be leaving afterwards. She's dealt with worse than him before.

The shotgun pair found dead were Jimmy the Louse and his de facto, Teresa Mitchell. The Louse's death wasn't unexpected. He was a talker that would pin you down at the pub and fill your ears without let-up, pumping you full of chatter, turning you to liquid nonsense inside your own skin. He wanted to be liked, and with him it was pathological. What he knew and who he might tell put the wrong people on edge. Nobody was surprised that he met his end with a hole in him but he should've died alone.

The Fidget downs the remainder of his pot in a gulp and belches the gas into a closed mouth, hissing it through his nostrils. He inclines his head towards the door, signalling his intent. He nods a few goodbyes and is gone. Those he has left behind shake their heads and wheel their conversation in the direction of his shadow.

The Louse was fair game but the Mitchell girl should have been left out of it. This too is understood. You could mete out what violence a man was due, but the price he paid was his alone. The Fidget knew that. Maybe she wasn't supposed to be there when he blasted a hole in the Louse. Maybe she got a good look at him, good enough to ID him. But he knew the rules and he did something stupid anyway, and all the excuses in the world wouldn't help him now.

Bartlett gets out the door and is grateful for the cooler air. He breathes it deeply. He knew the girl. Not well, not as a woman. Her old man and his worked the docks together. They were mates. When Bartlett was ten and a heart attack claimed his father, it was Mitchell that mowed their lawn, split their firewood and gifted them fresh-killed rabbits for stewing.

For some time now though, Mitchell has been an entry in Whelan's log of old and infirm dockers, the bedridden and the ill. The union looks after its old men regardless of what factional allegiances they might have held. All are equal when the years catch up, and the union shares among them such money as can be raised from their membership for the purpose. Old man Mitchell can't even stand to piss anymore. He mourns from his bed and apologises for his tears.

Someone from the Louse's camp would sort the Fidget or make the attempt. From that Bartlett takes no comfort. He needs the old man to know that the price the Fidget pays is for his daughter, that she is not simply incidental to a score settled for another.

Fidget's Farewell

Dusk has settled into place over flaking paint and overgrown gardens. Battered cars wait for rust to have its way. A cool breeze raises small bumps on his arms. The place he catches the Fidget is not private but nor is it the type of neighbourhood inclined to share its secrets. At the hand on his shoulder the Fidget turns, but there is little he can do to stop the blade that plunges into his gut. He looks down to where a fist is held against him, the knife buried to the hilt. Blood blossoms into the fabric of his shirt.

Bartlett leans into him and speaks quietly into his ear. This is for the girl, he says.

The Fidget looks up into the face of his assailant, and this time the blade is drawn across his throat. It takes him a moment to fall, as if his own death is something beyond comprehension.

Bartlett squats over the body and wipes the blood from his knife. He checks the Fidget's pockets for a wallet or something that might identify him. There is only the pay packet and a union card that belong to a man that never was. Again the riddle starts to loop inside his skull. If you kill a man that doesn't exist, is it really murder?

One hand clapping and all that shit.

Fallen Woman

JANE SULLIVAN

They say the long train on her gown tangled around her feet. What do I know. I'm good with horses, but not so good with women. Maybe that's because of this notion of mine that I was made to love my little brother.

He was an uncommon large baby, weighed ten pound. At last, said Ma and Pa, a big strong boy to work the farm. Not like me, bonny Rodnia, named after my father, a sturdy lad with a bumpy brow and tight whorls in his hair like a young billy goat's, but not tall, not even at four years of age.

To love means to protect. I stood on tippytoe to peer into the crib at the baby's curling fingers and vowed that I would take care of George Washington Morrison Nutt, even if George would one day tower above me.

I grew slowly and made it to forty-nine inches. George stopped at twenty-nine inches. So I did the towering. When George wanted to see the world, he sat piggyback on my shoulders and together we were as tall as a big boy. Then he felt free to shout all kinds of rudeness at his boy enemies. We roared around the town of Manchester, New Hampshire, me scowling and George crossing his eyes and poking out his tongue. We were so like an Indian totem pole that some folks started and crossed themselves in the Roman way when we rampaged past.

We weren't much use around the farm, so Ma and Pa fixed for us to join Mr Lillie's travelling circus and show of wonders. My brother at fifteen was the wonder — Tiny George, the smallest man in God's creation — and I at nineteen was *Hey, You*, to work for my keep at whatever came up. I had some notion to save up all my money and run away from the circus, but I had no idea where to run, and in any case I couldn't abandon George. Whenever I thought of my little brother, the muscles in my arms went tight, and I breathed hard and locked my hands together and pulled, one arm against the other. I had taken on all the bullies at the Manchester school and I would take on any blackguard, were he as big as an ox.

George's ambition was always huge. He wanted to be the biggest little man in New Hampshire, in America, in the world, bigger even than General Tom Thumb. But Mr Lillie would have none of it. He wore a ring on every finger and he turned purple when provoked. He turned purple a lot around George. 'I must have tone,' he said. 'Your antics, George, they will shut us down. No profanity, no trousers down, no farting. Stay in your booth and doff your hat to the ladies.'

'Aw, Mr Lillie, can't I go in the ring? Can't I wear a red nose and big shoes? I will be a sensation.'

Mr Lillie's jowls darkened. 'Roddie, can't you keep this rascal under control? George, you don't understand. You are not a sensation. You are a wonder.'

I did my best with George, I lectured him and cuffed him about a bit when he misbehaved, but he knew full well I'd never hurt him bad and he took no heed of me.

Meanwhile, I sought my own trick and thought it might come from study. So I studied Miss Emmeline and her brother Mr Ludovic at practice, to and fro on the trapeze above my head, to and fro. Their strength was not just in their arms or arched backs or their streaks of red hair. It was in their ankles, insteps and toes. And in Miss Emmeline's smile.

I don't know what it was about Miss Emmeline. You could say it was her queenliness or her grace or her beauty, and you'd be right, but that wasn't it. It was maybe something in her eye when she looked down or looked away, when she thought nobody was watching her. I'd seen that look with a horse that's been trained too hard, too cruel, but its spirit is still there, deep down. And then she'd see me watching and she'd put on her smile. A dazzling smile, even if it didn't quite reach her eyes.

With the brightest of her smiles, Miss Emmeline got me to take charge of their trapeze apparatus. Every night after the show, I took a lamp into the circus tent and took down all the rods and poles, ropes and ladders. I held each load-bearing part and connection close to the lamp and tested it by hand for fault or weakness. Then I put the apparatus up again for the next day's performance, spread and pegged the safety net, checked it for holes. I climbed ten, twenty, thirty foot, nimble and hard-handed as a sailor in the rigging, worked my way arm over arm along the horizontal poles. But I would never take to the trapeze. That was Miss Emmeline's place.

Another task I had was to clean out the Sapient Bear's cage, and there I could practise my speechifying. *I can offer strong arms and a true heart. One day I will inherit a half-share of a farm. I want you to be free. I want to save you from hard training, from a dangerous trade. I want to save you from …* The bear yawned, showed its yellow teeth. I caught a blast of mucky banana.

Sometimes Miss Emmeline would listen to my wisdom about struts and ropes and weights as she did her callisthenics on the grass. At least, I fancied she listened. I would hold samples of poles and leather straps in my hand and tell what load and stress they might carry while she stretched and swung. Sometimes she gave me a breathless, 'Yes, 'twill do,' over her shoulder, and *twang*, my chest swelled.

Alone in the circus tent, I practised my trick. Over and over again I leaped across a short gap from one rope ladder to the next. Sometimes I leaped to a single rope. I braced myself for the landing. I gripped hard to stop the slide that might scorch my palms. I flung out one fist, hard as iron, twirled lazily on a rope and smiled at the upturned faces, the drum roll, the clapping hands, Miss Emmeline reaching out her white arms. Then I looked down and saw a spider stretch of netting, a circle of sawdust, tiers of blank seats.

At the end of each day, I collapsed onto the straw pallet I shared with George and fell into a void of sleep. But one night George kept me awake to whisper to me his new plan.

'It's all worked out.' He was trembling with excitement. 'Only keep mum, so Mr Lillie can't stop us. I'll mount the trapeze with Mr Ludovic, and he'll fling me to Miss Emmeline to catch. To and fro, to and fro. My costume will be red and green silk. I'll tumble and fly like thistledown, like a hummingbird. Think of it, Roddie — Tiny George, airborne! How they will gasp and cheer!'

'Are you crazy?' I said. 'You're no acrobat. One slip ...'

'No slips. Maybe my trousers will fall down though.' He was jumping on our pallet.

I grabbed him, forced him down, hissed in his ear. 'Forget it. I forbid it.'

He looked at me, panting, all sly. His hair bristled with straw. 'Roddie, I love you, lord knows. But you ain't Pa.'

I knew I'd get no more sense out of him. I couldn't go to Mr Lillie; I was not a snitch. Nor could I go to Emmeline's brother Ludovic, who always looked at me as if I were a scraping from the Sapient Bear's cage. But I made up my mind to talk to Miss Emmeline while she did her callisthenics.

She listened, stretching her leg above her head so I grew faint to see. 'Tiny George will be safe with us, never fear.'

'He is not a sack of potatoes you can toss about. He'll wriggle and twist out of your grasp. He'll fall.'

'I don't think so. But if he does, he'll land in the safety net.'

I shook my head. I could not see it. George was never one to land in safety.

Miss Emmeline smiled and stretched her other leg. 'It does you credit though, how you care for your brother.'

'No more than you care for yours, I'm sure.'

She frowned, put her leg down. 'I have no brother.'

'But I thought ... Mr Ludovic ...'

'Then you thought wrong.'

Her voice, and the dark roses in her cheeks, made me cold. I picked up a leather strap and pulled it tight between my fists. When she spoke again, she sounded brisk, practical.

'If we don't do this, I will have to offer Ludo something else. He is very insistent. It is not enough to entertain, he says. We must astound.'

I swear, I was so near to saying something foolish about how she astounded me already. But then Mr Ludovic slid by, as he always did sooner or later, with his panther's ease and his soft call — 'Come, Em' — and clicking his tongue twice. She stopped in mid stretch, folded herself up like a tent and followed him.

I watched their shadows behind the canvas. No brother?

It was time to take down and put up the trapeze apparatus. I trudged slowly to the circus tent. High up, feeling my way along the poles, I wondered for the first time what it would be like to fall, to have the ground rush towards you. Would there be time for terror, for pain? Or would it all be the ecstasy of speed, of letting go? My eyes blurred; I reeled, dizzy. I waited for the fit to pass, then I turned, leaped from the ladder towards the guy rope.

Dozens, scores of times I'd done it, launched into nothing, slammed into the rope, knotted my fist tight around the heft of it, my body jerking back from the fall. Nothing different about this time. Yet I sailed past the rope, several inches wide, my outstretched hands clawing at empty air.

Much later, I heard a thin whispery voice.

'Lift up your heads, O ye gates; even lift them up, ye everlasting doors; and the King of glory shall come in.'

I am told the pious Living Skeleton found me lying still as a statue, but not in a statue's pose. I was half on, half off the safety net, my left leg thrown wide, my head under the front row of seats.

When they pulled me out, my head was full of nothing but swamp reek. They carried me to my pallet and sent for a doctor. I kept my mouth agape. I was choking on the stench of rotted grass under the bleacher seats. I gulped for air, for words.

'Calm yourself,' said George, attacking my arm with anxious little pats. A mountain of pain was growing in my left leg.

Sometime after that, George peered at me over the foothills of my mountain.

'We are tough Nutts. It takes a lot to crack us.'

I didn't answer. Cymbals crashed. I rose through the cooling air to the trapeze, where Emmeline waited for me. We were both naked as babes. Side by side we swung on the same trapeze, to and fro, to and fro. Emmeline reached out and grasped the bar. She swung onto the platform as my swing moved back. Everything moved slow as molasses. She turned towards me, her arms high, one hand holding the second trapeze — she was tiny, so far away — and took off. Now my trapeze swung towards hers. We rushed slow, slow, towards each other. Blood pounded in my veins. Trumpets blared. Slow, slow. I saw her smiling face, with her dark nipples and dark triangle beneath like a second face. I knew that when the trapezes met, our bodies would melt together. Closer. I reckoned my nose would reach and touch her between the eyes of her second face. Sweat sprayed off her hair, sparkled in the lights. Closer. A drum roll. My nose was there, between the eyes. Nothing but mushy apples and bananas, and rotting grass, and a pimply hairy snout and rough tongue. No Emmeline, just the Sapient Bear gripping the trapeze with his paws, hard as iron, and Mr Ludovic laughing, and light flashing in my eyes, and George buzzing round, just his head with wings, a pestering cherub, saying, *Please get better, Roddie*, and my leg on fire again.

When the doctor took me off the laudanum, he said there was a difficult break in the femur, it might take some time to heal. He had put a splint on my leg, said it was a miracle I had not hit my head, I must have fallen into the safety net and then bounced or slid half off it. I had escaped with one broken bone and a mass of bruises.

In time, the pain faded and I learned to swing my body around on crutches, with George running round my feet and threatening to trip me up.

'You still here, you pest?' I said. 'Not tumbled from the trapeze yet?'

'Oh, that.' He sighed. 'Roddie, I changed my mind. Seen you lying there, day after day … I'm figuring, I ain't about to put you through what I felt then. No, sir.'

Something swelled in my chest.

Then George grinned. 'But you still ain't my pa.'

I swung a crutch at his shins, and he shrieked as he scampered away.

Mr Lillie grumbled about mouths to feed and insisted I take up all my duties again. George threatened to walk out on the circus unless Mr Lillie waited until I could walk without support. They shouted at each other until I dropped my crutches and hobbled towards them and said I was ready for work.

My leg still ached in wet weather and I could not help limping. But I could do most of my tasks. So I went into the circus tent to the rods and poles and ropes of the trapeze. There, something cold seeped down my veins into my fingers and toes. I could not lift my feet even by one step onto the rope ladder. I sat down, still as a statue. A sour taste rose. The ring spun round. A rotten-grass smell clogged my head.

Miss Emmeline stood and listened as I hung my head and told her I could no longer take down or put up her trapeze for her. I wondered if she might despise me for a coward. But she nodded gravely. She seemed quieter and smiled less, though everyone said she was performing better than ever. In her arms she cradled spanking new pink boxes.

'New costumes?' I said.

Those dark roses again in her cheeks. 'We are announcing

it today. We are engaged. We will have our wedding on the trapeze.'

Something fell down, down inside me, and kept falling. I put on a smile, said a glad word or two. I wanted to tell her that I did not blame her for marrying Mr Ludovic, that the circus was outside the rules, a special place for special people who belonged together. Or again I could tell her that she should run away from the circus, and especially from Mr Ludovic. But I looked and said nothing. Her hair was drawn back under her bonnet, her arms were in wide sleeves, her thighs hidden in her skirts. Her miraculous strong ankles were all buttoned up in boots. The secret second face I had seen in my dream was no more than something for dirty boys to guess at.

I told myself she was no different after all from the New Hampshire misses who strolled the showgrounds on the arms of their beaux, mouths hanging open at the wonders.

The wedding took place as planned. The circus was packed; we all looked upwards. The couple stood on high trapezes, facing each other across the ring: he in black, she in white satin with a veil and a long train. A priest shouted the service from the floor. Then the band struck up the wedding march, and the happy newlyweds began to swing towards each other. Perhaps he would put the ring on her finger as the trapezes met. She stood high and worked her arms and knees, and her veil and train flew out in a silver arc behind her.

It was so fast, no one even had time to scream. At the top of her longest swing, she sprang out and up, silver thrown into space. Her arms were out as if to meet a lover, but she had already passed Mr Ludovic, still clinging to his trapeze. I saw where she would fall, way beyond the safety net, and I ran forward with my arms up and out, but there was no time. I could not meet her, could no more stop her than I could stop a horse bolting.

That was a few years ago. Now I drive a little walnut-shaped coach, wrinkled like a golden brain, drawn by two miniature ponies, and George sits inside and waves at the crowds. He's Commodore Nutt, he performs with General Tom Thumb in New York. Mr Phineas Barnum bought him from Mr Lillie for thirty thousand dollars, with me thrown in. Mr Barnum's face is pink to middling red and I took that as a good omen. He says I am the stoic of the walnut carriage. In the glory that was Greece, he told me when he first showed me the coach, the stoic was the still, calm fellow who held up a lantern to folly. He disdained riches and rewards, he welcomed poverty and suffering. Nothing, no one could perturb him.

I said to beg his pardon, but I could not be a stoic because I had too much feeling in me.

'Perhaps,' said Mr Barnum, all genial. 'But your feeling don't show, that's the trick of it.'

My chest swelled and my arm muscles went tight. I had a trick. I wanted to swing out on a rope, across the courtyard, over the golden brain.

Sometimes when I drive the carriage and ponies round and round the streets of New York, and the people shout, and George sits safe in his shell, thoughts go round and round with me too. I had to take George from her and Ludo, had to, had to, could not let him be the one to fall …

The thing is, I'm good with horses. And if I'm quick, I can stop a horse bolting.

I don't remember what I felt when I fell. I hope she felt the ecstasy, the letting go.

Four-Letter Words

RYAN O'NEILL

Cock
My father was very fond of telling the story of how he first met my mother because of a cock. He would always begin the same way, explaining that he had been born in Scotland (though this was obvious enough from his accent) in a small village near Aberdeen. He had come to Australia at the age of twenty-five, and settled in Newcastle because it had the same name as the English city. After some odd jobs, he found work as an apprentice glazier. His employer liked him because he was never heard to say a bad word about anyone, not thinking this might be because my father lived in a glass house himself.

One day my father was sent to a property in Bar Beach. The owner was a wealthy lawyer who kept a large greenhouse, vegetable garden and chicken coop, which he liked to potter around in on weekends. There had been a storm, and my father was to replace several glass panes in the greenhouse. At first, the owner tried to chat to my father about his prize chickens, but eventually went back inside when he couldn't understand my father's replies. My father took this opportunity to have a cigarette break. As he leaned on the fence, smoking, the gate gave way behind him, and a rooster ran out of the coop. Closing the gate, he chased after the rooster, which ran down the driveway towards the beach. My father dove at it, and the rooster leaped in the air and over a high wall into the garden of the house next door. My father jumped up, too, and pulled himself over the fence, falling onto his feet a few inches from my mother, a twenty-two-year-old girl, sunbathing in her underwear while her parents were away for the day.

Out of breath, my father said, panting, 'Excuse me, miss. Have you seen my cock?'

This word, derived from the Old English *cocc*, is commonly used in Scotland to describe a male domestic fowl, but my mother did not know this. She screamed, and slapped my father in the face so hard that she burst his nose. At that moment the rooster came squawking from the open door of the house, and my father was able to catch it. He held the struggling bird with one hand and his streaming nose with the other. My mother, realising that he wasn't a pervert, went to fetch a handkerchief. While she was gone, my father noticed that one of the lounge-room windows was cracked. When my mother returned with the hanky, he pointed out the broken window. Fearing her parents would notice the damage, my mother became upset, until my father explained his trade and offered to repair it free of charge. That afternoon, he asked my mother out. They were married two years later.

Fart

When I was a small boy, my father taught me his national anthem, 'Scotland the Brave'. My mother loved to hear me sing it, especially the chorus:

> *Land of my high endeavour*
> *Land of the shining river*
> *Land of my heart forever*
> *Scotland the brave!*

Whenever her relatives came to visit — which wasn't often, for they didn't like my father — she would have me stand on a chair and sing, while my father would accompany me on the mouth organ. Shortly before my grandparents came to call one day, my father told me he had forgotten to teach me the chorus properly, and so together we rehearsed the new words:

Fart, fart, my bum is calling,
Must be the beans I ate this morning,
Quick, quick, the lavvy door,
Too late, it's on the floor.

After my grandparents arrived, my mother, as usual, requested me to sing 'Scotland the Brave'. I never reached the second verse. At the end of the chorus, my mother snatched me from the chair as my father spat his harmonica across the kitchen, bent double with laughter. She took me to my room and spanked me with the *Macquarie Dictionary*, to teach me not to say bad words. She seemed both angry and embarrassed. (My mother's face never showed one emotion, but always a mixture of two, like a portmanteau word.) Later, my father crept into the room with a smuggled lollipop. He flicked through the dictionary and said, 'This isn't a proper dictionary. It doesn't have any of the best words.'

And he took a pen and wrote *Fart,* in between *Farrow* and *Farmer,* with the definition *to make a bad smell from the bottom.*

I told my father much later that *fart* was one of the oldest English words, with many cognates in other languages. He found flatulence hilarious. One of his favourite tricks was to have pie and beans for lunch at work, then return home and close all the windows and doors in the living room. For twenty minutes he would sit and break wind, only then calling my mother in from the kitchen. I would hear her shout 'Oh, Jimmy!' and my father's roar of laughter as she ran from the room, retching. He boasted that he had complete control of his bowels, and would challenge me to say 'when!', at which point he would instantly break wind. Sometimes I would wait for hours, then cry 'when!' and he would let out a loud fart. My mother would shake her head in disgust and run around the house, opening all the windows.

I wasn't allowed to say *fart,* so my father taught me the Doric for it: *braim.* Doric was the dialect of Aberdeenshire, where my father grew up. Even as a child I was fascinated by the different sounds and meanings the words had, and I began to realise, dimly, that language was shaped by place. By the age of six I could talk to my father in dialect in front of my mother, and she would have no idea what we were saying.

My father rarely swore at home. Sometimes if he was talking about his bosses at work, he would say, 'They're a shower of bastards, the lot of them,' and my mother would shoosh him. Even then, it was difficult to catch him swearing because his accent seemed to make even the mildest words profanities.

My mother and I glued together a little cardboard box and cut a slit at the top. This was the swear box, and my father had to put in twenty cents every time he swore. My mother made the mistake of promising me the money from the box when it was full, so I would try to provoke my father. The easiest way to do this was to break wind myself. Often I was unable to and just gave myself a sore stomach, but when I did my father would cry out in amusement, 'Was that you, you dirty wee bastard?'

And twenty cents would go in the box.

Poof

When I started school, I had a pronounced lisp that my mother believed was due to all the strange sounds I made when practising Doric with my father. She was very worried about this lisp, but my father insisted I would grow out of it, as I did, in fact, a year or two later. But in my first week at school, a boy three years older than me caught me on the way home and, calling me a poof, punched me in the face. I ran home with a split lip. My father came home to find me sobbing in the bathroom as my mother dabbed cotton wool on my lip.

'What happened, son?' he said, putting down his newspaper.

'Have you been drinking?' my mother asked him, but my father ignored her.

I told him what the boy had done, which seemed to me the most serious part, and only as an afterthought what he had called me. My father's face, normally red from the sun, turned pale.

'Fucking bastard,' my father said quietly. 'Little fucking bastard. Calling my son a poof? No one calls my son a poof!'

'Jimmy!' my mother cried.

My father went out through the kitchen to the shed, and returned a minute later holding a hammer.

'What's his name?' he asked me.

'Stelio Grivas.'

'A fucking wog, is it? Well, we'll see what his father has to say about it. Come on.'

'Jimmy, don't,' my mother said, holding on to me.

My father grasped my wrist so tightly that it hurt, and hauled me away from her.

'Come on!' he said, pulling me outside.

He began walking down the street, and I had to run to keep up with him.

'Where does he live?'

'I don't know,' I said, holding my nose, which had started to bleed again. 'Waratah, I think.'

'Right, then.'

He hid the handle of the hammer up his sleeve, its head in one clenched hand, and my hand in the other. We walked in silence, except that every ten minutes or so he would mutter to himself, 'Poof,' and then spit on the ground. (He would not have cared that this word dated back to the nineteenth century and had begun as French slang for a prostitute.) When we finally came to Waratah I was exhausted, and my father lifted me on his back and asked what street the boy lived on. I told him again that I didn't know.

'All right,' he said. 'We'll look for him. Tell me when you see him.'

My father walked with me on his back for four hours, peering into every garden and, if he could get close enough, every window of every house in every street in Waratah. After a long time it grew dark, and I fell asleep as he walked. When I awoke, we were at home again. I was lying on the couch, and my father was holding my mother, who was crying.

'Stop greeting,' he said. 'Stop greeting, now. I couldn't find him.'

'And what if you had?' she said, looking relieved and angry. 'What would we have done with you in jail, for assault, or worse?'

'All right.' He kissed her cheek. 'Will you not make us something to eat? We're starving.'

The next day was a Saturday. My father got dressed for work as usual, as he said there was a chance for some overtime. While my mother was hanging out the washing, my father rummaged in a kitchen cabinet where we kept all sorts of odds and ends. After he left, I went and looked in the cabinet. Among all the old bills, receipts and blunt scissors, the phone book was open, with the page for Greene to Gruenwald ripped out.

No one at school ever called me a poof again.

Tits

Shortly before my twelfth birthday, a salesman came to our door selling volumes of the *Oxford English Dictionary*. For a very reasonable rate, one of these thick volumes would be delivered to your home every month for a year. My mother, though she never bought anything from travelling salesmen, always invited them in, perhaps to make my father jealous. In fact, he arrived home from the pub that day when the salesman was having a cup of tea. I was lying on the floor, with the *C* volume open before me, so immersed in the dictionary that I didn't notice my father until he nudged me with his foot.

'Whatever it is, we can't afford it,' he said. 'Give the book back to the man, son.'

My mother apologised to the salesman, and my father saw him to the door. When he came back into the room, he whispered something to my mother, and she smiled. A week later, for my birthday, I got *A to Bea*.

I would spend hours with the dictionary, learning all of the abbreviations, *v.t. n. pl. colloq. def. MLG conj.*, and following words back in time to the places they were born. I discovered that many English words had come from other countries, like my father. I began to keep a notebook in which I would write down the new words I invented — *umzob*, *caramot*, *grebulous* — and their imaginary meanings. By the time that *Ga to Hee* was delivered, there were too many volumes for the bookshelf in my room, and my mother moved them into the garden shed, where they would be out of the way.

One afternoon, I went to look up *carrion*, a new word I had come across while reading *The Count of Monte Cristo*. *Caf to Dar* was kept on a low shelf beneath my father's workbench. I kneeled on the floor and pulled out the volume. As I did so, a large loose square of chequered linoleum came away. Underneath the lino was a magazine, and the front cover showed a topless woman cradling two gigantic breasts in her hands. The magazine was simply called *Tits* and was dated the month before. I began to look through it. After a few pages I was bored of the breasts, all of them huge and thick-nippled. But I read on to examine all the different words for breasts. There were Bristols, titties, jugs, boobs, boobies, funbags, mammaries, pillows, baps. (The word *tits* itself has an uncertain origin, but is similar to *titten* in German and *tieten* in Dutch.) I had never before seen so many synonyms for one word. I had just opened my notebook to write some of them down when my father came in. He looked at the magazine, then glanced away for a second, embarrassed, before he realised that it was only a pen that I held in my hand. I stood up, and he came towards me and kicked the linoleum back over the magazine.

Then my mother was at the door to the shed, holding a dishtowel. She was wearing a flowery yellow dress, and I noticed, for perhaps the first time, that she was flat-chested.

'Dinner's ready,' she said. 'What are you boys up to?'

My father said nothing.

'I was just showing Dad some new words I learned,' I said.

'You can show him at the table.'

After dinner, I wrote in my notebook: *filicate n. a species of lie which a son tells for his father*.

Piss

During my last few weeks at secondary school, my father had an accident. He was putting a new window in a house and was standing on some scaffolding ten metres up. It began to rain heavily. ('Absolutely pissing down,' my father said when he told the story, ignoring my mother's frown.) As he hurried to finish the job, he slipped and fell onto the muddy ground below, breaking all of the ribs on his right side. He had to stay off work for two months. His employer was very good about it and continued to pay his wages. My father would lie in bed all day, smoking cigarettes and watching the television, which we had moved in from the lounge room. My mother took my room because her tossing and turning kept him awake at night, while I slept on the sofa.

My father never complained of the pain, though for the first couple of weeks getting up to go to the toilet was an agony for him. I had to support him as he urinated, hissing with the hurt. Often his workmates would visit with slabs of beer. My mother didn't like drinking. We didn't even have a corkscrew in the house. But she saw how the visits cheered my father, so she said nothing. She didn't know that his friends would leave a dozen cans of beer under the bed, which my father would drink, one after the other, when my mother was out. He said they were better for his ribs than the painkillers, but I think he often swallowed down the pills with the beer. He relied on me to air the room, buy him breath mints, and dispose of the cans — and not to say anything to my mother. By now, I was very good at telling filicates.

One morning, my father sent me on an errand to his friend who ran the local bottle-o. (This word formerly meant a person who sold and collected bottles: it came from the cry, *Bottle-oh!*) After I paid him, he took me to the back of the shop and put a bottle of whisky in my bag.

'Remember, not a word to anyone,' he said. 'I would lose my job.'

I rode back home on my bike and gave the whisky to my father. He sent me out to buy us some sausage rolls for lunch, and when I came back, the bottle was half empty. He saw me looking at it and said, 'Don't be such a pessimist. It's half full. Now, what new words have you learned today?'

After drinking, he always enjoyed a good sleep, and I would hide the bottle away in my bedroom. It wasn't long before my father was sending me to the bottle-o every other day. I tried to stay away from the house so he couldn't ask me, but my mother wanted me to be near home in case she needed me. A few weeks later, my mother went to visit her sister. I was studying in my room but, after a while, I heard my father singing my name. I groaned, and ignored him until he began shouting. When I went in, he smiled and patted the seat beside the bed so I would sit down.

'Do you have any new words for me today?' he asked.

'Yes,' I said, still standing in the doorway. '*Dipsomaniac.*'

'That sounds like … That sounds like a … good one. What does it mean?'

'It's from the Greek *dipsa*, meaning thirst; and the Latin *mania*, indicating an extreme desire for something. Its short form is *dipso.*'

'I don't understand. What does it mean again?'

'You should know it,' I said. 'It means a drunk.'

My father nodded, and then as he understood what I had said, he tried to sit up in the bed.

'You don't know …' he said. 'You don't know anything.

How about you break a few of your ribs, see how you feel?' He took another drink of the whisky. 'Jesus Christ, you're a poor excuse for a son,' he muttered. 'You and your books.'

I stared at him. Like a word that you look at for too long on the page, he began to lose any meaning for me.

'Well, here's a question for you,' he said at last. 'How many syllables are there in *piss off*?'

In fact, I knew that *piss* came from the Middle English *pissen*, itself linked to the French *pissier*, and descended from vulgar Latin. But I said nothing. In response, he shouted at me, 'Go on, then. Piss off!'

I went out of the house to look at my books in the shed. An hour later, my mother came running from the kitchen.

'Come quick!'

My father was unconscious on the bedroom floor. Having drunk the rest of the whisky, and all the beer left under the bed, he had vomited on the bedsheets and on himself. Then he had fallen out of bed. The carpet around him was soaked with urine.

'Oh, Jimmy,' my mother said, weeping. 'Not again.'

(It was not until much later that my mother told me my father had had problems with drink before, but had gone teetotal when I was born.)

I helped her strip him and wash him. He groaned but didn't wake up. Between the two of us, we got him back on the bed after my mother changed the sheets, and we took turns watching him through the night to make sure he didn't choke on his own vomit.

When he awoke, he was penitent. Tears in his eyes, he swore to my mother that he wouldn't touch drink again. For the next two weeks I spent a lot of time with my father. Playing Scrabble kept his mind off the pain, he said, and we had endless games together, though when we changed the rules to allow Doric, he won every time. In a while he was able to walk again without much pain, and within another month he was back at work.

On my way back from school soon after, I saw my father sitting at the window of the pub, drinking whisky. I rode home, and searched my bookshelves until I found a particular notebook. I opened the notebook and crossed out *filicate*. Then I went to tell my mother what I had seen.

Slut

I was in my second year at university when my mother left my father. In the past three years his drinking had gotten worse. If my mother begged him, he would stop for a week or so, then start again. He was a good drunk for a long time, in that he was never violent and not usually unpleasant. Very often, if my parents were with other people, it would just be my mother who would notice he was drunk. The only outward indication of the alcohol was a certain jerkiness as he talked. As he told all his old stories (including, inevitably, the one about the cock) his body seemed to react, giving physical representations to parentheses, commas and question marks. By the end of an anecdote, he was often on his feet, clapping his right hand against his leg to mark full stops, and stamping his feet for exclamation marks.

The only place I could study etymology was in Brisbane, so I wasn't able to come home often. During the holidays, I rarely had enough money for travel; even if I did, I still made some excuse not to visit home. At Christmas, however, there seemed to be no avoiding it, and as it turned out, this would be the last time we were together before my mother left.

Christmas morning was quiet, my mother cooking an enormous lunch, my father watching television, while I boxed up some books I wanted to take back to Brisbane. I found the dictionary that my mother had spanked me with all those years ago. When I showed my father the words he had written there, he was delighted.

'I mind that day well,' he said, and he began to hum 'Scotland the Brave'.

My mother heard him from the kitchen and laughed.

After lunch, my father said, 'I'm going for a walk.'

As soon as he left, my mother said simply, 'He'll come back drunk. I never thought I'd have a drunk for a husband.'

I realised then how little I knew about my mother. I had often thought that the only way to truly understand a word was to know its past, but I knew almost nothing about my mother's.

'Who did you think you would marry?' I asked her.

For the next two hours, we talked about the boys she had been in love with before my father; about her own mother and father, whom I barely remembered; and about the good times she had had when my father was courting her. It was then that my father came home. He was, as my mother predicted, drunk. Having overheard her talking about my birth, he said, 'Yes, that was some day, some day. The best day of my life,' and my mother smiled at him.

'Almost as good was the day we conceived you,' he continued, winking at me.

'Jimmy! Don't!' my mother said, but my father had already started tapping his hand against his thigh as he told the story. 'And it was the first time we did it. I remember you blushed, didn't you, Mary, and I said, "But you've seen my cock before," and then you laughed. Of course, we had to get married after that, when your father saw your belly. You said it was your first time, didn't you, Mary? But that wasn't what I'd heard. You see, son, your mother was a bit of a slut in those days, and —'

My mother slapped him. It must have been the first time she had struck him since that afternoon in my grandparents' garden all those years before, and the result was the same. The blood started leaking out of my father's nose, but this time my mother left the room and didn't come back, and it was I who fetched a dishtowel for him. Without a word, my father took the towel, held it to his face, and went out again, probably back to the pub. I found my mother in the shed, sobbing against the fourth volume of the dictionary,

Caf to Dar, a place where I had always found comfort. In the volume *Ske to Tar*, it was noted that *slut* was first recorded in English in 1402, originally meaning an untidy woman. It was only later that the word developed a sexual connotation. I tried to tell my mother this, but she wouldn't listen. So I put my arms around her, and for a long time neither of us said a word.

Gook

After finishing uni, I got a job in Sydney working as an assistant lexicographer for the *Macquarie*. I had just become engaged to Phuong, whom I had met in my first year at the university. We drove down from Brisbane, stopping off at Coffs Harbour, where my mother now lived in a small unit, close to the ocean. When I introduced Phuong to her, she was delighted and immediately began to talk about grandchildren. Then she asked me when I had last seen Jimmy. For a moment, I didn't understand whom she meant. She had never spoken my father's Christian name to me before. He was always 'your father'. I told her we were going to stop by his place on our way to Sydney.

'I write to him every week,' she said. 'But he never replies.'

It was still Christmas at my father's house in Newcastle, as it had been for three years. My father had never taken down the decorations after my mother left. There was a broken windowpane in one of the front windows, and the lawn was weedy, the grass long.

I begged Phuong to wait in the car first. 'You don't know him,' I said. 'I have to see what state he's in.'

I collected the mail and walked up to the house. I wondered if one of the envelopes contained the latest issue of *Tits*, or perhaps one of my mother's letters, and then I wondered which would be more welcome to my father. I knocked on the door and waited for some time before he answered.

My father was wearing a frayed dressing-gown my

mother had bought him years before, and he had a cigarette in his mouth. He had become an antonym of himself. The last time I had seen him he had still looked quite young: thin, tall and with a full head of hair. Now he was old, fat, stooped and balding. He saw me looking at his belly and said through the smoke, 'Do I still have two feet, then? I haven't seen them in a while.'

He offered me his hand, which trembled a little, and I shook it.

'So where's this girl of yours?' he asked, stepping out onto the front porch.

I waved at Phuong and she started to get out of the car.

'I thought Phuong was a funny name.' He squinted so he could see better. 'You never mentioned she was a gook.'

Without a word, I left my father on the porch and hurried down the path. Taking Phuong's hand, I led her back to the car.

'Son,' my father was calling, as he carefully made his way down the porch steps. 'Son, I'm sorry. I didn't mean it. I don't know why I ... She looks a lovely girl. Son!'

'What is it?' Phuong asked.

'We're going,' I said, opening the car door.

'Why?'

An 1893 dictionary of slang defines *gook* as a low prostitute. It was adopted by American marines in the Philippine–American War to refer to all Filipinos (perhaps taken from *gugu*, a mocking of Filipino speech) and expanded throughout the twentieth century to embrace all South-East Asian countries, including Vietnam, where Phuong's parents had come from.

'I'll tell you on the way.'

'Son!' I heard my father again as we drove away. He jogged awkwardly after the car, then stopped, and leaned over, holding his knees.

I didn't speak to my father for five years.

Fuck

My mother called me from the hospital to tell me my father had had a stroke. He had telephoned her earlier that day, shouting gibberish into the phone. At first my mother thought that he was simply drunk, but there was a tone to his nonsense that scared her. She immediately caught the train down to see him. On arriving at the house, she found him in the bedroom trying to pull his work overalls on. He had retired the year before. When he saw her, my father said thickly, 'What's for tea, Mary? I'm fucking starving.' His mouth was horribly twisted, and his right arm hung limp at his side.

I found my mother sitting by his bed at the hospital. My father was asleep among the various lines and tubes that were keeping him alive. He was completely bald now, and his skin had a yellow, coarse look, like the old newspapers you find under carpets. I kissed my mother, then leaned over to look at my father. He opened his eyes, said quite clearly 'Fuck!' and closed his eyes again.

'The doctors said the stroke has affected his speech,' my mother explained. 'They told me the name of it, but I can't remember. Dys-something. Or a-something-ia. It's the bit of the brain where you form words, where you choose them. The doctor said he can't censor himself. He's been swearing the whole time he's been in here. They said, in the scans, there was evidence of older lessons in his brain. Lessons. Is that right?'

'Lesions?' I suggested.

'Yes, lesions. That maybe he had a small stroke years ago, and we never noticed, not with the drinking he did. And he said things ... He couldn't stop himself from saying those bad things.' She began to cry.

'What's that fucking racket?' my father said, drowsily. 'I just want to sleep, for fuck's sake.'

We took my father home three weeks later. He had lost much of his memory of the past ten years, and his speech was confused. He would ask for a fork when he meant a knife, and call my mother a 'silly tart' when she brought him one. But then he would shake his head, saying, 'I'm sorry, hen. I can't help it. My fucking brain is fucked.'

When he was stronger, I introduced Phuong to him. My father took to her straightaway, and Phuong was fascinated by his swearing, especially the infinite uses he made of *fuck*, a word that could be traced back to the eighth century.

'Och, I don't give a fuck!' he would say when he disagreed, or 'Get to fuck!'

When she heard him, my mother would cry from wherever she was in the house, 'Oh, Jimmy! Can you please mind your language!' She had returned to look after my father. I don't think he ever realised that she had left him: my mother never mentioned it to him.

After the stroke, he never smoked or drank again. His speech gradually became more coherent, but no less filthy. When I visited him he would stand up and say, 'Come here, you daft bastard!' and then embrace me. Then he would turn to my wife and, kissing her cheek, say, 'I don't know how he was smart enough to get someone like you, hen. He never had any common sense. As thick as pigshit, unstirred and undiluted. Except for his words. I'll give him that, the bastard.'

In my father's curses was his blessing.

Damn

My father came to live with us after my mother died. She was killed by an aggressive form of cancer that, up to the end, she was unable to pronounce. My father stayed at her side the entire time in the two months she was dying. When she was asleep, he would pray to God, unconscious of his blasphemies.

'Our father who art in heaven,' he would plead, 'for fuck's sake, help my wife.'

One afternoon my father began to tell, once more, the story of the cock.

'Oh, Jimmy,' my mother said feebly. 'Not that again.'

'Just listen,' he said. His recollection of the story was remarkable, although he had to stop half-a-dozen times when he couldn't find the word he wanted, and then my mother would help him.

'Greenhouse,' she would say softly. 'You were fixing the greenhouse.'

As he neared the end of the story, I straightened up as — for the first time — he deviated from the well-rehearsed script of decades.

'Well,' he said, 'your mother went away to get a ... What is it? Damn! Ah, a handkerchief because of my nose. And I thought ... And I thought to myself, Jimmy, you've got to see this lassie again. So I took a whatdoyoucallit ... a rock. And I put a fucking crack in the lounge-room window!' He laughed. 'I cracked it, and I showed it to your mother so she would have me back again to fix it. So she would have me back ...'

He looked down at her, and my mother took his hand.

'You never told me that part,' she said, smiling.

She died the next day.

My father was silent at the funeral, perhaps afraid of swearing in front of my mother's friends and relatives, and making her ashamed of him once more. So he didn't say a word throughout the service, or in the car, or at the cemetery where he stood holding my son's hand as his wife was laid to rest.

I drove my father back to the house to pack his things. When we got home, my father sat on the back deck as I shifted boxes into a truck. It was after sundown by the time I had finished, and my father was still sitting there, in the dark. I went out and sat beside him.

'Damn,' he said.

'What is it?'

'That's the only time your mother ever fucking swore at me,' my father said quietly. 'Just the once. She said, "Damn."'

I didn't tell my father that *damn* came from the Middle English *dampen*, itself derived from the Latin *damnare*, to condemn, to inflict loss. He already knew exactly what it meant.

For a moment I could think of no word to comfort him. Then I cried out 'when!', and without a second's pause my father farted, loudly, enormously.

And he threw back his head and roared his laughter at the darkness.

The Sixth Cycle

JACINTA HALLORAN

From her chair in the day ward, Teresa looked out over the elm trees in the park across the road. The first time she'd been there the trees were bare. By her third chemo cycle there were new leaves budding, like little tumours, on every twig on every tree. Now it was mid December, and the leaves were thick and lush, and the trees threw dense circles of shade onto the grass. This afternoon, if she felt well enough, she'd say goodbye to everyone then cross the road and stand under one of those trees for a minute. Her little farewell ceremony. 'All finished before Christmas,' the oncologist had said the last time she'd seen him. 'That's nice timing.' As if she'd somehow planned it.

Lucia, her yoga teacher, had suggested a mantra for chemo days. *It is what it is, no more and no less.* When, at the end of a Wednesday-night class, Lucia had first whispered it to her, Teresa had felt drowsy and warm, but perhaps it had been the heat in the room, or the way Lucia had said it: all brimming with confidence, her soft Scottish brogue so soothing, her hands lightly resting on Teresa's temples. *It is what it is, no more and no less.* Lucia wasn't young, but she seemed it. She'd travelled the world: South America and India, years of her life spent in places that weren't home. She was open to everything. Now, as the nurse — Joanne it was today — wheeled the IV towards her, Teresa wished for Lucia's flexibility of outlook. A flexible body and a flexible mind: six months' worth of salutes-to-the-sun and breathing — *so* much breathing — yet, still, she didn't have either.

'Your last day,' Joanne said, tightening the tourniquet on Teresa's arm. Joanne had round cheeks, a Cupid's bow of a mouth, and a blunt, brown bob that swung like a curtain. 'You must be happy.'

Happy? Was she happy? Was that what it was; this strange anticipation that sat, like a bubble of air, just under her sternum? But she was being too literal: an English teacher's habit. 'Yes,' she said with a smile. 'Very happy. Though you've all been wonderful here.'

'We do our best,' Joanne replied, tapping confidently at a vein on Teresa's left forearm. She picked up the IV cannula and steadied it against Teresa's skin. 'Okay, here goes. Lucky last needle.'

From time to time during the morning, Joanne walked past and asked Teresa how she was feeling.

'As well as can be expected,' she'd reply, or 'Pretty good, thanks.' The nausea was manageable, so long as she didn't think about it.

She'd learned that trick during her first cycle, on her way back from the bathroom, where she'd been vomiting her heart out. She'd stopped to fix a twist in her IV tubing when a man in the chair nearby had spoken to her.

'Keep your thoughts above your stomach,' he'd said. Just like that.

'Are you offering me advice?' she'd countered irritably. Her hands were tingling uncomfortably — the nurses had warned her they might — and she was still feeling sick.

'Yes.' He looked at her over the top of his reading glasses. 'I've found it's best to think abstractly, or to look out the window, or read something you love.' The book on his lap was *A Passage to India*. 'Just don't let your thoughts drift down to' — he patted his stomach — 'you know where.'

She smiled at the familiar tone of his voice. 'Let me guess. You're a teacher.'

'More or less. University academic. Botany. And now a self-proclaimed expert in chemotherapy. Last dose today of my second course.' He was thin, and as bald as a billiard ball, but he had a kind face.

'*A Passage to India* is one of my favourites, too,' she'd said.

'What are you doing for Christmas?' Joanne asked as she changed the IV bag.

'Having lunch with my brother and his family.' Teresa smiled so that Joanne could see she was looking forward to it. 'He has four teenage sons: can you believe it? The youngest are twins. All lovely boys.' She was gilding the lily: Callum, the fifteen-year-old, had been a handful all year, and lately the twins were at each other's throats. Just last month their mother, Meredith, had talked to Teresa about it. Should they change schools? The all-boys thing had worked well for the oldest one, but perhaps the others would do better to mix with girls. What did Teresa think? 'The best thing you can do for boys is to integrate them socially,' she'd told her sister-in-law. 'Some of the most positive friendships I've seen at school have been between boys and girls.' She'd been surprised at her directness, but Meredith had taken it well. Her diagnosis had made her more forthright, and Meredith less so.

Joanne flicked at a bubble in the IV tubing. She had lovely nails, Teresa noticed; all the same length, perfectly shaped and lacquered with shiny clear polish. 'What about you?' Teresa asked. 'What are you doing for Christmas?'

Joanne raised her eyebrows. 'We wanted to go to Thailand on the twenty-second, me and my boyfriend. You know, just forget about the whole thing. But my mother had a fit when I told her. So we're flying out Boxing Day instead.'

The night before, Meredith had dropped by Teresa's house with a plastic container of chicken-and-sweetcorn soup. 'It's light,' Meredith said. 'Good for summer.' She'd also brought two magazines: *Vogue Living* and *Marie Claire*.

'You really shouldn't have,' Teresa told her, as she put the soup in the fridge. 'You have enough to do as it is, and with Christmas coming.'

Meredith was dismissive. 'It's no trouble. I have to cook anyway, so I just make a little more. Six or seven: what's the difference?'

So Teresa had her magazines, and she always brought a book or two along with her. Today it was two of the texts for next year's literature class: D.H. Lawrence's short stories and *A Passage to India*. Last month, when she saw the Forster novel on the Year 12 reading list, she remembered the man who was reading it the day she'd felt so ill. The botany professor, she called him. She hoped he'd got back to work, to his plants and his students. She imagined him in a glasshouse, whistling while he worked, with dirt under his fingernails.

She read quickly through one of the Lawrence stories: the imagery was all well and good, but his attitude to women! The girls at school would hate it. She could just imagine the arguments in class: the girls articulate and indignant; the boys stirring them up for a laugh, yet secretly enthralled. And she, their teacher, trying to keep the peace, to get them to focus on themes and characterisation, all the while a little in love with them all; with their energy and youth, their possibility.

She picked up *A Passage to India* and began to read.

'So it really is a favourite of yours.'

She looked up to see the botany professor, dressed in khaki shorts and a checked short-sleeve shirt. He was no longer bald: instead a hopeful white fuzz, as fine as fairy floss, crowned his head like a halo. He pointed to the book in her hand, and she felt dizzy, unmoored, as if the two of them had suddenly changed places. 'It's a Year 12 literature text for next year,' she said. 'I'm just refreshing my memory.'

'Then I hope your students enjoy it as much as we both do.'

He hadn't asked if she was a teacher. She liked that he didn't seem to bother with redundancies. He simply put two and two together and got on with it.

'Are you here for a check-up?' she asked.

'Preliminary blood tests,' he said, sitting down next to her. 'I'm back for another course of the best stuff next week.'

'Another full course?' He'd barely been away. Just five short months.

'Yes, the works. So long as I can manage it. Which I will.'

He stayed to have a cup of tea with her. There was a plate of fruit too, brought by Joanne; thin cantaloupe slices and cubes of watermelon and grapes, cold from the fridge. The professor ate steadily while they talked about books. He was a fan of the modernists, he told her, reaching for another slice of cantaloupe. His appetite seemed infectious, so much so that she surprised herself by eating a whole bunch of grapes.

When the fruit was all gone, and she was afraid he might at any moment get up and leave, she found herself saying, 'I don't know what to think about it: having cancer, that is. I don't think it's given me any wider perspective, any great insights. I don't feel particularly spiritual.' She stopped. Had she upset him? He didn't look upset. He wasn't squirming in his chair. 'But there's one thing,' she went on. 'It sounds ridiculous really.'

'I don't mind ridiculous.'

'It's something I've been thinking about lately. Not analysing in any way, but I often find the thought has drifted into my mind. It's about these two men.'

'Ah! Sordid confessions.'

'No, quite the opposite. Terribly mundane.'

'But still you keep thinking about them, so that's interesting in itself.'

Teresa hesitated. What could she tell him? She didn't have a story in mind: rather a ragbag full of memories. No, less than memories: hazy recollections and vague interpretations of things that had happened so long ago that she sometimes felt they'd happened to someone else. He was looking at her, waiting. It was her move. She took a deep breath.

'I knew them both once, neither of them very well. Two acquaintances, really, and yet I keep running into them. Thirty years of our paths crossing, again and again. What do you make of that?'

He seemed to think about it for a moment. 'Coincidence, I'd say. You might all live near one another.'

'Yes, although I've moved around a bit since my student days. But perhaps the three of us are always moving in the same direction.' She poured a glass of water from the jug on the side table and sipped at it slowly. Two men from her past. One could say, at fifty, that one had a past, a history on which to dwell or forget. More past than future at fifty, cancer or no cancer: that was the plain truth of it. 'I met them both through different part-time jobs. The first worked as a dishwasher at the restaurant I waitressed at when I was eighteen. My first year at uni. Sometimes we'd sneak outside for a few minutes during the dinner service, and I'd have a cigarette with him. Not that I was ever much of a smoker.'

'You have to say that in here.'

'No, it's true. Neither a smoker nor much of a drinker. Not that it's helped.'

He tapped her lightly on the arm, and she knew what he meant. No self-pity allowed. 'Come on,' he said, 'keep talking.'

'After that I used to see him around; mainly pubs in St Kilda or Fitzroy, wherever there was a band playing. We'd nod to each other in an offhand way; sometimes we'd exchange a few words, if we could hear one another over the music. Then there came a time, in my early thirties, I think, when he walked right past me and didn't seem to know me. I probably hadn't seen him for a year or two before that, but I knew exactly who he was. After that he never recognised me again.'

'Do you still see him now?'

'Yes, more than ever. Outside a pub that I ride past on my way home from work.' That winter she'd seen him every Tuesday and Thursday, around five p.m., standing under the eaves of the Builders Arms Hotel, his black coat buttoned against the cold. She would ride past, thinking, *Today he won't be there*, but then she'd see him, dragging on his cigarette, a stubby in his other hand.

'And earlier this year, just before my diagnosis, he came past my house. I was outside, at the letterbox, the exact moment he walked past. Don't you think that's weird?'

'Coincidence, again. He might often walk down your street. That just happened to be the first time you saw him.'

'I guess you're right.' It was comforting to put it all down to chance.

'It's possible he's thinking the same thing about you. Who is this woman that I keep passing in the street? Why does she seem so familiar?'

She laughed. 'Somehow I don't think so.'

'Why don't you say hello next time? You could tell him you've been stalking him for thirty years. He'd be flattered.'

'Believe me, I've thought about it. But no: too much water under the bridge, and all that.'

When she'd seen him at the letterbox, in his black winter coat, she'd been surprised by how much he'd aged. Up close she could see his face was speckled with red and purple capillaries, and he had the watery pale-blue irises of an old man. She heard the clank of bottles in the plastic bag he carried, and wondered how well he was.

'And what about your other man?' the professor asked. 'Where does he fit in?'

There was an edge to his voice. Teresa thought he sounded tired. 'I'm boring you,' she said.

'If you were boring me, I'd leave.' He looked at her the way he might look down his microscope, Theresa thought: steady and serious and, behind the steadiness, a slow-burning curiosity. 'I've never been one for small talk. So, go on. Please.'

She began again. 'I worked with him during the university summer break, at a home for disabled children. Not that you call them that, these days. But they *were* disabled: kids with cerebral palsy so bad they couldn't sit straight, let alone walk. A boy of thirteen, as big as a man, with the mind of a two-year-old. We used to pour custard on his roast lamb and tomato sauce on his dessert, then feed it to him with a teaspoon. It seemed wrong to me, disrespectful, but the full-timers told us it was how he liked it. And he ate it, too, every mouthful.' She smiled, remembering more. 'Another girl, Karen, used to play the piano for the kids, and Dominic — that was his name — would play his guitar. We'd sing silly songs and get those kids who could to stand up and dance, until the full-timers told us to stop.'

'Why did they tell you to stop?'

'Because there was work to be done. Nappies to be changed and mouths to be wiped. Singing and dancing wasn't seen as good use of our time.'

'You were the young radicals, upsetting the status quo.'

'Yes, that's it. We felt so righteous, so enlightened.' She sighed. 'Anyway, Dominic went overseas soon after that, and I lost contact with him. Then, just this year, between my third and fourth cycles, I saw him again, at the National Gallery — the Dali exhibition. He was with a young woman: his daughter, I think.'

For no particular reason she'd followed them around the gallery, just for a few minutes. Once, he'd turned and looked at her, and she'd held his gaze for a second, waiting to see what would happen. Nothing did. Of course she hadn't expected him to recognise her. She was wearing her black velvet cloche hat and drawn-on eyebrows, and lots of foundation to cover the rash that had spread, like a butterfly's wings, over her nose and cheeks. So much time since she'd last laid eyes on him. He'd grown stouter and his eyelids drooped a little, but he was still the Dominic she remembered. When she'd worked with him, his thick, dark hair had been long enough to tie back in a ponytail: at the matron's request he had done exactly that. Now his hair was cut short, and sat against his scalp in smooth, old-fashioned waves. He looked, she'd thought, just as his father would have looked when she and he were nursemaids together, all those years ago. He had probably vowed to himself, back then, that he would never resemble his father, yet there he was, fatherly enough, strolling through the gallery with this straight-backed, pretty girl who, despite her nose ring and the blonde streaks in her dark hair, looked every inch her father's daughter.

'You're crying,' said the professor. He reached into his shorts pocket and pulled out a handful of tissues. 'All clean,' he assured her, pressing them into her hand. 'Just crushed.'

'Thank you,' she said, and dried her eyes. 'I don't know what came over me.'

'Blame it on the drugs.' He waited a while, then asked, 'Did you see this Dominic again, or is that the end of the story?'

'No, I saw him again. I've been going to a yoga class on Wednesday nights, for six months now, and two weeks ago I saw him there. He was there again last week.'

In the short meditation at the end of last Wednesday's class, she'd opened her eyes to see Lucia speaking softly to Dominic, her hands on his temples. The next time she'd glanced at him, he was crying.

'Of all the yoga classes in the world …' the professor said.

'Exactly.'

'Well, I don't know what to make of it. Of course it could still be explained by chance, but I understand that it might feel like something else.' He stretched out his legs. He was so achingly thin, and his bare knees so bony.

She touched his arm. 'I'm not asking you to explain it. Really, I'm not. It's enough that you listened, so thank you.'

When the IV bag was empty, Joanne removed the drip with a little flourish and bandaged her up. 'That's it,' she said brightly. She looked at them both. 'I didn't know you two were friends.'

'Oh yes,' Teresa said. 'Old friends.'

Down in the hospital lobby he asked her, 'How are you getting home?'

'I usually get a taxi.'

'I have my car here. Will you let me drive you?'

She hadn't told him everything. She hadn't told him that on the night before her nineteenth birthday, after the restaurant had closed for the night, she'd gone with the dishwasher to a bar to have a drink. As they left the bar in the early hours, he'd pushed her against a wall and tried to kiss her. She hadn't told the professor, either, that for one entire summer she'd been in love with the ponytailed Dominic, but that he'd passed her over for another. So many details, half remembered; so many threads, unravelled, left hanging. She hadn't told him everything, but perhaps he'd already guessed.

The day after the surgery to remove the cancer — and, along with the cancer, her uterus and ovaries — the surgeon had sat on the end of her bed and told her he'd taken as much of it out as he could. Now it was up to the oncologist. 'Six cycles of chemotherapy,' the surgeon had said, 'and then we'll see. But I should tell you now there's a good chance that the cancer will come back.'

'And what happens then?' She'd been dopey from the painkillers.

'More chemotherapy. And maybe more surgery.'

'And then?'

'Then we wait and see, again.'

Outside the hospital the day had grown hot and the north wind had sprung up. 'The car's on the other side of the park,' the professor told her. 'Do you think you're up to walking? We can stay in the shade.'

'Yes, I'm up to it,' she said, taking the arm he offered. While they walked he could tell her about the elm trees that lined their path.

Inseparable

MELISSA BEIT

There was a big kafuffle when we were born; cameras and magazine reporters camped all over the front lawn, just like we were the kids of singers or royalty or something. Dad was still reeling from the shock of our birth, but pulled his nose out of his schooner when he saw all those flashbulbs. There's some footage of him on the old video camera, standing awkward and frowny in front of the hibiscus bush, all but hiding Mum holding Meg and me in our tiny grow suits, special-made. He doesn't say much, just nods or shakes his head earnestly whenever the invisible interviewer asks him something, but for years he'd get the bloody thing out whenever someone new came to visit, and make them watch his thirty-four seconds of fame.

Poppy doesn't appear in any of the reels or photos, and Gretel says our grandfather holed up in his shed until the whole racket was over, muttering and weeping and throwing up his hands and lunch both. Gretel was five when we were born, so she remembers everything. Even Danny swears he remembers us being born, but he wasn't quite two at the time, and probably he just wants in on the excitement too.

We were good babies, considering, and Mum said it was enough that we didn't lay ourselves out with the colic or fevers, although Meg fussed a bit to begin with, trying to get that right hand free all the time.

It's my earliest memory: Meg and I, two years old, going for the same red cup, and me getting it first, because it was up high, and with her dominant hand tied up, she had to make do with snatching clumsily with her left. I remember Meg tossing a paddy on the kitchen floor and taking me with her, all spilled over with apple juice.

Possibly I remember it because things were usually the other way round, with me yelling and frothing and striking out at everyone and anyone, while Meg stroked my hair, the closest thing she could reach, and made that tuneless noise like the fridge starting up, until I calmed down.

Our house was far from peaceful. There was always someone around: Danny or Gretel; or Poppy, sad-mouthed and weepy; or Mum, of course, lifting and rearranging and wiping us clean; or Dad, clumping around in his dirty boots and getting on everyone's goat with his grousing and language. There were others too: that med student with the red hair who turned up every few months and cleared his throat so often it gave us the nervous giggles. And the seamstress, old Mrs Bogg, who clucked around us like a hen and managed to fashion double-necked garments out of purple terry cloth and pink stretch cotton. And doctors, of course, by the dozen.

Doctor Jack was the head honcho, and the biggest, with those shoes like boats, that great blob of a nose that Meg liked to pull, at first. There was Doctor Roseleaf too, and you hardly even noticed him to start with, all silent and dry and watchful. They were the two big guns, the movers, but there were dozens more, some around for a gawk who you'd see just the once.

'You have a responsibility to the future of medicine,' Doctor Jack told our parents, and Mum just shook her head, but Dad drew himself up to dizzying heights like he was totally responsible and reliable and not just some old boozer blowing his dole cheque on the nags.

Only at night was it just the two of us, Meg and I; even though Danny shared with us from the word go. From our cot we'd hear him snoring away in his bed and talking too, and Meg'd wriggle right around so our shoulders fit across the pillow and our legs went up the wall. In the dark room we could hear all the other comforting sounds: Gretel's violin wailing like a pulled tooth; Poppy hawking and spitting in the outside shower; all the neighbourhood dogs winding

Inseparable

down for the night; and Mum, clunking away with the iron while she watched the television, getting teary and thanking her stars that nothing really bad ever happened to our family.

Dad stuck around because he thought me and Meg would make him rich. He saw offers for film rights and royalties rolling in long before they actually did; had visions of a two-storey house, a speedboat. But after that initial fuss, Mum made the paparazzi bug off. She sent every journo packing and Returned-to-Sender all the wheedling propositions in their buff envelopes. And with Dad at the races or half-sunk at the pub most days, he was never home at the right time, so it was years before he figured out that we hadn't really been snubbed: we'd been snubbing.

Poppy came round in the end, round about the time we turned two. It's one of the stories Mum tells me at night when I can't sleep, but I swear I can remember it for myself. He was sitting in the shade of the jacaranda tree in the old camp chair, looking at nothing while Mum pegged our funny-looking clothes on the line, and Meg and I grovelled around in the dirt under her feet. I preferred to err on the side of caution when it came to bodily functions, but Meg always liked to push the envelope, so when I started off, heading back inside for the loo, Meg had other ideas, being not quite finished with her peg house and confident that the bladder could hold out a bit longer. So we set up a squabble, Meg holding grim-faced to the hoist, and me kind of rolling my way towards the house, and what with all the rumpus, Poppy looked up and beheld us, and for a wonder he didn't commence weeping like usual but laughed instead, a crusty bark that surprised him as much as the rest of us.

'It's the push-me-pull-you!' he croaked.

And Meg, who always knew the right thing to do, beamed out a big Oh-*hello*-there! smile at him and tucked us straight into his heart.

We could move pretty fast by the time we were four. If Danny started across the room towards some toy or book, Meg and I could scoot round him and snaffle it before he got there or even realised there was competition. We were top-heavy, so walking was never going to be our locomotion of choice, but we could go lickety-split on carpet or grass, and we loved the sandpit. Mum used to shake her head in wonder and say, 'Ah bubs, you're a blur of limbs, you make me head whirl.'

But most people were like Poppy had been in those first years, and it hurt them to see us living squished up together. The doctors were no different. Doctor Jack and Doctor Roseleaf started up again, first with Mum, then with Poppy once they saw that he'd come on board, but in the end, mostly with Dad. 'With prosthetic limbs, both girls could walk independently. Run perhaps. Why they could even walk to school together!' It was the launch of the last campaign to separate us, and I don't doubt that it had a seductive tune to it.

Now I walk. I make my slow and lonely way across the room, and I never beat anyone to anything.

When we turned five the clamour from the outside world became a roar. We were going to school next year; how would we cope, how would we even sit at the desks, all skewiff like we were? How could they stop us cheating on tests? No matter that we were happy now, what about when we reached adolescence and realised we were *different* from everybody else? What about when we got interested in boys? (In sex?) It was selfish of our parents to deny us the operation — no, it was more than that; it was wrong. An infringement of our basic rights as human beings.

And Poppy, red-faced and just about inarticulate with indignation, would shove pictures of Chang and Eng under their noses and shout, 'Both married! Both had kids!' and the doctors would smile patiently and turn their attention back to Dad, where they were at least making some progress.

'It is imperative that it happen soon,' said Doctor Jack in

his rumbly, assured voice. 'The sooner we separate them, the faster their bodies will heal, and the more successfully they will compensate for any deficiencies.'

He turned his head, and we could see the frustration scrambling up those smooth, moisturised features. He muttered, 'It should have been done years ago,' and Doctor Roseleaf threw him a warning look from across the room.

One time Doctor Jack turned to us and crouched down, all smiles, and said, 'Wouldn't you girls like to be able to give each other a big hug? Play hopscotch together? Ride a bike?' but we just stared back at him, mute, for didn't we give each other hugs all the time? And only little kids played hopscotch; we played marbles and, what with my aim and Meg's grit, we were just about unbeatable in our street. And we rode Danny's bike all the time, with the trainers on, and with just a bit of help from him and Gretel.

Mum showed the doctors the door and hurried straight back to us. 'It's all right,' she said, wiping away my tears and Meg's scowl. 'I won't let them.'

And Dad banged out the door and went to the pub with a face like a pound of tripe.

Meg was the strong twin, so when it came time to say goodbye, out there in the prep room, Mum barely gave her the time of day. It was me she was worried about, with my tiny scrap of liver, my single kidney and dickey heart. It was me she thought she might not see alive again, so she wept all over me and kissed my face wet and gripped my hand, then at the last minute, as the nurses made to take us, she remembered Meg and pecked her on the cheek. 'Take care of your sister,' she said to her, fierce. 'You keep a good hold on her!' And then she was gone, poor Mum, with her sad face, grey and lined from all the months of court and fighting, and we were on our own.

They wheeled us through some metal doors into a room bright with overhead lamps and smelling badly of bleach, and

Meg, the bold one, tucked her head under my chin as best she could, and whimpered, and it was me who had to be brave. With my good arm I reached around and cuddled her to me, tight as I could for courage, and with the hand we shared, I stroked her hair. Underneath the din of clanging and beeping and busy people turning knobs, I started up a humming, low and steady, a bit like the noise a fridge makes; and like that, we went under the gas.

Writing [in] the New Millennium

DEBRA ADELAIDE

Professionalising the Creative (11.00 a.m. – 12.15 p.m. Sem. Rm 3): When someone in the audience asked how long it should take to write a book, all the authors exchanged glances. I expected the answer to be depressingly precise, but not this depressing. Nor this precise. Ten years, said one author, not missing a beat. Six weeks, said the author next on the panel. The first elaborated: ten years from early notes to final draft but another two before publication, so strictly twelve. Her book was a nervous-looking volume of fiction that sounded more like poetry. In the book display it sat disdainfully to one side of the embossed historical novels and the fiction with perky covers and one-syllable titles. *The Lonely Flight of the Soul*. It looked a lot like its author, a lonely soul clad in muted tertiary shades, sitting apart from the rest of the panel. The author who said six weeks went on to explain that he only wrote in the evenings, as his real job was in finance. He held up his book, a fat action thriller well over 120,000 words called *Code Six*.

My evenings were spent in front of the television. Sometimes after Rosie and Jay settled down for the night, and Curtis and I were done throwing clothes in the washing machine or cleaning up the kitchen, there was no point even switching it on. If I ever got to bed with a book, I couldn't seem to stay awake. It had taken me three years to write my manuscript and it was still fewer than 30,000 words. I wondered how late the finance guy worked? Six weeks of 120,000 words came to 20,000 words a week, or 2,857.14 words per day. Not so bad if you said it quickly.

But I wondered how many words per hour he wrote. And were all those words good ones?

Hothousing New Talent. Mentoring and Marketing. Furthering Your Manuscript. I chose all the sessions that sounded like they meant business. I wanted action, results. When the assessor confirmed our details for the program, eight of us, all expenses paid, she added a final comment in her email. More like a warning. Our manuscripts had been chosen for their potential, but the rest was up to us. Even if we were to secure a book deal at the end of the conference, we had to understand that afterwards we would be on our own. With a deadline. She recommended we approach agents on the first day. Potential alone would not be enough.

The agents were all very tall. Twice, I lined up to speak to them after sessions (*Managing a Literary Career*, *Breaking through the Paper Ceiling*), but even seated they towered over me. One of them had severe cheekbones and shorn white hair, under which her skull protruded. I could almost see her thinking how she would rather be back in her office overlooking the water while on the phone to New York finalising a deal for a client, a real author. Instead she was in this small town, which had doubled in size for the week of the conference, talking to people who thought that because they had been told they had potential they were special. Waiting in line, I overheard her saying something dismissive about potential writers. Potential started to sound less like a quality with inherent power, and more of a handicap. Each time I walked away before reaching the front of the queue.

At the first session after breakfast, someone said, 'You know the Annals woman is still in her room? She's written a thousand words this morning!'

Oh, the Annals woman. So famous she did not require a name. Like a duke from Shakespearean drama, Norfolk or Gloucester, so powerful that she went by an abbreviation of her estate instead. *The Annals of the Golden Children*. Five or six books, all with two definite articles in their titles, just to make sure. A body of work almost legendary among fans even though she was still so young. She dressed like an extra in a fantasy film. She could have been Galadriel's understudy. Everything about her was bountiful: flowing hair, long velvet skirts, the thousands of words. Before breakfast.

Another writer, a bearded vegan from the mountains, said to no one in particular, 'Apparently Trollope wrote three thousand words every morning. Before going to work. And he didn't even have a laptop!' He slipped a banana from the breakfast buffet into the pocket of his coat, which had telltale leather patches at the elbows. He looked like a nib-pen kind of writer.

Annals had a silver laptop. It really did seem made of precious metal. On opening night, when the rest of us were laughing and drinking too much wine, she clutched her laptop close to her chest, talking with head bent to her editor. She departed early in a way that announced, *I am going upstairs to write now; that is what writers do*, while the rest of us quite obviously were not writing. Unless you counted the flirtatious text messages criss-crossing the room. Arts bureaucrats, literary professionals, let loose for a week together. Even I caught on to that.

And writers. A writers' conference is full of them. Why such an obvious thing took so long to strike me, I didn't know. There were books and people to sell them, but no readers. We were all writers. Dozens of people attending each session. Here to learn writerly things. I was so eager. A great sheet of blotting paper ready to soak up everything about the writing life. And yet all the writers, the ones with books on display, seemed a different species. Everything they told us was contradictory. Write no more than three drafts, otherwise you overdo it. At least ten drafts. Twenty. Write with your eyes shut and let the words flow. Don't censor yourself. Learn how to self-edit. Don't even *try* to edit yourself. Be ruthless. Cut, cut, cut. I began to suspect they were all telling lies. The thin nervous author and the mountains poet whispered over skinny soy lattes during the morning coffee break, though on stage they seemed to despise each other. Maybe they were conspiring to keep us potential authors out of the scene.

And for a writers' conference there was some very sloppy language around. I studied the program posted up at the information desk. I couldn't knock out thousands of words in a day but I did know my grammar. Why was everything a gerund?

'A what?' Another Potential Writer, next to me.

'*Writing the New Millennium. Professionalising* everything. All these verbs without subjects. And nouns posing as verbs.' She looked at me and moved away.

Streamlining and Storytelling. Approaching Publication. Writing the New Millennium. That was the keynote session: only top-shelf authors participating, we privileged mentees up in the front row, part of our fabulous opportunity. The authors had hardcover editions and overseas agents and Commonwealth Prize shortlistings. The audience questions were vetted beforehand. I dared not offer mine. Writing about, writing in, even writing for the new millennium. But what was *writing* the new millennium? The missing preposition bothered me.

The top-shelf authors were all unsmiling males over sixty. They read from their books in wearied drawls, making comments about dead European writers I'd never read. They wrote historical novels, and somehow we all knew that did not mean Regency dramas or anything with a bodice on the cover. Everything they said was addressed to the corner of the room somewhere past our heads, as if there hovered a better quality audience, a more appreciative and deserving one. The writing life of the new millennium sounded like afternoon tea in the staff common room of a boys' school. I left the session early. The millennium wasn't even new anymore.

Again in the bar I knocked back two cold beers before moving on to red wine. Behind me on the wall was one of the conference posters. After my second drink I took out a felt pen and added the word *in* between *Writing* and *the*.

Annals wore her flowing clothes and silver jewellery at breakfast. Looking closer when I fetched my coffee, I saw she was also wearing full make-up. Her hair was sleek. Like a waterfall. An advertisement for hair conditioner. She drank decaffeinated tea and ate only a tiny wholemeal roll and an apple. Her figure was perfect. Her voice calm, well-modulated. I knew her study back home would be organised with document trays and proper bookshelves. Her kitchen cupboards would be tidy, her bedsheets always fresh. I didn't need to see photos to know that her husband would have slightly greying hair and project an aura of stern kindness. Actually, I was certain he would resemble Hugo Weaving. And her children, one of each. Sebastian and Aurelia. They would have excellent teeth and school reports.

Even the university where she worked was a magical place, on a hill. Evergreen trees, misty mornings. I expected that on teaching days she also wrote a thousand words before breakfast. Hugo was probably something in design, or advertising. They would pay their bills on time and upgrade their cars every five years and have family holidays at coastal resorts. Curtis and the kids and I holidayed at the coast too. But somehow I couldn't see Annals in a tent, the whole shower-block, burned-sausages thing. Where would she write her morning thousand words for a start?

Between sessions, tall young men stalked the grounds, phones clamped to their ears. Impossible to decide if they were successful young authors or successful young publishers, agents or editors. Producers or consumers. It didn't seem to matter. Suits worn nonchalantly with T-shirts. Shaved heads. Ray-Bans. Once, you could pick authors by their straggling hair or unfashionable floral skirts. But here only the bearded mountains poet seemed to be playing the part. Everyone else had a corporate look. These young men with phones were doubtless negotiating deals with New York, Frankfurt, Hollywood. One of them had thick black hair that he pushed back from his forehead, but in petulance, not despair, for surely he was too successful for that. He pulled his phone away, stared at it, then reattached it to his ear while gazing into the distance. As if he were listening to the sound of the sea in a conch shell, the sound of a faraway sea, the Atlantic, or the Nordic. The immense swell, the crashing waves of success and prosperity, the white caps of book sales cresting in triumph before pouring into a bank account.

Another of these men emerged from a doorway as I walked past and we almost bumped. He was looking at the floor while talking on the phone, uttering single words punctuated by brief silences. Ambiguous (pause). Deficient (pause). Vulpine. So he was talking to his publisher or agent. Accommodate (pause). Windfall (shorter pause). Yo-yo. Or maybe providing answers to crossword-puzzle clues. His voice was soft, and the hair on the back of his neck curled endearingly just like Rosie's when it was damp, but I did not let that fool me. I was sure he was a deeply focused, humourless individual who wrote five pages each day and secured literary fellowships every other year.

Not fast enough at leaving one session, I became trapped in the first row before the next started. *Contemporary Mythical Narrative* (4.00 p.m. – 5.30 p.m. Sem. Rm 1). My eyes started closing though I willed myself to remain awake. Luckily the lectern hid me from most of the panel. The author at the end was reading in a piping monotone from his new novel. The story was all about a woman walking across a windy mountain pass that seemed to go on for miles. He read for twenty minutes, and still all she did was brush some grit from her eye. She never got anywhere near the end of the rocky path. The roaring wind did not abate. I was alarmed when I noticed he was only halfway through a very thick volume, and it was while speculating on what might lie ahead in the novel (a speck in the other eye? another mountain after this one?) that I fell asleep.

Afterwards I decided I must make a greater effort. I returned to the book display and selected one of Annals' books from the piles of them under her photograph. Unfortunately I could not read past the second page of *The Annals of the Soothsayer*, which contained the phrase *Alamandra swooned at the feet of Alaric*, because a) I did not believe that anyone had swooned since 1801, and b) I was already confused by two characters' names commencing with 'Al'.

I was allotted a half-hour, one-on-one session with a Strategic Marketing Consultant. His head was polished to match his shoes. At the start of our session he placed his BlackBerry beside his appointment book and pressed a button firmly. Possibly he was activating a timer.

'And what genre do you write in?'

Genre.

'Umm. Well, it's a sort of children's story.'

'But what genre? Fantasy? Adventure? Crime?'

'Not any, really. Elements of all, I guess. Maybe.'

'Children's or young adult?'

'Oh, definitely children's. I mean kids from any age. If they want.'

'We need a specific target audience. What age exactly?'

'Around twelve? Ish? Maybe younger. Eight, nine. But then teenagers might —'

'Children or teens. You don't do both.'

It was the first I'd heard that kids aged eight and thirteen weren't allowed to read the same book.

'Look around you,' he said. 'What are you doing here?'

'Well, my manuscript was selected …'

'That's not what I mean.' He glanced behind him. 'I mean,

look at all the *successful* authors here.' He emphasised the word in a way that showed contempt for the handful of writers, like Thin Nervous, whose book might have been translated into French but whose sales remained under four figures. These writers were not even bothering anymore to turn up for their book-signing sessions, whereas Code Six and Annals sat there signing and smiling every day. Their publicists slid well-padded chairs underneath them and stood by with supplies of bottled water, as if book-signing were an Olympic event. 'These authors understand exactly their place in the market.'

Author? He meant I really was an author?

'*They* are focused.'

No, clearly he meant I was not.

'Your target audience,' he repeated, closing his appointment book just as the BlackBerry buzzed. 'You need to define your target audience.'

No one could confirm when and where I was to meet my mentor. Or if she was even there. I carried my manuscript around all week, expecting anytime to start the hours and hours of blissful intensive hands-on work that I had anticipated ever since I applied for the program. My manuscript began to have a dog-eared look to it. Then I noticed that few people had manuscripts with them. As if it were impolite, or show-offy, hawking a folder of paper around. Writing the new millennium seemed a very private affair.

At dinner one night I was seated next to an author from Los Angeles called PB, who wrote for twenty-somethings.

'What do you have there?' She tapped my folder.

'It's really just a first draft.' This was not true. I must have rewritten it fifty times.

She did not step in to ask what it was about or had I been published, but took a bite of her cheesecake.

'No one here seems to be doing much writing,' I said. Apart from Annals, but I knew better than to mention her to someone called PB. Not with her hot pink wig and tartan miniskirt.

She laughed. A sudden barking sound like gunshot at daybreak.

'We all do it but don't admit to it. Like picking your nose, or masturbating.' Seeing the shock on my face, she leaned closer. 'Listen, kid, writing sucks. Getting your name out, that's what counts. Do you blog?'

Kid? I was at least ten years older!

She got out of her chair. 'Are you going to the *WordSlam*?' But it was not an invitation.

Writing the new millennium was clearly for a different kind of writer. I wanted sessions on the problems that bothered me, such as choosing names for characters and keeping my desk tidy. Or advice on posture and diet. And I wanted to know how to inoculate myself against the contagiousness of style that I once read about. I didn't want to be told that writing sucks. I hoped my mentor was not like PB, with her interactive texts and Californian advice.

Not only was my mentor unable to answer these questions, she looked at me as if I were a species of vermin. Finally, on the last day, I'd found her seated at the back of a small room smoking a cigarette out of the window.

She told me to sit and pushed some forms at me. 'Publishers. Conference committee. They're after details,' she said.

'More details?'

She shrugged. I had already filled in forms and answered questionnaires, when I was selected. When my manuscript was selected. She shrugged again, saying she was just a freelancer, funded by the conference trust and the local council, just doing what they asked. I signed the forms and pushed them back. I wondered how much she was paid to sit here on the last afternoon and blow smoke in my face. The mentors were meant to be professional writers and editors.

I asked if she had written books too, if she was an author.

'Freelancer,' she said ambiguously.

Somehow I already knew that she would ignore my folder too.

* * * * *

When I got back home on the Sunday night I threw my suitcase into the corner of the bedroom and headed for the spare room with my notes.

'I'll have to be set up properly in here,' I called out to Curtis in the kitchen. 'Your friends won't be able to stay the night anymore. And the kids' toys will have to go back in their room.' I kicked a plastic dinosaur out the door and tossed three stuffed animals onto the bed. Then I took them and the other toys off the bed. I needed it to set out all my notes and drafts. I was dismantling the Thomas the Tank Engine train set that took up half the floor when Rosie walked in, sucking a finger.

'Sorry, petal. All this has to go. Clean sweep. Mummy's gotta write.'

'So you got the book deal?' Curtis appeared in the doorway.

'Yeah. Well, I signed something.' I pulled Rosie's finger out of her mouth.

Over the next few weeks I learned that the greatest impediment to writing was not the children, not the television, not even the lure of the refrigerator, but the telephone. The phone calls anywhere between three and eight-thirty, from telemarketers, consumer researchers and someone offering me a free holiday if I attended their investment seminar. I couldn't unplug the phone and I couldn't ignore it. Sometimes I did ignore it. But after five or six rings I would give in then, after I'd growled into the phone and returned to my desk, forget what I was going to write. If Jay had been a few years older I'd have asked him to take messages. Curtis had not a clue what I was going through.

'You try being creative at home,' I told him. 'You try pulling an entire story together and keeping the household running. And that bloody phone. What do we need one for anyway?'

But I knew why. The third week back, still no contact.

'Haven't you already written it? Isn't that manuscript what they contracted?'

The ignorance of some people. 'Duh. As if I won't be pressured for the next one. Gotta have that ready when they want it. Besides' — I gestured at the dog-eared folder — 'this needs a complete rewrite.'

One afternoon I was staring at the blank space on the screen where I had just deleted two paragraphs. They had to go but then I panicked at the sight of this big hole which needed filling in. My head felt as empty as the page before me. If I stared at it long enough maybe the words would bore through to the screen from my pupils.

When the phone rang, for once I was grateful. Though I quickly regretted agreeing to take part in the survey.

'How much of your weekly income is spent on takeaway food?'

Instead of answering, I asked, 'What are you reading right now?'

'Pardon?'

'What book are you reading? You are reading one, aren't you?'

She mentioned a title I had never heard of. The author's name sounded fake. Edwina Montgomery. Either that or she died in 1939.

'Name her other titles,' I demanded.

'*Return to Galaxy Red. Journey to the Edge of Time. The Starship Propheticus*,' she said. 'Science fiction.'

'Speculative fiction,' I hissed into the phone. That much

I'd learned from the conference.

What I did not learn from the conference was why so many of these authors were stuck in the old millenniums. All those books about medieval travellers, the taming of dragons, the quests for sacred swords and magic stones and shimmering portals that transported unlikely heroes to other worlds … What did this have to do with the new millennium? When someone mentioned adult fantasy I examined these titles in the book display and, no, they were not sealed and black with R-rating stickers, though I couldn't help imagining leather bras and purple glow-in-the-dark dildos. They were fat and colourful, the covers embossed in gold. The blurbs mentioned battles, lost jewels and magic talismans. Fiery hearts and pure minds and kingdoms and keys and ravens. I wondered what the difference was between adult fantasy and children's. I flipped through each one, scanning the storylines. No sex. Chaste embraces. Kisses on rings or hands, when warlords met or wise men bestowed blessings. Adult fantasy seemed very innocent.

I became obsessed with organising my time. I spent so much time planning my days I did not have time to write. I was stuck between ten (or twelve) years and six weeks. I alternately despised both Thin Nervous Poet-Novelist and Code Six, but then I knew that Thin Nervous had won two literary awards while Code Six had sold over 80,000 copies of his book.

In ten years Thin Nervous had devoted herself to writing 26,000 words. (While at the book display I had counted them — it was easier than reading them.) That was exactly fifty words a week. But fifty words a week divided into 7.12 words each day, and how could you write a fraction of a word? And she must have written half or quarter sentences since some of her sentences were much longer than that. At what point did you divide words into fractions?

As for Code Six, I imagined him sitting there with the

clock set like Trollope and laughing at us all while running off just under three thousand words every evening after dinner. Probably all before eleven p.m., the bastard. Well, of course, being in finance he wouldn't have to muck around with the washing-up or the kitchen floors after dinner; he could just disappear into his study. But I still wanted to know how he did it. Six weeks. Faulkner wrote *As I Lay Dying* in six weeks, but then he cheated. One of his chapters was only five words long. *My mother is a fish*. If only I could write chapters like that and win the Nobel Prize.

The phone rang. There was the familiar lag and crackle before a voice said, 'Good morning, madam, how are you?' but it was not a Bombay accent.

'It's afternoon.'

'Oh sorry, ma'am. How are you this afternoon?'

'Who is calling, please?'

'I am calling from Mordern.'

'Where?'

'Mordern. Have you heard of Mordern, ma'am?'

'No. Where is it?' It sounded like a place in a fantasy saga. Perhaps Annals created it. Or Code Six. I didn't mind, I would have liked to go there.

But Mordern was not a place, it was a company that made roller-shutter blinds, and I said not interested, thanks, and placed the phone down as the guy was asking me to reconsider.

How hard could it be? They were only words, after all. Not anything difficult like microbes or atomic particles. And it was not like developing a vaccine for testicular cancer or isolating the gene that causes Down syndrome. I was not meant to solve any of Fermat's remaining theorems or even understand them. Writing a thesis on the Brahmagupta–Fibonacci identity or completing the Gold Coast triathlon or interviewing Tom Cruise or discovering a way to reverse baldness — all those things were *really* hard.

What about those people who engraved pictures on grains of rice, or built entire sailing ships inside bottles? If they could do that, then I could write a second children's story of under 30,000 words by the end of the year.

'What book are *you* reading?' I demanded of the person who called to sell me tickets in an art-union lottery.

'Tom Clancy's *The Archimedes Effect*,' he said as if it were right beside him.

Even so, I was a step ahead. 'Incorrect. Are you aware that Tom Clancy did not write this book? That his name is a brand for the Net Force series?'

'Ah ... no.'

'And that the real authors of this novel are writing under sub-licensing agreements?'

'Really?'

'Yes. Their names are Steve Perry and Larry Segriff.'

'Oh, okay.'

'Can I help you with anything else today?'

'Er, no.'

'Thank you for calling,' I said before I hung up.

I began to see my target audience. They were lashed to a frame by the ankles and wrists, while my story arrowed its way right through a bullseye painted on their chest. Shoot, shoot, shoot. I reached my target audience again and again, until they slumped on the frame, blood leaking down to pool at their feet.

You are not a writer, said the convenor of *Professionalising the Creative*, if you don't write every single day of your life. If you don't wake up and write your dreams or make notes or plan your day's work. I ensured that I had a notebook and sharp pencil beside the bed. When I woke up I grabbed them — but before I fixed my glasses and stopped yawning, Jay raced in and jumped on the bed, and my dream vanished like water out of a bathtub.

PB was right. Writing sucks. Words were sly, mendacious, untrustworthy, treacherous, dirty, rotten, scheming BASTARDS OF THINGS! I hated them more than anything. I wrote and wrote and these slippery words, these stinking lousy mongrel BASTARDS, disappeared from the page sideways, upwards, anyways. Anything but stay in place on the line, forming nice tidy sentences, one after the other. Pinning them down on the computer screen was like trying to pick up mercury with chopsticks. They rolled and slid away from me whenever I got close. I yelled at the screen. 'I hate you I hate you I hate you I hate you!' Why couldn't I write my story with numbers instead?

'I hate words so much!' I told them one night, slamming the keyboard up and down on the desk. Rosie was doing well with books up until that point. I grabbed *The Very Hungry Caterpillar* from her hands and tossed it aside. 'Forget it, they'll only turn around and betray you when you're older! Look at me, all these words around and do you think I can get a single one to make any sense?'

She started to cry. Curtis hissed at me, 'Grow up, why don't you! You're only trying to write, for god's sake, not trying to solve the riddle of the fucking phoenix.'

'But I have a deadline,' I wailed as he slammed the door to the kids' room in my face.

'Whatever.'

'And it's sphinx,' I said. 'It's the riddle of the sphinx.'

Thank you for attending the Writing the Millennium Conference. Please note the conditions for the submission of manuscripts:

The date of final submission is not negotiable.

Manuscripts received after this date will not be considered.

Manuscripts must be hard copy and not emailed.

Please indicate by return email if you will be complying with these conditions.

No, it didn't sound like a contract. Curtis used the same email address. I printed the email out, then deleted it, then hid the printed email between the pages of a second-hand copy of *Gone with the Wind*.

'No distractions!' I announced. 'No distractions until I've finished my final draft.' I listed all the things I wouldn't do: the ironing, picking up toys, making beds, changing the sheets unless it was absolutely essential. Within a week I refined my list: no more washing, shopping, cooking anything. I looked in the cupboards. There was plenty of tinned food, cereal, rice, instant noodles, packets of biscuits. We had enough food to last for months. Millions of people in other countries lived off barley soup and plain rice; so could we.

One evening Curtis came home to find Jay feeding Rosie peanut butter on stale Mini-Toasts while I gazed at the computer screen and scratched at my dandruff.

'I'm going to the supermarket for fresh food,' he said, picking Rosie up as if she needed an emergency infusion of green vegetables. As an afterthought he asked if I needed anything.

'Yes,' I said, deleting the ninth sentence for the last half-hour. 'I need adjectives. Bring me some nice fresh adjectives.'

He shut the door.

'No, make that verbs,' I called out.

I had a deadline.

'You make it sound like something bad,' said Curtis, he heard it so much.

But it *was* bad. How could something called *deadline* be good? Pages and pages of prose, and what for but a deadline. As if their fate was to be killed, victims of some distant war. All those words, tens of thousands of them. The infantry of prose, the front line. How could I have hated them so much? Poor little soldiers, lying flat and lifeless on the line, their letters dripping off the pages, clotting and staining everything beneath. I would have felt more sorry for them if I hadn't been so worried about my manuscript. Maybe those dead lines could join my target audience, shot through the head, the heart, left to bleed out there somewhere, under the pitiless sun. In the mud. On the beach.

'What an imagination,' he said.

'Thanks.'

'It's not a compliment.'

One day Annals materialised beside me at the washbasins in the women's toilets. We rinsed and shook our hands in unison. She leaned over the basin to inspect her perfect face in front of the mirror. Her hair fell forward in a silent swoosh then rippled over her shoulders and down her back when she stood straight again. The water wound down the plughole, as if reluctant to leave her.

Please note the following additional conditions:
  Authors whose work is accepted will be contacted by telephone.
  We are unable to provide feedback to unsuccessful authors.
  The editorial team's decision will be final.
  No correspondence will be entered into.

Curtis would never think to open the pages of *Gone with the Wind*.

Reckless, Susceptible

A.G. McNeil

Years ago, when I was a young boy, I went through this phase during which I was fascinated by animals. I insisted on having animal-themed bedsheets and pyjamas. My room was filled with stacks of books about animals, photographs of me in front of various enclosures at the zoo, rubber birds strung from the roof in formations, that sort of thing.

I cherished a collection of plastic animals — sixty-two at last count — which I would arrange on the dining-room table. I imagined them in congress, discussing the fate of their kingdom.

My older brother, James, tried to paint a kind of jungle scene on the ceiling just above my bed. He lacked basic technique and understanding of colour. None of his creatures was recognisable. Still, I knew that science was always discovering new species, so I thought of those strange, deformed beasts as inhabitants of some exotic island. They talked among themselves as well, I fancied.

One day I overheard James talking to my mother in the next room. His voice was muted by the walls and so mostly indistinct, but I was able to make out a few sentences.

'You are right though,' he said. 'The animal thing is a bit weird. Childish.'

Mixed with my distress, I think, was the unsettling realisation that my brother was an adult. And that adults had meetings of their own, in which my fate was discussed.

The following day — this is the most vivid of my early memories — I took my collection out to the swimming pool in the backyard. Ribbons of sunlight played in the water, forming spirals and separating.

I set about the business of drowning my animals. I was

systematic. Their deaths were unspectacular. I wouldn't have them struggle. Instead I held each one just below the water's surface, counted to ten, then added it to the terrible little pile beside me, as if I was flash-frying them. Their expressions didn't change. Tigers and sheep alike went to death without protest. It occurred to me that they might have been prepared for this day. I thought them noble.

I had all of this in mind as I was running a bath recently. I was examining a small, four-legged wooden carving that had just arrived by express post. I turned it in my fingers.

The hot water coming from the tap was a flawless white column. Steam was starting to cloud the mirror by imperceptible degrees.

I'd woken up late in the afternoon, having slept for only a few hours, and was feeling the residual effects of a bottle of wine as a sort of thready, nauseous guilt. I'd fallen asleep watching an old horror film, and at some point the disc had reverted to the menu screen, so it was looping one brutish soundbite. I set the carving down beside the sink and went into the lounge room to switch off the television.

There was a newspaper dismembered on the coffee table. The cryptic crossword had been solved. The solutions were written in my handwriting. I read the first clue, then my answer, but was unable to follow the logic. On the floor beside the couch was an empty wine bottle. It wasn't the bottle I remembered opening. It was much nicer. I stared at it for a while, reasoning with the thing.

At length a sequence of images came to mind, none fully formed. I remembered being down in the garage and struggling to unlock the lattice door that leads into the space below the house, then crawling past stacks of firewood and rusted bicycle parts, over to the boxes of wine that my girlfriend's father had stored there years ago.

My girlfriend, Jess, she'd been in Bangkok for several weeks. She was studying aquaculture, conducting experiments with barramundi.

Back in the bathroom, as the water pooled at one end of the old bathtub, two or three chips of paint came away from the metal and drifted to the edge like snowflakes.

That my short-term memory was poor was no revelation. It had been steadily worsening.

Also beside the sink was the portable phone and a book of poetry by Aleksandr Pushkin, the Russian poet. For four years I'd been writing a thesis on Russian literature. I was still a long way from finishing. I gazed momentarily at the frosted-glass window and could just discern the outline of the garden outside — some plants animated by the wind, some melted colours.

I undressed. Then, as I eased into the water, the phone rang. It was Jess.

The line was pretty bad. Her voice had an ethereal quality. 'They're dead,' she said.

'Who?' I slid down in the tub so that everything but my face and hands was submerged. I always pictured her there in long rubber boots, a numb choir of industrial filters going in the background.

'My fish.' She sighed loudly.

I frowned and held the phone away from my ear. She was probably pressing her palm against her forehead.

'… just such a waste of time,' she said.

The line was cutting out intermittently. I reached for my book, trying to open it and hold it at a reasonable angle with my free hand. She was waiting for me to say something.

'So, you didn't get any results or whatever?'

She sniffed. I decided against asking her to hold the phone away from her face when making those kinds of noises. 'We didn't even get that far,' she said. 'It's only a few days since we've even been able to see them.'

I waited before saying: 'What?'

'It isn't important now. They're basically invisible until the fourth week. The larvae. They're less than one millimetre long and they're translucent. We don't really even know if they've spawned or not. But we still have to feed them.'

'Without knowing whether or not they exist?' I considered this for a few seconds. 'That's kind of nice.'

'No. Anyway they did *exist*.' She emphasised the word as if, lacking substance, it didn't fit. 'But then they died anyway.'

'Still,' I said, my mouth tightening to prefigure a little smile. 'It's a nice idea.'

There was a period of silence in which, I thought, we seemed almost to be analysing each other's willingness to let that silence continue. We didn't always see things the same way, Jess and I, which could result in some disjointed conversations. She'd just ignore some of the things I said, or else wait quietly until I returned to good sense.

'Sorry,' I started to say, or had decided to say, but she spoke at the same time.

'Anyway,' she said, taking a deep breath, composing herself, 'so I'm coming home tomorrow. I'll email flight details.'

'Right. Well, that'll be good.'

Then she asked if I was okay. I sounded weird, she said. There was a hint of maternal reserve in her tone.

I looked up at the patterned, pressed-tin ceiling and recited from memory: '*Such, as I was before, I'm now left to be: reckless, susceptible.*' She didn't respond. 'Aleksandr Pushkin,' I explained. 'Eighteen twenty-six.' Then I noticed the wooden carving beside the sink. 'Hey, did you send this fucking wooden thing?'

'… think it was?' was all I heard. I squinted as if to put right the squalling connection. '… like it?'

'It's fucking grotesque,' I said.

She laughed, I think, then said, 'It's the likeness of some animal they found up in the mountains or something. A few months ago. A bad omen, they reckon. Part human, part something else, totally hairless. Supposedly they've got it in a cage somewhere.'

I sat up a little. The bathroom light, coalescing with the steam, seemed to take on some physical properties. So, I found myself thinking, they finally found the island. I shook that thought from my head, then asked: 'Why did you send me a bad omen?'

'It isn't *actually* a bad omen,' Jess said. '… tourists. It's fun.'

The interference grew louder, now containing a thin continuous whine, finally culminating in silence.

Later I walked around the house mindlessly collecting bottle caps and pieces of scrap paper, pausing to scrutinise some trivial thing: the pair of dusty old pedestal fans by the front door, for instance. Even the slightest details seemed to suggest some fearsome consequence of my existence. I'd acquired a thoroughgoing fear of terminal illness. I opened all of the doors and windows, wanting fresh air.

The days had all been the same. I seldom left the house. I'd gotten into the habit of reading and writing until the early hours of the morning, or later, then cooking some noodles and falling asleep, drunk, in front of an old film. Jess had only called a few times. Once to tell me she'd made some friends, another time shouting and slurring and urging me to listen while she sang karaoke. I heard male voices in the background.

I resented her for leaving me alone for so long.

I sat down to reread my work from the night before. I lit a cigarette. I made some notes in the margins but couldn't concentrate, eventually deciding to walk to the pub for a meal.

The air was cool. I took a long coat from the wooden hatstand by the door and set out, imagining myself as some Russian. Our street was lined on both sides by tall peppermint trees which almost joined above the middle of the road to form a remarkable canopy, and all of it was glowing deep pink with the beginnings of sunset. The sky seemed like a great, stitched wound.

The bar was quiet. I ordered a bottle of house wine and a basket of bread. I stayed there reading for several hours.

As I was finishing the last glass of wine a woman approached my table, offering to buy a round of drinks. I accepted without thinking. Trying to picture her now I can only conjure an impression of sorts, something near formless and shifting in the half-light; first convulsing with garish laughter, next pressing up against me, smelling stale.

We talked for a while, and she kept buying the drinks. When the bar closed I invited her back to the house and poured us both some whisky.

'What do you do?' she asked. At the end of each sentence she addressed me as *darl*. Her eyes, I noticed, were small and dark and alert.

'I'm a writer,' I said, affecting total self-confidence, handing her a glass. 'A writer and a doctorate student.'

Her reply was basically unintelligible.

'You have an accent,' I said. 'Where are you from?'

'American by birth.' She turned the glass in her hand, looking into it for her responses. 'Manhattan,' she added. 'Ever been?' I said that I had. 'Weird island,' she said, which I thought was a dull assessment. Still, I nodded.

'Surreal,' I said. We stood quietly in agreement.

In fact, Jess and I had visited Manhattan only a few months before. We rented a place in SoHo. We walked the streets, interpreting. Banks of blackened snow, frozen solid, lined the sidewalks like geological formations. Christmas trees, out with the trash and wrapped in black plastic, were mob victims. The yellow cabs, I said, were herd animals at a standstill and honking as if to gauge one another's position, or just to declare their being. One day, outside the Museum of Natural History, there was a spooked horse running uptown through the traffic. It came into sight — at first a monstrous, changeable thing — two blocks away, seemingly fashioned from the commotion surrounding it. It got to within a few metres of us. What might have been fear shone from its eyes as purpose, and Jess, I remember, was remarking upon its beauty just as one of its legs buckled and the poor creature skidded a short distance, all limbs, attempting recovery, then collapsed in front of us, making a terrible sound unique even to that city. At length a police officer covered the animal's trembling head and shot it. He straightened up, the officer, apparently having mistaken necessity for heroism, and searched our faces for appreciation. Impossibly hungover, I vomited in the snow. That evening was the first time Jess mentioned my drinking.

The American woman — I never got her name — kept making advances, and finally I let her stay, more out of interest than anything else. Her skin was mottled, brown and hairless. Unwrinkled but spongy. When we kissed, her lips were dry and, I realised, slightly asymmetrical. A faint scar ran between her upper lip and her nose. She had long bleached-blonde hair and fake, stone-firm breasts.

More than once her manner struck me as inconsistent. Her generally dizzy, flirtatious bearing was prone to frank interjections. At one point she was straddling me, keeping her eyes closed and making small, breathy sounds. Then, as if startled, she halted, looked at me and — newly lucid, her voice an octave lower — said: 'No anal.'

I repeated those words in my head until they lost their import, then their intonation, and soon I was certain she'd said, and was maybe still saying, as the room spun: 'I'm real.'

Afterwards we lay on top of the bedspread in silence. She was on her side with her left arm in an angular figuration, her open hand supporting her head. I was tracing her curves with my index finger, more brooding than affectionate, watching ripples of skin swell, roll and level out.

The windows were still open. The room was incredibly cold.

The best thing to do, I thought, would be to call James.

I drank the last of the whisky and went into the bathroom to find the phone.

James is married. He lives on the other side of the country with his wife and two children. I realised when he answered that it was well after midnight.

'I just worked out how late it is, man,' I said. 'I'm sorry. I can call back.'

'Drew?'

'Yeah. Yeah, sorry man. I didn't want to wake you. I didn't want …'

'What do you want?' He was clearing his throat a lot.

'If you have a second. Just, like, one minute.' My mouth felt inordinately small. My tongue was mostly unresponsive to commands. James was waiting for me to speak. 'I thought you'd want to know,' I managed to say, 'that your animals have come to life. Or they've been discovered. Or whatever.'

'Drew,' he said, more loudly, in rebuke, 'what the fuck?' I thought I heard his wife say something in the background.

'The mural,' I said, feeling at my jaw as if to recalibrate it. 'That you painted on my ceiling. The animals are fucking alive man. At least one of them is here. Two maybe.' He didn't answer. I lost balance, then steadied myself against the wall. My hands were trembling. 'Is it cold where you are?' I asked. I could hear him breathing. I was seized by this fear that I'd disappointed him. 'All right, forget that. I'm sorry, man. But one … another thing.' I suppressed a hiccup, unsubtly. 'Is it possible that you don't like Jess? Like, you can just say it. You know what you think means a lot. More than you know.' I paused, then added: 'I can get rid of her.'

There was no response. James had hung up. I dropped the phone and sat down on the cold tiles, listening to the steady hum of the retractor fan, shivering uncontrollably.

At one point I heard the front door close. A while later I got up to make some coffee. I spent the rest of the night trying to tidy, reciting poetry to the empty house.

Sometime around dawn I drove Jess's car to the airport.

I had no idea what time her flight was getting in, so I just found a seat in the arrivals lounge and tried to read. The west-facing wall was composed entirely of windows. I watched the planes as they negotiated the sky with what seemed an impossible weightlessness, and I waited, unable to shake the idea that the sunrise was some kind of celestial wreckage.

Birdsong

MYFANWY JONES

When he should be turning sausages with the others, patting backs, he is instead in the rented shed at the back of the rented garden in Lalor with a six-pack. He won't be going anywhere today.

One of the slat windows is rusted open, but he shuts out urban birdsong with country music. He still can't listen to the birds, cannot tolerate their high-pitched hopeful calls. They don't sing of wildfire; of death and devastation, homelessness and starvation. It's not in their repertoire. He can't listen but at the same time he misses them, with an ache that feels strangely like unrequited love, as if his joy in them will forever now be out of reach. He turns up the volume on Adam Brand and cracks open the first can.

This reminds him of playing truant as a boy in short pants: the thrill of taking off up the bluestone alley near the school at the final lunch bell. *I'm outta here! Just try and stop me!* It was an eleven-year-old *fuck you* to the world. All too soon, the buzz would wear off and the fear would set in, and he'd spend the stolen afternoon loitering in the back streets with a bag of mixed lollies, scared and bored and lonely. But it didn't stop him from doing it again, anything for that first rush, and probably, too, he half hoped he'd be caught, get the strap and some of his mother's attention. *Would you just stop me already?*

The light in here is bad, so he sets up the two long-necked lamps, one at either side of the workbench. They glow hot and yellow. He takes down a small square of sandpaper from the shelf and starts working on the latest piece, rubbing away at the wood in a gentle, circular movement. It's small, this piece; fits neatly into the palm of his left hand. This one's his favourite so far. Leigh calls this his therapy and says at least it's cheap, though she is set on a holiday when the money comes through. Somewhere like Bali with lots of water and sand and not too many trees, all blue and yellow and non-combustible.

It's just gone midday. The shed is warming up. Today they are predicting low thirties, barely a flutter of wind.

He drinks and sands, keeping time with the music. Out of the corner of his eye he can see Leigh moving about in the garden. She planted a vegie patch before Christmas, but he'll have nothing to do with it. This is not home, these flat grey streets with their piddling nature strips. Leigh is trying to build herself a new nest, but he is dreaming, every night, of running away. Through the burning trees. The rushing, roaring heat. But to where?

They say the more sedentary birds are always the hardest hit — the thornbills and scrubwrens, treecreepers and lyrebirds. The cockatoos, the honeyeaters, they can sometimes outfly the flames.

He puts the sandpaper down and scrutinises the piece, turning it over and over in his hand. Then he takes up a knife and starts whittling again. There is something not quite right with the head.

Leigh is coming up the path. He opens another beer.

'Won't you come out?'

'No.'

'They've had their minute of silence.'

'Good on 'em.'

'We could go for a drive. Just you and me.'

'Gotta finish this.' He holds up the piece in his hand, but she is staring at the corner of the shed, at the heap of salvaged, blackened timber, his raw material. It smells of wood and smoke in here.

She is frowning, her two worry lines just like her mother's, crooked and deep. 'People are ringing in on the radio, you know, praising the CFA.'

He doesn't say anything. He reaches to turn the music louder. When he turns back she is already walking up to the house.

He wouldn't switch the radio on today if you paid him a year's salary. He will not watch the TV, or listen to the latest from the Commission. He will not light a candle, or talk about it, or observe a minute of fucking silence. All this pantomime is for the pollies and for the people who weren't there but who bang on nonetheless about the indelible scar and the great Australian spirit. They turn up at funerals, in their suits, standing up the back, putting their arms around grieving families, uninvited. They are the kestrels and kookaburras that move in after wildfire to exploit the open canopy, all the dead and injured animals.

He drinks, and takes up the sandpaper again. This is the best part, the smoothing out. He folds the paper to make a cone, uses the point to get into the crevices. He is nearly finished. This one is definitely his favourite. He looks at the others, lined up on the narrow shelf between the rusty jars of screws and nails. They look back at him with their charcoal faces of red gum and yellow box and mountain ash. One year today. He moans, a low growling moan like a dog's.

Sometimes he thinks if he could just get back there and rebuild it would be all right. It's the transience that's hard. Then in the early hours of the mornings when he can't sleep, he makes very different promises to himself, to still his heart: that he will never return; that he won't ever, again, be caught out like that. And so he goes, back and forth, like a tennis ball, with the rubber underneath beginning to show. He has fallen behind at work. Leigh's patience is running out. No one complains — to his face.

He drinks. The music in here is much too loud. *Would you just stop me already? Please?*

He is soaked in sweat. The piece is finished. He turns off the lamps, and the music player, and the tears, for once, stream silently down his face.

Pulling the shed door closed behind him, he walks up the garden path, past the vegie patch with its neat little rows, and the lorikeets and house sparrows, raucous in the almond tree and still, somehow, sounding like lost love.

'Leigh?' he calls out.

'In here.'

She is ironing in the living room, with the radio on. He walks over and flicks it off, then hands her the wooden bird, perfect, with its small, beautifully rounded head, its wings outstretched in flight, burned black.

She bursts into tears. He holds her. 'Shall we go for that drive?'

And as they head north-east on the back roads towards Strathewen, where the boys will be drinking beer on the oval by now and the women cleaning up, he thinks of the five lyrebirds that were found in a sheltered gully just after the fires, far from their natural habitat; huddled together, alive.

How My Father Dies in the End

PATRICK CULLEN

My father didn't die the night he left my mother and me alone in our house on the outskirts of town. No, he did not die then. Instead, he left my mother for a woman he'd met in the office where he worked. It was his job to watch over the hours kept by construction workers; it was not his job to reluctantly dole out their wages as though they came from his own pocket, but it's said that that's how he did it. Like my father, the woman — the daughter of the man who owned the construction business — was married at the time. But maybe she was more inclined to leave her own marriage because it was without children and the pleasure they are supposed to bring.

What happened — all that really happened — was that after he left I lay in the darkness of my room, wondering if it was not something between my father and the other woman, or between my father and my mother but, instead, something between my father and me.

He may have left that night but he did not die, not then.

He died a week later, the day of my tenth birthday. At the urging of my mother — 'Whatever you want!' — I had made my birthday wish and I imagined that she'd be as pleased as I was if my wish — the return of my father — was granted.

But that morning, I crept down the hall and found my mother alone and weeping in her bed. I knew that the day I faced at school was one of awkwardness, and that the awkwardness would follow me after school and into a party with friends who would already know — just a week later — that I was from a 'broken' home and — even at the ages of nine and ten themselves — know that it meant *something*.

Something big and insufferable.

Rather than suffer the likely day ahead, I feigned illness: stomach cramps, intense but widespread; something hard to pin down, and less pointed than the hint of appendicitis. My mother had to work that day, and I knew that there was no one on whom she could call to care for me. The greatest suffering, for both of us, was those few seconds she hovered beside my bed, that awful expression on her face as she weighed up what she would lose — or if she would even gain something — by not going to work. And my greatest joy was when she drove away; I'd never felt better. She left me with more space and silence and solitude than I had ever known. I wandered around the house, entering rooms as though for the first time. The newness of things was fixed in those moments and in those same moments disappearing, because as I left each room I felt that I would never return.

In the bathroom, the prints of my father's fingers were smeared across the mirror from when he'd last lost himself there amid the steam. In the lounge room, the indentations of his shoes were still in the carpet, emerging from the kitchen linoleum and disappearing out onto the concrete verandah. I walked backwards through the room, reversing over his prints with long clumsy strides, until I was in the kitchen. There I saw the scuff of his shoes on the linoleum and followed it through the room to the laundry and, from the laundry, around to where his dull markings morphed into prints blurred in the hallway carpet. I continued backwards in his footsteps until I reached my parents' — my mother's — bedroom.

The impression of my mother's head was still on her pillow, and on the far side of the bed, the side on which he had slept, there was no trace of my father. I had always known that to be his side of the bed and I remembered, then, what had always been under that side. I crossed the room and kneeled beside the bed and grinned foolishly, so surprised I was — no, relieved — to find that it was still there.

On my tenth birthday, I slid my father's rifle out from under my parents' bed, opened the drawer of the bedside table and took out a thin cardboard box, the bullets tinkling like loose change as I tipped them out onto the covers. Still dressed in my pyjamas, I stood in my parents' bedroom and briefly thought about what had happened in my own small life, and in that moment it made perfect sense that leaving was sometimes the best thing to do. So, I loaded the rifle and went out into the backyard.

I stood there struggling under the rifle's weight, my cheek against the stock like my father had taught me, and I sighted every window in that empty house. I sighted each window and I watched. I waited for him to show his goddamn face — I wanted him to; if he was ever to return then that was surely his moment, but he was not there for me.

My shoulder burned. The rifle became too much and the tip of the barrel fell forward, digging into the ground. I inverted the rifle and placed the butt of the stock between my bare feet and picked long blades of grass from the barrel. It reminded me of toy rifles I'd seen on television, on shows I'd watched with my father, back when he got home from work on time — the trigger was pulled and, after a puff of harmless smoke, a little flag would unfurl: *Bang!* Ha, ha. You're dead. Joke's on you. And everyone would laugh — my dad and me together.

Alone in the backyard, with the tip of the barrel right there in front of my face, I slid my hand down onto the trigger and I stared into that dark hole and fired. Ha, ha, Dad. Joke's on you.

My father died much later, after days, weeks, months of suffering. By then his new girlfriend had left him — and not for anyone else either: she'd just left him.

He drank and smoked more than ever, and he did nothing to look after himself. He got cancer and ended up in hospital. He called my mother, desperate to have someone with him, and I heard her tell him that he'd made his own bed and it was time that he lay in it — even if he was going to have to lie in it alone.

But my mother did go and see him over his final weeks. 'Only because he's dying,' she told me. His cancer was what the doctors called *fungating*. My mother said to think of it as a cancer that comes out of you, and at night I would lie in my bed with my hand inside my pyjama top, knuckles pushing out between the buttons, my fist like an alien bursting out of my stomach. The thought of him dying like that used to make me laugh. Ha, ha. You're dead.

No. My father didn't die then. My father died years later, during the Gulf War. He'd gone there as a reporter, and a convoy in which he travelled came under fire and my father was the only one to survive. He was captured, held for months and for much of that time we knew nothing — my mother was only told that he was missing. And then, one night as I sat mulling over some geography homework, there he was: barely recognisable because of the beard he'd grown or, rather, had been unable to shave off. He was saying that the war was wrong and that he would rather die for his mistake than come home to his own family. And then a man stepped into the frame and the footage froze as a pistol was held to my father's head. I waited for a flag to unfurl from the barrel; I really thought it would, but it didn't. No matter how many times that scene was replayed, there was no flag, no *Bang!*, no Ha, ha. My father died a victim of his circumstances.

He died a joke that had lost its punchline.

No, my father didn't die like that. He died much more simply. He died on my first day at high school as I walked through the maze of corridors and lockers and hormones. He died when my first girlfriend's friend told me that … like … she — my girlfriend — didn't want to be my girlfriend anymore and that she — my girlfriend (but maybe her friend too) — wasn't sure if she ever really did … like … want to be my girlfriend. He died when I first turned the key in the ignition of the car in which he himself had learned to drive. He died the first time I ever drove that car alone, and every time I drove some girl — usually an ex-girlfriend's friend — someplace to be alone with her, knowing that she would make me feel that if I died that night I'd at least die happy.

My father died more times than I can remember: he died the night he left my mother and me alone in our house. He died each and every time I was injured or afraid or for some reason felt that life was not worth living. He died each time I was ever a failure at anything, and he still died any time I was ever a success at something. And he died one last time the night my own son was born. That night, as I cradled my son against my chest, in awe of how he could be so small and fragile and so in need, I knew in the space of one tiny breath that I could lay down my own life for him: I knew then that a father could die for his son and, if he could, he would do it more than once.

My father still lives in the town where we were both born, the town where he has spent his whole life and where I spent all the years of my childhood — all of what I jokingly call my … like … *de*formative years. Ha, ha.

I haven't been home for so long, and I can't imagine a time when I'll ever return.

In the end my father will surely die, and when he does he will die not knowing how I wished he'd lived.

Outback

RUBY J. MURRAY

Today is the first day of the rest of your life.
　Mark stares at the Siamese cat, and it looks back at him knowingly from under the brim of its top hat.
　The calendar was a gift from River Jones. There's an inspirational quote on every page. And a picture of an animal. It might be a horse in a Heidi outfit, frolicking in a field of daisies somewhere high in a range of neon mountains, or a Shihtzu in a dressing-gown reading a book and smoking a pipe like Sherlock Holmes. Today's Siamese, with its wise black eyes looking over its shoulder, is walking into a luminous sunset.
　It's Monday, and Mark is sitting behind the counter in O'Carroll's Australian Outback Adventure Outfitters on Ryrie Street, Geelong, Victoria, Australia, population 132,770, sipping his coffee out of its cardboard cup, and waiting.
　From the outside looking in, this particular Monday would seem like any given Monday in Mark O'Carroll's life. Although if you *were* outside, and you could look at all the Mondays in all the lives of all the people in the world, like so many snow domes lined up in a storefront, you wouldn't spend much time in front of Mark O'Carroll's.
　Mark's life is no sparkling globe of bright beads. It's akubras, Hard Yakka and Driza-Bones; a small semi-detached in Geelong; a cat called BooBoo that makes him sneeze; a wife who suspects she could have done better. The water in his snow dome is sort of cloudy, the contents:
　　1. A shoe display wall.
　　2. A cascade of dust from the stock piled out the back.

3. A ceiling fan in a bedroom that slows ever so slightly every third rotation.

But today is different.

Mark's shoes are too tight.

His wife bought him the shoes for Christmas, in an attempt, he suspects, to make him look more like a small-business owner and less like an outback outfitter's shop assistant.

'Don't call yourself a shop assistant,' says Mark's wife when people ask him what he does. 'It's *your* shop. Say you run a small business.'

Mark's wife, whose name is Sandra, is always buying him clothes that are too tight across the chest, jeans too short in the leg, jackets that leave his wrists exposed. In his wife's mind, it seems, Mark is a much smaller man than he is in reality.

At 10.03 a.m. River Jones comes spilling through the entrance, trailing shoelaces and hairpins and a faint smell of ozone, moisture, bindi smoke. Mark is crouched on the floor before the first customers of the day, a gay couple down from Melbourne who want matching cowboy boots. Mark doesn't look up as River comes in. He doesn't need to look at her at all, not anymore. The last four months have left him with the pieces of her in perpetual motion inside his head.

Once the couple leaves, clutching their awkward boxes, Mark joins River behind the till.

'Am I late?' she asks.

'No.'

'Oh, that's fantastic. I've lost my phone again, see. It's driving me crazy.'

'You weren't late.'

They stand next to each other. River runs her hands absently over the fake wood of the countertop. Mark stares out at the morning traffic on Ryrie Street.

Mondays are slow.

River edges around the counter, says something about going out the back to stack stock. Mark knows that her face is: quizzical; a little amused; one eyebrow exasperated and the other slightly droopy and resigned, two arcs separated by a perfectly smooth expanse of skin three and three-quarter centimetres wide.

Mark nods, and River goes. Her fingers on the bench have left small marks of condensation, and he covers them with his wide palms. His palms are sucking up her moisture.

River is from San Francisco, California, in the U.S. of A. That's how she says it. Her full name is Maria River Escobar Jones. Her dad is Mexican, and her mum is a Buddhist who used to be a communist who used to be a WASP. River went to high school in The City, which is what she calls San Francisco, and then she went to the University of California at Berkeley where she studied economics, which she dropped after two years to study shiatsu, which she dropped for a boy, who she dropped because she needed to travel and find herself, which is how Mark came to find her on a soggy Tuesday afternoon four months ago, when he walked out of the storeroom to see a tall woman standing at the counter and glaring up at Andy, the stuffed moose-head over the shoe display.

'Can I help you with anything?' he asked her.

'What's that?' She gestured with long, bare fingers at the moose-head.

'That's Andy. He's our moose.'

'Well, I think it's cruel.'

'He's not real. It's not a real moose, it's a fake,' Mark said, setting down the stack of plastic-shrouded Hard Yakka shorts he'd been carrying. Rain blew in through the open door.

'Oh.' The woman ran a finger over her top lip. 'Well. I guess that's okay then.' She paused. 'Mooses. Moose. They're Canadian, you know.'

'I know.'

'Okay. You don't have them here. Anyway, my name's River, and I was just wondering if you're looking for anyone at the moment?' And then Mark saw the folder clasped under her arm, its clear, wet plastic showing a thick wad of photocopied CVs. Was he looking for anyone?

He hired her.

When Mark told Sandra about it that evening, she was exasperated.

Sandra said, 'Well, Mark, you should have asked me, if you were looking for someone. You know Magda's sister Linda needs summer work.'

And he said, 'She's got experience, this lady.'

For the next week, he watched River knock around the store, muddling receipts, putting shoes back in the wrong boxes and hanging plaid shirts backwards on the hangers.

River wasn't funny. Not funny ha-ha, as Sandra would say. River made jokes, but they trailed away, segueing into stories about mustard or ingrown toenails or the Year of the Pig. It wasn't her jokes that made him laugh; it was how she lived. River lived in full, screaming technicolour. Life clutched at her. And once, when she saw that Tibetan guy down on the waterfront with one leg who hula-hooped with tinsel round his neck for hours over the summer, she clutched at Mark.

'OhMyGOD!' she yelled, yanking on his arm so that he spilled coffee down his shirtfront and onto the new leather shoes. 'Ohmygaaaawwwd, Mark, would you just check that guy out?'

Mark felt, through the scalding coffee, that life was clutching at him too.

The morning is passing. Mark is staring at his diary. Monday. The day is blank. He hasn't filled it in. Normally, on Fridays, he takes the shop diary out of the drawer and fills Monday in, so that he can arrive and look at a full, productive day between the small inked lines.

River emerges from the back of the store.

'Have those Caterpillars come in yet?' she asks.

'No.'

She stands for a moment. Mark knows she is looking at him, knows she is running her finger over her lip, which means: nervous, unsure, undecided. He keeps his eyes on the empty Monday in the diary, on the diary on the bench, on his hands on the bench, on the moisture spots that spread out from under the fingers on his hands on the bench.

He has one thing to do today. The blankness of the Monday on the page says nothing about the Monday he is living in his gut.

'Okay,' she says. 'Okay then.' Which means: Whatever. Be like that.

Mark concluded a while ago that some part of him must have known her straightaway. Maybe it was his spinal cord, maybe his fingernails, maybe his clavicle. Whatever it was, it had controlled him for the nine and a half minutes it had taken for them to organise her pay, her shifts, what she should wear, and for her to walk back out into Ryrie Street, popping open a bright pink umbrella.

He's not sure when the rest of him achieved the same level of self-awareness that his clavicle seemed to possess. It happened in pieces. First, a week after she started, he found himself picturing her as he masturbated, and he had to stop, releasing his penis and holding his hands out in front of him in the water. He stood, flat-footed in the bathtub under the slap of the shower, staring blankly at Sandra's pastel collection of body puffs, those weird half-sponge things that slide over your skin without cleaning you at all.

After his initial shock, what briefly paralysed him was the thought that it might have been sexual harassment, somehow, this picturing of your co-worker during masturbation. That scared him, that and how quickly River had appeared unbidden in his skull, her long thighs in their firm jeans leaning over the fitting bench.

Then Sandra thumped on the door. 'There's a bloody drought on, Mark.'

Sandra was obsessed with the drought. According to Sandra, the drought was responsible for, among other things: higher food prices, Mark's lack of sexual drive, and also his dry skin, which she was always caking in various tonics and creams in an attempt to get him to suck stuff up.

It's lunchtime, and Mark leaves without telling River that he's going. He doesn't do this intentionally; he just walks out the door on autopilot, holding his ten-dollar note to buy a pastie and a tall hot strong soy latte. He sits in the window on a green Starbucks armchair and watches his shopfront. The Starbucks Summer Mix plays over the café's sound system: Louis Armstrong, Burt Bacharach. *Do you know the way to San Jose?* croon the speakers.

River would know the way to San Jose.

Across the road, River walks out of O'Carroll's Australian Outback Adventure Outfitters and, shading her eyes against the afternoon glare, squints through the exhaust haze of Ryrie Street. She is looking straight at Mark looking at her, but she can't see through the reflections on the plate glass. After a moment, she lets her hands fall to her sides, turns, and walks back into the shop, disappearing from view.

Mark eats his lunch.

Across the road, River's hands fall over and over and over, and she turns away over and over and over, and Mark chews on the vegetable paste that fills his pastie, and swallows.

Mark isn't sure if he's a hero, or a coward.

It's hard to know.

It was already Christmas by the time Mark realised what was happening to him. Customers elbowed in and out of the shop, and he and River brushed up against each other in the storerooms out the back, and she sang flatly to herself and crawled into swags on the shop floor to show people just how totally comfy they were, and he realised he loved her.

Not that he'd *fallen* in love, because there was no motion in it. He'd probably always been in love with her.

When he wasn't looking at her, her body played itself out in his head all the same, and her disembodied voice became America: long empty roads, petrol stations sparkling in the blue distance across the plains, diners with blinking lights, teenagers jumping on MTV, cheerleaders and civil rights and Oreo biscuits.

They started going for walks along the Geelong waterfront after closing up the shop. Sitting on the hill above the sea baths in the evening, wreathed in sonic clouds of mosquitoes, they talked and ate Calippos, sucking the juice out of the bottom of the cardboard tubes. He'd never considered himself smart or funny, but with River he found himself full of anecdotes. He saved small happenings from each day, and these pieces of his life grew smooth and polished under the pressure of his mind so that when he told them to her, and she threw back her head and snorted, he knew that he had achieved perfection.

After the first of those evenings, he sat on the couch with Sandra watching *Thank God You're Here*, wracked with guilt. They had sex later that night, much to Sandra's surprise. It was the least he could do. He tried not to focus on anything while they fucked. He felt the press of the covers on his back and the pillow riding up and down against his nose. Face down in the bedsheets. Three months ago. December. The month that he'd finally met River.

December.

Which, Sandra told him yesterday, was also the last month that she'd had it.

'What?' he asked, flipping the dinner plates onto the drying rack and absently imagining a hundred ways of making love to River in the back of the store, surrounded by crunching cardboard and the boom of falling fixtures.

'I said, I haven't had my period in three months, Mark.'

Mark turned to her, feeling the water dry up on his hands. 'It might be the drought,' he said.

Sandra made a half-laugh half-sob, and then she put her arms around him.

'I know we didn't plan it,' she said, 'but when you think about it, it couldn't really have come at a better time, don't you think? We're ready for it now. We've just about paid off the mortgage. You've got that American girl who can take over the shop for a bit if you need. I'll be able to get good maternity leave. Our careers are at the right points. It couldn't be better if we had planned it, really. Mark?'

After she counts out the till, River asks Mark if he has time for a Calippo.

'Not today,' he says. 'We have to talk about something.'

'Are you okay, Mark?'

She reaches out her hand to touch him — ozone, Oreos, smoke, moisture, the blue light of diners in the middle of the night on a highway he's never travelled. For a moment, he thinks that she is going to put her hand on his face, and he moves away even as his body goes forward, and his snow dome spins, and the dust falls off the boxes out the back, and he is letting her go.

Like a Virgin

TEGAN BENNETT DAYLIGHT

There is a part of your life, I now realise, in which you are so clean and fresh-looking that you can wear the oldest clothes and still look pretty. I noticed this stage passing after my children were born. I still went into second-hand shops. I was good at finding the right things, running my eyes along the rows of dresses, pulling something out with red in it, a bold pattern, a geometric neck. One day, with my son in his pram, I tried one of these dresses on, and I looked as though I had been born when the dress was made. No more a doll, a gorgeous baby doll dressed up in pretty doll's clothes. And I no longer had that strong, eager, possible look that had made it hard for me to meet my own eyes in the mirror. Now, staring straight back at myself, I was just a woman in a piece of clothing whose cut did not disguise my widened hips, whose stained fabric made me look stained as well.

When I was fifteen I went to a party given by one of the girls in my year, the kind of party everyone was asked to. She had a new record which we hadn't heard. It was Madonna, *Like a Virgin*. I didn't like it much. I was given to anachronistic musical passions inspired by my parents or my older brother. The Beatles, of course. An Australian recording of *The Rocky Horror Show* with Reg Livermore and Kate Fitzpatrick. David Bowie. I stopped at the doorway of Katie's sunken living room and looked down at the girls writhing on the carpet.

Of course, I didn't know what it meant: like a virgin. No — I knew what it meant, but I didn't know what it was to be reclaimed like that, to find a love so fresh that you felt like you were doing it for the first time. Doing it for the first time was something I wished could happen while I took leave of my body. I wanted a beautiful anaesthetist, a drug to make me swoon. I watched the girls dancing like Madonna, wriggling and shifting as though they had a pole to hang on to, a sort of shiver from top to bottom, running through their bodies like a ripple through water.

I couldn't stay there watching them. I was needed somewhere else; my friend Judy had drunk nearly half a bottle of tequila, and I had to take care of her. I found her on the bed in Katie's bedroom. I tried to get her to sit upright, to drink the water I had brought her, but she wouldn't. I stood up and tugged firmly at her arm, put one hand behind her head and tried to lift her up to sitting. But she just groaned and threw herself backwards, so hard that she cracked her head against the wooden bedhead, and the girls who had followed me into the room screamed and laughed.

I was ashamed of us. Judy was exposing us, showing everyone how unable we were to deal with being at a party; to stay on our feet, talk to the boys, dance to 'Like a Virgin'. All the privacies of our friendship were a joke here. I regretted everything: the lunchtime retreats to the library, the secret language, the matching bead bracelets. I was sweating. I was wearing one of my father's jumpers, nearly to my knees, with a belt round the waist, and stockings. It was summer. The wool gaped away from my body so that I could feel the sweat coursing down between my breasts. I wasn't wearing a bra because I hadn't been able to stop the straps from showing. I pushed the sleeves of the jumper up past my elbows and kneeled down beside Judy and bellowed her name in her ear, but she turned over, away from me, so that I could see the vulnerable back of her neck and the broad rolls of her waist, where her T-shirt had ridden up.

I had been with Raffaello when Katie came and got me and said Judy was vomiting. I loved him. I had started loving him properly one day at assembly when I'd been standing behind him and happened to look down at his legs. There were legs all around me. The prettiest girl's legs belonged to

Vanessa Wilson, indisputably — they were long and brown and the thighs were nearly as slender as the calves, but not so slender as to give her that horse-riding gap between her legs that you see in some slim women.

The boys' legs were always interesting to me. Dean Meyer's: solid flesh, with no bone or muscle showing, blotched with freckles, ginger-haired. Matt Wilmott's: tanned and stringy. The boys at our school wore dark blue shorts, King Gee brand, perfectly flattering to a bum the right size. Raffaello's bum was not very big, and his King Gees hung a bit, but his legs, I'd realised that morning, were beautiful. They were brown and had dark hair, though not a great deal. He had very white socks, pushed down, and sneakers, and his bag dangled off one shoulder. I felt helpless, standing there in the sun while the vice-principal harangued us, almost as though I might fall on my knees.

But how would I persuade Raffaello to love me? Could it be done? Everything was out of kilter. I was clean and fresh-looking, embarrassingly ample-bosomed. I had no pimples. My mother's friends were always leaping at me with index finger and thumb at the ready, shrieking, *'Doesn't* she have beautiful skin!' But there was Sarah Lamplough, for instance, bony, with lank hair and a face that looked like a dirty fist — she had a boyfriend. Paul Bosch, not a boyfriend I would have wanted, with his pudding-bowl haircut and sneering assertions about Πr^2 and the speed of sound, but still a boyfriend. Once, outside English, Raffaello's friend Andrew accused Paul and Sarah of not really *doing* anything.

'You're afraid to pash,' he said, and they seized each other without a beat and locked together, tongues twining. Then they parted, panting, facing us triumphantly.

Judy's mother was at the opera that night, so I rang mine, and she came to get us. My mother is smaller than I am; we needed help, to get Judy to her feet and into the car.

'I'll get a couple of the boys,' she said, and disappeared, coming back with Andrew and Raffaello in front of her,

her hands in the smalls of their backs. She was impatient, unsurprised. It was hard for me to tell whether there was something she was storing up for me. Part of the terror of being my mother's daughter was that she would not show anger in front of other people. And then she would close the front door behind you and turn on you, take you apart for your faithlessness, your rudeness, your stupidity.

Judy could not be made to stand, or even to open her eyes. I was sweating very heavily by now. Andrew took the shoulders and head, and Raffaello took the bottom and legs. A group had gathered to watch and give useless instructions. Judy sagged between the boys, her weight beyond what they had expected; Raffaello had to use his knee on the backs of her thighs to lever her up again. Katie's house had a steep driveway and my mother had parked her Saab at the top of it. I ran effortlessly up the drive in my woollen jumper and stockings, and opened the car's back door. The boys staggered up after me and jammed Judy in. I had to go round the other side, open that door and try to pull her by the shoulders. I hissed, 'Come *on*!' and she moaned, turned her head, and was sick into the footspace behind the driver's seat. At the same time she released a terrible, noisy fart.

I went back round. I bent her knees up and closed the other back door. I didn't check to see if she had shat herself, and I didn't speak to the boys, who were retreating down the drive, Andrew already shouting the story to the group below. I climbed into the front seat and wound the window down immediately, putting my face out into the jacaranda-scented air to stop myself from being sick too.

My mother got into the car, and I said, 'I'll clean it up. I'll clean it up. Take us home.'

She wound down her window, and we pulled out into the dark, leafy street.

I was born in the 1970s. I was a late child, coming ten years after my older brother, when my parents were just taking their last steps together, just finishing themselves off as a couple. My father already had another family, though my mother didn't know about that at the time. When he left, my mother took, in a way that makes perfect sense now, to serious drinking. She weaned me, deliberately; her intake of wine from those round glass flagons (the kind with a handle you could hook two fingers into; I can still feel the pressure of it on my index and middle finger) was too high for someone breastfeeding. I learned this from my brother, who helped her look after me, in ways I couldn't imagine. I know now that there was more to do than change nappies and give bottles. But he was a strong, adaptable being; besides, he needed someone to care for.

My mother and Judy's mother were in a women's group together. It was the women's group that saved her life, my mother said, collecting second-hand clothes for me, taking James to and from school, coming once a week to clean the house. And they were people to drink with. Every Wednesday at midday they met, well into my memory.

So I'd always known Judy, but until we started high school together it was in that way of someone not quite understood, not seen regularly enough for her personality to make a strong impression on me. I remembered that she was fat, because my mother talked about it, how Judy and Barbara always had trouble with their weight, and that was all. Once or twice we were both at women's group, because we were sick or there was a strike at our schools. Then we were left to play with each other, to try to work each other out. Judy's mother put out a wedge of heavy brown bread for us to make ourselves sandwiches with while the women went upstairs, their platform heels clunking on the wooden floor against the bird-like cries of laughter and clinking of bottles. Judy got some honey. They kept it in the fridge. I held my knife above my piece of bread, and the honey slowly lowered itself onto the butter.

When my father left, before I was old enough to know

Like a Virgin

I had a father, he did not take everything with him. I think this is because when he first said *I'm leaving*, first stepped out the door, my mother bolted it behind him, and that was it. Locks changed, and he never set foot in the house again. I don't know that this is exactly what happened — nor does James, who was at school that day — but it is easy to imagine.

My parents are the sort of people who shed most things as they go through life, except books. I would not, when I got older, have caftans and platform heels to dress up in, left over from my mother's youth, but I did have piles and piles of books. My father liked American humorists from the first part of the century: S.J. Perelman, Robert Benchley, James Thurber. I used to take my copy of *The Thurber Carnival* to school when I first started Year 7. I showed it to Judy. We had been put in the same class, and we sat together gratefully, looking at my book under the desk. The book started to come apart within weeks — it was an orange Penguin, more than thirty years old, and it had sat on the shelf without being touched for a long time. But I stuck one of the cartoons on the front of my folder; the famous one, with the angry-looking woman on all fours on top of a bookcase, and a man saying: *This is the present Mrs Harris. That's my first wife up there.* I had read about how the cartoon was a mistake: the woman was meant to be at the top of some stairs, but he'd got the perspective wrong. I didn't ever find out what she would have been doing at the top of the stairs, but there was something I liked in the way the cartoon came out of a mistake.

Judy was an only child. Her mother hadn't ever been married. I knew that. My mother had told me, not with any special emphasis. Emphasis was not needed. It's hard to describe the quality that this information gave Judy — not illegitimacy so much as unwantedness. Judy herself once said to me that her father had never bothered to find her, that he had a real family somewhere else, in another state.

My father's other family were in the same city as we were. I refused to consider myself the same as Judy. I had a brother. My parents had been together, they had fought and fought, and then divorced. The insults they still conveyed to each other through me were part of their connection. I had an older half-sister and a younger half-brother, one born between James and me, the other after my mother got my father out the door. I lived in a drama, a TV show, with my mother as the bitter, sometimes drunken leading lady, but Judy, I thought, lived in a kind of emptiness, peopled only by her eating and her mother's angry singing.

Monday was much worse for Judy than it was for me. We had English first, together, and when we walked down the concrete steps to the bottom of the school, boys from our year bumped past and made vomiting and farting noises. Sarah Lamplough was sitting on the railings outside the classroom, with Paul Bosch caught in the scissors of her skinny legs. They were whispering to each other with their foreheads together, but as we approached they looked up, Paul blew a soft raspberry, and Sarah giggled.

It went on like that through first period, second period, recess, lunch. By the end of the day the people in the years below knew too. Judy kept her head down and did not cry. At home time I held her arm and steered her through the bus lines to the gate. I said, 'Ignore them, ignore them,' over and over.

The temptation to jump ship was very strong. But it would not do; there was nowhere for me to go. Judy and I toiled up the hill with the sweat running down our legs. It was an overcast day, hot, the sort that had you checking the back of your uniform to make sure your period had not started. Judy was walking a little ahead of me. The tops of her thighs were mottled with heat. I hated her. I wanted to hit her on that stupid big bottom, push her over, shout at her. We would never escape. We had two more years of school. We would never get to the end of this.

I had gone to that party hoping to see Raffaello. I talked to him most days at school; we sat next to each other in maths. But I was hoping that he would notice me at Katie's party, more than he did at school, which was also why I was wearing my father's jumper. I'd taken it from Dad's house without asking on my last weekend visit, months ago. It was fashionable then to wear belted shirts or jumpers with stockings, and this jumper was red, thickly and strongly knitted. It covered a lot of me. I was resolved to wear it, however hot the weather.

Raffaello was not tall. He had dark brown eyes, curly dark hair cut close to his head, and a sunny smile, rare in a teenage boy. I could make him laugh, and did, often, until our maths teacher threatened us with separation. She told me I was ruining his concentration. I was more careful after this.

The best thing about maths was that Andrew was not there. Andrew was shorter than Raffaello, skinny, spotty-faced, rat-like. He never got bullied, despite his size; the bigger boys were frightened of him. He was a savage mimic. He could be horribly funny. He found out things about your parents and said them in front of everyone. He would go through your bag, find your diary, point out that you were not wearing a bra, hold his nose and say, 'Have you got your *period*?' when you had to push by his desk.

I took Raffaello to sleep with me every night. It was a small ritual, an imaginary play made simple by my lack of experience. We went walking. There were lanes near my mother's house — this was the kind of suburb I grew up in — lanes over which the trees met, to make a tunnel of green. We went walking, down the lane, towards the bush, and Raffaello took hold of me, and turned me to him.

That was it. I took that back to its beginning as many times as it was needed. Raffaello turned me to him, and I fell asleep.

Before the party, I'd filled my bottle — an old Jim Beam bottle that I'd found at the bottom of James's cupboard when I was looking for a tennis ball — with tequila from my mother's liquor cabinet. It was easy enough to do, and just as easy to top up the tequila bottle with water. I was almost used to drinking. We had a great deal of alcohol in the house. I wasn't allowed to drink it, but I did, testing myself on different kinds to see which made me feel best. Tequila was quick and sharp, and its disappearance was easy to conceal.

Judy and I walked to the party, over the bridge that looked down on our school, and up the steep hill to Katie's place. There was a moon, coming up orange over the trees. We passed the bottle between us, Judy coughing and laughing and miming drunkenness with each sip.

'You're not drinking enough,' I said, as we reached Katie's street. I looked at the level in the bottle. 'You'll never get drunk. You have to scull it.'

'I can't. It tastes foul.'

'We'll mix it with something. We'll find something in the fridge.'

'Do I look okay?'

We were at the top of Katie's driveway. Judy stood so she faced me, and I did what I usually did — tweaked at her, pulled things into place. She was wearing a Frankie Goes to Hollywood T-shirt over black stirrup pants which brought her legs down into a kind of point, making her V-shaped from the feet up.

'Titian hair,' I said to her. It was our code; it was about possibility. Her long red hair was beautiful, gold when it caught the light. We had built it into our mythology of the future, when she would be discovered by an artist and painted, nude, with her hair falling over her breasts.

We made our way down to the house. There was orange juice in the fridge. Katie's parents didn't seem to be there. No one said hello to us as we came in; we just went to the kitchen. There was music, and kids smoking on the verandah. The moon was higher now, and paler. Sometimes there would be a surge of noise from the cicadas. I poured the rest of the tequila — still nearly half a bottle — into a tall,

Like a Virgin

patterned glass and topped it up with orange juice. I took a huge, burning swallow and passed it to Judy. She took a deep breath, put it to her lips and drank the lot.

'That was for me too!' I said, but when she'd finished coughing she grinned at me and wiped her lips and eyes.

'Now I'm ready,' she said.

We had agreed to separate. Judy's goal I secretly scorned: she was in love with Michael Brown from Year 12, a boy who was legendary for his beauty and kindness, who would probably not even be there. I was in love with him too. You couldn't not be. He'd once stood up and offered me his seat on the sport bus, when hockey and football were being played at the same ground. The seat was warm when I sat down on it. Michael smiled at me, and I kept my thighs carefully propped up, so that they did not touch the seat, spread and look fat.

Judy's goal was to talk to Michael, so that he might remember who she was, wonder about her, choose her, with her Titian hair, to model for his final work for art. This was the thing about Michael — he played sport like a hero, but always came top in art and English. After the modelling, he would not be able to get Judy out of his mind. Then he would get a scholarship to a school of art in Paris, and beg her to come with him, not even finishing her HSC. She would, and they would be so poor in Paris, on a single scholarship, that they would not have much to eat and she would lose a great deal of weight. It was a very satisfactory story, to which I'd contributed quite a lot. We'd come up with the weight-loss part together.

Judy went out one door of the kitchen and I went out the other. There was a can of beer on the floor outside, which I picked up and shook. It was half full. I peered into it to see if there were any cigarette butts. There were not, so I drank it. It helped with the warm and pleasant feeling I was beginning to have from the tequila. Hearing Raffaello's voice from outside, I went to find him.

It was the tequila, undoubtedly. I said something which, years later, still has the power to make me shudder. It was unforgivable, as though I had learned nothing in the last four years of high school. I said: 'Would you go out with me?'

This wasn't an invitation to the movies or to see a band. It meant, *be my boyfriend. Love me.* I don't think it had ever been said, in the history of North Hills High School, ever, by a girl.

Before Raffaello could answer, Andrew exploded next to him. I'd seen this performance before. It consisted of laughing so hard he cried. Of smacking his thighs, holding his aching sides, wiping his eyes.

I was still, suspended in myself, watching, waiting for the thigh-slapping and shrieking to stop. Even Raffaello did nothing. Eventually Andrew fetched back up against the wall of the house, panting, one last wipe of the eyes with the back of the hand, and said to me, 'You! You think he'll go out with *you?*'

Other kids were looking at us now, though none approached.

I was still waiting to fall dead on the spot, the effects of the tequila flushing downwards, leaving my head sore and clear.

'I can't see it,' said Raffaello, looking at his feet.

'Why not?' I said. I had nothing left to lose.

He took a breath, and stared straight at me. 'We've got nothing in common,' he said; then added, 'Everyone thinks you're a lesbian.'

Andrew was silent now, arms crossed, eyebrows raised. I gave a push with my backside, heaved myself away from the wall. Someone, a girl, was calling me, in a stupid singsong voice that promised insult. You get so that you can identify this.

'Tash-a,' said Katie, as she came round the corner of the house, 'your friend needs you. She's spewing.'

Like a Virgin

On Thursday afternoons Judy's mother went to her singing class and Judy came to my house. She was old enough to be left alone, but it had been happening so long, and it suited us both. Friday was the day homework was always due; on Thursdays we sat at the kitchen table, stuffed ourselves with toast and peanut butter, and did our work together, comparing, criticising, helping each other.

My mother hadn't been able to castigate me for drunkenness — I was too old to let her get away with that — but I'd had to get Judy's vomit out of the car myself and then pay for it to be cleaned. I used a trowel from the garden and a pair of washing-up gloves. Then I had to look in the yellow pages for the car-cleaning service. It was six weeks' pocket money.

And of course my mother was not above making Judy feel terrible. The smell would never go away, she told us, and she was too poor to be thinking about buying another car. She said this while she was looking in the back of the pantry to see if she had forgotten any bottles of wine or scotch. She was on her hands and knees, moving the tall jars of flour and rice that never got used up. She had that look on her face — belligerent, preoccupied, but ready to be angrier if it was needed. She looked exactly like the woman on top of the bookshelf in the Thurber cartoon.

'Look, Jude,' I said, nudging her. *'That's my first wife over there.'*

Judy looked, and some spit went down the wrong way, and she choked with laughter. My mother glared at us. Of course there were no hidden bottles of scotch or wine. There had been, but I'd drunk them.

It didn't last forever. It was easy to see that no one would ever forget, and if Judy ever made another mistake, if she ever did something like fart in class or vomit from bus-sickness (which she'd been known to do), we would be back at the beginning again. But she was careful, and so was I.

It hadn't surprised me that Raffaello had moved seats in maths that first week. I was on my own now, looking out of the window, staring so hard at the eucalypts in the playground that they had silvery edges.

I was outside English one afternoon, waiting for the teacher, not even thinking about it, thinking about Jane Eyre and her small, plain self, when Andrew ducked up next to me. He had been trying to catch my attention, I realised. It was another performance: he was singing, and now that I was looking at him, I could see that he was singing 'Like a Virgin'.

He went on singing, doing little twists in front of me. Other kids were watching us, glad they weren't the object of Andrew's attention. I kept still. And the longer I was still, the more it started to look like Andrew was serenading me rather than harassing me, his little dance becoming more and more elaborate. I looked at him, his rodent's face. I could see his teeth as he sang, and they did not look clean.

It was a decision, a sudden accession to adulthood. It was like when I'd decided not to speak to my father. It was absolute power, if I wanted it. It came like so: I was not going to be a success at this, and so I was going to stop trying. I had found a virtue in stillness, in watching — in ceasing, at least for the moment, to care whether or not I was acceptable to others. In this silence, while Andrew's dance wound down — you could see him considering how to leave, whether it would be better to spin away from me as though I had never been there or come to a stop in front of me and see what I would do — I realised that it was not just me who was a virgin.

I have looked at a photograph of myself from that time. I see a girl with pale skin and short dark hair, with arms folded over her breasts. I am wearing something else of my father's, an old painting shirt, and I look pretty, and angry, a lot like my mother. Judy, who is standing next to me, is not so fat as we thought. But we were right about the weight loss, though it was Judy's own scholarship that took her away, that left her little time or money for food. We are still friends.

We dress as ourselves now. I wear jeans, and T-shirts. Judy is tall and bosomy and recognisable in public. She wears old-fashioned dresses with sculpted bodices, long boots that lace up, and dark glasses if we are going out. Judy comes over from the eastern suburbs to sit in a café with me. If my son is on Judy's lap he will bury his hands in her hair, still streaked with red and gold.

Tales of Action and Adventure

MARK O'FLYNN

We're throwing a small dinner to welcome my wife's old friend Russell back from his long trek around the globe. The kids are at a sleepover so we think we might be able to get in some adult conversation for once. I am cooking. Russell Stanley is Shona's first boyfriend. Someone she has known since high school. His postcards, from various parts of the world, are pinned to the noticeboard beside the fridge. They have arrived with enviable regularity, adorned with vistas of colourful stamps. Grace, our daughter, is too young, or too cool, to be interested in stamps, or her mother's old boyfriends.

Shona talks about Russell frequently, relating his news about the part of the world from where the latest cards have issued. I can't keep up. Now that I come to think of it I have never heard Shona say a bad word about Russell. I have heard her say plenty of bad words about other men from her past, but not Russell. It's almost like she still loves him, but that couldn't be correct, because that was years ago and she married me, right? Right? I recall her saying that Russell was distantly related to Stanley, intrepid explorer of Stanley and Livingstone fame. That may be true, but the test of a man's character is relative. We shall see. I have always thought it quaint the way she has managed to maintain friendships from her school days; that sense of shared history. It must be nice. I know no one from my past. They're all ghosts. The past is a haunted place for me. Shona thinks the most intimate knowledge one can have of another person is if you knew them when they wore braces. Shona has perfect teeth now. I have studied the photos — and there is Russell, at her side, with braces of his own.

I confess a part of me has been a little jealous of Russell. Of his physique. Of his hair. Of how the last seven or eight years, more often than not, he has been travelling overseas. Lucky beggar. I wonder how he has been able to afford it? It can't have been cheap. Another way of looking at it might be that in the last seven or eight years he has been out of work more often than not. Alternatively, perhaps Shona sees in both of us the same outdoorsy, adventurous type.

I am still setting the table when the doorbell rings. Suddenly I am struck by the banality of the sound. Shona is still getting ready. I open the deadlock. Russell is early. The prodigal boyfriend. There is nothing else for it but to shake his hand.

'Welcome home.'

'Home?' he says, philosophically, considering all the nuances of the word.

'Come in. Would you like a beer?'

Russell gives a little shrug.

'No? Wine then? Or juice?'

'Juice.'

I go into the kitchen, open the fridge, pour a flute of orange juice. The fridge is full of alcohol, but all he wants is juice. When I return, Russell is still standing by the front door.

'Would you like me to take my shoes off?'

'No, no. That's fine. Come in. Make yourself at home.'

Russell wipes his feet, then shuffles in and takes off his coat, which I hang by the tall mirror in the hallway. He still cuts a strapping figure. There, that's a sentence from a tale of action and adventure. A strapping figure — despite the tinge of salt and pepper at his temples. He stands at the entrance to the dining room and watches me finish setting the table. The doilies in place. The serviettes. I notice that he peers into his orange juice, examining it closely.

A toilet flushes in the distance. In a moment there is a squeal from the far end of the hallway, and I take this to mean that Shona has at last spotted her long-lost friend. She throws herself into his arms, and I find myself counting the seconds of their kiss. She has reverted to a schoolgirl. I think about candles, then dismiss the idea. Candles are too intimate. There are only a few little birthday candles anyway.

I have met Russell before, of course. I could not have married Shona without knowing something of her past dalliances, just as she knows mine. Russell's name has always cropped up at the most significant moments in her history. I don't know exactly how I feel about this. Once, before I met her, Russell drove Shona to an abortion clinic. Afterwards he took her home and listened to her sob in the shower and made her a cup of tea even though he was not the father. He came to our wedding, of course, and after our daughter was born a few years later he gradually faded from our lives. Then, when he had disappeared overseas, the postcards began to arrive. I think it is good for a woman to have male friends, friendships of a platonic, non-threatening nature. Friendships that would be perfectly fine for me to have too.

I have mashed an avocado, mixed with garlic and tomatoes to make guacamole. I have crushed chickpeas and garlic to make my own hummus. I have julienned carrots and celery as instruments to dip and dig into these concoctions. Russell looks at them and sighs. He explains that the jet lag is still catching up with him. He hopes he'll be able to stay awake. Shona seems to find this inordinately funny, and giggles. I pour some wine for Shona and, as he doesn't appear to be drinking, another juice for Russell, which again he examines with forensic attention. During this momentary silence the whine of a mosquito is clearly audible. Shona flaps her hand. She hates mosquitoes. I don't mind them because they always bite her and leave me alone. I jump up to put on some music so as to camouflage any future intrusion I fear silence may make into proceedings. Shona apologises for the mosquitoes.

'That's all right,' Russell says, 'mosquitoes are nothing. In Honduras, near Tegucigalpa, I was bitten by a vampire bat.'

'A vampire bat?'

'I was camping in the jungle and there was a hole in my sock. It bit me on the toe. There was blood everywhere.'

'Weren't you in a tent?'

'There was a hole in that too.'

'Don't they give you rabies, those things?'

'I don't know.'

'That's amazing,' Shona says.

'Not really. They're very common.'

He takes a celery stick, digs and dips, and pops it into his mouth.

I say: 'I hope you don't mind the garlic in the guacamole then.'

'No. It's very nice.'

We listen to the music for a moment.

Ambience.

'Shona didn't tell me if you still eat meat or not. We're having lamb, but there's plenty of vegetables as well.'

'Yes, I eat everything,' Russell says. 'In fact in Brazil I ate a howler monkey.'

'A howler monkey?' Shona is not quite sure if she has heard right.

'Yes, we were travelling overland from Imperatriz and got disoriented in the jungle. We had no food and after a few days my companion, Jacques, shot a monkey.'

'Aren't those things jumping with parasites?' I ask.

'Are they? I don't know.'

'What happened?'

'We cooked it first. It was very tough.'

'Did you get sick?'

'No. My friend got sick. But I was fine.'

'What happened to him?'

'He got better.'

I excuse myself. Duty calls. With industrial-strength oven mitts I fetch hot plates out of the oven. I carve the leg. I serve the slivers. I bring out the main course, garnished with rosemary and mint. Pumpkin. Sweet potato. Lots of spuds in a ceramic bowl that Shona made during her pottery phase. A clichéd Australian meal to welcome back the lonely traveller.

'Careful, the plates are hot.'

Russell chews every mouthful diligently, thoughtfully. I see that candles wouldn't have been amiss. Something to look at while he is finishing each mouthful. Shona tries to tell him about a holiday we had last Christmas down at Batemans Bay, but there is not much to tell. Grace stubbed her toe so badly the nail turned black and fell off. Framed photos of the happy, sunburned children gaze down from the walls. Russell reports that he was stung by a stingray in the waters off the coast of Luzon and spent two weeks in a Philippine hospital with the lepers. He offers to show us the scar, but Shona declines. She is still eating.

I say: 'I guess you won't have heard about Steve Irwin then?'

'No,' Russell says. 'Do I know him?'

When he was discharged, Russell continues, he was ordered to rest and recuperate, so he was laid up in a beach resort near Tuguegarao. The ash from a volcano simmering nearby kept falling into his orange juice and the waiter took twenty minutes to bring a fresh one, even though there was no one else staying at the resort. When it arrived it was brought personally by the manager who said that all the waiters had evacuated, and perhaps sir might like to consider evacuating too, but Russell had already paid up front and was determined to get his money's worth, so he said he would stay put until the volcano erupted if he had to, only it didn't erupt.

Shona says: 'Wow.'

Over dessert, peaches and cream, Russell asks about a mutual schoolfriend of his and Shona's. Shona is sorry to report that the last she heard their friend, whose name I don't catch, broke his ankle falling off a ladder and was on crutches.

Russell tells of how, while riding a motorbike near Cuzco in the Andes, he hit a condor that hadn't seen him coming, and nearly fell into a ravine.

'Didn't it knock you off your bike?' I ask.

'Nearly. It broke the mirror and I lost my deposit. I had bruises the size of dinner plates.'

I clear away our dinner plates and, for the moment, am happy to potter about in the kitchen. I put on the kettle and stack up the dishes. We have a dishwasher, but I am thinking perhaps tonight I will do them by hand. I can hear the music perfectly. When I return with the coffee, Russell is telling Shona a story about how he spent six days in a police lock-up in Lushnje in Albania.

'What did you do to deserve that?' I ask.

'Nothing. It was a misunderstanding.'

'I'm afraid there's nothing very exciting about our lives,' Shona says.

'Least of all the coffee,' I add, placing the tray on the table.

'That's all right.'

In Montijo, Russell says, a gypsy touter sold him a quarter ounce of Lebanese hashish. Why did he buy it? Because it was a good price, and the Australian dollar was so much better than the escudo. It wasn't until he reached the Spanish border a few days later that he remembered it was in his pocket. As the guards were checking passports, he quietly sat in his train carriage and ate it. After what seemed like an hour, they opened the carriage door, and he vomited a foul-smelling goop into a plastic bag, which was enough to make the guards, after a cursory glance at his documents, move quickly on. Russell spent the rest of the journey studying the luggage rack overhead, sitting very, very still.

More music.

After finishing his coffee, Russell has another. He has several chocolates and several biscuits. I see that I have finished the wine. I think, may as well be hung for a sheep as a lamb, so I open a second bottle, even though I will suffer for it tomorrow. I return to the dishes in the kitchen, again leaving the school chums to catch up on old times, only I am coming to suspect that there are not too many old times being chewed over. There seems to be a big loud silence coming from the dining room. Like flat champagne. I clean everything in the kitchen. In fact I give it a thorough scrubbing. I sweep the floor. I clean the oven. I change the music a few times. I overhear Russell say, in response to Shona's question, that one of the things he has learned in his travels is that the native Inuits from Inuvik in Canada always take a long time over their meals so as to strengthen the social and familial bonds. They have a word, *sunasorpok*, which means to clean up the food left unfinished by others. I am glad I have removed the plates — there was only fat left on mine. A part of me wonders if Russell is making this up, if he has, in fact, been lying. I have never really swallowed the Stanley–Livingstone story. So I sneak into the study and quickly google *Canadian Inuit eating rituals*. This search yields zero results: *Did you mean Canadian Restaurants?* Such a dead end proves nothing, which merely reinforces my more general suspicion that Google is a great way to prove nothing. I'll have to take Russell's word for it.

When I eventually return, Russell is still sitting with his hands around his coffee mug, as if it is still warm. The school chums have run out of conversation. The old flame is flickering. Shona is looking decidedly weary, and Russell does not seem as though he wants to leave, ever. I see he has kicked his boots off. The couch appears far too comfortable. Thank goodness he hasn't been drinking. I sit down beside Shona and give an enormous, prefabricated yawn. Russell tells us how he was robbed at gunpoint in Rybinsk, but only had about thirty roubles in his pocket at the time, so everything worked out for the best. I realise, with the aid of my peripheral vision, something Russell has not: that Shona has fallen asleep. She gives a little, soft snore.

'My god you've had some adventures Russell,' I say, 'in

these exotic places. I don't know where half of them are.'

'Not really,' he replies. 'It was all pretty boring.'

The sound of my laughter wakes Shona with a start. The dream-word she drags out of her snooze is: 'Curriculum.'

She's clearly got other things on her mind.

'Oh, Russell, I'm sorry. I'm afraid I'm going to have to go to bed.'

'Me too,' I add. 'We've both got work tomorrow.'

'Oh,' he says. 'Bummer.'

Shona clambers to her feet and shows him to the door. He does not look at the photos on the walls.

'Don't forget your coat.'

'Did I tell you about the time I forgot my coat in Keflavik in Iceland? It's the most expensive place I've ever —'

'Perhaps next time.'

'Oh … okay … When?'

'I'll give you a ring.'

Russell puts on his coat and, reluctantly, leaves. We listen to his footsteps, but there is no sound of an engine from out on the quiet street. I wonder if he is out there, waiting for us to change our minds and invite him back in. I clear away the coffee mugs. The kitchen is sparkling. I am so good. I go to the bathroom and brush my teeth. I do it with my left hand so as to stimulate alternative neural pathways and thus avert the potential onset of dementia. While I do this, I stand on one foot, like a stork, for thirty seconds at a time so that my body will retain its physical memory of balance and not leave me bereft when I am older. I am thinking ahead. Shona comes in behind me. Like the children, she no longer asks what I am doing. She already has on her nightie. She hoists it and sits on the toilet unselfconsciously.

'You cooked a lovely meal,' she says, 'my dear, sweet adventurer.'

'Me? It's all I can do to get the car started in the morning.'

She must have been adorable with braces. After she washes her hands she gives me a sleepy hug, her mouth humming against my neck, which I take to be a manifestation of her love, love that is not humming against the neck of her old school flame.

'Did you enjoy seeing your pal?'

'What a dreary man,' she says, yawning again, as content as I've seen her.

Blue Watches

BROOKE DUNNELL

Michael is standing in front of the aquarium in the lobby of the Diamant Grand Hotel in Basel. The fish are magnificent. Gliding slowly, soft fins wafting, cool as anything: when a large one drifts by, blinking, he can almost hear the whoosh-pop of the eyelid. Head cloudy with jet lag, he feels as if he is submerged too.

'Come here, Michael.' His mother is sitting on a bumpy leather couch, and her face has a twist in it. An eel floats by, shuddering.

'Michael!'

He joins his mother on the studded seat and she softens, smiling and placing a starfish hand on top of his head. 'Daddy will be down soon.'

Michael's father makes expensive watches. Michael can't pronounce the brand name, but he knows they are all blue: smooth blue tiles for the strap and a shiny blue panel for the face. They all look the same, except the ladies' ones are narrower. Michael thinks that's boring, but his father says it's about brand recognition, which means people knowing a watch is Michael's father's without having to be told. Also, if he ever wants to, he can bring out a red-tile-and-face watch in a limited edition and blow everyone away. 'The ace up my sleeve,' his father calls it.

They are in Switzerland so that Michael's father can attend a watch conference with all the other watchmakers in the world. His father says this is a big deal, a very big deal, because here he can get new distributors, new outlets. Michael isn't sure what was wrong with the old ones. His father says his brand recognition will be through the roof by the end of the conference. He says everyone will want an unpronounceable watch, and then what he'll do, he'll restrict the supply, make fewer so people want them more. (Michael thinks that's kind of mean, taking the watches away from the people who want them.) And then, when demand is strongest, his father says, he will release the red watch and the marketplace will go ballistic.

Michael has no reason to doubt this, only he's never seen anyone outside of his own family wear a blue watch. His mother and father wear theirs every day, and Michael will get one of his own when he turns thirteen, his father has promised. 'The best watch the company ever made,' he says, though Michael isn't sure how this is possible, since all of his father's watches are exactly the same. Maybe he'll get a red one. Red is okay.

The hotel hums imperceptibly. There are so many brown couches it's like a shop. Michael wonders how a place with such awesome fish can have such ugly furniture.

He and his mother haven't been at the first few days of the watch conference because Michael didn't want to miss the school swimming carnival. Michael is one of the best swimmers in his year. He swam in every category, emerging from the lanes red-faced and gasping. In the end, he came second overall and got a shiny medallion, which in a lot of ways is actually better than the trophy for first, since he can wear it around his neck all the time.

He lies back and yawns. The plane ride was boring. He'd been on planes, but never for such a long time. Beforehand, while his father was packing for his own flight, he talked about the plane Michael would fly on, which was the biggest in the world. He said he went on a big plane like that, when he was younger, and they let him into the cockpit to hold the controls. Michael liked the sound of that but, when they boarded, the flight attendant said no. 'It's a security issue,' she told his mother. Flying is full of security issues, Michael knows. The machine beeped every time he went through it because he forgot the swimming medal still nestled under his T-shirt. He held up the whole line. His mother was so embarrassed she tried to give the man a tip, but she wasn't allowed. They said it was a security issue.

The whole trip his mother had the twisty-face look, and every few minutes she would rub antibacterial on her hands. Even though the smell made Michael feel sick and he couldn't sleep, she wouldn't let him sit up and play with the TV in the back of the seat instead. 'You need to be well rested for Daddy,' she said. 'Just close your eyes.' She didn't sleep at all, as far as Michael could tell.

The hotel lobby has the same nothing feeling as the plane. It's like being suspended from a coat-hook, or diving deep in the pool and stopping there to watch your limbs lift lifelessly in front of you. Everyone walking past them glides like the fish.

His mother strokes his hair. 'Tired?'

An elevator pings and there is his father, smiling. Michael's father has thick grey hair and wears only suits. Walking out of the lift, he smooths down his tie and then opens his arms. 'There's the intercontinental traveller!'

Last year his father took him to Melbourne for his birthday. They saw the *Lion King* musical (which his mother had taken him to ages ago but his father had forgot) and went to the cricket and the zoo. It was pretty good. On the last day they visited the markets, which had mostly koalas for the ends of pencils, and bad leather jackets, but around one corner there were DVDs and bags and watches. Michael began looking for a blue watch in the hope that his father would buy it for him — even if he hadn't turned thirteen.

He looked everywhere for one of his father's watches. He thought he saw one, but when he reached out for it the stallholder shrieked, 'Rolex! Best ever made!' and scared the heck out of him. Michael's father looked over from the purses. 'What's up, Mikey?'

Hand still extended guiltily, Michael said, 'I wanted one of your watches.'

Smiling, Michael's father walked over and told the man that his son wanted an unpronounceable watch. 'But we'd want an original, of course,' his father said merrily, the way he did when he was joking, only Michael didn't get it.

The watch-seller frowned. 'No.'

His father beamed. 'That's refreshingly honest.'

'No, we no have that watch. All original. No watch.'

Michael's father's smile began to sag. 'Sold out?'

'No one want that one. Rolex! Best ever made!'

Michael could see the shock crest his dad's face like a wave. They left the markets after that.

But if no one wants the watches, Michael thinks, seeing the blue on his father's wrist as he rushes wide-armed from the hotel lift, why are they in Europe?

The hug is tight, kind of choking. Michael hasn't seen his father in three days, but still. When he is released he looks back at his mother, who is smiling plastically, as if her photo is being taken. This is the way she usually smiles. Before she got married Michael's mother did modelling, so there are a lot of pictures around the house of her standing with her hip out and offering that smile. Michael prefers the smile she gives without planning it ahead of time, the one where she shows her teeth.

'How's it been?' she asks his father politely.

'Good. Really good.'

'Blowing them away?'

His father is still looking at Michael. 'How do you like this, eh? Our room is even better. Almost as big, too.'

'I like the fish.'

'Michael,' his mother says.

They have dinner in the hotel restaurant, where the aquarium is less interesting, since it only has crabs. When the waiter comes over, his father orders seven courses and then looks around the table eagerly. His mother gets several dishes with tiny, elegant piles of food in the centre and squirts of lime or crimson sauce patterned around the edges. Every time she goes to dismantle them with her cutlery she pauses, as if afraid to cause damage, and asks Michael's father a question instead. 'Has there been much interest?'

'Things are chugging along.'

His mother's knife and fork quiver in the air.

Michael tugs on his medallion and says, 'Are you increasing demand, Dad?'

His father looks at him, and his face breaks into a smile that widens and widens, like a ripple across a lake. 'I'm stockpiling, Mikey,' he says. 'I'm stockpiling.'

Later, despite his tiredness, Michael wakes at four a.m., his body crying out for the lunch he should be having in Sydney. He lies in bed, stomach squirling. His father was right; the room is enormous. Michael doesn't like it. He asked to stay in the same suite as his parents, but they told him what a privilege it was for him to have his own. 'You're a lucky boy,' his mother said. 'Your father is spoiling us.'

The giant empty room is starting to scare him. There are things in it that shouldn't be there. It stretches out so far, and there are heavy curtains and odd corners. Finally, his stomach hurting, he gets out of bed and slips outside, carefully pocketing the swipe card for the door on the way. The hallway is bright, and he realises that he could have just turned on a light, except he didn't think of it at the time and the lift has come to his floor anyway. Michael steps in and presses the *L* like a grown-up. As the floor drops, he looks at himself in the mirror and smooths down the front of his pyjama top over the reassuring lump of the medallion.

The lobby is slick and softly lit as before. Michael marches importantly over to the reception desk, where there is a pretty lady, her blonde hair tied with a scarf and curled on her shoulder like a seahorse tail. Her voice has a light accent. 'Can I help you?'

'I'd like room service, please.'

'Of course.' She smiles gently. 'Although most guests prefer to order that from their rooms.'

At this, Michael's shoulders droop, but the receptionist continues. 'How about some French fries? You can eat them down here, if you like. We shall call it lobby service.'

Michael beams. 'Can I watch the fish while I wait? Please.'

'Certainly.' The lady gets up from the desk and leads him over to the aquarium, which is still awake and alive. She taps on the glass as a fat grey fish chugs by, pouting. 'This one is Henry. He is the oldest of all the fish.'

'That's my dad's name,' Michael tells her. 'His hair is the same colour.'

'Well.' She smiles again, like a breeze. 'I'm sure you can learn a lot from both of them.'

The chips come quickly, hot and delicious, and Michael eats them in handfuls while staring at the fish. Henry moves stately through the water while the other fish ignore him. There is a bit of moss growing on his belly, as if he spilled his dinner and didn't notice. He reminds Michael of the story of the emperor's new clothes: pompous and ridiculous. Michael loves him.

The endless light of the hotel lobby, the constant negotiation of fish around fish make time disappear. Michael could be anywhere, at any hour. His stomach is warm and full, his eyes bright and searching. Sometimes the lift pings and whooshes, but it's just punctuation. His fingertips brush the glass. He is drifting, like Henry.

A hand sweeps his shoulder: the nice receptionist. 'He is delightful, no?'

'I just want to pick him up and hug him,' Michael says, then blushes, thinking how girly that sounds.

'Ah, but you would kill him with kindness.'

'I know.' Michael's fingers linger on the glass. 'They breathe water.'

'Not exactly. They do breathe oxygen, like us, but their gills, they have been made perfectly to find it in the water. That is their natural environment. They cannot function in the air; in a way, they drown.'

'Drown?'

Henry the fish stares at them through the glass. His hanging lip is like Michael's father's when the watch-seller yelled, *No one want that one!* They got home to Sydney and his dad started talking about the conference. Distributors. Outlets. Brand recognition. Everyone with a chunky blue watch barnacled to their wrist by Christmas.

The receptionist folds her hands at her waist. 'I think perhaps it is time for bed?'

At the suggestion Michael's eyelids feel heavy. He thanks her for the food and exits the lobby, whisked skyward by the silent elevators. Back on the top floor, he swipes open his room door and gets into bed, but he can't quite sleep: the combination of warm snack and enormous down quilt make him feel too hot, like being suffocated in a desperate hug. He tries throwing off the sheets, but then all the radiant heat is confined to his back, where the electric blanket has been cranked up for the northern spring. Groaning, he slides out of the bed and onto his knees to fumble below the mattress for the controls.

His hand has barely disappeared beneath the bed before it hits something. A few somethings, in fact. Half asleep, Michael lifts one, and the slight weight in the base of it immediately reminds him of when his bird died and they buried it in a little perfume box of his mother's. Frightened, he drops the something and scoots back across the carpet to flick on a light.

It is a box, white and rectangular and made of thick card, with the unpronounceable name in slanted gold in the corner. He needn't open it to find what he knows is there, but he does anyway. There is the velvet pouch, a blue watch nestled in the centre. It is set on midnight and doesn't tick.

All the heat in him suddenly rushes to his breastbone. Michael presses the side of his face to the carpet so he can see below the bed: dozens and dozens of white boxes are lined up like coffins after some terrible disaster.

The watches, all of them, are meant to be in the display cases at the conference centre. Michael knows this because his father has been through every last detail with him, talking about it constantly since they got back from Melbourne. The conference centre is wound up tight as a prison, he explained: guards with guns on night patrol, complicated laser systems like James Bond, alarms that could deafen the whole city. There are a lot of security issues at a watch conference. His father's watches would be behind bars for the whole week, unless they sold out in the first couple of days, ha ha ha.

Michael doesn't know what to do, so he turns off the lights and climbs back into the overheated embrace of the bed, clutching his swimming medallion in one hand. Above him hangs a heavy grey balloon holding all the things he isn't supposed to know: the watches, the two hotel suites, his mother's anxious hands.

To distract himself he thinks of Henry, wiggling importantly through his perfect blue world, and what the girl at reception said about fish needing water to breathe. Squeezing his eyes shut, Michael pictures Henry lifted from the tank, the great grey goliath gasping and flipping and bashing itself senseless on the ground. Pulled from his aquarium, and left to drown.

The Place Between

JULIE GITTUS

I shade my eyes and look towards the sun. Against the steep rise of the valley the plane has the dimensions of a toy, the type my brother used to make out of balsa wood and rubber bands.

'Must be the aerial-mapping guys I heard about in town,' Cohen says.

He's standing on the boulder above me, watching the plane zigzag across the creek line. I lay my sarong on the slab of rock above the water and sit down. The granite's gritty texture needles through the cotton into my thighs, so I prop myself back on my elbows to redistribute my weight. It doesn't help.

'Look at me!' shrieks Marigold.

Cohen turns. Assured of her father's attention, she does a running leap from the rise above the swimming hole, the rope clutched in her hands. Her skinny legs pedal the air until she gathers herself into stillness, then she plummets with her toes pointing downwards. The splash is minimal. She's already looking towards Cohen when she surfaces. He gives her the thumbs up. Water streams off her skin as she hauls herself onto the ledge below us.

'What's the score?' she calls up to him.

Cohen was just telling me moments ago how since following the Olympics on her mother's television Marigold has become obsessed with scores and comparisons. But he's watching the approaching plane again and doesn't answer.

'Nine and a half,' I call back.

She makes no comment, just crouches in the dappled shade and begins sorting through a pile of river pebbles. I know my opinion doesn't count. I'm a relative newcomer to the Farm plus I live on the opposite side of the valley. So far I haven't had much to do with either Marigold or Cohen.

The plane is close enough now for me to make out the wing struts and wheels, yet the noise isn't as loud as I thought it would be. I cover myself with the edges of my sarong. The plane's shadow slides over us, a dark cross. I watch disbelieving as Cohen waves upwards, a whole body wave that sets his cock swinging slightly.

'What was that about?' I ask.

The sound of the engine recedes to a drone. He stares at the plane skimming over the rainforest towards the head of the valley.

'Thought I'd give them the archetypal hippie performance.' He turns to me smiling. 'Something for them to have a laugh about over their beers tonight.'

The missing front tooth, the full-on beard, the nakedness combine to make him look like a crazy man. Nothing like the dignified teacher who led the meditation retreat last Sunday. That was the first time I met him. Over the communal lunch he happened to mention how he always swam in the Turtle Head swimming hole. I've come every day since, hoping to see him again. He crosses his arms. I can feel my skin going tight in the sun.

'You're mottling pink across your shoulders,' he tells me.

He doesn't mention that my breasts are also burning. I roll over so that I'm lying on my stomach.

'Daddy, look! These tadpoles have got legs!'

He doesn't shout back, but instead seems to speak from somewhere deep in his chest.

'Bring one up here for me then.'

Her voice takes on a whining quality. 'But they're too hard to catch.'

'You've got to be patient, sweetheart.' His voice drops. 'Wait till you and Felix have kids,' he says to me. 'It's a tactic you learn. Saving your energy till it's really needed.'

I press my nose against my arm and breathe in the smell

of the river trapped in my skin. The mention of Felix reminds me of the watering I have to do before dark. And because the pump broke down yesterday, it's going to take hours. I count out the days in my head till Felix is back from his trip to Fraser Island — eleven.

When I told Cohen earlier about Felix being away for a month, he laughed.

'Sounds like the *we need some space* number that couples go through after arriving here. The one-year itch, we call it on the Farm.'

I blushed then at the way he'd so succinctly nailed those earnest conversations between Felix and me over the last few months.

That afternoon in town I learn how the light plane that zigzagged across the valley wasn't an aerial-mapping company at all, but the police searching for dope crops. The laundromat is alive with talk about the paddy wagons now blocking the valley road.

'You should have seen the cops swarming over the Farm!' says a woman I've never seen before.

I turn away and watch my doona somersaulting over itself. The rest of her words are swallowed by the hiss of plastic as the laundry attendant bags up wet clothes. Before Felix left for Fraser Island he estimated our crop had a street value close to four thousand dollars. Almost enough to build a one-room shack. But now the notion of another wet season in a leaky army tent seems a vague inconvenience when I think of what I might be facing when I drive home. The waiting police. The escorted trip to the station where the charges will be laid. There'll probably be a court conviction, even a jail term. And then I think of Cohen with his zero-tolerance stance about growing on the Farm; what he will say when he finds out.

The dryer stops. I plunge my hands into the folds of hot cotton, trying to find comfort in the warmth.

I sit out the raid in the Rainbow Café, not leaving for home until after dark. When I turn off the valley road towards the Farm, the moon edges over the range, a saffron-coloured moon that's more magnificent than any sun. I creep the station wagon in first gear through the hairpin bends. The tyres wallow in the slush of gravel. It seems obvious now that the raid was planned to coincide with a full moon: that way, the police can nab those of us who thought it safe to return. I imagine a whole squad of police cars positioned at the Farm gate, the officers flagging me down. I see it clearly in my mind: the policeman gripping the roof above my window as he peers inside, the smell of his perspiration embedded in his nylon shirt. *No, officer, I don't live here. I'm only visiting from Victoria.* I feel absurdly pleased how the details on my driver's licence, which I haven't got around to changing since Felix and I shifted up this way, will support my story — despite the fact that lying is in breach of the Farm precept number four. Then I will point to the plastic bag in the back. *I've been to the laundromat in town.* I will smile again, comment on the beautiful night, the whole time conscious of the gun slung low on his hip. But then what?

The moon is poised above the mountains now, illuminating the valley with a light so strong I can see the barbs on the fence wire, even the mesh of a spider's web slung between branches. From here lantana smothers the undulations of the old dairy paddocks in brambles, the perfect camouflage for growing dope.

It was only September when I watched Felix place damp cotton wool balls into matchboxes. *Like a miniature hospital*, I said. He didn't comment. For days the rain had fallen in silvery veils, the run-off trickling across the kitchen's dirt floor close to our bare feet. I understood what he was doing when he began plucking individual seeds from a foil packet with tweezers, but I chose not to say anything. One seed per matchbox that he stored in our tin Coolgardie safe, away from the rats.

The Place Between

I remember his excitement when every seed sprouted; the delicacy of his movements as he transferred the tiny plants into separate pots, which he lavished with fertiliser and spring water. After planting them out he led me down the path to the creek, challenging me to find the entrance in the lantana thicket or a sign of cultivation, but I couldn't see anything.

As the road loops down towards the Farm gate, my heart begins to trill like a dawn-crazed bird. I force myself to focus on my breathing, the way Cohen instructed at the meditation session last weekend. Pranic breathing, he called it. *Inhale the breath through the right nostril, pause and be present in the place between coming and going, the bridge between worlds, then exhale slowly through the left nostril. Now inhale through the left nostril...* I can hear Cohen's voice; feel the calm spaciousness of the meditation room. I can almost see his straight back, the perfect placement of his buttocks on the orange cushion up on the dais. My pulse begins to settle.

I ease the station wagon around the council grader jammed on an angle against a bank of lantana. The shovel is poised in the air like a prehistoric creature about to pounce. The mounds of gravel peter out. Now the road is thin and hard, the centre covered with bony corrugations. The steering wheel shudders in my hands, and as I round the final bend, I lean forward and peer through the windscreen, waiting for the police cars to come into view.

But nothing.

The parking space beneath the white gum trees has the familiar utes and battered Volvos. The Farm gate is shut, the chain and padlock intact. I switch off the engine and wind down the window. The air is thick with the smell of soil and moist leaves. Behind the silence is the distant rustle of the creek over the stones. Now a mopoke: *hoo-hoo, hoo-hoo*. There's the faint twinkle of lights high on the ridge, the hamlet where Cohen lives. I think of the things I have to do down at the campsite: the bed that needs re-making, the lamp that needs filling. Maybe I should chop some wood and light a fire to keep the silence at bay. But I don't move, I just sit there staring at the gleam of moonlight on the cyclone mesh gate.

As soon as I step into the clearing above the campsite, I know that someone has been here. Not police though. The scene before me is too orderly, too calm to have been raided. I roll the laundry bag to my other shoulder, trying to discern what's different. I notice the guy ropes first, the way they've been tightened so the old tent doesn't sag any more. Now the stack of chopped kindling, pale in the moonlight beside the blackened stones of the fireplace. I pick my way down the steps that Felix cut into the slope and dump the laundry bag in the tin shack we use as a kitchen.

The lamp has been filled with kerosene, and there's a new box of matches beside the gas stove. I lift the glass flue off the lamp and strike a match. I don't dare guess who the visitor was, in case I'm disappointed. The dirty bowls I left piled in the sink are now clean and upright in the dish rack. They've been arranged in a funny way — facing the back instead of the front so that they look like the roofs of the Opera House.

The piece of paper is on the bench beside the Coolgardie safe, anchored by a jar of lantana flowers.

Picnic at the Turtle Head around midday tomorrow? Just bring yourself. Cohen.

Below the words is a drawing of a mandala.

Over in the army tent I unpack the washing bag slowly, savouring the pockets of warmth, the sweet clean-laundry smell. I tuck the corners of the fresh sheets under the double mattress with careful deliberation. Bush rats scamper on the canvas overhead, but they don't worry me tonight. The thought of the note sets up a humming sensation inside my chest. I stretch out the time by re-folding clean T-shirts as I plan tomorrow's schedule; how I'll do the watering in the morning so I'll be free to spend the afternoon with Cohen. Just for a moment I think about ripping up the plants at dawn, dumping them in the old mineshaft near the creek, but it doesn't feel right to destroy the crop, to leave Felix with nothing.

As I fling the doona over the mattress, my shadow billows upwards on the tent wall. I'm startled by the way it completely fills the space.

Static

CATE KENNEDY

'Anthony,' says his mother, 'what's this we're drinking?'

He'd known this was going to happen, the minute Marie showed him the punch recipe.

'You know they're hyper-conservative,' he'd said. She'd rolled her eyes, put a post-it note reminder on the recipe page and added it to her list.

'For crying out loud, what's not to like about melon ginger punch?' she'd muttered. The glossy magazine bristled with post-it notes, annotated painstakingly by Marie with dozens of clever and simple Christmas lunch suggestions for people with more to do than slave over a hot stove, et cetera.

Now his mother pokes at a perfectly spherical melon ball in her drink, and looks at him like it was a floating dead mouse.

'It's punch,' Anthony says, smiling hard.

'Just something cool and refreshing,' adds Marie. Anthony's father, Frank, puts his down and pulls himself off the lounge chair.

'How about a beer, son?'

'Sure, if that's what you're after.'

Anthony listens to the asthmatic wheeze of the leather chair his father's just vacated, sucking back air into itself as if desperate for breath, the only noise in the room for a few seconds.

In the deoxygenated silence, he feels what he thinks of as Evil Rays, like something in one of his old comics, jagged lightning bolts shooting across the room. They're crackling from the fingertips of the archenemies seated on either side of him. *Take that, Ice Maiden! No, you take THAT, Bitch Crone!*

Then both of them, his mother and Marie, turning the

Evil Rays onto him, as if the whole thing is his idea, his fault, when all he's done is get out his credit card to pay for the whole bloody shebang: the punch and the Peruvian glass punchbowl it's in and the gourmet chestnut stuffing mix in the organic free-range turkey out there, rolled and boned for easy slicing — Anthony knows exactly how it feels — and the sighing, put-upon lounge suite still on the interest-free-nothing-more-to-pay-for-ten-months plan, which Marie is already obsessing is the wrong shade of taupe. Are there actually different shades of taupe? It's news to Anthony. Hell would be like that, he thinks, gulping punch. It would be shades of taupe that drove you screaming into eternal torment, not the flames.

'Let's open the presents,' he suggests.

'But the children haven't even arrived,' says his mother.

'I meant just ours,' he answers feebly. True, for a few seconds there, he had forgotten the children were coming. The Children. His sister's offspring, always referred to in capitals, who would dominate the day. It wasn't the kids' fault — they'd be desperate to escape into the study as soon as they could to play with the Wii he'd bought them, the poor little buggers. No, they would be used, The Children, as deflector shields against the Evil Rays, as ammunition against the day's parries and thrusts of emotional blackmail. Hannah and Tom. They'd have to be twelve and ten now.

Marie hadn't even wanted them to come; she'd made a big fuss about having to plan a special menu for them and how they'd turn the house upside down, but Anthony, ducking his chin and ploughing through a veritable snowstorm of Evil Rays, insisted that if they were going to have a family Christmas, his sister and her husband and kids had to be there, or his parents wouldn't show up.

'I don't care if we have KFC,' he'd finally said, gesturing to the pile of magazines hawking sunshine and patios and people in uncrushed white linen shirts. 'If we've agreed to do it, they have to come.' And Marie had slammed off into the study to channel her fury into pumping six kilometres out of the exercise bike. You could bounce a coin off her calf muscles, if you were game to try.

Rays, rays. One drills into the back of his skull as he leaves the kitchen, another counter-attacks with a punch square in the solar plexus as he carries in a platter of smoked-salmon blinis. Marie's doused them with chopped dill, and his mother looks at them like they've been sprayed with grass clippings from the mower. She can get every secret weapon into those rays — contempt, accusation, disdain, puzzled faux-innocence, the works. Anthony is determined, fully determined, to thwart her with unrelenting good cheer today.

'Pikelets, eh?' says his father, eyes swivelling back to the one-day match, luridly coloured on the plasma screen. 'Well, well.' He folds one into his mouth to keep the peace while his mother refuses, mouth like a safety pin. Vol-au-vents, that's his mother's style. Cheese straws and a sherry.

Anthony starts eating the things so that when Marie comes back it will look like they've been a success. He's got four in his mouth when a stray caper lodges itself in his throat and forces him to cough a spray of ricotta and dill and masticated pancake into a Christmas napkin. For a second he's terrified he might actually throw up, and wouldn't that be a wonderful start to the day, but he swallows down a mouthful of punch and his stomach settles.

Where's Marie? If there's one thing those magazines kept promising, it was that even though you were a hostess you wouldn't need to be tied to the kitchen all morning; with your new fresh and fun easy-peasy celebration menu you'd be relaxing with those you loved on this special day.

He can't go back out to the kitchen yet. It wouldn't look right. 'Who's winning, Dad?' he says.

'The Pakis.'

On the screen the tiny bright figures move as if they're underwater. Bowl and deflect. Go back, wait, run up slowly, bowl and … block. Christ, it's like watching paint dry.

'I got all my shopping done early and out of the way this year,' says his mother. 'And what a relief that was. I can't stand having to shop when the place is such a madhouse just before Christmas.'

'You're right. It's crazy, isn't it?' He recalls going to Safeway just the night before, running up and down the aisles searching for cranberries in syrup. The person ahead of him at the check-outs was buying four barbecue chickens, salad mix and a big tub of choc-chip ice-cream, and Anthony had felt an overwhelming, childish longing to follow them out and curl up in the back of their car and go home to their place.

'And I got everything boxed,' his mother is saying, 'just big square boxes. I'll never forget the terrible problems we had wrapping that rocking horse for Tom.' Seven years later, and she's still talking about it.

'What did you get him this year?' says Anthony. He can see the packages under the tree — all the same red paper with military-tucked corners.

'A walkie-talkie set.' She looks at him shrewdly, and Anthony does his best to simulate admiring delight.

'Oh! He'll ... Was that something he said he wanted?'

'You know how much he loves all his electronic games. He'll be able to play police games with this, with his friends. You know, hiding round the house.'

'Terrific.'

She's on to him in an instant. 'What? Don't you think it's a good idea? Lord knows it cost me enough. I just try to keep up with what the children seem to want; I don't know all the latest gadgets. I just do my best.'

God, where is Marie? 'No, no. It's a great idea. He'll love it.'

When Tom sees the Wii, Anthony knows, the walkie-talkie's going to get dropped like a dud Tamagotchi.

'I'll just see if Marie needs a hand,' he says, weaving through the lounge chairs to the kitchen.

'Honestly,' he hears her tut as he exits, 'how hard is it to roast a turkey?'

Listless applause trickles from the TV as someone finally hits something, and the lounge chair exhales a gust of weary depression.

Marie's eyes, as she glances up, are murderous.

'Pit those,' she snaps, flicking her eyes to some cherries. 'If your father cracks a filling on a cherry pip I'll never hear the end of it.'

She's ... what the hell's she doing? Anthony stares at his wife's hand, vanished to the wrist inside a Christmas ham.

'I'm getting the fat and skin off. I'm not going to drop dead of cholesterol even if they all want to.' She extracts her hand like a doctor completing an internal exam and peels back the great flapping layer of fat. 'Look at that. Disgusting.' She wraps it in a plastic bag, shuddering, and drops it into the bin. 'We'll just have this ham cold, sliced and arranged on the platter with some rocket garnish and a scattering of cranberries.'

Anthony grimaces. He can hear the pitch rising in her voice, the manic brittleness that has nowhere to go but up up up into hectic hysteria. It will break later, after everyone has gone, and the tic that's jumping now under her eye will somehow afflict her whole face and pump itself down her arms and legs.

'Try not to get upset,' he says as calmly as he can. 'I'll do all that before we eat, just come in and sit down for a while.'

She's scrubbing ham grease off her hands in the sink. 'I hate that lounge suite,' she mutters. 'I told you it was the wrong colour.'

Anthony scrabbles in the cutlery drawer for the cherry pitter he remembers buying at Ikea. 'So I'll just do these cherries then.'

'I'm not going back in there by myself,' says Marie, who fronts a whole courtroom five days a week.

'Well,' says Anthony, keeping it light with everything he has, 'I'll bring this bowl in and do them in there.'

'Are you serious?'

'Sure. It'll give my mother something to correct me about. Make her happy.'

She flashes him a smile as she heads for the door. The ghost of an old smile, one he misses; she's trained herself not to do it because it shows the tooth she's convinced is crooked. He's told her he loves that tooth, but she just rolls her eyes. In every one of their wedding photos, stored over there in the hand-tooled leather albums, she has on the other smile, the trained one — lips closed and chin raised like a model of cool serenity, a perfected study of herself. But somewhere in a drawer, Anthony has an old photo of her, pulling off her mask and snorkel at the Great Barrier Reef, just out of the water, and her grin broad and unselfconscious. Years ago.

'I don't have any explanation for it,' she'd told the fertility specialist last week when they'd had their first session. 'I'm doing everything right: diet, exercise, monitoring ovulation …'

How reasonable she'd sounded, how rational. That lawyer's tilt to her head, the voice pleasant and determinedly non-aggrieved. And the specialist nodded and said, 'Sometimes these things take more time than we expect,' and she replied, in a voice a shade or two firmer, that she'd done her own research and was ready for the first stage of conception enhancement.

That was the term she'd used: *conception enhancement*. Like they were joining the Scientologists rather than trying to make a baby.

Anthony takes the cherry bowl and the Ikea pitter and an extra saucer into the lounge room and sits at the end of the dining-room table. Marie is at the stereo, riffling through the stack of CDs for something suitable, his mother pointedly brushing dill off a blini she holds in her palm.

'Aren't you the domestic one?' says his mother when she sees him, and he waits, counting tiredly to himself and getting to seven before she adds, 'Just watch you don't splatter that shirt with cherry juice because it's the devil's own to get out.'

He starts on the first cherry, and his mother writhes with the discomfort of not interfering.

'Would you like me to do it?' she blurts when she can no longer endure it after ten seconds.

'No, thanks but no. I'm enjoying the challenge.'

The cherry stones drop onto the saucer, and the repetition of the task lulls Anthony into a light trance. The cherries are huge, bigger than any he remembers from his childhood. He and his sister Margaret used to sit on the back step and eat them, collecting the stones for that rhyming game about who you'd marry, and Margaret would always eat the exact number required to get her past *tinker, tailor, soldier, sailor*, all the way to *rich man*. He remembers spiking her pile with an extra stone, just to bump it up to *poor man* and drive her crazy.

It's worked, too, that trick. She and Ian are in some dire financial straits. He's under oath to say nothing to their parents, but it makes him feel uncomfortable, having the big new house, and that's what made him overcompensate, probably, with the presents.

Thunk, thunk, go the cherry stones, sliding obediently from the dripping flesh. Slippery as hard little rocks you'd remove from someone's gall bladder. In fact, one time he'd had his ears syringed after they'd blocked up during a bad cold, and he was astonished to hear a thunk into the kidney dish the doctor had instructed him to hold beside his head. Looking down as the warm solution sloshed around inside his ear, he saw a hard ball of wax just the size and shape of one of these cherry stones lying there. Anthony couldn't believe something like that had been wedged in his ear all along, slowly building up like a small, solid boulder. And what amazed him even more was the sudden clearing of sound as the water drained from his ear canal. It was like finding the treble knob on your stereo system at last and hearing, really hearing, everything that had been dulled and muted before.

'I hope you don't mind our funny little present to you, Marie,' says his mother. 'It's just that you're so hard to buy for, the two of you — I mean, my goodness, there's really absolutely nothing else you need, is there?'

'No,' says Marie, smiling that gracious close-lipped smile. 'We've both worked hard to get the house the way we want it, haven't we, Anthony?'

Tinker, tailor, soldier, sailor, he counts before he answers. 'Yep, but it's been worth it,' he says. *Rich man, poor man, beggar man, thief.* You couldn't have that rhyme now — kids wouldn't get it. You'd have to update it. *Consultant, accountant, banker, defence-force personnel ... human-resources manager ...*

She used to call him Ant. He can't put his finger on when it started being Anthony. It was like his attention had waned momentarily and then there it was, a new name and a new smile, to go with the new granite-topped Italianate kitchen bench and the whole brand spanking new house. He'd closed his eyes signing the mortgage, suffering a brief swooping dizzy spell of nauseated disbelief, and he thinks of that title document now stacked away in some bank vault somewhere, his signature slumping below the dotted line like a failing ECG.

The front doorbell rings its two-gong Tibetan chime, and he jumps up.

'That'll be Margaret and Ian!' he cries, making for the door just as his mother rests her hand thoughtfully on the upholstered lounge chair, readying herself for the next bout, and says: 'What colour do you call this, Marie?'

At the table Anthony is crouched, looking through the viewfinder of his digital camera. He's starting to breathe a bit easier now, with lunch almost finished. He looks at the group of them reproduced in pixels, their movements at the table making the image shift and shimmer like a 3-D postcard.

'Oh, good, get some photos,' calls his mother, a little loud now after three white wines. 'Get one of all of us, Anthony. There's so few occasions we're all together like this.' She waves her hand extravagantly to bring Tom and Hannah over beside her and gestures again at Anthony. 'Put it on the timer thing and be in the photo too; get a record of all of us before we all change forever.' She's gone a bit slurred and maudlin, he sees with alarm — blinking hard and giving her eyes a surreptitious blot on one of Marie's linen napkins. 'Time goes so fast,' she says to nobody in particular.

Anthony stands tilting the camera a few millimetres back and forth, mesmerised, as the group arranges itself before him. The pixellated image oscillates, scanning and reading the shifts of light and shade. One moment he sees his sister overweight and worn and dowdy in her Target outfit, frumpy beside the immaculate blonde Marie who outshines them all. The next he sees Margaret kind and comfortable, touching Ian's arm and smiling warmly, with Marie pale and cold and stick-thin, face grimaced into a close-mouthed rictus. Back and forth the shimmering image goes; how she sees them and how they see her, this life and that life, with Anthony in the middle, trying to hold the camera steady and depress the button for auto-focus at the same moment. He's looking at the faces of his niece and nephew as he takes the picture, the way they're holding their smiles frozen, crouched compliant beside his mother, waiting for it to be over. Where do we learn those smiles from, Anthony is thinking as he preserves it all, megabyte by megabyte.

'Now, Tom,' he says to his nephew as they're clearing away after lunch. 'I really hope you enjoy your presents and everything, but I just need to have a quiet word with you, man to man.'

'Okay,' Tom says. He's trying hard to behave himself today, dressed up in new shirt and jeans. Brand new, like he got them that morning, and it makes Anthony's heart constrict in small, suffocating aches to think the kids have got good clothes this year for their Christmas presents.

'I've bought you a present I reckon you'll love, and I think you'll really want to play with it, but the thing is, Grandma's also got you a present she'd like you to play with, and I think it would be nice if just for today you played with hers. Okay?'

'Why?'

Why indeed? Why is he pandering to the domineering old harridan? She's just spent Christmas lunch behaving as if it's a cardinal sin not to serve roast parsnips. Asking for a cup of tea, of all things, instead of dessert, sending Marie back out to the kitchen to make it specially. Why is he trying to embroil Tom in this too?

'Well, she's tried hard to get you something she thinks you'll like, you see. The thing I've got you' — he gives Tom a big indulgent-uncle grin — 'let's say you need a TV for it, but we can play it anytime, my place or your place …'

'I don't think we have the right attachment thing for it,' says his nephew, his face beginning to fall. 'Our TV's too old. If it's a Wii, I mean.'

'Right,' says Anthony, owner of three plasma widescreens, possessor of a seven-figure debt, master juggler of every line of credit. He's smiling hard again now, his face feeling numbed with it. 'Right, well. I'll have a talk to your mum about maybe … um …'

How to broach it with Margaret, how to offer? Tell her he never uses the one in the bedroom? Yeah, tell her it's been sitting in the guest bedroom gathering dust, be great if she could take it off his hands. A loan. As long as they'd like it. His fault for buying the gadget. Anthony has to squeeze his hands together between his knees to stop himself grabbing Tom and hugging him as hard as he can. A thin boy. Too troubled for a ten-year-old. Reading out those stupid knock-knock jokes at the table, trying his best to do just what's expected of him, to decode all those signals and stand in the firing line of all those deadly rays.

Later, when they're assembled in the lounge opening the presents, he winks lightning fast at Tom as he eases the sticky tape away from the walkie-talkie box.

'Thanks, Grandma!' the boy says, getting up to give her a dutiful kiss, and Anthony's praying for her to just shut up for a minute, just one fucking minute for once in her life, but she can't, of course, she has to start in on how he's got to look after it because it cost a lot of money and he can't take it to school, it's just to be played with at his house. She accepts Tom's muted kiss on the cheek without even looking at him, not really, because what she wants is babies, she only likes them when they're babies; by the time they're Tom's and Hannah's ages they've learned to be wary and submissive and not to trust her, and who can blame them?

Anthony squeezes his hands between his knees again and looks over at Marie clasping her gift basket of toiletries. He thinks of the kilometres she tries to cover each night on that stationary bike, the endless net surfing she's done on sperm motility and ovarian cysts, like someone gathering evidence for a case they have to win. Does she love him? She lets him see her in the morning without make-up, does that count?

'Batteries,' he hears himself saying as Tom takes out the two handsets from their foam boxing. 'I've got just the thing over here, wait a sec ...' and he's tearing a corner off the wrapping on the Wii to dig inside for the pack of AAs he's tucked in there for the remote control.

'Do you want to have a go with Tom?' Margaret asks Hannah, who screws up her nose and shakes her head with the exquisite disdain of a twelve-year-old girl.

'Me!' Anthony says, leaping up. 'Let's check out the range on these things!'

Once he leaves, he knows the conversation could go two ways — his loyal sister, God bless her, keeping the peace and staunchly championing him as being great with kids; or his mother, voice flat with disparagement, claiming that he'll never grow up, no matter what sort of high-powered job he seems to find for himself. And what would Marie say of him? Which side would she take?

'Outside!' he calls to Tom as he sprints down the hall.

He's suddenly desperate for fresh air. 'Switch yours on, see the rocker switch?'

'Yeah, I'm on to it,' Tom replies, disappearing into the laundry. Anthony hears him stop and begin to negotiate the squadron of deadlocks on the door that leads outside. He does the same with the sliding doors onto the patio and jogs down the steps to the house's north side.

They'd paid a landscaper to do the garden, and he'd dug up the grass along this whole stretch and laid down a bed of stones. Anthony's feet crunch on it now, staggering slightly. The stones are too big, really, to be called pebbles. It's like wading across a big, empty, bone-dry riverbed. 'Absolutely zero care,' the landscaper had said, and he'd been right.

Anthony flicks on his walkie-talkie, holds it to his mouth. 'Securing the zone,' he deadpans into the mouthpiece, stifling a grin. 'Agent Two, do you copy?'

He flicks the switch and hears a snow of static, moves his arm in an arc to clear it. Rays, he thinks absently, are holding them together. Currents zapping between the aerials. He flicks the switch back once the static clears and tries again.

'Commando Two,' he barks. 'Do you read me?'

He hears a gurgle on the other end. His nephew, laughing. Anthony sinks to a crouch, raises the walkie-talkie to his ear, and listens. Tom's voice, when it starts through the chuckling, is so loud and tinny he almost jumps.

'Reading you, Uncle Ant,' he says, and starts laughing again.

'Commando Two, request information — who is Uncle Ant? Please repeat code name.' He lowers his head in the shade of the pergola, his ear pressed to the handset to hear the smile again in his nephew's voice. Instead the voice he hears is Marie's, her tone hard and skating on pain like it was ice: *Well, Anthony, tonight's the night, this is the window — do you want to have a child or don't you?* and his chest tightening as he tried to think of what to answer her. Then her voice again, rising bitterly from her side of the bed: *Just say, just tell me, so I'm not wasting my time anymore*, and then Tom is giggling again, saying, 'Commando Two here, sir, reading you loud and clear,' and Anthony — gazing at the stones at his feet, then up at the glazed pots full of massed blue-grey succulents on the patio with its two canvas chairs arranged just so — finds his voice has deserted him. His throat has closed up.

Static and space wash over the line, a sound like the inside of a shell. He can see into the kitchen from here; Marie at the granite bench, arranging mince pies on a platter. She's using tongs to lift them from the cardboard box, like the woman at the ludicrously expensive bakery did, placing them reverently down in a line.

He watches his wife's face pinched with dark concentration, remembers her voice at the end of its tether in the darkness. But tethered by what? He hears a sharp catch of breath — his own, coming through the headset. *For fuck's sake*, he tells himself, *pull yourself together*. He watches as Marie takes the sifter and starts dusting the pies with icing sugar and something dislodges in him with a delicate gush of pressure, something shifts to let bright sound in.

He watches her wrists flex, the air going out of him, sure suddenly that nothing of him will ever take root inside that thin, tightly wound body, nothing.

Tom's voice comes through the handset again. Clear as a bell now, the clearest thing he's ever heard.

'Agent One?' it says, tentative. Like he thinks Anthony's given up on him already and tired of the game.

'Copy,' rasps Anthony, flipping the switch. 'Ambushed here, Commando.' Marie turns and turns the sifter's handle, the muscle twitching in her face, resolutely dousing the pastries that nobody will want to eat with a deluge of white, a blanketing snowfall of sweetness, covering every track.

'Do you require assistance?' comes the voice at the other end of the line.

'Yes,' he says. 'Man down here. Man ... inoperative.' Jesus,

Static

what's he saying? 'Over,' he adds hastily.

'I can't really hear you, Uncle Ant,' says Tom's voice. There's another bubbling of static, the distant squeaking of some other low-band frequency interfering with the line. Anthony thinks he hears Tom add: 'Can we go and play with the Wii now?'

He means to say yes. He wants just to lose himself in the big benign glowing screen, crack open Cokes for the kids, and have that quiet word with Margaret and Ian, have the day mean something. He's exhausted, suddenly.

'Man down. Mayday,' he hears himself croaking instead. 'Mayday.'

Okay. He's got about forty seconds before Tom comes and finds him. That's all he needs to hold this together, summon the good energy, get up off his knees and blame the static. But he finds, in the luxury of those seconds, that he can't take his eyes off the cacti in their pots. They don't seem to have grown an inch since they were planted there at the advice of the landscaper six long months ago. Totally unchanged. Zero care.

Anthony puts the handset down onto the stones and gazes at them, so steely and barbed and implacable, something that even neglect and drought put together can't seem to kill. He reaches out with a fascinated finger to prod a curved spike, hard, against the cushion of skin. He just wants to see a dot of hot, red blood well reliably up, as if he needs proof that such things are real.

Papas' Last Command

JANE McGOWN

Suction lived next door. He was my best friend despite our thirty-year age gap. *The town idiot*, the schoolchildren called him, frequently trailing behind, chanting his name, mimicking his long ungainly strides. There was no denying he looked the part, with his elongated ears, beak-like nose and upturned chin — not to mention his lips, which seemed to have disappeared inwards, leaving a wrinkled smudge of a mouth that sometimes resembled a cat's bottom. My older brother Bernie told me Suction probably breathed in so hard one hot summer's night he accidentally swallowed his lips. For a while I believed him.

Once, when I asked my mother what was wrong with Suction, she told me he'd got stuck between his mother's legs when he was being born. As the youngest, I was never too sure when Mum was giving me the real story. Bernie confirmed it though, telling me they'd needed a tractor to haul Suction out. I'd seen the farmers do this with calves that refused to budge, their skinny legs sticking out at odd angles, so it seemed logical enough. Bernie told me to make sure I married someone with wide hips; the kid stood a better chance that way. I had a look at Suction's mother's hips the next time she passed our gate. She was a thin, grey-haired woman who looked like life was gnawing away at her from the inside.

I decided Bernie had a point. I remember writing it in my notebook: *Marry someone with big hips.*

Then adding *(Suction)*, just as a reminder.

But Suction was far from stupid; I can say that with certainty as I knew him better than anyone. From the time I learned to walk I followed him everywhere. He couldn't talk but he taught me about a world that didn't need words, yet wasn't a world of silence: it was full of the sounds of nature. He would take me down to the riverbank where we would lie under the willows and watch for wildlife. He knew the call of every bird in the district and, although he couldn't form words, he could mimic them. In fact Suction could mimic any sound. That's what saved Costa's sister that night. The cry of something injured really got Suction going. He couldn't stand to see anything hurt.

Bernie said there was nothing much inside Suction's head so that whatever brain he had just sloshed around in a big empty space, accounting for the strange noises he made. But he was wrong. There were no empty spaces in Suction's head. It was full to the brim with kindness. I saw it in the way his big hands gently scooped up Costa's sister. The way he carefully laid her on the table in my father's surgery.

I was too young to fully understand what happened that night. It took me many years to put it together but I'm sure Suction knew. He must have known a lot of secrets in that town. A lot of people must have been grateful Suction could neither talk nor write.

Costa belonged to the only Greek family in the town. Papas, his father, owned the local café. I remember it well. I remember the faded lace curtains and the drone of blowflies as they buzzed in the corners of the shop window. Trapped, they'd eventually die there, their dry bodies littering the sill. Occasionally Papas would give them a dismissive flick of his duster, but it was only ever half-hearted, and there'd be more to replace them the next week.

Every Friday I'd sit perched on one of the stools in the café, Suction beside me, both of us slurping strawberry milkshakes. Papas would roam around, wiping up our drips with a grotty old rag, talking about his village in Greece. He must have been lonely, as he seemed to get a lot off his chest. He didn't seem to care what he told us, probably thinking one was too stupid and the other too young to understand.

The first time I met Costa he'd barged through the shop door, breathless and panting, his shirt ripped and bloodstained, both his eyes swollen.

'You fight back this time, son?'

'I told you, Dad. I'm not going to fight. It's not my way.'

'What's *your* way then? To just stand there? Let them belt the hell outta you? You make it real easy for them, boy!'

Costa hadn't answered, but stood there with his head down, still catching his breath. He was about seventeen, slight for his age.

Papas held up his own fists and pranced back and forth in a mock fight. 'I'll show you how to do it, son.'

He lifted one of Costa's fists, but his son pulled away.

'I told you I won't fight!'

'All right. Up to you. You wanna get bashed everyday, go ahead. Where's the honour in that? Go and get changed before you make me real mad. And tell your sister to come down and clear the tables.'

Papas threw his hands up in despair then leaned over the counter. 'Something wrong with that boy. Bring him to a new country and what happens? He becomes weak. If he not fight back they make it worse for him. You see.'

Papas was right. Over the next few months I lost count of the number of times Costa received treatment in my father's surgery. The attacks became more and more vicious, more and more frequent.

'If this doesn't stop you'll have to report it. Bring charges. This can't go on. Something bad's going to come out of it,' I heard my father say as Papas guided Costa, yet again, out of the doctor's rooms.

'But he refuse to fight back, and if I bring charges then no one come to my café. Business bad already. No one wants to help us in this town. Especially those Italians! They bad news.'

After the war, the Italians had settled in the hills outside the town, taming the land then growing grapes. They'd worked hard and done well but had transported historical gripes with them. Costa, being the only Greek boy in the school, bore the brunt of it.

We were finishing off our milkshakes one day when Costa appeared earlier than usual. His father looked surprised. His son was clean, undamaged.

'What happened? You outrun them or fight back at last?'
'Neither.'
'What then?'
'The wog boys are going to protect me.'
'Protect you! In return for what? I thought they were the ones thumping you.'
'Not always.'
'Wogs never help Greeks. They're setting you up. They want something. What they want?'
'Nothing.'
'Rubbish. You don't get nothin' for nothin'.'

As Costa walked away, Papas tapped the side of his head. 'That boy weak up here as well if he thinks wogs wanna help a Greek boy. Ever since we come here that boy not listen. He never obey his father no more. In Greece he a good boy. He do as father say.'

'Maybe he just wants to try it his way.' I circled the straw around the base of the metal milkshake container to collect any stray drops. Suction had already finished his milkshake and was blowing through his straw, sending fine milky spray all over the counter Papas had just wiped.

'No, he weak all right. Those boys out to get him for sure.'

The night Papas' world fell apart, Suction had taken me down to the river to collect yabbies. We were making our way back through the bush when we heard a ruckus going on. Suction stopped, his head tilted in the direction of the noise. We turned off our torches and crept towards the clearing ahead. The moon had ducked behind a cloud, but there was just enough light to keep us on track until we reached a boulder where we could crouch unseen.

The men were making such a racket I couldn't work out what they were doing.

'Come on, man ...'

'Yeah, man. She's all yours.'

'Don't worry about her carryin' on like that ...'

'... the bitches all kick and scream when they want it.'

'Yeah, just means they want it real bad.'

Even I could tell they'd been drinking. I'd seen the drunks on Friday nights leave the local pub, stumbling down the front steps, shouting out their slurred farewells and reeking of beer.

'Come on, mate, get a move on! If you don't screw her we'll *all* have a go at her!'

Beside me, Suction chomped nervously on his gums. I could feel his muscles tensing. There was one boy much bigger than the rest who seemed to be the leader.

'Hear that, guys? He wants to know who she is! You don't worry about that, mate. All bitches are the same.'

I could tell Suction was agitated. He was rocking backwards and forwards and making the humming sound he always made when something upset him. I didn't understand what was going on but I knew it felt all wrong. I stood closer to Suction, seeking reassurance from his body warmth.

The voices in the dark were getting louder, more insistent.

'Get some grog into him. That'll fix him.'

'Come on, mate. Screw her and we leave you alone in future.'

The men were grouped in a circle blocking our view. Then, without warning, they started cheering and whistling. A few stepped sideways as they hauled a carton of beer closer, opening up a gap that enabled us to see what was going on. In the middle of the circle, kicking and struggling on the ground, was a girl. Her hands were tied and a hood had been firmly secured over her head. Two men were holding her down and on top of her was another man. I felt Suction flinch and start towards them.

'No, they'll kill us. There's too many.' I pulled him back. 'I know. Make your siren noise. Make it real loud. They'll think it's the police. I'll flash the torches.'

Suction's imitation of a siren was so convincing he often had people running out into the streets.

When he started, it was so loud it nearly deafened me. I turned on the torches and twirled them above us. Well, you've never seen a group scatter so fast. They ran like scared rabbits. Even the guy with his pants down somehow managed to hobble along and cover some distance before he hauled them up. Boy, did he bolt then. Suction kept the siren going until we were sure the coast was clear then he ran to the girl. He untied her hands and removed the hood, and the tape from her mouth. Gently, he put his large hands under her back and gathered her up. Trotting like one of those show ponies, he carried the trembling bundle all the way to my father's surgery, a couple of blocks away.

We didn't realise it was Costa's sister until Suction laid her on the table. She was shaking and sobbing uncontrollably.

I could tell from Dad's expression when he turned to me that it was bad.

'Go and get Papas as fast as you can!'

At the time I didn't even know what 'rape' meant. When I crept back into the surgery later and looked it up in one of Dad's medical books, I doubt I still properly understood. I understood what it did to Papas though. Upon seeing his daughter, the colour left him; and when it returned, his face was so red I thought he was going to explode. In a way he did. He started kicking the walls of the surgery, then banging his head against the doorframe until Dad jabbed him with a needle. That quietened him for a while, but when Costa turned up with his mother, Papas started carrying on again, shouting at Costa at the top of his voice.

'You find the boy who done this to your sister! Hear me!'

'What d'you mean? The kid said there'd been an accident.' Costa stood there bewildered, trying to make sense of the scene in front of him.

'That kid too young to understand what happened. But I'm telling you now, son … *rape* ain't no accident!'

Costa lost colour then as well. I thought he was going to faint, but he managed to lurch outside and just made it to the porch before spewing everywhere.

'See, Costa a good brother. He real upset because he close with his sister.' Papas followed his son outside. When he came back in, Costa was nowhere to be seen.

'Where's Costa?' my father asked.

'Told him to find and kill the bastard that did this to his sister. Then chuck him in the river.'

'Not a wise thing to do, Papas. Leave it to the police.'

'No. Maybe this time that boy do as I say.'

I never saw Costa again. They found him in the river the next morning, a boat anchor strapped to his waist. Papas stayed in town a few more months, his behaviour becoming more and more peculiar. Then suddenly, overnight, he shut up shop and left. Not even Suction saw him go.

The Chamber

MEG MUNDELL

If she'd quit smoking the week before, like she'd planned, Penny never would have found the gun. That summer a heatwave was crisping the hedges, killing old people and making the birds pant helplessly, beaks agape. Bushfire smoke drifted into the city, tinting the daylight amber and giving the air a sweet, woody scent. Walking home from work that night Penny was pissed off, and she'd flicked her cigarette butt into the bushes without thinking.

As she stamped out the butt, she spotted something nestled in the parched shrubs, a shape glinting under the streetlight. At first she thought it was a toy, some plastic replica lost in a game of cops and robbers. But when she picked it up, the weight of it sent a quick thrill skating through her. She checked the street: empty.

The gun was L-shaped. Its body had a blue-black sheen, a grooved cylinder and a textured handgrip with indents for your fingers. The barrel had tiny writing printed on it. She was careful not to touch the trigger. The metal felt warm — how long had it been there? But it was a hot night, she reasoned; everything was warm.

A childish thought skipped across her mind: finders keepers. Penny put the gun in her shoulder bag and walked away quickly, her blood banging out a loud pattern. Maybe it was a good-luck omen; what had her fortune cookie said this morning? *It is better to be the hammer than the anvil.* She smiled: some good luck was way overdue. She rolled another smoke and decided not to head home just yet. Her housemate spent his life inhaling bongs in front of the twenty-four-hour news channel, and she wasn't in the mood for him.

A siren wailed to life nearby, and Penny made a quick

decision to cut through the unlit park. You weren't supposed to walk here at night, but nobody could fuck with her now. Dead grass crackled underfoot, cicadas shrilled from all directions and a plane rasped overhead, blinking upwards and out of sight. She walked faster than usual, taking long strides, a new confidence welling up inside her. Her bag swung heavy on her hip, and she felt strong.

Next morning she phoned work to ask about the roster. The manager picked up. A sour man with a neurotically thin moustache, Greg liked to play favourites, and Penny wasn't one of them. His answers were curt, and he kept saying her name like it tasted bad. No shifts available next week, *Penny*; I'm in the middle of a stocktake, *Penny*, we'll be in touch if we need you. She hung up and swore at her bedroom wall. She'd like to punch that asshole right in his stupid moustache.

Five weeks into the job she'd balanced the till wrong twice, and yesterday had lost her temper with two pimply jerks in the fruit aisle who'd made repeated enquiries about 'them melons' while gawking at her chest. Penny was sick of it, all the ogling and moronic comments, and her reply had been quick-witted and lacerating. It had also been loud. The two creeps slunk away, but Greg appeared at her elbow. Next thing she was in the storeroom listening to him cite a long and viciously exaggerated list of her shortcomings as a grocery worker. He didn't need to remind her she was just a casual. He refused to let her explain, so she'd been reduced to glowering.

Out in the lounge room her housemate Derek was hunched over a breakfast of Cheezels, watching TV with the curtains shut. The ceiling fan spun sluggishly, stirring the bong-scented air around like soup. Onscreen the bushfires devoured whole swathes of the map; the camera panned across the blackened shells of homes, and emergency workers led weeping people through the smoke.

'Hey,' said Penny.

Derek grunted a hello.

She took her daily fortune cookie to her room: *Today is the tomorrow we worried about yesterday*, it informed her. What the hell was that supposed to mean? It was no help at all. Today she should re-jig her CV, look for another job and sign up for the dole. Glumly she fired up her laptop, angled her desk fan for maximum sweat evaporation, and began her weekly email to her mum.

Everything was great, she reported: her housemate was really laid-back and into current affairs, and uni was going well. She hit send without getting too elaborate. The lies had begun two months ago, with the discovery that she'd missed the application date for her design course. Sorry, the admin person had said, try again next year. Three weeks later she was packing groceries under Greg's militant gaze: not a great result for moving halfway across the country. Most nights she had a recurring dream: she was stuck on a train that ran a circular loop of track, over and over. It wasn't that hard to interpret.

Her sketchpad lay on the desk. Penny regarded the gap beneath the wardrobe for a while. Then she kneeled down and slid the gun out, positioned it in the sunlight, and began drawing. This was the first gun she'd seen up close, and it was a beautifully designed thing. She sketched its outline, blocked in shading, copied the curlicued logo and the tiny writing stamped into the metal: 38 S&W SPECIAL CTG. / REG. US. PAT. OFF. / MADE IN USA / MARCAS REGISTRADAS / SMITH & WESSON, SPRINGFIELD MASS. She held up the final result: not bad. At least she could still draw.

The firing mechanism was hidden somewhere inside. Fiddling with guns was a bad idea, but if she was careful … A childhood spent dissecting household appliances and copping whacks around the head from her stepfather had taught her how to put things back together properly, to treat machinery with respect. She tested the cylinder, but it wouldn't budge; must be a lever. The one at the back stirred vague memories of crime shows, the bad guy cocking it just before squeezing the trigger. She tried a smaller catch below, and the cylinder gaped open. A light tremor went through her. There were six bullets inside.

That night she opened all the windows wide, but the house would not cool down. Derek was sucking at his bong like an asthma patient taking bottled oxygen. On TV a suspected arsonist was being taken into police custody, a towel draped over his head as the cops held back an angry crowd who bayed at the man like starving animals. All that pain, so ugly to see.

'Don't you get sick of watching that stuff?' Penny asked. Derek, busy packing a cone, didn't reply. The furniture was placed at awkward angles; she had to step around the couch to reach the front door. 'I'm going for a walk. Have a good night,' she said, not bothering to hide her sarcasm.

Penny set out for the field by the airport, where you could lie back and watch the planes, pale bird-bellies exposed as they rose or sank towards their destinations. Two months after moving here she was virtually friendless. Derek, obviously, didn't fit the bill. Miranda, the chatty girl she'd shared shifts with at work, had not returned her last two text messages, but maybe she was busy or had lost her phone. Penny crossed the bridge over the aqueduct, a dry concrete avenue with a channel running down its middle, a strip of black water at the bottom, and slipped through the wires of an old farm fence. She followed the faint track, her way lit by the eerie glow coming off the airport, and settled into the grass beneath the southern flight path.

A big jumbo lumbered over the tarmac to the runway entrance, then squatted under the lights as if gathering up courage. It rolled towards her, gathering speed, but lift-off always looked impossible from here — the runway inadequate, the machine too slow and heavy. The engine screamed as the spindly front wheels left the ground, then the heavy back end rose up too, and the huge beast heaved itself clear and tore right over the top of her. Its stomach slid past, white and vulnerable, and the landing gear folded in like little claws. She watched the plane climb steeply into the night sky and wink away until it was no longer visible.

When she reached into her bag to roll a smoke, there it was, wrapped in a scrap of velvet. Carefully she held the gun aloft, keeping her fingers well clear of the trigger. Its blue-black metal gleamed in the airport lights as she weighed the heft and menace of the thing. She'd searched the online news for recent crimes in the area: a knifing weeks ago, a local bottle shop knocked over, and a string of 7-Eleven burglaries by a druggie with a bloody syringe — all unsolved and no mention of a gun, abandoned or otherwise. She'd read up on the model: the bullet calibre and firing pin, its double-action mechanism, the spring buried deep within the handle. The cylinder contained six chambers where you loaded the bullets; when the gun fired, one bullet shot out, the cylinder spun, and the next one was right there, ready to go.

How would it feel to point a loaded gun right at someone, someone who had it coming? Once she held it in her hands the thought came unbidden: you couldn't help wondering. Couldn't help imagining the look on their face, the fear dawning as the situation switched and they lost their hold: Greg's smirk fading, those assholes who'd taunted her falling silent, backing away. Her stepdad losing the upper hand for once, his gaze wavering, palms held out all helpless, saying, *No, don't* ... Yes, she thought, a cold kind of pleasure blooming inside her: she had some idea how it would feel.

At home Derek was watching a documentary on terrorism. He nodded hi, so Penny flopped down on an armchair. The credits rolled over shots of bombed-out buildings and military checkpoints.

'Full on,' observed Derek.

Penny looked around the lounge room, at the slow-spinning fan, the mismatched furniture set at odd angles, the boxes piled in one corner. On the way home she'd texted the girl from work again, Miranda, but no reply.

'Let's rearrange the furniture,' she said suddenly. 'Sort out the feng shui in here.'

Derek peered at her. 'I dunno. I was planning on taking it easy tonight.'

But now she could see it, the difference it would make. She was on her feet, making brisk suggestions; bossier than usual, halfway between insistent and cajoling.

The TV was showing a documentary about voles. 'All right.' Derek sighed. 'Just don't smash the bong, that's all I need.'

Two days passed in a blur of heat. Penny left her CV at a couple of cafés and registered for the dole. There'd been a long wait before her number was called. The woman behind the desk asked questions and noisily banged Penny's replies into her computer.

'What was the reason for leaving your last job?'

'It wasn't really a proper job,' Penny said, 'just shifts here and there. They've got none at the moment.'

The woman looked up. 'They just stopped calling?'

Penny nodded, and the keyboard clattered for what seemed like a long time.

Her mum had emailed: the cat had had a lump removed from his ear, someone had set a car on fire down the street, and she hoped Penny was making friends at university. No mention of her stepdad. Miranda still hadn't replied to any of her texts. Fuck her, thought Penny. Stupid cow had probably dobbed her in about that face cream — one measly jar. You couldn't trust anyone.

In the hot afternoons she stayed in her room, parked by the fan in her underwear, reading up about ballistics. *Go confidently in the direction of your dreams*, one fortune cookie had instructed. But her dreams all starred that aimless train, stuck on its circular route to nowhere. And sometimes that other dream came: the one where she lay wide awake, motionless, feigning sleep as she watched the silent shape of a man standing at the foot of her bed. Her dreams had nothing good to say.

Now after dark she'd go out walking. 'Later,' she called to Derek as she left that evening. She kept a quick pace on these night walks, as if it wasn't just wandering around, as if she knew exactly where she was going. The air was still sweet with woodsmoke, and the day's heat radiated up off the footpaths, sending hot swirls around her bare legs. The streets were empty and TVs flickered through windows as she crossed the road to cut through the park. It was a decent-sized park, about five minutes' walk from one side to the other. She was less than halfway across when she heard the footsteps.

The man was behind her and gaining steadily. He made no effort to lighten his step; it sounded as if he was wearing heavy boots, like the ones tradies wear. She could just make out the path ahead, hemmed in with tall shrubs and stretching into blackness. Walking faster would do no good; she was still a long way from the far side. She had two choices: run, or turn around to face him. She slid her hand into her bag and felt her fingers slot neatly into the gun's handgrip. As she turned she heard him speak: 'Hey. You got a light?'

He stopped a couple of metres away. Penny could not see much, but the man's outline looked tall and heavyset; she could hear him breathing. She kept her voice level. 'No,' she said, 'and you better just keep walking.'

It wasn't until he laughed, a dry noise with no humour in it, that she took the gun from her bag and held it low against her leg.

'You were the one *just walking*,' said the man in a pleasant voice. 'Now you've stopped, so I'm asking if you got a light.'

She thought fast: should she pull back the hammer, or

was the first shot primed to go if you squeezed the trigger hard? She couldn't remember. 'No, I've quit,' was all she could think to say.

'What you doing out here by yourself?' he asked, and this time he made no effort to sound friendly.

She had no idea where the words came from: 'I'm looking for assholes. Are you an asshole?' The gun was raised now, pointed at his middle.

The man didn't answer at first, just hovered there. 'What's that you got?' His outline shifted, craning a little closer. 'What is that?'

Then he backed off and she could just make out his hands, lifted up in front of him. 'I just wanted a light,' he said. 'You need to fucking relax.'

Penny tried to keep her voice strong. 'Go away. Just go, right now.'

He stood there a moment, then his footsteps began retreating. 'Crazy fucken bitch,' she heard him call back.

Penny listened until there was nothing but the high screech of cicadas and her own shallow breathing. Then she turned and ran, her heart slamming in her chest and the tears already coming, blurring the lights from the highway on the far side of the trees.

Out under the flight path she lay in the grass and tried to slow her breath. She had been lucky, she reasoned; if she hadn't had the gun, if she hadn't thought so quickly on the spot, it could have happened to her all over again. But she knew it was not quite that simple, because without the gun she'd never have cut through the park at night in the first place. The thing that had saved her … it was the same thing that had led her to take the risk. And what if she'd pulled the trigger and shot him, right there in the dark? How would that really feel, afterwards?

One split-second decision, one chance encounter, and your whole life could switch course, events tumbling on uncontrollably like those rows of falling dominoes. You can't reverse things: once the bullet drops into the chamber it's too late.

In the sky a plane was circling, coming in to land on her runway. She cradled the gun against her stomach and tuned in to the approaching roar.

Next morning Derek was watching the bushfire coverage again, a satellite image showing a cloud of smoke so vast it was visible from space.

'Can't we watch something else? This is depressing,' said Penny.

'There's a cool change coming through,' he said. 'I wanna see what happens.'

In the kitchen she snapped open a fortune cookie: *Something you lost will soon turn up.* She was thinking this over, trying to recall all the stuff she'd misplaced over the years, when the TV noise cut off abruptly and she heard Derek speaking on the phone. Something in his voice, an anxious note, brought her back into the lounge room.

'So they got out?' Derek was asking. 'They're safe, they're going to be okay?' He let out a long breath, nodding. On the silent screen a journalist was standing by a charred letterbox, its metal face partly melted.

Penny waited until he'd hung up. 'Everything all right?'

'Cousins. My mum's sister. Probably lose the house, but everyone got out in time.'

She wasn't sure what to say. He'd never told her he had family up in the hills; but then again, she'd never asked. She felt a faint sense of shame. How would it feel, sitting there watching the fire devour whole towns, knowing someone you cared about was in its path? She got two icy poles from the freezer and offered one to Derek. 'Thanks,' he said.

It was mid morning when Penny left the house. The sun leaked across the sky like something bleeding, and in the amber light her shadow on the footpath took on a strange terracotta hue. She walked out to the bridge over the aqueduct. For a while she stood there in the heat, watching the planes take off and rise up into the hazy air, get smaller and eventually vanish.

She took the gun from her bag. Down below, in the centre of the aqueduct, ran the thin channel with its dark streak of water. She opened the cylinder and positioned herself carefully. One by one, she took all six bullets from their chambers and dropped them into the water, which swallowed them with barely a sound. Then she placed the gun on the ledge of the aqueduct and walked away: not slow, not fast, just heading home.

Leaving the Fountainhead

ZANE LOVITT

The rain has kept people away. I'm planted on a stool at the end of the bar and I'm halfway drunk on bourbon that burns in my lungs and in my throat, but it's cheap and this place is across the street from my office, so checkmate. For all the days and nights I've worked out of that office, I must have come here to the Fountainhead Hotel on only a half-dozen occasions. It's always so peopled. I'm usually peopled enough.

But tonight the rain has kept them away. The stools stand empty, and the bartender has nothing to do but polish glasses, slowly, taking pride. Most nights there'd be seven or eight men seated here, lungs burning, flushing the day away. Tonight it's just me.

Way off in the lounge there's a couple of kids, barely old enough to drink, talking in hushed voices, ignoring their beers. Breaking up maybe. Or getting back together.

But that's it. I've been easing into the quiet for about half an hour, keeping my weight on the points of my elbows, looking up only to watch the water cascade down the front windows like there's an actual fountain on the roof of this place, true to its name.

I'm doing this, watching the water, when the barman speaks.

I say, 'What?'

Tiny pineapples and bananas decorate his shirt, which is easily the happiest thing in the room. The pores on his big friendly nose look like they've been drawn on, and his big friendly face smiles at me with an openness that must earn him a nice tip from anyone who comes in here alone and lonely. He's got the kind of moustache you don't see much anymore, and beneath it there's a smugness, like he's immune to what affects his moping clients and what's more he knows it. Or just thinks it. Or maybe I just think it. I can't read people the way I used to.

He says again, louder, 'Why the long face?'

And I force a grin. Bartender humour.

He snorts pleasantly, puts the glass he's been wiping on the shelf behind him, draws another from the dishwasher.

'You okay, bloke?' he asks, polishing again.

'I'm fine.'

'You don't look fine.' With an elegant swoop of his arm he pours a shot of bourbon into that same tumbler and puts it on the mat in front of me.

'This one's on the house.'

It's a throaty voice, comforting, like a lawnmower when it finally starts. I don't say, 'Thanks.' I say, 'Thank you.'

His shoulders push back against my gratitude. 'I can tell when someone's having a bad day.'

I neck the bourbon I've already started and clutch at the new drink, feel the glass still warm from the dishwasher, just as friendly as the man who poured it. It makes me turn back to the window, the rain outside.

He follows my gaze. 'It's a wet one, hey.'

'Yeah.'

'My word,' he says. 'What do you do, bloke?'

I look back at my glass. 'I'm a delivery boy.'

'What do you deliver?'

'Legal papers, mostly. Financial records.'

'You enjoy it?'

Maybe the answer is inside my drink somewhere. I peer in. 'I don't think so.'

'Yeah …' He pulls another glass from the dishwasher and says, 'What are you going to do?' Only it's rhetorical, so it comes out: 'Waddayagunnadoo.' And I'm hoping this is his way of ending the conversation.

But then he shelves that glass and says, 'Where you from?'

'You're used to a lot of people sitting here, talking to you … right?'

'My word.'

The way he keeps saying that, it's like his catchphrase. He delivers it with stern conviction.

I say, 'Well, I guess I don't really feel like talking.'

The bartender nods, arches his mouth like a Chinese businessman agreeing on a price, turns his big round body away to the stack of ashtrays behind him and puts one on top with just enough delicacy to give me a rush of guilt.

I say, 'But thanks for the drink …'

He goes back to the dishwasher, pulls out another glass without looking at me, and I sigh at the awkwardness. There's a distant rumble of thunder. Beyond the window, headlights and neon signs flash at each other, and I don't want to go out there, so I figure it's good when a silhouette crosses the window and comes into the bar, ringing the bell above the door, splashing water from his umbrella onto the linoleum and giving the bartender something to think about apart from how I'm a jerk.

But seeing who it is gives me something to think about too.

Our contact was so brief and so long ago that he won't recognise me, which I'm thankful for. I almost didn't recognise him in that well-cut suit and those polished black shoes, his grey beard and hair trimmed to imply someone corporate. The last time I saw him he didn't imply someone *bathed*. As he approaches the bar, glancing at me with those fat black eyes and looking around the place to see how empty it is, I'm thinking this is like his face has been cut-and-pasted onto the body of an effeminate city executive, complete with a strawberry red umbrella. Also, I'm thinking he could reinvent himself as an air hostess and anyone in Melbourne who isn't brain-damaged would still recognise Kevin Tomlinson.

But then the bartender says, 'What can I do you for?' with that same good-natured smile and there's no hesitation in his voice or eyes. So what do I know.

'I'm looking for the Boatswain's Club,' says Tomlinson. 'Isn't it around here?'

The bartender scratches his nose. 'The what, sorry?'

'The Boatswain's Club. Do you know where it is?' It's a voice like he was raised by foghorns.

'My word,' says the bartender. 'You're on foot, are you?'

'Yes.'

'No problem.' He points emphatically, stretching his hand as far back and away from his body as it will go and waving a finger out there. 'You go six blocks along Russell Street until you hit Victoria Road. You go two streets west along that until you come to Locust Street, where you take a right. It's a laneway, really. Go all the way to the end. The Boatswain's Club is on the corner there, next to the Parkway-Spruce Hotel.'

Tomlinson squints. His eyes twitch, one at a time.

'So … six blocks along Russell, left onto Victoria, right onto Locust.'

'It's a popular place. You can't miss it.'

'All right. Thank you.'

'No probs, bloke.'

The exchange is over in all of thirty seconds, then the bell above the door rings again and Tomlinson is gone. Back into the rain. I watch his umbrella open and float away past the window.

Then I look to the bartender, waiting for him to look back.

When he does, he misinterprets my face. 'You want another?'

'Why did …' I'm about to ask the obvious question, but then I don't. Instead, I say, 'Sure.'

He pours me another. There's silence while he does it. Then he goes back to drying the glasses from the dishwasher.

In that rain, walking that distance, it'll take Tomlinson about twenty-one, twenty-two minutes to get where he's going. The bartender, he's not doing these calculations. Even as I watch him, serenely shelving mugs, he might already have forgotten about the stranger who just came and went, carrying a red umbrella.

I ask, 'Do you know who that was?'

'Who? That bloke?'

'Yeah.'

'Is he famous?'

'Kevin Tomlinson?'

He doesn't recognise the name either.

'Spac Attack Tomlinson?' I offer.

This time he scowls and his gaze drifts past my ears. 'Sounds familiar,' he says. 'What's he famous for?'

'He's a psychopath.'

'You mean, like, he's a footy player?'

'No, he's a real-life psychopath. And a thief.' I take a sip, glance back to the door. 'And it looks as though he's doing well for himself.'

The bartender slows the polishing of the glass, comes almost to a stop. His eyes search the floor. After two seconds of thinking, he snaps out of it, looks back at me.

I say, 'He stabbed his home-economics teacher in high school, spent five years in a youth prison, got out and made a career robbing houses, and somewhere along the way he blowtorched his own nipples off. He's got a tattoo on his left arm that says *Rebecca*. He's also got Hepatitis C, mild narcolepsy and once he won twenty-seven thousand dollars on a horse named Rent Arrears …'

I drink. The bartender doesn't move.

'… which is what it says on his right arm.' The bourbon roars in my throat.

'How come you know so much about him?'

'I used to know this kind of stuff for a living.'

'Were you a cop?'

'Not really. I worked privately. The first client I ever had was someone Tomlinson robbed. At least, the police said it was Tomlinson. We never found out for sure. This was a long time ago.' I laugh to myself, feel the passage of time right in my stomach the way a boat feels rust.

The bartender keeps polishing, pretending he isn't worried about what's just happened. I'll let him pretend for a while.

'They invited me along to a raid on Tomlinson's flat. I was supposed to identify a stereo and TV belonging to my client. But I never got to do that.'

I expect stealth, but they just walk up to the door and knock. It's about as *not* like the movies as it can be. Seven uniforms plod along the second-storey catwalk, one of them's even whistling, and when they get to his door they knock politely and wait, in the midday sun, for it to open.

I'm at the back of the group, hanging so far behind you'd think I lived in this block of flats and I was just curious. The raiding party eye me with indifference. Some of them smirk at the distance I'm keeping, some of them don't try to hide that they're smirking. Some of them, I can tell by the way they chew their gum, are freaking out just the same as me.

We all know whose home this is.

The door opens, and it's a woman, her hair pulled back tight, and there's lots of green shadow around her eyes. It's obvious she hadn't bothered looking through the peephole because she makes a face when she sees who's out here.

'Oh, *fuck off*.'

The senior constable at the head of the group, the name on his pin reads Gant. He offers her a folded sheet of paper and says, 'Becky, we've got a warrant to search this flat. Is Spacca at home?'

'No, he's not here,' she says back, louder than she needs to.

'You're going to have to let us in.'

Already other officers have their hands on the door, ready to push it open.

Her lower jaw is stuck out in thought, like she's actually wondering whether to take on these men hand-to-hand. It's a perfect, fraught moment. Then she rolls her eyes, drops her hand from the door and disappears.

The uniforms pour into the flat. As I creep towards the doorway I take a final look around to make sure Kevin Tomlinson isn't coming up behind me with an axe. This catwalk is one side of a courtyard, and the doors and windows of the other three sides are peppered with faces, craning at doorways, peeking through half-drawn curtains. They've come out to see the cops finally catch up with the madman who lives next door.

It's a dim, barely furnished place and I'm at the entrance to a short corridor. At the other end, Tomlinson is sitting on a torn-up couch, drawing on a water pipe. Two officers approach and he draws harder, sucking back as much smoke as he can before they reach him. When they do, and when they wrench the bong from his grasp, he exhales up into their faces. The big bad wolf blowing down a house.

I stay right here at the door.

I don't know what makes me look over, but when I do I see that the couple in the far corner of the lounge are kissing. They can't hear what I'm saying. They're caught up in their own story.

'So what happened then?' the bartender asks, watching me. He's still drying that same glass.

'Well,' I say, scratching my head, 'what happened then I had to piece together after the fact. I saw it, but I couldn't hear it. I only found out later what was actually said. And it got recounted at the trial. But I don't know if what was said really matters in the end.'

'So ... he went on trial?'

'Yep.'

'But you said they didn't find the stolen stuff.'

'They didn't,' I say, sipping frugally from my glass. I look up at the ornate wooden clock above the bar. Beside it there are two bottles of Old Forester. One of them is half empty, the other unopened. A bottle like that, he and I could get to be good friends.

'There was nothing there. And I mean, apart from a few of Tomlinson's things, the place was outright empty. There was a quarter ounce of marijuana on the coffee table but, as it turns out, Tomlinson didn't go on trial for that either.'

It's been three minutes since he left the Fountainhead.

Senior Constable Gant, he's trying to hide his disappointment, angling the bowl one way, then the other, like it contains an unimpressive stool sample. Around him the other uniforms would be turning the place upside down if there was anything here to do that to. They wander aimlessly, checking behind furniture and under loose flaps of carpet, trying to seem busy.

'It's a hell of a parole violation, Spacca.'

'Big whoops.' Tomlinson is still on the couch, his eyes stained red with the drug. He wears a flimsy tattered singlet showing the words on his arms. His shorts are shiny green and gold, crowning skinny, impossibly hairy legs. The choppy fuzz that grows out of his face is caked with food and it's wet from who knows what. Becky sits next to him, marginally more clothed, eyes still green.

She says, 'It's not his mull, it's mine.'

'No kidding.' Gant is barely listening. He puts the bowl back on the table.

'Yep,' says Becky.

'Yep,' says Tomlinson, grinning.

Becky adds, 'I bought it and I own it, which makes it mine, right?' She knows the script.

'I'll go down for less than a month if it's not my gear,' Tomlinson taunts.

Gant sighs. 'It's on your coffee table in your flat and you're smoking it, Spacca, so we'll just see …'

He catches the eyes of several other uniforms, who shake their heads, shrug. They've found nothing.

'All right,' he grunts, waving at one of the officers, then

pointing to the pair on the couch. 'Get them out of here. Everyone else, five more minutes.'

The officer who strides to the couch, he's got black hair and a crooked nose and he's the one who was whistling on the way to Tomlinson's door. Fast as he can he's got his handcuffs out. He gestures at Tomlinson and says, 'Up.'

Tomlinson stands, achingly slowly, still grinning at Gant. Not even looking at the cop with the black hair though they're face to face. The name on the officer's pin is *Correll*, and he's handcuffing Tomlinson, hands in front.

What makes Tomlinson look at Correll is Correll whispering, 'A month is long enough to make a special friend inside, isn't it, Spacca?'

No one else hears it. Not Spacca's girlfriend, not Senior Constable Gant who's turning away now, looking mournfully at his watch. Not me, standing at the door, trying to keep hidden from even the police because I'm just a reminder of what they've failed to find.

Tomlinson stops grinning. He blinks twice and his eyes go dead. Correll stares back into those eyes and says, 'I've heard that's what you're into.'

None of us hear that either.

But Tomlinson does.

His face spasms, like those uninhibited moments right before you belch. His lips and eyes squeeze shut and his head jerks back and forth in tiny chicken pecks. But all his preparation is over in an instant and he lunges forward, not at Correll but at a sandy-haired giant who isn't looking when Tomlinson rips his name pin from his breast and wheels it into Correll's left eye.

He might be handcuffed, but Tomlinson stabs Correll twice in that eye and once in the nose before anyone turns to look.

Correll screams and Becky screams, but over the two of them Tomlinson screams the loudest, a throaty cackle with the psychopath right there inside it. The giant and Gant grab hold of him but he stabs Correll two or three times in the other eye before they get control of the arm holding the pin and blood is spouting like spring water from Correll's face but he's not making any noise now because the shock has overwhelmed him and he hits the floor and Tomlinson's trying to get down there to hurt him some more but six uniforms are holding him up and Gant has got Tomlinson's hair and everyone's shouting for an ambulance or for help and Becky's shouting that they're all bastards.

The way Gant pulls on Tomlinson's hair, Tomlinson's face is angled at me. Amid the storm of struggling and shouting, his body tense with fight, Tomlinson locks eyes with me, this little person all the way over here. For a moment.

Me, who's not a cop, who's peeking around the door from outside the flat.

Me and my boggle-eyes. Me with my myth of Kevin Tomlinson that's been proved violently true.

And he smiles at me, hungry and joyous, like he knows everything that's going to happen to me from this day on. And it tickles him.

'Jesus,' says the bartender, softly. 'How was the cop?'

'Blind. And apparently he went a little nuts. I suppose you would.'

'My word,' he says, distracted. He's been polishing that glass right through my story. But not because I'm a good storyteller.

'Didn't this Tomlinson bloke go to jail?'

'Sure. He got eight years. But this all happened a long time ago. He's back out again.'

It's been eleven minutes since Tomlinson left the Fountainhead. He'd have reached Victoria Road by now.

'A lot of criminals act like they're crazy,' I say, getting ready to ask the obvious question. Properly this time. 'Then it turns out they're just ordinary people, only they want you to *think* they're crazy. But Spac Attack Tomlinson is the real deal. A genuine maniac.'

The bartender's wrinkled brow furrows.

I watch him now, with his big happy shirt and his big friendly nose. This big man with his big pores, he's wiping the same glass like he'll get three wishes if he just does that for long enough. I bet I know what one of those wishes would be.

I say, 'So?' And rest my face on my hand, propped on the bar.

He looks up from the floor, glares back. 'What?'

I have to raise my head from my hand to speak. 'Why did you give him the wrong directions to the Boatswain's Club?'

'Hey?'

'You sent him to the Blue Fandango.'

'No.' He shakes his head urgently, laughs. 'I didn't.'

'The Boatswain's Club is on Piermont Avenue, not Locust Street.'

He laughs again, shakes his head. Shrugs, shakes his head again, shrugs again. 'That's what I told him. I told him Piermont —'

'You sent him to the Blue Fandango. A bondage club. A bondage club that's got a sign right there on the street that says: *No Women, No Straight Men*.'

'No …'

'All right,' I grunt. My elbow slumps off the bar. 'But when Tomlinson comes back and stabs you in the neck with that umbrella of his, don't go telling me *then* you didn't —'

'I used to work at the Boatswain's Club,' he blurts, gripping the wooden edge of the counter, staring at it.

That cuts my annoyance short. I sit up.

He's finally stopped polishing that clean clean glass. He says, 'It's one of those pretentious joints, right?' His voice has lost that friendly, lawnmower tone. 'Like when you buy a pack of cigarettes and the bartender opens them for you and pulls one out of the pack. I was always crap at sucking up to patrons … I hated it. And they sacked me. Some teenager with big boobs got my job and now I'm stuck pouring drinks in this shithole.'

A car horn bleats right outside and a shrill voice responds, '*Fuck off.*'

The bartender doesn't seem to hear them. He says, 'People come in here all the time looking for the Boatswain's Club, but I send them to that faggot bar instead because … Just to get my own back, you know?'

His words hang there, glued to the air around us.

He says, 'I guess you think I'm a bloody idiot.'

'My word,' I say.

I take another sip, then another small one, and I shake my head, try to change gear.

'It's no big deal. He'll get lost in the rain. Someone will give him directions. He'll find his way to the Boatswain's Club.'

The bartender nods, trying to believe it. His tongue works back and forth across his bottom lip, seeking reassurance. He says, 'Maybe he isn't that crazy anymore.'

'Maybe not.'

He waves the glass in the air as he speaks. 'Maybe prison sorted him out. Maybe he got treatment. He looked good, yeah? Well dressed. Maybe he's a normal person now.'

'Sure,' I say.

'Like you said, all that … that stuff …' And he points at me. 'That was a long time ago, right?'

But even as he speaks, his eyes skip over to the door, wondering if it's about to open.

I say, 'A long time ago. Yes.'

He nods, satisfied, then turns to shelve that glass with the rest. He reaches it up to the wooden mantel above the register.

The girl over in the dining area laughs, a shrill giggle that's not too loud — but it's enough to make the bartender flinch.

He drops the glass. It smashes on the floor.

For a moment he doesn't move, like he's paralysed while standing. Then he lowers his hands to his knees and he stays like that for several moments.

The rain isn't getting any lighter. If anything it's more intense. The noise of the street is like a meteor approaching.

I finish the last of my drink. 'I can go find him for you.'

At first he doesn't respond, still bent over like there's something on the floor that's more interesting.

Then, softly, he says, 'Really?'

'Yes.'

'What will you do if you find him?'

'Spin him a line. Get him to the Boatswain's Club. Make sure he forgets all about you.'

Slowly, he straightens up and rests himself on the bar. 'You can do that?'

Not being able to hadn't occurred to me. I say, 'Yeah.'

'You'd do that for me?'

I try not to smirk. 'I'll do it for that bottle of Old Forester up there on your top shelf.' I point.

He turns to look. When he turns back he's thinking. 'Will you get to him in time?'

I say, 'He's probably on his way back here right now. But he shouldn't be hard to find.'

The bartender tries to see through to my deeper layers. 'How do I know you'll really do it? How do I know you won't just take the bottle and go home?'

I lean forward on the bar. 'I've got a better one. How do you know the story I told you is even true? Perhaps I made it up to shake a bottle of whiskey out of you and I've never seen that guy before and I don't even know his name.'

'Is that what this is? Are you having me on?'

'Nope.'

He sifts through it all in his head — the clock, the Old Forester on the shelf, the half-drunk stranger who, as it turns out, isn't the one having the bad day. Then the tension evaporates, and there's nothing in his eyes but cool acceptance.

He goes back to the shelf and, tiptoeing briefly, brings down a bottle of Old Forester whiskey. I'm trying to show him my disapproval, but again he can't interpret it, so I tell him, 'The sealed bottle.'

I can imagine he wouldn't last long at the Boatswain's Club. He's a man who doesn't like to be at a disadvantage. Now, as he swaps the half-empty bottle for the full one, he exhales, gentle and long, like I'm testing his patience. Like this is the last favour he does for me, and I should quit asking.

Before he offers me the bottle he says, 'You *are* going to find him, right?'

The bell rings, and the fear is back in his face. He squints at the door like it's a horde of Indians come to ransack the camp. But it's two businessmen fresh from the office, dripping wet. They trot to the counter, and one of them says, 'Two Johnnies, rocks.'

I yank the bottle from the bartender's grip, don't say anything. I feel his eyes on my back as I reach the door.

Tomlinson's red umbrella should stand out well enough.

The man says, 'Hey barman, two Johnnies, on the rocks, please.'

As I step out into the rain I hear him say, 'Hey barman, why the long face?'

And I hear the two men laugh.

Louis

CLAIRE AMAN

It's six forty-five in the morning. I ignore the police car outside my house and turn instead to the cage where Squizzy the cockatoo lives. Rain splashes on my hands. Carefully, tenderly, I feed the banana through the wire. Squizzy grabs it in his drab beak. Fast, I push six muesli bars through and they drop to the floor.

It's not strictly speaking a cage. It's a galvanised iron lean-to, about as tall as a phone box but narrower than a wheelie bin, with chook-wire from waist-high up. My son is in there, hunched down in the dark with his knees around his ears. The cops will never find him: I am his mother and wilier than them. If it would just stop raining I'd be able to think straight. But as the water trickles down the back of my neck, all I can do is wonder who'll look after our children when we're gone.

The silver Commodore was there when I woke up. I'm absolutely certain it's an unmarked cop car. In this drizzle I can't see how many detectives are sitting in it. My house is on a corner block. There's just a wire fence all the way around because my scab of a landlord won't build a proper fence. This means that from where the cops are parked, they can see not only my front and back gates but also everything in my backyard — my clothesline, the lillypilly tree, the dead washing machine and Squizzy's cage. Brilliant.

My boy pokes his head out from under an old bird-pellet bag. I whisper that the cops are outside but not to worry. I fill Squizzy's water dish with the hose, and my son holds up his water bottle. I overdo it and spill some water on him. He doesn't say anything but his mouth turns down like a sad beak. None of this is easy.

I go back inside and ring work. I say I have a migraine. It's close to the truth. We're stuck: my son in the cage, the cops in the car, and me in the kitchen listening to Elvis and chewing on my fingernails. To make matters worse, it's been raining for five days, rain's forecast for the rest of the week and it looks like we'll get a flood. I have a lot to worry about.

I'm not saying I've never broken the law, but I've never had anything much to do with the police. Apart from speeding tickets, I've always managed to stay out of trouble. I thought my son had too, until last night.

He gave me the fright of my life when he turned up sopping wet at my bedroom door at three a.m. I was so relieved it was only him that I burst out laughing. But he didn't laugh back; he just stood there hugging this green backpack and looking spooked, so I jumped up, hauled him into the bedroom and shut the door.

He plonked down on my bed, hung his head and dangled his hands, and he told me he didn't do anything, said it wasn't him. Then he said the cops might be looking for him. What does that mean, I asked, and he said he'd need to hide for a while because of the backpack. Then he dived under my bed, the great galoot, backpack and all, with his boots sticking out the end.

I grabbed his foot and dragged him out. I told him that's the first place they'd look, stupid. What's going on, I asked him. He just lolled back on the floor looking up at me all pale around the gills, waiting for me to do something. My poor son with his shining blue eyes, silly fool with the cops looking for him, a fool jumping under his mother's bed. I thought he'd been going alright in Coffs Harbour. That's what he'd been telling me for the three months since he'd left home.

Show me the backpack, I said, and he pulled it away. He said the dude next door gave it to him to look after. What dude? I said. Mick. Mick who? Dunno. Mick said he'd give him three hundred bucks to keep it safe. What's in there? I asked, and he said just a bit of gear. I know what gear is.

I grabbed the thing and pulled down the zip. Surprise, it was chock full of dope, all bagged up in Glad bags. He told me he saw the cops take Mick away last night, and he got scared when they returned later and drove up and down the street. He thought Mick must have dobbed him in. So he jumped over the rear fence with the backpack and ran. Ran off to Grafton to see his mum.

Well. Why would he think I'd know what to do? I asked him where his car was, and he told me he'd caught the train, pleased with himself for this strategic thinking. Pity he hadn't been strategic to begin with. Pity he's so hopeless. He watched me thinking this. It made me feel like crying, and I held his big sad body close and hammered at him with my fists, and he held me tight. He'd grown a billygoat beard since I last saw him. I gave it a little tug. He pushed me off and told me again he never did nothing.

I told him those bags were going down the toilet now, and he said no Mum, and I said yes, and I took hold of the backpack, but he snatched it away and headed for the front door. I'm fine, he said. You don't have to worry.

Okay, I said, come here. There wasn't enough time for all that. We went into the kitchen, and I gave him leftover spaghetti bol and eight slices of bread and butter. While he was eating I checked outside for unfamiliar cars. I made him change into a pair of my black trackie pants and my big black jumper. Then I gave him a blanket off my bed and a bottle of water, and I led him out to the backyard and unlatched Squizzy's cage, and he squeezed inside with the pack. Squizzy didn't mind.

It was the only place I could think of where they wouldn't get my boy or the backpack. Squizzy's a psychopath when it comes to other people. He would have shredded anyone else. Then I went back to bed. I must have gone to sleep in the end, because I didn't hear the cop car pull up.

Now it's seven-thirty a.m. and I'm still waiting for the knock on the door. I don't know why they're taking their time. One night on *The Bill* they were parked outside a house waiting for a drug dealer to come home. Maybe these ones here are waiting for back-up. Or they need the okay for a search warrant. They want to go strictly by the book. This is serious.

I pour my third cup of coffee. The rain's a tapping patter. I didn't get enough sleep. I should be at Caroona Villa now settling the oldies for breakfast, not this. Elvis is singing 'Kentucky Rain'. It's a forlorn song, and the little trembles of piano sound like raindrops. I wonder if they have cameras at Coffs Station. Watched my boy get on the one forty-five a.m. train to Grafton. I should have driven him out to the state forest last night and left him there with a tent. Too late now. At least I can keep an eye on him here.

It's just a matter of time before the cops get the okay for the search warrant. My son must be very uncomfortable by now. He might not be Einstein and he might not even be innocent, but he wins the prize for sheer fortitude. That cage is far too small for an adult. That's the beauty of it.

I go into his old bedroom and find his wet t-shirt on the floor where he dropped it last night. My heart thuds into my stomach. If the cops found it they'd be like a cat with a mouse. You're not keeping up with your housework if you haven't seen your boy for three months, Mrs Gargan. Still finding his dirty clothes lying around? Well, no, I'd say. It's mine. My Big Day Out shirt. And it's Ms Gargan. Mzz.

I press the shirt to my face and inhale the sweet reek of my son. I know that in his numbskull brain he thinks all this is worth three hundred bucks. Through the venetians I see they're still out there with the water streaming down their windscreen. It's a cop car for sure. No one in this street would have a car like that. I poke the shirt behind my wardrobe.

Would you hide your child from the law? If you thought it would help? I have a hot shower and put my pink dressing-gown back on. The car's still there. I wait for them to come splashing up the path. They'll never get anything out of me.

Louis

I'll pull a shawl over my head and slip on big spectacles and act like a poor old gran, don't know anything. Sit up in bed in my nightie clutching at my heart. I'm a crafty old thing, cunning as a wolf's mother. Too clever for them.

There's a trick to everything. I left school at fifteen but I'm no mental slouch. I'm a person who likes to have a plan. I'm trying my best here.

If they show up at the door I'll be okay. I'd let them in, lounge room, sit down nice and calm. Discuss the rain. The cops'd be on the sofa, me sitting up in my chair looking concerned. Oh, really? I'm sure it's a mistake. They'd ask if I knew where he was. Your son, able to assist us in our inquiries. Maybe he's here, one of them might say. Could have reason to believe, and they'd stare at me, but I'd keep steady. I'd stare right back. I hope he's not in any trouble, I'd say.

I'm a steamroller baby, sings Elvis, *roll all over you.* The rain changes pitch.

Whatever happened to my laughing blue-eyed boy?

The bastards are playing mind games with me. Why don't they just come in? When they do, I'll ask them to hand over the search warrant and I'll have a good read. That'll stall them. I suppose they'll search the house first. Then they'll go marauding about in my backyard. Squizzy would scream blue murder if they go anywhere near his cage. But they might shine a torch into the cage and see my son's ginger hair down there, all mussed up like a nest.

What if I had a gun? I wonder if I'd shoot them. Kapow. A bucket of trouble. I wouldn't know what to do with a gun anyway. It'd probably go off in my face.

A black Falcon with an outsize spoiler fishtails on the wet road and skids around the corner, straight past the cops. They don't bother with him. This town is full of hair-trigger boys with hot cars.

Our street is filling with water. The low spots are joining up and turning into small lakes. I'm sure the river's going to pop its banks. We haven't had a flood for years. It'd be just my luck to get one now. I get out of my dressing-gown and put on my jeans. It's ten to eight.

I knew something bad would happen ever since last Monday morning when I found a little silver baitfish lying on the Grafton Bridge. The dead eye stared up as if to say this is the world: this is how it goes for a small fish. And further on, a baby's sock lying there. Dead fish, baby sock. My son's a Pisces. Think about it. I'm not superstitious, but there are some omens you can't ignore.

Under the bridge is a footway with a steel deck and chain-wire sides. You can walk over to South Grafton in three minutes with the cars and trucks rumbling above you. There's a good view over the river, but most people don't like to go there, especially at night.

One thing I have always protected my son from is this: I conceived him on the footway under the Grafton Bridge.

He's nineteen years old. That makes him three years older than the boy who fathered him up there. He doesn't know his mother was a drunken girl on the bridge, and he'll never find out either. I wonder how many girls still get pregnant on summer nights up against the chain wire, with the river below. The wire leaves red diamonds on your skin. Everyone looks down their nose at you. Deep down, there's only ever you and your kid.

These things pierce me about my boy. He never had much. At school they said he was impulsive. But he'd never harm anyone. Life is more complicated for some people. None of us are bad; some of us born at the wrong time or in the wrong place, but never bad. I haven't always been the best example but I'm glad I had my baby.

It's eight o'clock. I switch over to the radio again. It's weather on all stations and they're saying the Clarence River's at seven-point-five metres and rising. They're saying everyone who lives between the showgrounds and the river should evacuate. That's me. I go to the back veranda and look up. The sky's like a big weeping backdrop to my life.

Louis

Once was enough. Getting pregnant rattled me; I made sure I never got caught again. And anyway, I have a habit of getting into relationships with bastards. No one's been nice enough to be a dad. Dave, my last ex, said I should have thrown my boy out of the nest when he was born. What did you call him Louis for anyway, Dave asked me one day. No reason, I said. Louis the fly, I said. Joe Louis. Louis Armstrong. Louis waste of space, Dave said.

Someone's knocking at the front door. I bang my knee as I run to the window. But it's not a detective, it's a fireman. There's a fire engine outside. The fireman at the door tells me the levee's going to fail at nine o'clock this morning. Everyone has to leave. Didn't I listen to the radio? He tells me to go up the South Grafton hill to the high school. He asks if there's anyone else in the house. Any pets? He says to go now while there's still time. It'll be a big one.

I just stand there looking up and down the street. The fireman turns and goes splashing down my path. He sets off for my next door neighbour's place. He won't find anyone home there – they're in Brisbane for a wedding - but I don't bother calling out. My head's pounding. The rain's clattering out of the sky, and I can't understand how the world could have become so wet. Everyone's packing their cars and driving out of the street. I'm sick of Elvis, I'm sick of the rain, I'm sick of the cops, sick of all this. I have always protected my son through thick and thin. There's nothing I wouldn't do. Nothing is stronger than love. But who'll look after this clumsy boy when I'm gone?

I pack all my photos and some clothes in a suitcase. Then I sit down on the sofa. The street becomes quiet. Everyone's gone except the cops, me and my boy. None of us are giving up.

I make a plan.

I carry the suitcase out to my carport and get into the car. I shut the door loudly so the cops notice. In my glovebox is an isolation switch for the ignition. My son had his mate install it for me. Cars are always being stolen. When you press the isolation switch, the car won't start even if you hotwire the ignition. The engine will turn over but it won't start.

There's a trick to everything.

I push a fifty-dollar note and the spare car key into the glovebox and make sure the isolation switch is on. I turn the engine over a few times. Don't flatten the battery.

Out I get, slam the door, squelch over to the cop car. I'm going to ask if they know anything about Datsun Bluebirds. I rehearse as I go. Excuse me, I've got a problem. Car won't start. A lift, officer? Thank you so much. Trying to evacuate, cutting it fine. You're a lifesaver. That's what I'll say.

That's my plan. I'll start to get in the cop car, then I'll say, oh, but I need to let my cockatoo go. Let him take his chances, I'll say. I don't want him trapped in the cage if the river comes rolling down the street. Then I'll run back. I'll unlatch the cage and get Squizzy on my arm. They won't be able to see the cage door because it's around the other side, the house side. I'll pretend I'm talking to Squizzy but I'll be telling my son to wait until he hears the cop car drive away. I'll be telling him to take the Datsun, key's in the glovebox, don't forget the switch, go to your uncle Paul in Inverell. That's my plan. I realise it might not work but I don't have anything else.

Watch out, I'll say. Keep your eyes open. Make sure you always know what's happening around you.

My legs are like jelly by the time I reach the cop car, and I'm thinking it's not such a good plan at all. It's strange that the cop car has tinted windows. I tap on the glass. Nothing. When I go to the passenger side I see the window's broken. I try the door and it's unlocked. There are wires hanging from under the dashboard, and someone's left crushed-up potato chips all over the seat.

It's eight forty-five in the morning. I lean against the car, this abandoned car, and close my eyes. I don't know if I'm glad or monumentally shitted off. What I need now is a new plan.

Blackbirds Singing

KAREN HITCHCOCK

A man's cuffs should graze his heel. You button a jacket from the top down and stop one button from the end. A Windsor knot will always mark a man as well groomed. We do our best to help, but the moment a customer's wife says he looks good, then he looks fabulous. We aren't responsible if they've ignored our advice. We aren't responsible once they wear the stuff downstairs, outside, at home, out for tea, away from our golden lights. Since when do we live up to our own expectations anyway?

Sixth floor, men's collections. It was a move up for many. It was not exactly what I'd imagined for myself, folding jumpers and chit-chat chit-chat. But it wasn't manning the reception at Frank's garage. In men's collections, no man wolfed Chiko rolls for lunch, there weren't those bloated shiny tits plastered on every vertical surface, the toilet was not a piss-splattered steel vessel with neither seat nor paper. The sixth floor smelled good. There was no grease. I just had to breeze in, look neat, and never ever point: I directed customers with my fragrant, moisturised palm.

Men's collections shimmered with mirrors. My reflection had a reflection of its reflection. We knew how we looked from vistas supernatural. And if now and then I was oblivious to myself and the soaring expectations, the other girls would let me know: sweeping gazes, harsh as steel brooms. And then I'd be bent over the Country Road rollneck display table, breathing fast and hard, my palm buried in navy blue lambswool, wondering what the hell I'd been thinking, leaving the house dressed *like this*. Then I'd be dreaming of my apron and my cakes and a quiet place where I could work with jam smeared along a cheek and flour in my hair and no one would give a damn.

But I rode the elevator each day and stood folding and hemming, hanging and fetching — stabbing the floorboards with my stilettos — as I waited in that infinity of mirrors, smiling like my teeth would suffocate if I accidentally closed my lips.

I didn't want to be a front-girl in a department store. I wanted to hide away in the back of a boutique bakery that specialised in cupcakes displayed on gilded plates and old-fashioned lace. I'd even bought the parchment cards on which I'd write their names in black ink. Like:

Interpretation Of Dreams

I had no one else to cook for so I carted the cakes to work. Set them out on the tearoom laminex table every Friday morning to see if they passed the test.

Tonight's composition was a study in tart mashed berries and chocolate ooze I'd named *Manhattan Murder Mystery*. I slid butter and cream from the fridge and frozen blackberries and cherries from the freezer. The bittersweet chocolate was in my handbag. The sweet vermouth under the sink.

Friday morning, 9.36 a.m. and in waddled Claire. She always could smell a cupcake at three hundred miles. She was my most dedicated fan despite her 'diabetic diet' but she'd never meet my eye: she'd talk to me, and her eyes would roll around their sockets and then flee up behind her forehead, leaving me staring at the membranous whites. So, in rollicked Claire and she started swallowing cupcakes, throwing them down onto god knows what else she already had in there, while she flicked through an old *Women's Weekly*. I stood and watched, feeling a strange mix of satisfaction and despair.

'*Manhattan Murder Mystery*,' I said when she looked up from the mag.

She showed me the whites of her eyes, slick as boiled

eggs. 'What?'

'It's the name of the cakes.'

'Oh ... they're divine,' she said in a distracted kind of way, as if what she really wanted to say was: *Cakes? What cakes? And who the heck are you?*

The real test was whether or not I could get the other girls to eat them, ascetic congregation that they were. It was like tempting a pack of monks: bit of cleavage, bit of ankle, stroke their forearm gently and maybe they'll start imagining, maybe they'll take a lick.

One cake for morning tea once — that's all it took — and they hurled austerity out the window permanently. The first cakes I ever got them to eat were a batch of *Breakfast at Tiffany's*: savoury semolina cupcakes flecked with spinach, corn and ricotta. I sold it to them as a high-protein, low-carb breakfast, and for once Claire didn't get to take home a plate full of her own leftovers.

'Oh god,' they'd usually say, 'my hips, my gut, my bum.' But then they'd say 'Oooo!' and 'Cindy!' and take a cake straight to their tongue.

The successes: *Strawberry Fields Forever* (fresh strawberries and cream-cheese folded through vanilla cake), *Nuts about You* (caramel cake with pecan butter praline) and *Don't Blame It on the Sunshine* (pineapple and passionfruit upside-down cupcakes). If they were gone by morning tea, I knew they'd been a success; any left by four, Claire took them home 'for her demented mother', and I'd scrap the recipe. Notable failures: *Your Place or Mine* (it was the jaw-shattering chopped dates), *Grandma Takes a Trip* (a cupcake filled with rainbow-coloured whipped cream that leached out into unappealing puddles of food dye and grease).

There were three other full-timers besides Claire and me: Sue, Tara and Ange. Sue had been on the cover of a magazine for *Losing Half Her Weight AND Her Husband!* For that headline they gave her five thousand. For three years she drank black coffee and only ate her fingernails. She'd remarried and now supplemented the coffee and nails with three protein bars a week and a Friday carb-loading cupcake: 'I have to keep up my strength,' she explained.

Tara was tall and skinny and loud. She'd had a bit of lipo here and there, and two boob jobs (A to C, then C to E) and she'd let us feel them. For a few years now she'd followed the only-one-type-of-food-a-day diet. It was usually apples or chicken breast or low-cal soft serve, and on Fridays it was a cupcake. 'Being a skinny bitch is no walk in the park,' she'd say, laughing, then slip off to solicit husbands in the change rooms.

I mostly spoke with Ange. We'd hide from our reflections in the dim-lit clothes reserve, lying on piles of soft jumpers. When Ange spoke she'd look at the bone of her wrist and take licks of her lip gloss between words. Ange was different, Ange ate anything, Ange ate everything. But then she'd go and spew.

The week after *Manhattan Murder Mystery* I invented *Cloud Nine One One*. It was a complicated cupcake that I knew would be difficult and expensive to produce commercially. The lemon-scented cake was filled with raspberry puree, then coated in meringue and baked until crunchy. A shard of toffee pierced the meringue, allowing dribbles of escaping raspberry to slip down the side. They looked like little bleeding clouds. And they were a triumph at morning tea.

'Ohmygod,' said Tara, dissolving meringue on her tongue. 'You should totally go on *Masterchef*.'

'What's *Masterchef*?' I asked, and everyone turned to me with mouths agape, as if I'd just declared that white carbs make you thin.

'*Where* have you *been*?' said Tara. 'It's only like the most popular show in the world or something.'

Sue nodded, eyes wide.

'It's not that good,' said Ange.

Sue looked at Ange like she was a bag of sick, then looked

back at me and said, 'You audition, you get on the show, and if you can cook really good stuff then you win! You should see what they make ... Unbelievable stuff ... Stuff just like that.' She pointed at the *Cloud Nine One Ones*.

So I watched the show online in one huge binge, the first episode to the last, and it made me so excited that my lips went numb from the hyperventilation. If I could get onto *Masterchef* then *everyone* would see my beautiful cakes, then I'd open my own kitchen and I'd get my recipe book published and — the relief of it — I would get the fuck out of men's collections.

I didn't sleep for a week; I lay awake dreaming up new recipes and cooking them for massive black cameras and awe-struck, salivating studio audiences. Thursday night I assembled the ingredients for *Bitter Almonds and Sweet Revenge*: an almond-meal cupcake with chips of marzipan and Turkish delight swirled through the batter, and with the palest pink, rose-flavoured frosting. I considered *Bitter Almonds and Sweet Revenge* a masterpiece, but they didn't fly in the tearoom. Tara refused to 'eat flowers' and everyone — even Claire — claimed that marzipan made them gag.

'How about plain chocolate next week?' Sue said, with big gaps between each word, as if I was three years old, or retarded.

Tara gasped. 'Or even better! *White* chocolate!'

'Yes!' squealed Sue. 'I *love* white chocolate! I had white-chocolate mud cake for my wedding!'

'That's what I want too!' said Tara.

Meanwhile, my little dream-cakes sat in lonely sophistication, and my heart sank like an amateur soufflé. If I couldn't entice a tearoom of half-starved shop-Sharons then I had zero chance of getting on TV.

Sue said, 'Hey, Ange, isn't it your birthday next week? *You* should pick the type of cake!'

Claire put her hands on her massive hips. 'I'll make your

birthday cake, Ange. Name the cake. I've cooked a few good 'uns in my time and I should practise.'

'Practise?' I asked. 'Practise for what?'

Claire hit me with her rolling eggwhites. 'Oh, didn't I mention?' Her voice had gone all singsong. 'I sent in my entry for the *Masterchef* auditions yesterday.'

This snap-froze my thorax.

'Wow!' said Tara. 'That's awesome!'

Claire examined her fingernails with feigned nonchalance.

'Blueberry cheesecake,' whispered Ange.

Claire and I both turned to Ange and said, 'Okay!'

'Oh, don't worry, Claire, I'm more than happy to make it,' I said.

'Oh no, it's too much bother. You concentrate on your fancy cupcakes, *I'll* do a normal old birthday cheesecake classic.'

'But I'd *like* to do it.'

'So would I, doll, and I, as I said, need to practise.'

'Girls, girls,' said Tara. 'Don't fight over making cake, for god's sake. Both of youse can make one. We'll take any leftovers down to Dawn in lingerie … then maybe she'll start giving us the heads up on their sales!'

'So,' I said. Ange and I were dressing the dummy we all called Max. 'What do you reckon about Claire entering *Masterchef*?'

'What? Oh well, she's not exactly … she basically hasn't got a hope in hell of getting on.' Ange dropped Max's cuff and rolled her eyes back, and we both laughed. 'And besides, they reckon twenty-five thousand people are going to audition for the next series.'

I swallowed. 'Twenty-five thousand?'

'Yeah, it's the housewife's new lotto. Win the jackpot and all your dreams will come true.'

'Except lotto is about luck, and *Masterchef* is about skill.'

'Is it?'

'Of course! I'd love to go on that show … The contestants

are all talented, and they all have a true passion for food.'

'Well, Cindy, why don't those twenty-five thousand passionistas go do their chef apprenticeship if they really want to cook?' She raised her eyebrows at me. 'Why don't they work for what they want?'

I tightened the tie so tight around Max's neck that I heard stitches snap. *What would you know, puker*, I suddenly wanted to hiss.

I let go of the tie. 'I'm going to the loo.'

On Thursday night, feeling competitive and resentful, I assembled my ingredients. A cheesecake is a complex beast, and I wanted to turn it into a cupcake.

I stared at my materials and gently settled into the zone where there was no Claire, no girls, no me and no men's collections. And there I came across *Blackbirds Singing in the Dead of Night*: a thin disc of pastry, purple with blueberry juice reduction, supporting a buttermilk cupcake strewn with blueberries, frosted with a tower of whipped vanilla cream cheese. On top I set an orb of blueberry jelly in which a single blueberry was suspended. *Blackbirds* was a stunner.

Friday morning I walk in and all the girls are in the tearoom drinking green tea. In the middle of the table is a massive hulk of a cheesecake with an inch-thick biscuit base, blueberry gunk running down the sides and a dozen crooked candles. I set my *Birds* on a plate and slide it beside this wretched beast.

'Pretty!' says Tara.

At morning-tea time Claire volunteers to man the floor while we sing an ironic sort of happy birthday for Ange and eat cake. They all look at me apologetically and take a hunk of Claire's. Ange, though, takes both; eats mine then Claire's. She eats as she always does, just like a squirrel: fine fingers to tiny mouth, disassembling the food bit by little bit until it's no longer on the plate, but you aren't entirely sure if it's inside her body or has turned into thin air. Then she usually excuses herself and is gone for quite a while, during which time we'd all avoid the loos.

And so the cakes disappear from her plate — we all try not to watch — then she stands up from the table and smiles like an angel.

'I think both of the cakes are gorgeous. Thank you, Cindy. And now I will go and thank Claire.' She opens the door.

I follow her — the door swings closed behind us — and I grab her by the forearm. 'Ange,' I say.

She stops, looks down at my hand and sets her calm eyes upon me.

'Please don't spew.'

She looks at me for what seems like a long time, and I don't let go of her forearm though I feel nervous and a bit sick. You see, we all know each other's secrets, but we aren't supposed to interfere. We ignore Tara's soliciting and don't suggest Sue should eat; we pretend Claire really is following her diabetic diet and leave Ange alone in the loos.

And now there's a hard thing on Ange's face that I haven't seen before and her arm's still stuck out and in my hand and she says to me, sweet as sugar, 'I really liked the name of your cupcakes, Cindy, that Beatles song about the blackbirds waiting? I think it's really fitting ... under the circumstances.' She wrenches her arm free. 'After all, *Cinders*, who knows? Wait long enough and someone might walk in that door, lead you to a shop full of ingredients and *beg* you to turn them into cake.' And she slaps me with her pity-smile then spins from me, towards the bathroom.

Harry

EMMA SCHWARCZ

Harry surveyed the breakfast buffet. Tropical fruit manned by an Indian with a cleaver; canned fruit, its pallid cousin, sitting alongside mueslis and yoghurts and, oddly, salad greens and hard cheeses. He turned to his right: lamb sausages, roasted tomatoes, hash browns, bacon crisped to buggery, scrambled, gelatinous eggs, fried rice and onions. To his left, the carbohydrate display: breads, pastries, pancakes, muffins and cereals in small boxes. He and Ruth had once discouraged these miniature cereal boxes in their household. Caitlin pointed to them in the supermarket, and Ruth shook her head, listing the additives that had been shown to mutate cells and cause cancer. In rats, Harry had thought; there was no definite causal link in humans.

    He could never keep up with all the perils in his way after they married, perils that changed each week depending on who was finessing the test tubes. One week it was tartrazine, the next saccharine and aspartame. Coffee was banned in January only to be reinstated in June, when its antioxidant properties emerged. Ruth had put him on a Pritikin diet for a few years after the full extent of his family's cardiac history came to light one beach holiday — a father and two brothers with telltale chest scars — but then someone discovered the risk of thyroid malfunction and the diet was turfed. Ruth had panicked, palpating Harry's neck at the breakfast table, looking for signs of a goitre.

    When the salt had returned to the table, Ruth decided to cut red meat from their meals. Chicken went swiftly and silently a month later. They were down to fish, which stank out the kitchen and left Harry's wallet lighter. There were days when he would have given his thumb for a nice rib-eye.

After that, it was anyone's guess which food was no longer considered ripe for consumption. Families on the breadline were able to dine out on buckets of fried chicken and soft drink, but Harry, who had finally reached a level of fiscal respectability, existed on brown rice and seaweed. His gut, Ruth claimed, would thank him. 'You watch,' she said, dishing up some mirin-soaked sweet potato and quinoa, 'while all your friends develop bowel cancer, you will be squeaky clean.'

Now, scanning the acres of food, he felt weak. He could eat any of this, if he wanted. He could pile his plate high with danishes or create a tower of bacon rashers. He could drown everything in maple syrup and cinnamon sugar and fail to brush his teeth. The space left him gasping, and he had to grip the bench for a moment until the room came back into focus.

'Dad?' Caitlin reached past him for some papaya. 'Aren't you hungry?'

'Just struggling to decide, I suppose.'

He looked around. On all sides, young families, retirees, honeymooners — kids so new in their skins and relationships that they were wide-eyed just eating cornflakes together.

It was mostly couples. The resort was made for them, what with all the loveseats on the sand, flaming torches dotting the perimeter and frangipani carried along the warm breeze. He was loath to sit down with Caitlin, the expectation was so great; twice already he'd had to correct the assumption that they were a couple. A couple! She was half his age and could do much better for herself than the grey ghost he had become. He watched her open a tiny box of Coco Pops, spilling the small beans across the table in her haste. She'd lost weight — the result of stress, she said — and while Harry didn't want to encourage any unhealthy habits, he had to acknowledge that the architecture of her face was more readily available to the world now. She was, if not the spitting image of her mother at a young age, then a high-functioning facsimile. He could see his own influence somewhere — the nose was his,

Harry

and the small ears, which on a woman worked better — but Caitlin was mostly Ruth, at least in appearance. He couldn't work out if this was now a source of pain or consolation.

'Dad? You sitting down or what?'

He took a seat and picked at his muesli with a spoon. 'So, what's on for today?'

'Same as yesterday, I guess. Sit by the pool, read, swim. Not much else, is there?'

'We could go into town. If that's something that interests you?'

Caitlin waited until she'd finished her mouthful. Ruth had taught her well. 'Is that something that interests *you*?'

Harry shifted his muesli around in its bowl. He didn't know why he'd chosen it; of all the options, muesli was the one most likely to cause him to bloat, which was not an attractive thing at the best of times but especially not in Speedos. He never could remember which foods prompted which complaint, but he had never needed to before. He was the caretaker of the banking, the stock market, Medicare and private health insurance; Ruth was the one who knew the ailments. *Chickpeas give you gas, boats make you seasick, the rogan josh was too spicy for you last time, don't you remember?*

Caitlin was staring at him, but he'd forgotten the question. He was too busy registering the sidelong glances from a woman at the next table. She was roughly his age and sitting with a man who was also roughly his age. The look on her face suggested that this, and only this, was a suitable arrangement and that seeking refuge from the instabilities and indignities of age in a younger offer was beneath any respectable citizen.

He squirmed in his seat. 'Listen honey, you'll need to call me Dad a bit more often, and probably louder too.'

She glared at the other table. 'Forget about everyone else, okay? This is not about them.'

This Harry could confirm, but who it *was* about was anyone's guess. Caitlin had suggested the trip. 'It's your thing,

Dad, you do it every year. And this year, well, I think you need it more than ever. I'll come with; it'll be healthy.'

But it wasn't just *his* thing.

'I can't leave now. What if something changes?'

Caitlin had placed a hand on his. 'Dad, nothing has changed in ten months.'

'Yes, but that's not an indication of the next few months.'

But it was, at least according to the doctors. 'She's stable but non-responsive, Mr Rogers. You go on your holiday.'

He looked at his daughter, now idly dunking a teabag in her cup. Her forehead had a malarial sheen to it, the result of hasty sunscreen application, and her hair had started to frizz from the humidity, expanding and separating in a slow-waking fan. He noticed a few superficial creases in her décolletage, which he'd taken for sleep marks the day before, but here they were again. If he'd stopped to think, he wouldn't have pointed them out to her; he might have instead mentioned the colour of the water or how well she seemed to be doing in her job. As it was, she covered her chest with one hand and muttered something about wrinkles and getting old.

'You? Old? Ridiculous. You don't even have any greys yet.'

'Yes, I do.'

'Where? Show me.'

She placed her fork down and stared. 'Dad, I dye my hair.'

'Do you? But it's the same colour as when you were born. Why would you dye your hair the same colour?'

She looked at him as if he were slow, which he was beginning to think might be the case. 'To cover the greys.'

He never had these sorts of circular conversations with Ruth. They always seemed to travel quite directly from one point to the next, until one of them reached a conclusion and they settled into silence. He wasn't sure he was ready to give that up.

The woman at the next table was shooting daggers at him, and the muesli had lodged in his intestines and would no doubt be looking for an exit strategy before long.

'Cait, I'll meet you at the pool, okay?'
'Finished already?'
He motioned in the direction of the hotel rooms. 'Old-man prostate.'
She shrugged and went back to her breakfast, opening up the local paper.

Caitlin was swimming underwater lengths of the pool when he emerged from his room. Long, powerful strokes that pushed her past the toddlers in inflatable rings and couples in paddling clutches. She was stronger these days, back to her usual self, or at least close. He supposed that he was meant to follow suit.

'Dad!' She was topside, waving a wild arm like she had as a child, and pointing to the seats she'd saved. He waved back and settled onto the lounge, adjusting it so that he had full sun. He and Ruth had always found seats under the palm trees on previous visits, in the shade so that their gooseflesh didn't crisp and wither. As if it was skin cancer that would get them! Not when arteries thickened like old cream. He lay back and let the warmth wash over him.

By the time Caitlin sat down next to him, Harry was under the umbrella. The sun was unpredictable and, besides, he wasn't suddenly free to do anything he liked.

'I was thinking of going parasailing,' Caitlin said. 'What do you think?'

'Well, if you want to, you should.'

'I was hoping you might come with.'

They'd seen them each day, little dots hoisted to the horizon by colourful sails, and each time Caitlin commented on them — *Oh, how wonderful* or *Oh, that'd be so much fun* — but Harry only saw them as a semi-interesting backdrop. If Ruth were here, she'd place a hand on his arm and remind him of his vertigo.

'Oh, I don't think I could do that, Cait.'

'Of course you could.'

'No, no. I'm happy to watch you do it, though. If you want.'

She tilted her head to the side and squeezed the water out of her ponytail. 'Maybe you'll change your mind in a few days.'

The breeze picked up, and Harry was assailed by the scent of frangipani, sunscreen and French fries, ordered by a guest a few seats down. The man was thick-set and paunched, with a complexion suggesting endless tiers of sunburn. His white hair was balding at the crown, and a finger on his left hand was in the vice of a wedding band fitted sometime in his youth. When he sneezed, his shorts bulged dangerously at the sides. Harry smiled and turned to share an unkind word with Caitlin, but stopped short. She wouldn't appreciate it as her mother would. Not that Ruth was mean-spirited — she volunteered at a charity and fostered four seeing-eye dogs — but she couldn't abide sloth and didn't mind when Harry poked fun at it occasionally.

A graceful, fine-boned woman of about sixty sat down next to the white-haired man and reached a hand across to his cheek. He smiled and took another fistful of fries while she fussed over him, applying more sunscreen, handing him a water bottle, checking the menu for an afternoon cocktail. They laughed about something and then settled into their separate books.

Harry looked away, feeling a clench in his abdomen. He tried to focus on the individual strands of thatch on the roof of the bure, the carvings on the supporting poles, the markings on the tapa cloth stretched to its limit on the wall, but all the details, separate or combined, couldn't stave off the growing feeling that none of this was right, none of it, not the warmth or the holiday-reading or the faint thrum of a ukulele from across the sand. He shouldn't have come.

The nights were the worst. By day, one could roam the beach, swim laps, play cards at the Tikitiki Lounge; at night, the children were parcelled off to their rooms to watch cable TV and eat burgers while the adults wandered two by two. The clamour of the day was replaced by crickets, frog song and village singers who channelled Tony Bennett and Burt Bacharach. He'd never noticed how alienating a place it could be.

Before dinner each night he'd rung the hospital, and before dinner each night the duty nurse had told him that nothing had changed. Now he sat by the phone, staring dumbly at the little tabs alongside each number: reception, laundry, room service. In thirty-seven years of marriage, he and Ruth had never ordered room service.

He stared hard for a moment at the message light — dim and unactivated — and then left for the restaurant.

Caitlin sat opposite him, nursing a pina colada and studying the menu. Candles dotted the tables, and when a breeze huffed theirs out, Harry hid it among the condiments.

'When we were here last year, your mother ordered the wahoo steak every second night.'

'Was it that good?'

'It must've been.'

Caitlin shrugged. 'Still, she could've tried other things.'

'Your mother is a woman who knows what she likes.'

Caitlin smiled tightly and closed the menu. 'I think I'll have the salmon.'

They sat there in silence; Harry tried to discern if it was comfortable, and after a moment he decided it probably wasn't. They had said all they had in them in the first few days, and the resort hardly provided extra stimuli. He was starting to repeat himself, and Caitlin, with her thirty-year-old memory, was starting to remind him of it.

'Why don't we try the curry place tomorrow night, Dad?'

'It's too spicy for me.'

'You've never tried it.'

'Yes, I have.'

'Mum never cooked curries and you never eat at Indian

restaurants, so when exactly have you tried it?'

'I've had a rogan josh before, I remember it clearly.' But he couldn't. He knew that Ruth always steered him away from curries, and she usually had a good reason for these things. He put his menu down. 'It was like *fire*.'

'It's not too late to try new things, you know. You're not dead yet.'

Harry clenched his fork. 'No. Not yet.' He noticed Caitlin's cheeks, now flushed. 'And how many of those drinks are you going to have? I didn't know you were a drinker.'

'Oh, Dad.' She crossed her arms and looked out over the pools. In this light, her face seemed on the gaunt side. Ruth wouldn't have approved; she always said that a woman had to choose between her figure and her face. Ruth chose her face, and even as she lay prone and blanched of make-up at St Vincent's, her facial routine — cleanse, tone, moisturise and slip into bed each night smelling of cucumber — shot to hell by the tubes passing over and into, even then she looked a full five years younger than her age.

The food arrived and they ate without a word. The wahoo steak was a little overdone, he thought.

The next day they caught a taxi into town. At the local market, Caitlin sifted through knick-knacks while Harry looked on, his vision glazing over in the heat. 'Can I help you with anything, sir?' A young woman was suddenly by his side, gesturing at a display of tropical lotions.

'No, no. I'm just looking.'

'Something for your wife, perhaps? The frangipani is very popular.'

Before he could decline, the saleslady had popped open the lid and dabbed a little on his hand. The smell was sickly, not at all true to the flowers on the resort, but it got into his nostrils and under his skin and made him tear up for a moment so that he had to turn away from the girl and pretend to be checking his wallet for enough cash.

Harry

Caitlin was inspecting piles of fruit at another stall, picking up pineapples and limes, asking how much for a bunch of sugar bananas. She settled on a mango and exchanged money with a tiny woman who clinked with rows of bangles as she moved.

Caitlin held up the mango to him and mouthed, 'Gold.'

'You can have mango at the breakfast buffet, you know.'

'I know, but this I can have whenever I like. Plus, it's helping out the local economy.' She reached into her bag, pulled out a tub of lip balm and was about to apply it when Harry grabbed her wrist and stopped her. 'Dad, what are you doing?'

'You've just touched everything in that market. Do you think you should be putting that same hand to your mouth now?'

She rolled her eyes. 'Seriously? Dad, it's not like there's cholera here. Stop being ridiculous.'

'I'm not being ridiculous.' He felt the heat rise to his cheeks and wished for some support. 'I'm just looking out for you. You should wash your hands before you transmit all those germs to yourself.'

She stood there and stared at him. 'Where is this coming from? This isn't you, Dad. You don't fuss and bother about germs. Mum does.'

'Maybe it is me. Maybe I've always fussed about germs, but your mother has been the one to voice it more regularly. How would you know? Only your mother and I know.' He pointed to his chest and then to his right, where Ruth's chest would have been. '*We* know.'

Caitlin, mouth agape, looked so much like her mother he felt doubly admonished. But there was nothing to be done; it was said, she was hurt, and now they would return to the hotel and eat another meal in silence.

Neither of them said a word in the taxi. The radio was up loud, and Harry could feel the pulse of the reggae through his forearm as it rested on the doorframe. The driver picked up speed, taking corners so quickly that Harry's grip fastened on the door. He reached behind him for a seatbelt but felt only the pinholed leather of the seatback. These old models came without them, he realised, just like the ones in his youth. He watched each turn on the drive back, his chest bare and unbolstered.

By their second-last day, Harry and Caitlin were swimming in different pools. One of them would make a vague attempt at unity — 'I'll probably be around the Tikitiki Lounge if you feel like lunch at some point' — but then 'island time' afflicted them and the opportunity passed.

Harry read the local paper by the main pool, browsing the jobs section and calculating what he might need of a salary to make a life here. It wouldn't take much if it was just himself he had to support. That thought alone made him put down the paper and close his eyes.

His silence was broken by a tinny rhythm, a constricted, muffled buzzing. He opened his eyes to see a woman lying next to him — really a girl — nodding along to the music from her iPod. She was black, a point Caitlin was always saying Harry shouldn't notice, but how could he not when a) she was so black it was extraordinary to him, and b) he had eyes? It wasn't as if you ceased to see someone's attributes once their background was deciphered, and this girl was the kind of smooth brown that Harry had only seen on American TV shows. Her skin was accentuated by a hot-pink bikini and nails to match, and she was mouthing the words to the hip-hop track seeping out of her headphones.

Harry looked around. All the guests were either white or Asian; the only other black people were the locals, ferrying drinks or tending the garden. Her hair was plaited in tiny braids that moved in a swirl along the contours of her scalp. Caitlin had done that once in Bali in her early twenties, but on her it had looked like a cheap grab at childhood. On this girl, it was fitting. The soles of her feet were pale, as were her palms, but the rest of her was immaculately black. No mottling of the skin, no blotchy allergic spots — nothing like the varicose veins Ruth had on the backs of her calves or the strange new freckles, bound to be liver spots, now surfacing on the skin of his hands. She was incredible, and Harry had to monitor the glances he stole every so often so as not to appear either racist or perverted.

She was sitting alone, and Harry wondered who her companion might be. Perhaps parents, though she looked too old and brazen to be holidaying with family. The hoist of her bikini and the ease with which she sat there, half-nude, one leg crossed high over the other, toes kicking every so often to the beat, said lover rather than daughter. A small silver toe-ring glinted in the sun, and Harry decided that she might be a callgirl of sorts. She was pretty enough and there was a cheapness to her attire, and when the waitress came round to take her order, the girl seemed flustered and unsure, as if she might be caught out in a charade. Harry rapped himself over the knuckles. He was being uncharitable.

When a tall glass of something tropical was delivered to her, Harry took the chance to start a conversation.

'Oh, this? It's called a Malolo Sunset, but I have no idea what's in it. The lady told me but I clean forgot!' The girl's accent — all-American — was as refreshing to Harry as her presence. 'Maybe some rum with a whole lotta tropical juice? Did you want to try some?' She offered the straw to him, but Harry waved it away.

'No, no, you enjoy it.'

'You should get one, it's *amazing*.'

'I tend not to drink much during the day. Or at night, actually.'

'Oh,' the girl whispered, 'you in AA?'

'AA? Is that — oh, no! No, I don't have a problem, I just …' He thought about it. There was a reason, surely, but it eluded him. Alcohol just belonged to a different life, that's all, one he chose not to live.

'That's cool, you don't have to drink. I'm not a big drinker or nothing, neither; don't be thinking I'm a alcoholic. I just like to treat myself now that I'm on a island, sitting by this pool, not worrying about no rent or work or alarm clocks. It's a holiday, y'know? Time to do things you don't usually do.' She smiled, her teeth a revelation. 'I'm Alma, by the way.'

'Harry.'

'Nice to meet you, Harry. You here alone?'

Was that it? Was she here to solicit? 'No, I'm here with my daughter. She's at the other pool.'

'Oh, I get it. Embarrassed by her dad?' Alma laughed.

'Possibly.' Harry took a quick breath. 'What about you? Are you here with your family?'

'My family? Hell no! No, they back in California where I left them. I'm flying solo this time. I just want to eat, drink, swim and sleep.' She swept an arm out across the landscape. 'This is my treat to myself.'

'And what do you do normally? When you're not treating yourself, that is.'

'Me? I'm a travel agent, you know, booking trips for people who don't appreciate it.' She exploded with laughter and then quietened herself with a sip of the cocktail.

'I'm sure they appreciate it.'

'No, I don't mean me — who cares if they appreciate me? — I mean the *holiday*. Most of the couples who come in just want the safe option, something familiar, but it's never going to really rock them, you know? I offer them things like skydiving in New Zealand or hiking in Patagonia, but they never choose it. The husband leans over to the wife, or the wife to the husband, and says, "Maybe next year, honey." But who they kidding? Not me, that's for sure.'

Harry squinted at the pool, at the trees and bures and islands in the distance. Had he ever asked Ruth to go anywhere else? Would she have wanted to? Would he? The whole thing was moot now anyway, he was beginning to see that. He leaned over. 'And yet you're not in New Zealand or Patagonia either.'

'Ha! Harry, you are one hundred per cent right. I am not.' Alma ran a hand over her braids, shifting one that must have been pulling. 'And life is all about taking risks. But for me, this is a risk — coming here alone? With all the pretty honeymooners? You telling me that's not some sort of craziness?'

Harry smiled. There was certainly a craziness to her. Possibly no real logic, but that didn't seem important. He called a waitress over. 'Can I have one of those too?'

'A Malolo Sunset, sir?'

'Yes, please.'

Alma took a long sip from her drink and then placed a hand on Harry's arm. The novelty of it — that small, perfect hand on his — surprised him; that there could be any novelty, at this late stage, was a wonder.

'Good on *you*, Harry. You go and crazy it up today.' .

The duty nurse was curt when he called. In the background he could hear the clack of heels across lino and the rustle of papers accumulating at the nurses station. 'There is *no change*, Mr Rogers. No change. I think the doctors explained that there's no chance of change, didn't they?'

'Well, I don't know about that; they said there's little chance, which is different from no chance.'

She sighed, an exaggerated sigh that Harry thought inappropriate to the circumstances. 'What can I tell you, Mr Rogers? She is still unconscious. I have some paperwork here for you, for when you get back.'

His head started to ache, and for a moment he thought he might be about to suffer his own aneurysm; that Ruth had sent one back for him, a pigeon pair. He hung up and rubbed the crown of his head, where the pain was at its worst. He'd wanted to tell Ruth about Alma, about their chat and the newness of the Malolo Sunset, which had gone down remarkably easily, he thought, even though he wasn't used to the rum — but of course that was madness. It was all madness. Because either there was change or there wasn't change — it couldn't be both, and yet that was what the duty nurse was telling him, what the doctors were telling him, and what Caitlin was telling him. No change, mister; except for you: infinite change. He put his face in his palms. Caitlin, of all people. Ruth had wanted her so badly. They both had, but Ruth …

He lay back on the bed. The pain in his head shifted to his temples and he began to settle; it was no aneurysm, just the alcohol. He wasn't used to it, but he soon realised that if he didn't fight it, the haze would carry him off to a deep sleep.

On their last day, Harry woke with a dry mouth. Caitlin was already eating when he arrived at the buffet.

'Morning.'

'Morning.'

'Might just get some breakfast, then.'

'You do that.'

He waited for the multigrain to shimmy through the toaster conveyor belt, and then hovered over the bain-marie. The sausages glistened under the light, a thousand different wrongs wrapped tight in casing. He grabbed two and a scoop of eggs.

Caitlin raised an eyebrow when she saw the meat, but didn't say anything.

'I used to eat these all the time when I was a kid.' He cut a small piece off and studied it. 'Sometimes twice a day. My parents didn't know any better.'

He popped it in his mouth and felt the hit of salt and fat and flavour. He cut another slice, then another. When he'd finished the first sausage, he took a sip of juice.

'Not having the other one?' Caitlin's voice had an edge to it, but that would pass. It would all pass.

'I might leave that one.' Out of respect.

Harry

They packed their things, and Harry went to settle the account. He wouldn't be back; he knew this now. He made his way out to the beach, for a final look — beyond the couples passing sunscreen and checking menus, beyond the sunlounges and musicians and waiters, beyond everything, so that there was only the lagoon, spread out before him, calm but for the occasional school of fish changing direction.

Theories of Relativity

CHRIS WOMERSLEY

You learn things in this life, don't you, whether you like it or not. God, it's awful. I'm eleven years old. Our father fills the bath with cold water, orders me to dump a tray of ice cubes into it and tells my older brother Patrick to strip off his clothes. Father is tall, angular and taciturn, a man accustomed to being obeyed by his family, if no one else. His crucial error is to mistake disdain for respect. He has a stopwatch in one hand. 'We'll see what you're made of,' he says.

I stand in the dim hallway looking up at him, listening intently to his instructions; I know they will be issued only once and I risk a clip over the ear if I ask him to repeat them. Our little sister Janet lingers in a doorway with a strand of hair in her mouth, staring, like always. She's nine. Our mother is out somewhere. My brother's face is grim but stoic as he realises what is about to happen. It is midwinter. Rain is drumming on the roof. It dawns on me that I will remember this afternoon for the rest of my life.

Father is adamant that Patrick and I be toughened up and has devised a variety of techniques to ensure we will never be in the slightest bit girly. When we play soccer in the backyard, for instance, he never allows us to win because that doesn't happen in the real world. He refuses to help us up if we fall down ('Self-inflicted. No crying. Stand up, little man'). Years earlier — and this is embarrassing — I faltered one cold night in my toilet training and my father took me outside, yanked off my pyjamas and hosed me down as a method of instruction.

Father doesn't drink, doesn't smoke and thinks those who do are damn fools. He has no time for sentimentality and the few jokes he utters are usually at someone else's expense.

The world is a harsh place, and it's his job to equip his sons the best way he knows how. After all, it was good enough for him; we could do a lot worse than turn out like he did. Little does he know exactly what this will entail.

The bath test and the toilet training and so on happens long before the accident, of course. Afterwards, he wouldn't have dared.

There is a lot packed into a kiss. Even now, years later, it is one particular kiss I remember as the defining moment of my life. It wasn't even a kiss given or received by me, but one I glimpsed from a darkened hallway. It was then I realised a kiss is never only between the two people concerned: there are always others, out beyond the footlights, unseen.

The day of the kiss was a hot Sunday, ten years after our father's accident (or, more accurately, 'accident'). Everything became so clear that I blushed not only at my own naivety, but at the thought that everyone else in the street probably realised what had been going on all this time in my parents' house. It was a good, middle-class area that kept its reputation trimmed by the brisk, whirring blades of gossip. People must have suspected something. What had they seen that I had missed? Did they think *I* was in some way implicated? Jesus Christ. Just the thought of it.

I was twenty-one that summer, in many ways still an innocent. I had started going out with a pleasant, bovine girl called Julie who did deliveries for the bike shop where I worked on weekends. My brother Patrick was taller than me, more athletic, much better-looking and possessed a roguish charm that attracted the type of girl willing to do things nice girls were not. He played guitar. He had been born missing the tip of the little finger on his left hand, a disfigurement that only heightened his appeal rather than diminished it, as it might have done in other boys. My brother also had a competitive streak that prohibited him from gaining any real pleasure from his success with girls or sport. He could be cruel, as I knew only too well: he forgot people's names on purpose; he mimicked people mercilessly behind their backs; he told vicious jokes about neighbours and classmates; he had long called me Mr Einstein, on account of my interest in the great physicist's theories of time and space.

But this. This kiss. The knowledge of it almost made me swoon with its dark power. I thought of Robert Oppenheimer, and the dismal thrill the American must have felt upon discovering the technology for the Bomb. Like all discoveries, the information had been there all along, for years, waiting for someone to figure it out. God, I had been so blind.

After witnessing this particular kiss — and when I had composed myself — I eased away from the study doorway, crept down the hall to the lounge room, gathered my jacket and bag and left without saying goodbye to anyone. Long after the gnashing implements were out of earshot, I heard the *snip snip snip* of garden shears as Father hobbled about the backyard.

It hadn't always been like this. It seemed that everyone changed in the months after our father's accident, or that the entire family was reorganised in a way that was never clear to me. I felt I had lived through a revolution, say, or a natural disaster, whereby everything had become different, but in ways too seismic to define. Mother took up smoking for a start, and became dry-witted and elegant. She began to say things like: *Oh, that's marvellous* or *Sweetie, please don't do that, I have a headache*, while sitting on the couch in the afternoon flicking through a glossy magazine. Indeed, it seemed she had barely existed until the moment of Father's accident. Even her name, Marie, which had seemed rather pedestrian before, assumed a more cinematic quality. She took to wearing lipstick around the house and having afternoon 'kips', a concept she had picked up from an American magazine. At first — in addition to everything else that had happened — it was somewhat disconcerting, but Patrick and I both came to like this new persona. She became the type of parent the other kids probably talked about at home with their own, more mundane families; hers was a low-grade, schoolyard celebrity, like the Cambodian kid Nam whose brother had been shot by communists.

People admired our mother when she came to pick Patrick and me up from school. She had fallen pregnant with my brother when she was seventeen and so was only thirty-one at that time, even though Father was ten years older. She was still attractive, and the other fathers paid her quite a bit of attention. I didn't mind, but Patrick became furious if she flirted too long with Mr Jacobs and he would refuse to speak to her after we returned home. When this happened, Mother would expend considerable effort coaxing him from the cave of his mood, fetching treats from the pantry and swearing to behave herself in future. *Come on, darling. There! Have an Iced VoVo.*

Patrick changed into another, more restless person. He was fourteen, so he was hardly old, but now he refused to accompany me around the neighbourhood to see whose fruit trees we might climb. No more hide-and-seek. He even took to calling our mother Marie, rather than Mother or Mum, a practice she did nothing to discourage, even though Father disapproved.

Patrick and I still shared a room, and I would lie awake and stare at his sleeping profile, hoping to detect a clue to his sudden alteration. After all, it wasn't like the accident had befallen *him*. Sometimes he prowled through the house at night and occasionally even slept elsewhere, on the couch in the living room, or on the daybed in Father's study. On the single instance I crept after him, he turned in the hallway, pressed a hand to my chest and shook his head in such a way that discouraged me from following him ever again. 'Back off, Mr Einstein,' he hissed.

Our father was a captain in the army. Before the accident, he liked to talk authoritatively at barbecues about immigration policy and 'covert actions' in South-East Asia as if he were privy to secret information. In fact, he merely shuffled bits of paper from one office to the next and overheard rumours in the canteen, along with everyone else who worked in his building. He had joined the army with the boyish hope of being sent overseas to some exotic war zone to battle terrorists or communists but had never been closer to genuine military action than manoeuvres in Darwin one year (the highlight of his entire life), and he certainly wouldn't be deployed now, considering his age — not to mention his injury.

His own father, my grandfather, had been in the army and had been bitter about being sent away to shoot people in Vietnam; Father was bitter that he never had the opportunity to shoot at anyone. He was merely a public servant with a fancy uniform. If asked about his foot injury, he mumbled something about a 'hunting mishap', which was true, I suppose. Naturally, the accident changed him most of all.

The morning of the accident was wet and frosty. I heard my father moving about in the bathroom next door. Patrick slept in his bed on the other side of our room, blissfully unaware until Father burst in and roused each of us with a slap to the side of our heads.

'Come on, lads,' he said. 'We move out in ten minutes.'

The car interior was almost as cold as it was outside. Father didn't believe in excessive comfort. Besides, we were rugged up. We were going hunting; there was no point getting too cosy. In the back seat, I breathed on the glass and drew a face in the damp, silvery fog. The rising sun flickered behind trees.

He had been promising to take us hunting for some time, but my excitement at the prospect of shooting a real rifle was tempered with guilt. Mother thought we were too young for such an expedition and she didn't approve of shooting animals for sport — objections Father disdainfully overruled.

'My old man used to take me out here when I was about

your age,' my father was saying to Patrick, who was sitting beside him in the front seat.

Father didn't usually speak unless necessary, then only in a clipped manner that suggested he was keen to be done with talking as soon as he had made his point. But now I recognised in his voice the tone he reserved for speeches on The State Of The Economy, The Difference Between Men And Women or How To Tell The ABC Has Been Overrun By Lefties.

From the back seat I could see my brother's face in profile. Patrick was weirdly lit in the alien glow from the dashboard lights so that his skin appeared dusted with green phosphorescence. A crescent-shaped scar was visible on his right cheek where he had fallen during a game of chasey years earlier. Patrick inclined his head to show he was listening. I knew he hated these little homilies but endured them with the same stoicism he marshalled for the occasional strapping across the leg. He was a serious boy, introspective, given to harbouring grudges — none of which I really knew, or only dimly, on this cold morning. I loved and admired my brother even though he intimidated me because it seemed that, should it ever become necessary, he would get by very well without any of us, myself included.

My father changed down gears and slowed the car to cross a railway line. 'You never really knew your grandfather, but he was a great man. Really, a great man.' The car bobbled over the tracks. 'I loved those trips. Just me and him. The *men*, you know. Course we used to eat the rabbits. Take them home for Mum to cook. Make nice stews, she did.'

I listened over the thrum of the car's engine. Although directed at Patrick, I knew my father's speeches were intended for anyone in earshot. My own memories of my grandfather were vague: a grizzled muzzle; the smell of urine; a wing of grey, greasy hair pasted across his forehead. Patrick and I were both a little fearful of the late widower, who had lived nearby and visited every few days to have dinner and watch television. Although Father had often extolled his virtues and urged us to respect him, neither Patrick nor I had ever felt comfortable with our grandfather and avoided being alone with him. When he died a year earlier, Mother told us — as she told all family members and visitors — not to mention Grandfather's name in our father's presence in case we upset him.

'When I was your age,' Father was saying, 'we used to lay traps. Caught a wild dog once. Stupid thing. Those traps were hard to set. Always a chance of getting snagged …'

I stopped listening and wiped my bleary window clean with the sleeve of my duffel coat. My nose ran with the cold. I thought of my warm bed, and of Mother, who would by now be standing at the kitchen window in her dressing-gown, drinking tea with the serious expression she adopted for her morning ritual. Janet would be playing with her teddy on the lounge-room floor. The image prompted in me a flood of wild, helpless love, and suddenly I wished I were at home with them instead of sitting in this freezing car. A kookaburra on a wire fence watched us pass.

'… and I guess,' my father was saying when I tuned in again, 'I guess that the thing I would hope for us — for you boys and me — is you would respect me like I respected my father. That's why sometimes I'm hard on you. That's all. It's for your own good, you know.'

It was the most personal speech I had ever heard him make and I was amazed and almost terrified to detect a quaver of emotion in his voice. Neither Patrick nor I said anything, but my brother reached a hand over and patted our father gently on the shoulder.

'It's okay,' he said, and turned to me in the back seat. 'We understand, don't we, Nick?'

I mumbled agreement. For the next hour we drove in companionable silence, as if we had used all the words allocated to us for the morning.

We arrived at an isolated car park around nine a.m. and

piled out of the car. We unloaded the rifles and knapsacks and set out for the campsite, which was two kilometres away through the bush. The frosty grass crunched beneath our boots and our hot exhalations billowed around us in the glinting morning sunlight. Small birds darted about in the high grass. I felt anxious, as if my guts were aware of something hidden from the more articulate parts of myself, but perhaps this is just how I remember it.

Waking in the half-light one Sunday, I slid from the couch. Richie Benaud was calling the cricket in a droning voice that sounded like a small plane perpetually losing altitude. It was hot and I had fallen asleep after the roast Mother organised every few weeks. I had by this time moved out of home and was undertaking a degree in physics, but Patrick stayed on while he tried to be a rock star. The lunches were always desultory affairs peppered with small talk, and afterwards each of us dissolved into different parts of the house.

Half asleep, I followed murmuring voices and found my mother and Patrick huddled at the study window watching my father as he limped across the lawn doing odd jobs in the garden. He didn't know he was being observed, just as Patrick and Mother were unaware of me standing in the doorway to the darkened study. As they so often did, they were giggling at a private joke.

Although only twenty-three, two years older than me, Patrick seemed to live in a whole other world, to which only our mother had access. At that moment she had a cigarette in her right hand and she turned her face away from Patrick and exhaled the grey smoke up into the study's cool corners. It reminded me of a conical plume sprayed from a can of insect repellent.

'*Look* at him,' she was saying, referring to Father as he struggled to raise himself from where he had been kneeling to weed a garden bed. 'An old man in a dry month.' She had been drinking wine at lunch.

Patrick didn't say anything. She offered him her cigarette. He took it casually, barely noticing, drew on it and handed it back. I had never before seen my brother smoke a cigarette. It shocked me.

'Do you ever regret what happened?' Mother asked Patrick.

Patrick shook his head. He exhaled his cigarette smoke and looked at her as if something had occurred to him. 'Why? Do you?'

Mother rested her head on Patrick's shoulder and laughed. 'Hardly, darling. *Hardly*.'

And then the kiss.

My father tells Patrick the cold water is excellent for his circulation. He smiles his smile that shows no teeth. 'It's only *three minutes*. You don't even have to put your head under, like when I had to do it.'

I watch Patrick take off his clothes. He goes about it slowly, as if memorising each movement for later use. He leaves his watch on. The watch belonged to Grandfather — he acquired it in Vietnam — and he gave it to Patrick not long before he died, much to my father's chagrin. Father said our grandfather was half blind and demented at the end. *He only gave it to you because he thought you were me*, he would say, a comment guaranteed to rile Patrick almost more than anything else.

Finally, when my brother is naked, skin puckered, shivering, he walks down the hallway into the bathroom and steps gingerly into the bath, drawing a sharp breath as he does so.

I found it impossible to return to the family home after that kiss. Every few months my mother would ring to urge my attendance at lunch, but I always found a reason not to go: I had a report due, I was going to Wilsons Promontory with Julie, I was tired after a big night out at the pub with my mates.

'Oh, come on, sweetie,' Mother would slur down the phone line. 'You know your brother would love to see you. And we *always love* to have that Julie around the house.'

Only my mother could so effortlessly squeeze two lies into such a short speech. The thought of kissing her lips made me queasy. The thought of seeing Patrick made me furious. The thought of seeing my father made me feel, strangely enough, almost unbearably sad.

After we had been tramping for an hour or so through thick bush, my father stopped and threw up a hand for my brother and me to halt. My heart began thumping. My mouth dried up. Were we actually going to shoot something? Patrick hefted his rifle. I followed suit. Father crouched and peered into the undergrowth. Then he turned to us and mouthed the word *pig*. A pig? A wild pig. Now that *would* be something. He had told us how unlikely it would be to come across a pig but said rabbits would be fine for our first hunting expedition. 'Nothing wrong with shooting little bunnies,' he said. 'It's still hunting, after all.'

Our father shuffled backwards and indicated for us to do the same. He looked scared. Patrick smirked. Presently, I saw something move about in the thick bushes. My heart was really pounding, and my palms were moist. Again I thought of Mother and Janet, safe at home, listening to the radio. There came a grunt and my father raised his rifle, but what lumbered from the bushes was not a pig at all, but a huge wombat. Patrick cheered the creature's snuffling entrance. The wombat — which was the size of a short-legged, obese dog — looked around for a moment and waddled off into the bushes. I thought it was cute, but my father was displeased. He gave us a stern look, as if it were our fault.

We trudged all over the countryside but didn't have much luck that day. 'It takes a while,' Father said, 'to get your eye in, to be able to spot things moving about and realise what they might be.'

Night fell quickly and we returned to our camp. We heated a chicken stew Mother had prepared. My father hummed to himself as he ladled out the dinner and fiddled with the fire. He seemed possessed of a sense of wellbeing I didn't recall ever observing before.

Before we turned in, he got up and muttered something about going to the toilet, before picking his way into the darkness with the torch.

'You should go that way,' Patrick said, pointing in the opposite direction. 'There's a clearing through there. It's easier to find your way.'

Our father turned and stood still, as if Patrick had said something quite unusual. He looked at both of us and his face was strangely animated by the light from the flickering fire. At that moment he appeared wholly unfamiliar to me, like a stranger just emerged from the bush. 'Okay,' he said at last. 'Good man.' And he set off the way Patrick had indicated, ruffling my brother's hair as he passed.

The tree trunks trembled and twitched in the campfire light. My cheeks blazed from its heat. I was exhausted from the early-morning drive and the endless tramping through bushland. Hunting wasn't as fun as I had thought it would be, and we still had an entire day left. Patrick threw wood onto the fire.

Then an awful scream.

Even at the age of thirteen, my brother is genuinely tough. Not in a show-offish way, but you can sense it about him, and it is perhaps this quality that drives Father to devise ever more rigorous tests. With a hand on each side of the tub for balance, Patrick lowers himself into the freezing water. The ice cubes joggle about his knees and chest. I can see he is suffering, but my father won't activate the stopwatch until Patrick is fully immersed. Eventually, Patrick takes a deep breath and lies back with his hands across his chest. I feel humiliated on his behalf as his penis shrivels to the size of a witchetty grub and his nipples turn liquorice-coloured. Janet sidles away.

Our father clicks the stopwatch. 'Okay. We are … *Go!*'

It took Patrick and me only a minute to locate Father. He was lying on his back in a ditch. His eyes were clenched shut and his mouth set in a grimace of pain. 'Get it off!' he was saying. 'Get it *off*! Get it *off*!' His torch was on the ground nearby. Patrick picked it up and played the light over our father's face and down the length of his body. His ankle was clamped in a steel rabbit trap. His trousers were torn. There was thick blood, a flap of purple flesh. I squatted at his side, but Patrick yanked me back so hard that I fell to the ground. Father was by this time writhing in agony, pounding at the damp earth with a fist. 'Quick! Pull the latch, Patrick. Pull … the bloody … thing … back. *Quick! Get it off me!*'

When Patrick's three minutes in the cold water are up, Father says: 'Well done, little man. Out you get. Nick, fetch his towel.'

But Patrick doesn't move, doesn't say a word. He doesn't even open his eyes. All he does is lift a hand from the water to *scratch his nose*, as if he were on the couch in front of the TV. Again Father tells him to come out, but Patrick won't listen and he ends up staying in that bath for ages — maybe half an hour — until Mother comes back and asks what is going on. She is furious. By this time Patrick's entire body is the colour of a fresh bruise. His lips are grey. Father has stormed off, and Janet is slumped in the hallway crying. I help Mother lift Patrick out. He is shaking hard and he can barely walk, but his half-lit smile is the same one that will resurface the night of the accident, when he squatted down leisurely beside our screaming father, drew up the sleeve of his jacket to reveal his watch and said: 'Okay. Let's see what you're made of. On my signal … Three minutes from now. We are … *Go!*'

The Trees

LESLEY JØRGENSEN

When they hit the tree it was like a bomb going off. The orderly row of saplings along the farm drive whipped upwards into a whirligig of sun and sky, as if he and Val had been lifted clean out of the farm and the land and taken someplace where the old inescapable rules, of gravity and debt and ageing, did not apply.

But then, through the shivering electric haze of disturbed atmosphere, the pale blue bars of sky returned to surround them, and the saplings stood sentinel again. Art could see his arms stretched out straight on the wheel like a rally driver's, the veins on his forearms plain as fencing wire. His footwell had shrunk into a small pocket of space around his feet, as if he'd gone driving with his legs tucked into his swag for warmth.

Art turned his head to the left but his wife was not to be seen. In place of the ute's centre front seat was the bole of a tree, as large as a cannon, just where they would put the shopping on the way back from town, or their daughters when they were small. Art bent forward as far as he could, mindful of the pressure of buckled plastic across his stomach, and managed to catch a glimpse of Val on the other side of the tree trunk.

She was upright but leaning away from him a little, towards the side window, as if she'd nodded off, except that her eyes were half open. The front of the car had folded itself around her neatly and symmetrically, like the travel blanket she'd used in winter in the Austin, their first car after they'd married. It was the tree that looked unnatural: dangerous and out of place in the serene, accommodating flow of metal and plastic; its bark a mess of multicoloured pastels and its sharp-edged leaves in khaki and gunmetal blue, intruding on the space between them.

Art pushed forward harder, the dash's pressure against his belly oddly comforting, like the broad leather belt he was supposed to wear for heavy lifting. He took a hand off the wheel and stretched around the cold smooth front of the tree to touch his wife, but she was out of his reach.

He could hear her breathing, stertorous and guttural. As he listened, her breaths gained pace, continuing deep and rough, until she sounded like a man with a pack running up a steep hill. Then they stopped. For five beats of his heart there was silence, then an explosive inspiration, and another and another, racing faster and faster until another deadly breathless pause, the kind that he used to dread on patrol in Vietnam. He used to shut his eyes back then, or look down at his hands. No point in looking if you can't do anything. Doubtful suddenly whether he was sixty or twenty, he tried to see himself in the rear-view mirror, but mirror and windscreen were gone, replaced by air that shimmered with sunlit, suspended dust.

Val's breathing staggered on to another breathless climax, but when he struggled forward even further to try to see her again, pushing against the dash like a stubborn farm gate, she looked unchanged, sitting silently in her navy blue windcheater with the apple trees and clouds painted across her chest, and the cottage with a rose bush and a swing, sitting just below her heart. Her hair was still tidy at the front, though he remembered seeing, as he had half dragged her, stumbling and silent, into the car, that it was uncombed at the back, flattened into a sunburst of grey radiating outwards from a pink triangle of scalp.

She'd slept on the recliner last night, still in her clothes. For all that evening, she'd been restless and clumsy, walking around and around, shouldering the standard lamp to rocking on its stand so that its orange cover tilted and almost fell.

'What?' he'd asked. 'What are you doing, love?'

'Some paper. Where's the paper,' she'd said, her voice slurring as if she was too tired to talk.

'What d'yer need that for, love?'

She didn't reply at first, disappearing into the kitchen, where he could hear her opening drawers and cupboards but not shutting them again. He stayed sitting in his easy chair with a dull pain in his stomach, listening to her moving from room to room in the house, its yellow strapped ceilings echoing sounds back to him with such familiarity that he knew exactly where she was, and where she was going.

When Val returned to him, she was holding a pen and last year's agricultural calendar from the back of the toilet door and her left leg was dragging. She didn't head for the couch, her usual spot where she would pile up sewing or wool by her side as she worked, but instead stopped at the first chair she came to: the recliner he used when he had a beer. She pushed down on its back as she moved towards him, and Art felt an instinctive shrinking. But when she got to the end of the armrest, she half turned away from him and fell back heavily into the recliner, her hands grasping at nothing. He stared at the television while paper was rustled and her glasses case was fumbled open, then dropped on the floor.

'Making a list.' Her words came out strident and forced, as if she was on a long-distance call and trying to make herself understood through time delay and static.

He listened with dread. There was no money for shopping: she knew that. No money for anything anymore. But he couldn't say that, couldn't ask.

She seemed to struggle to answer him anyway. 'All the things.' She took a breath. 'All the things wrong with the farm.'

Art slid his hands off the armrests and into his lap and looked at them, upturned, the skin yellow with calluses and the creases on his palms dark as the weaving dotted lines that delineate an unsealed road on a map, forming chains and ponds of uncertainty and risk. Dry season only, perhaps.

Do not attempt when wet. Notify your loved ones before you commit.

He could hear her pen scratching now, her breathing heavy, and when he turned towards her, her tongue was protruding slightly from the fierce looseness of her mouth, as if she was one of their daughters doing her homework. The pain in his stomach rose again as he thought of their two girls, who did not want to come home anymore. School in Adelaide had turned from purgatory into paradise.

He watched as Val slowly printed on the calendar's blank and glossy back. Red and black lettering ran across the upward curve of the calendar's front. *For All Your Agricultural Needs*.

'Drought.' The word came out as if she was still on her long-distance call. Two years' worth, two failed crops in a row.

He cleared his throat. 'Drought's broken now.' But too late, with the wheat sown but not ready to be harvested, rotting in the ground.

'Now the rain,' she said. 'And our girls. Hate the farm.'

'They don't, love. They're young.'

The blank hostile gaze of his daughters, the last time he and Valda had insisted they come home for the summer break, the constant texting and flat, ironed hair, their refusal to help outside.

'The big tractor, and the truck.'

'They just need fixin'.' Three months now.

'Phone's off.'

'I'll be talking to the bank, love,' he said, reflexively, hopelessly. Glen Morgan, a good man with ties to the district, had gone years ago, replaced by a series of young men and women that never bought, just rented till they moved on.

Art had left her then, had hauled himself up and out of the chair, walked out to the front porch and sat on the step, peering through smeared glasses at the darkness beyond, feeling pointless and unbalanced without a beer next to his boot. After a while he heard her moving around the house again, the kettle going on and clicking off. That comforted him enough to pull himself up by the verandah post and go back inside, but in the kitchen, the kettle was sitting in the sink and a cup was on its side on the floor, next to a teabag. He went to bed then, walking with averted eyes past the occupied recliner, full of fear for what it might contain.

Art woke in the early hours, heavy-eyed and dry in the mouth as if he really had had a few, and then he forced himself to get up and go and look at her in the lounge. He saw the stiff droop of her mouth and said Val, best get you to the doctor, love. She didn't respond, just looked at him, one-eyed, her reading glasses still on, and he had to haul her up and she leaned on him heavier than she ever had before. As he half dragged, half carried her across the porch to the car, she dropped the calendar and, propelled by the wind, it moved in a series of shushing sweeps across the floorboards, like a subtle, fluttered signal to some watching enemy.

Pushing her into the car was a battle, her left leg unwieldy and resistant. As he strapped her in he thought of the last time he had done that, when she was six months pregnant with the girls and had to be driven to Adelaide for the last trimester. She'd smiled at him then, and he'd felt his own stomach, flat and tight, brush over the taut bounty of hers, with promise and strength.

But this time his stomach had drooped over her sagging breasts like an insult, and they'd driven off, strangely naked without the thermos and sandwiches, jackets and hats that always accompanied them on the two-hour drive to Wudinna or beyond, along with the letters to be posted and the cans for the recyclers, the fresh eggs for their friends in town and the tupperwared biscuits for those sick in hospital.

The doubled row of eucalyptus saplings lining the long drive had flashed past, Valda lurching further to the left each time the car bumped or turned. He couldn't understand why they'd been hit by the tree, the last of the big old trees on the boundary line, as if in leaving the farm he had broken some rule of nature.

Art moved back into his seat again, his stomach burning as the dash's pressure suddenly eased. He would have to drive the truck, and its tank was empty. He would have to get out of this car and leave Val and walk the two kilometres back to their house and then another five hundred metres to the sheds and untie the jerrycan from the tray of the truck and walk back down here and siphon petrol out of the tank and then walk it back to the sheds and fill the tank and then hope, hope it started and drive it down here and then try to get Val out of her metal blanket and lift her into the truck's cabin and drive two hours to town. He felt dizzy at the thought, the planning involved, trying to remember if the jerrycan really was on the truck or under the peppercorn tree where the tractor sat. Would the diff give out before they got there?

Art shoved experimentally on his door, and it grated open, letting in cold air and a side view of close-ranked saplings, and without thinking he pulled it shut again. He rolled his neck and cracked his knuckles as if preparing for one final assault or some irresistible attack, then twisted hard to his left and pushed blindly around and behind the tree's bole, wanting to touch his wife just for a moment. His fingertips met a warm stickiness that must have been at the back of her head.

A crow called, like a baby crying, or a shouted command, and he could see a single ant, like an advance scout, standing on a fragment of glass that edged the windscreen frame. I hate those crows on the road, flapping and pecking, she'd said once. I don't mind the roadkill, it's the creatures coming down after it. He leaned back again, trying to see what he could feel, but the pain in his stomach was worse then, and a wave of coldness rolled upwards from his feet to his knees. 'Don't worry, love,' he said, or thought he said, as the crow called again. 'We don't have to look if we don't want to.'

About the Authors

Debra Adelaide is the author or editor of over ten books, including three novels. Her latest novel, *The Household Guide to Dying*, was first published in Australia in 2008, and has now appeared in a dozen other countries. She works at the University of Technology, Sydney.

Claire Aman lives in Grafton, an inspiring town. She writes for pleasure. She has had short stories published in *New Australian Stories*, *Best Australian Stories*, *Island*, *HEAT* and *Southerly*. Her writing life has been nurtured by Varuna, the Writers' House.

Jon Bauer was born in the UK but has lived in Australia for ten years. He is the author of short stories, and plays for stage and radio. His first novel, *Rocks in the Belly*, was published in 2010. Visit him at www.jonbauerwriter.com.

Melissa Beit has had short stories published in various anthologies, magazines and journals. She is mere months away from completing her first novel, helped along by several visits to Varuna, the Writers' House, away from her very noisy children.

Tegan Bennett Daylight is the author of the novels *Bombora*, *What Falls Away* and *Safety*. She is currently at work on a collection of short stories.

Tony Birch writes short fiction, poetry and essays. His short-story collections are *Shadowboxing* and *Father's Day*. He teaches in the writing program at the University of Melbourne.

Georgia Blain is the author of five novels and a memoir, *Births Deaths Marriages*. Her work has been shortlisted for major literary prizes, and her first novel, *Closed for Winter*, was made into a feature film in 2009. Her latest book, *Darkwater*, is a murder mystery for young adults.

Patrick Cullen's first book, *What Came Between*, was published in 2009 and includes five stories that appeared in *Best Australian Stories* between 2005 and 2007.

Sonja Dechian works as a documentary development writer in Melbourne, and was previously a producer and writer with ABC TV in Adelaide. She is working on a novel.

ABOUT THE AUTHORS

Brooke Dunnell is completing a postgraduate degree in Creative Writing at the University of Western Australia. Her short stories have been published in the collections *Best Australian Stories* and *Allnighter*, and read on ABC Radio National.

Peggy Frew has been a musician and songwriter for over ten years with critically acclaimed Melbourne band Art of Fighting. She has recently completed a diploma in Professional Writing and Editing at RMIT. Her story 'Home Visit' won *The Age* Short Story Competition in 2009, and her novel 'House of Sticks' won the 2010 Victorian Premier's Literary Award for an Unpublished Manuscript by an Emerging Victorian Writer.

Julie Gittus is the author of the young adult novel *Saltwater Moons*. Her short stories have been included in *New Australian Stories* as well as *Best of the Best*. She is currently working on her second novel. Visit her at www.juliegittus.com.au.

Marion Halligan has published twenty books: ten novels, including *Spider Cup*, *Lovers' Knots*, *The Golden Dress*, *The Fog Garden*, *The Point*, *The Apricot Colonel* and *Murder on the Apricot Coast*; collections of short stories, including *The Hanged Man in the Garden* and *The Worry Box*; books of autobiography, travel and food; and a children's book, *The Midwife's Daughters*. Her most recent novel is *Valley of Grace*. She has received an AM for her services to literature.

Jacinta Halloran is a general practitioner and writer. She has published both short stories and a novel, *Dissection*. She is now writing her second novel with the assistance of an Australia Council grant.

Karen Hitchcock is a writer and doctor. Her collection of short stories, *Little White Slips*, won the Steele Rudd Award in the 2010 Queensland Premier's Literary Awards, and was shortlisted in the NSW Premier's Literary Awards and the Dobbie Award for women writers. Her first novel, *Read My Lips*, will be published in 2011. 'Blackbirds Singing' first appeared in *The Big Issue*.

Anne Jenner lives in Adelaide. She is currently undertaking an MA in Creative Writing at Macquarie University, while writing short stories and working on her first novel.

Myfanwy Jones has published numerous short stories and her debut novel, *The Rainy Season*, was shortlisted for the 2009 Melbourne Prize

ABOUT THE AUTHORS

for Literature's Best Writing Award. She is also co-author of the ABIA-winning *Parlour Games for Modern Families*.

Lesley Jørgensen is a medical-negligence lawyer and mother of two, based in South Australia. Her short story 'Pure Gold' was published in *New Australian Stories*. She is currently completing her first novel, just as soon as she can.

Cate Kennedy is the author of the highly acclaimed novel *The World Beneath*, which won the People's Choice Award in the 2010 NSW Premier's Literary Awards. She is an award-winning short-story writer whose work has been published widely, and her collection, *Dark Roots*, was shortlisted for the Steele Rudd Award in the Queensland Premier's Literary Awards. Cate is also the author of the travel memoir *Sing, and Don't Cry*, and the poetry collections *Joyflight* and *Signs of Other Fires*.

Zane Lovitt has a Masters degree in Screenwriting from the Victorian College of the Arts. He works as an adviser at the Tenants Union of Victoria and studies law at the University of Melbourne. 'Leaving the Fountainhead' won the S.D. Harvey Short Story Award in 2010.

Scott McDermott has had stories about invisibility, mouse herding, mermaids, the elderly, operational expenditure and old gods published by Cardigan Press, Sleepers, *Cutwater* and UQ's *Vanguard*. 'Fidget's Farewell' won the S.D. Harvey Short Story Award in 2009.

Fiona McFarlane is from Sydney. Her stories have been published in *Southerly*, *Zoetrope: All-Story* and *The Missouri Review*. She is currently pursuing an MFA in Fiction at the Michener Center for Writers in Austin, Texas. 'Exotic Animal Medicine' first appeared in *The Missouri Review*.

Jane McGown has travelled extensively throughout Asia and is a teacher of the Japanese art of ikebana. Success in short-story competitions has convinced her to pursue her craft more seriously. She lives in Sydney and is working on a discontinuous narrative.

A.G. McNeil is currently working on his PhD at the University of Western Australia. His work has appeared in *New Australian Stories* and *Best Australian Stories*.

Susan Midalia is a writer, editor and teacher. Her collection of short stories, *A History of the Beanbag*, was shortlisted for the Western

ABOUT THE AUTHORS

Australian Premier's Literary Award in 2007. She is writing her second collection with the assistance of a grant from the Australia Council. 'Parting Glances' first appeared in *Westerly*.

Jennifer Mills is the author of the novel *The Diamond Anchor* and a chapbook of poems, *Treading Earth*. Her second novel, *Gone*, will be published in 2011. Her work has appeared in *Meanjin*, *Overland*, *HEAT*, *Griffith REVIEW* and *Best Australian Stories*. She blogs at www.jenjen.com.au and at *Overland*. She lives in Alice Springs.

Meg Mundell is a Melbourne-based writer who grew up in New Zealand. She has published journalism in *The Age*, *The Monthly*, *The Sydney Morning Herald* and *The Big Issue*; and fiction in *Meanjin*, *The Sleepers Almanac* and *Best Australian Stories 2010*. Her first novel, *Black Glass*, will be published in 2011. Meg is currently completing a PhD and a trucking memoir.

Peta Murray lives in Melbourne. Her best-known work is the stage play *Wallflowering*. Other plays include AWGIE winners *Spitting Chips* and *The Keys to the Animal Room*, and *Salt*, which won the Victorian Premier's Literary Award for Drama. Peta's short fiction has appeared in anthologies, including *The Sleepers Almanac*.

Ruby J. Murray is a writer, researcher and co-founder of the-democracy-project.org. Her writing has appeared in Australian newspapers, magazines, online, and in Australian journals, including *Torpedo*, *The Lifted Brow* and *Meanjin*. Ruby blogs at rubyjoymurray.wordpress.com.

Mark O'Flynn's poetry and short stories have appeared in a wide range of journals. His novels include *Grassdogs*, which was published in 2006. He has had seven plays professionally produced and has also published three collections of poetry. Recently Picaro Press published a selection from these in *Wagtail 100*.

Ryan O'Neill's stories have appeared in various journals and anthologies. His collection, *A Famine in Newcastle*, was shortlisted for the 2007 Queensland Premier's Literary Awards.

Paddy O'Reilly is the author of a short-story collection, *The End of the World*; a novel, *The Factory*; and a novella, *Deep Water*. Her stories have won national and international story awards and been widely published and broadcast. 'How to Write a Short Story' first appeared in *Southerly*.

ABOUT THE AUTHORS

Kate Ryan has worked as a freelance and in-house editor, and has written a number of children's books. She is now completing a novel as part of a PhD in Creative Writing at RMIT, where she was selected for a mentorship with Robert Dessaix.

Emma Schwarcz is a Melbourne-based writer and editor. Her work has been published most recently in *The Age*, *harvest* magazine and *Hide & Seek Melbourne*, and she teaches writing at RMIT.

Jane Sullivan is a Melbourne-based writer specialising in literary journalism, who writes a Saturday column and features for *The Age*. Her novel *The White Star* was published in 2001. You can meet the characters in 'Fallen Woman' again in *Little People*, which was shortlisted for the inaugural CAL Scribe Fiction Prize in 2010 and will be published in 2011.

Chris Womersley is a Melbourne-based author. He won the 2007 Josephine Ulrick Prize for Literature with his short story 'The Possibility of Water', and the 2008 Ned Kelly Award for Best First Fiction for his novel, *The Low Road*. His second novel, *Bereft*, was published in 2010. 'Theories of Relativity' first appeared in *Kill Your Darlings*. Visit him at www.chriswomersley.com.